Sons of Steel

DOMINION

G. L. Keady

First published in Australia in 2023
by Big Island Publishing

Big Island Publishing
PO Box 3027, Tuross Head, 2537, NSW, Australia.
www.bigislandpublishing.au

ISBN:
Print: 978-0-6459738-7-7
ePub: 978-0-6459738-6-0

Edited by: Canon Doyle
Cover design and art: Brandon Evans-Keady

A temporal distortion occurs when two dimensions interact with one another. The observer may be able to catch a fleeting glance into another world. Seeing a ghost is perhaps an example of temporal distortion.

TABLE OF CONTENTS

CHAPTER 1
ZYGOTE

IT WAS AN ugly-looking thing, and though it reminded Alice of the Rooga, Lilith the humanoid bat, the Scorpion man, and other monstrosities he had fought over time, if there were an award for repulsiveness then this mongrel would've won it hands down. Al glanced down at Nimrod De Ville on the floor. He was a scientist who had gone missing, and Al had been dispatched to find him. The wounds the creature had inflicted on him were bad, possibly fatal. Sprawled out on the ground unconscious, all Al could do for him was to keep the monster at bay until a window of opportunity opened for escape.

The creature glared sideways at Al and then snarled. It was seriously agitated after having been belted in the head and having its eyebrow slit open, with its left eye swollen shut. Al could tell it was definitely a human who had either been horribly disfigured by radiation or a mutant born all messed up.

Standing seven feet tall with beady black eyes, it had no neck to speak of. Its grotesque head was sunk into a bulbous mass of deformed muscle and flesh that made up its shoulders. Little intelligence showed in its eyes, only ferocity and a need to kill. When its big mouth snarled, its black lips curled back to show a few pointed teeth. It snorted through a human-like nose each time it gnashed its teeth threateningly. At the end of its muscly arms were seriously clawed hands, and its dark pink hairless naked body was marked with brown blotches, open sores, and countless scars. It was impossible to tell whether it was male or female, as there were no noticeable sex organs. Its legs were the healthiest part; they were strong, long, muscly, and athletic but with clawed feet.

One thing Alice knew for sure was that it was fit and could run and jump like an Olympian because it had chased him through the forest into the old warehouse where it now had him trapped. Had it not been for a lucky punch that had knocked the thing silly and stunned it, he figured he would've come to a sticky end. At least when he ran into the dilapidated warehouse, he'd found Nimrod on the floor, and that had probably saved the scientist's life. This wasn't a mission to another time but to another part of the world that was too remote to get to by any other means. OTT had located Nimrod De Ville via his GPS signal and had directed a wormhole to him.

Al drew a WASP out of his pocket, pointed the sensor on its front at the creature for it to lock onto the target, and then said, "Sorry, buddy, but you leave me no choice." He flicked it up into the air where it hovered for a moment. Then, emitting a buzzing sound, it flew at the creature. With lightning reflexes, the bulky monster snatched the WASP out of the air and crushed it in a clenched fist as though it was an annoying insect.

"Argh! What did you go and do that for?" Al cursed.

It raised its claws, snarled, and with a murderous look in its eye, started towards him. Daylight was streaming in ribbons through the mostly smashed windows in the single-story building. There was plenty of room for Al to manoeuvre around and avoid the oncoming beast. He needed to divert it away from Nimrod. The scientist was the father of archaeologist Jax De Ville, whom Alice, his sister Vee, and the Oceana security agents Karzoff and Viktoria had met on a mission to Tahiti a few months earlier. When her father had gone missing on a research mission to the Chernobyl Nuclear Power Plant, Jax had contacted Viktoria for help.

Al felt he owed Jax one from their last adventure and so agreed to be dispatched through Kairos to Chernobyl, near the city of

Pripyat in the north of the Ukrainian SRR, to find and retrieve Nimrod. Chernobyl was the location of the 1988 nuclear disaster considered the worst of its kind in recorded history.

"Argh!" Al barked at it threateningly, trying to get it to back down. "Bloody hideous thing," he mumbled when it just kept coming at him. A shot rang out and a windowpane shattered. The creature ducked, glared panic-stricken at Alice, and then from a standing start, sprung fifteen metres into the air through a gaping hole in the ceiling and disappeared.

"What was that hideous thing?" Vee cackled, walking towards Alice with a smoking gun resting on her shoulder.

Happy to see her, Al said relieved, "You took the words right out of my mouth. Here, give us a hand."

Vee stuck the pistol in her belt and then moved in to help Al with Nimrod. While he was sprawled out unconscious, Al took the opportunity to check him for broken bones.

"He seems okay. Where'd you get the gun?" Al asked.

"When we split up to search for the camp, I found it, but no signs of the other four in the team there. I rummaged through their stuff and found the gun," Vee explained.

He looked endearingly at his sister. She was looking older, standing at five foot eight with shoulder-length wild jet-black hair shaved at the sides. Her sleek tattooed eyebrows framed big almond-shaped black eyes. Her face was pear-shaped with high cheekbones, and her left arm was tattooed in a sleeve that extended to her fingertips. She was pretty, but there was an ominous razor's edge about her.

"Thank the gods for that," Al said, with a proud grin. She was a chip off the old block. "No blood or signs of a struggle?"

"Nup, only that they'd left in a real hurry. The campfire was still warm. Reckon they bailed out during the night. Something must have scared the crap out of 'em. Reckon it might have been Mr Hideous we just frightened off?" she said, with a chuckle.

"Could have been. Maybe there's a pack of 'em?"

A murmur came from Nimrod.

Al was wearing a black beret, a black denim jacket over a white singlet, and black jeans. Vee's grey and black camouflage fatigues were capped off with a black beret.

"He's coming round," Al said, helping him sit up.

Nimrod rubbed his fingers through his short-cut salt-and-pepper curly hair. In his fifties, it wasn't difficult to see the family resemblance to Jax: the same eyes, Afro-American, good looking but with a black beard that only gave space to his lips, nose, eyes, and forehead.

"Nimrod De Ville?" Al enquired.

"Yes, yes, that's me," he groaned. "Why, who are you?" Not really expecting someone to be speaking English.

"I'm Black Alice, and this is Vee. We were sent by your daughter Jax to rescue you."

"Help me up, will you, Alice?" he asked, holding out a hand to be pulled to his feet. He rubbed the back of his head. "Got a lump the size of an egg on the back of my head. Someone must've belted me from behind and then carried me here."

"Maybe it was the hideous monstrosity we just chased off," Al claimed.

"If you're referring to one of the mutants, yeah. I'm an anthropologist. I've been tracking and observing them for two months now. This is the first time they've displayed any sign of malice."

"Malice? That's putting it lightly, isn't it? That thing had a murderous look in its eye if I've ever seen one... it was going to kill you," Al barked.

"Yeah, well, like I say, I've not seen any sign of that in the two months we've been studying them. Did you find the rest of my team?"

Vee answered, "No, the campsite was deserted."

"Let's get out of here back to your camp. Fill us in on the way," Al proposed.

Vee covered them with the pistol while Nimrod led them

through the desolation towards the campsite. Along the way, he explained how he and his team had been sent by Boston University to study the long-term effects of radiation fallout on life around Chernobyl. There had been rumours that at the time of the nuclear accident, there were homeless people living in the area who had never been evacuated. Because a generation had passed since the accident, along with a war, Nimrod's research tenure was to locate these people and study the effects on them. The creature they had encountered was a thirty-year-old, born of one of the homeless survivors, mutated at birth. The mutants had no means of reproducing and had a life expectancy of less than forty years, depending on the extent of the mutation, so it was critical to study them now.

"How many are there?" Vee asked.

"So far, we've found ten. The one you encountered is the oldest but the least mutated."

"Bloody hell, are you telling me others look worse than it did?" asked Al.

"I dare say so," Nimrod confirmed.

As they continued, Nimrod asked Al how he'd met his daughter Jax, and Al filled him in. Nimrod was fascinated by the explanation of how Alice and Vee had travelled to Chernobyl from Sydney through a wormhole. Though the extraordinary story sounded like science fiction, he had no cause to doubt the veracity of it.

Professor de Luz burst into Dr Secta's laboratory at Oceana Time Travel with an expression on his face as though he had just learned that the world was on the brink of collapse. A tall, slender scientist with cropped white hair looked up from his computer at the Professor and jestingly remarked, "What's bothering you, Vic? Did someone pinch your lunch money?"

Vic de Luz slumped onto the two-seater lounge, placed his laptop on his knees, and fixed a stern gaze on Secta over the rims of his round John Lennon glasses. In his late fifties, a tad weathered and undeniably worn, with long, untamed grey hair, the Professor—a Texan—had faithfully maintained his trademark unconventional academic appearance for decades. "I've stumbled upon a significant discovery, Secta."

Recognising that such a declaration from his esteemed colleague demanded serious attention, Secta rose from his workstation and settled into a comfortable armchair across from the Professor.

"Go on," Secta encouraged.

"As you're aware, I've been thoroughly investigating all of your sister's data, and it's utterly remarkable."

Secta's sister, Dr Hope, was a founding member of OTT and had recently fallen victim to an assassination by a Zen agent. She had developed the original formula that allowed for the disintegration and transmission of atoms—matter transfer—an experiment initially conducted on Black Alice. This ground-breaking experiment had propelled him into the future for the first time and had subsequently been refined and stabilized to ensure safety. Hope had truly been a genius.

"You're not revealing anything new, Vic. Spare me the babble and get to the point."

"She encoded a marker within the DNA of the zygote."

"What? Inside the embryo we sent Morri?" Secta exclaimed, springing to his feet and pacing the floor, struggling to fathom the magnitude of the assertion.

"Yes, within her own harvested egg, which she fertilised with Alice's sperm, that we sent to 2087 to impregnate Morri, with the intention of producing a child to ensure the survival of humanity. The egg contains an isotopic marker embedded in its DNA that can be traced. The marker code is 777."

Secta ceased his pacing and regarded Vic with a mix of disbelief and astonishment. "Such brilliance was so characteristic of her. God, how I miss her."

"Should we fear an attack by these mutants?" Vee asked Nimrod, as they were nearing the campsite.

"I don't know what could have ticked them off, but like I said, they're normally quite docile. There's the camp," Nimrod said.

They entered the clearing in the forest where five tents were pitched; everything was there Nimrod expected to find, all of it relatively undisturbed.

"So, you were asleep when that thing must have come in, banged you on the head and carted you off," Al speculated, looking at tell-tale tracks on the ground.

"It doesn't make sense. Why would he do that all of a sudden?... I honestly can't believe it was one of the mutants, they're vegetarians... and the one you met, even though he looks ferocious, is like a kitten. We call him Dodder, because of the way he dodders about. But what's really damn concerning is the whereabouts of the rest of the team?"

"Well, old Dodder sure had me fooled," Al said, surprised.

"Me too," Jax agreed.

"Look, we had an altercation about two weeks ago with a bunch of red-neck hunters that I fear are inextricably linked to this kidnapping. By their weapons, we figured they were off-duty Ukrainian Militia."

"What were they hunting?" Al asked.

"The mutants. It has been a sport of theirs for years."

"What, killing these people?" Vee protested, outraged.

"Yes. It had been reported the numbers were dwindling; we wondered why, blaming it at first on radiation."

"So, you knew about the mutants before you came here?" Al quizzed.

"Yes, it has been one of the best-kept secrets in anthropology, an opportunity to study the post-effects of high nuclear radiation over time."

"Ah, so Hiroshima and Nagasaki weren't enough for you?" Vee challenged, facetiously.

"Chernobyl and Fukushima present a different type of radiation challenge than what was derived from an atomic bomb, Vee. In simple terms, Hiroshima was a uranium bomb, while Nagasaki was a more powerful plutonium bomb. The fallout from a damaged reactor causes a considerably higher number of deferred victims for the simple reason that it releases a much larger and more toxic mass of lasting fission products than does a single atomic bomb, and also more heavily contaminates a much larger territory."

"Oh, I see," Vee muttered, accepting the correction.

"Alice, what are we doing here? This is a waste of precious time," En-Ki said in Alice's mind.

Alice ignored the alien that possessed him and asked Nimrod, "Are you saying Dodder led me to you?"

"Most probably, he's not stupid, you know. He might look seriously deformed and can't speak, but my observations over the last two months prove he's intelligent, and definitely shouldn't be hunted down for sport."

A series of loud cracks broke the silence.

"Gunshots!" Nimrod exclaimed, worriedly.

"Are there any more weapons?" Al asked, hastily.

"No, we only had the one pistol that Vee has."

Worried for the safety of the rest of the team and the mutants, the three of them headed off in the direction of the gunfire.

CEO of Zen Corporation in Oceana, Gorrick, who was possessed by the evil En-Lil, the creator of the fifteen hundred Gorrick clones that commanded the global chapters of Zen Corporation, called for an urgent meeting. This meeting took place at the new Zen/TWO joint venture time travel facility in Texas. Present at the meeting were Honor, the head of ZEO (Zen Espionage Operative), Professor

Adamski (head Zen Scientist and inventor of Aquila, now the scientific operations director of the new time travel facility), Dr Li (head of Zenisis, cyber-technologies), General Bull Bruckmaster (director of the US black-ops division TWO: Time Travel Works), and CIA operative agent Voltaris Idram.

With the former Desertron Particle Collider facility in Waxahachie, Texas, receiving a black budget and being renamed TWO, it was granted the same classification as Area 51, effectively making it non-existent as far as the US Government was concerned.

Seated around a large timber table in the spacious ultra-modern boardroom, Gorrick rose to address the assembled group. Standing at six feet four inches tall with cropped white hair, unblinking startling blue eyes, the absence of eyebrows, and a pallid complexion that spoke of a life spent away from the sun, he dressed entirely in black, presenting a sinister and alien appearance.

Speaking with a voice warmer than his appearance suggested, accompanied by a subtle Russian accent, he began, "This marks the inaugural meeting at our new joint venture time travel facility, Aquila-TWO. The primary purpose of this gathering is to establish the first time travel mission and select a suitable time traveller. I now yield the floor to our operations director, Professor Adamski."

With that, Gorrick resumed his seat.

Professor Adamski, a somewhat anxious-looking man from the Baltic region, embodied the quintessential scientist. He placed an iPad on the table in front of him and then stood up.

"Dimensions are akin to the pages of a book. As I stand here, I am situated in one timeline, alongside numerous others that run concurrently. Each timeline within each dimension yields a distinct outcome. At certain junctures, timelines intersect, leading to diverse futures. In the 21st Century, we're aware that Tibetan monks possess the ability to utilise astral meditation to open gateways to alternate timelines. Through the employment of Aquila, we've managed to replicate this process; however, designating a target timeline necessitates an item from that time to serve as a focal point for the wormhole projector. You might wonder how our adversaries at OTT have managed future travel. This is due to the fact that their time traveller, Black Alice, inadvertently entered a wormhole that transported him to 2087. Dr Secta was able to follow him thanks to a trackable marker encoded within Black Alice's DNA. Their second foray into the future, specifically Tokyo in 2047, occurred because Black Alice had been transported there by the power of En-Ki, who had somehow initiated a portal for him. Thus, the question arises: how do we establish a portal to the future?

"Well, someone else possesses the ability to utilise astral projection to glimpse into the future—our very own Gorrick," Adamski remarked, gesturing toward him. "I've developed a virtual holographic unit that will facilitate Gorrick's interaction with Aquila, thereby enabling the opening of a portal to any of the dimensions I've mentioned—the 'pages' in our metaphorical book. I pause to witness the expressions of astonishment on your faces."

Adamski continued, "Yes, by connecting Gorrick to Aquila, while he is in a meditative state and can focuses on a particular timeline, we will be able to open a wormhole to that time destination through which we can then send a traveller."

CHAPTER 2
IVORY TOWER

RIGADIER BRUCKMASTER WAS mighty pleased with the amazing possibilities Adamski had outlined. The big pompous man filled to the brim with arrogance and self-importance, was the top dog in the CIA's covert venture into time travel.

"Tell me Professor, what do you have in mind to utilize this process?" Bruckmaster asked, gruffly.

Adamski was still standing. Intimidated by Bruckmaster, he glanced sharply in his direction and said nervously, "When OTT visited 2087, Honor was still with them and she has a transcript of that mission. Honor?" Adamski nodded to her, and then sat, relieved.

A smug smile cracked on Honor's face, proud that she had such vital intelligence to contribute to the meeting. Dressed in a stunning black Carolyn Cooper business suit with her black hair up, she was elegant. However, the wicked look in her eyes betrayed her real inner demons. "Thank you, Professor. When the dissident Black Alice was accidentally sent through a portal for the second time, it was as the Professor said to the year 2087. This was a time following a seven-year war classified as the Cyberwars. When he arrived, it was inside the body and mind of a returning soldier from that war. His name was Turk and he was returning to his home on the east coast of Oceana. As a result of the war, the world had been reduced to a post-apocalyptic dystopia that was well-governed by Zen Corporation. The

Gorrick in charge of the Angel City global headquarters of Zen, had developed incredible cyber-technology that he was determined to use to police a world that had fallen into decay since the war. Zen of course believed the war was a necessity in order to cull the human race and create a sustainable society. Black Alice joined up with a group of dissidents and with the help of Dr Secta, who had time travelled to join him, managed to obstruct Zen's plans. Professor?" Honor nodded for Adamski to proceed and then returned to her seat.

Still looking self-conscious, Adamski stood, "We believe if we were to visit Zen Corporation in the future we could obtain technology from them that would put us well in advance of OTT. We aim to send a traveller to 2112, twenty-five years later, when we believe Zen will be at its peak of global power."

As he resumed his seat, Gorrick rose up and led a round of applause. When it had subsided Gorrick said, "Which brings us to the second item on the agenda. We need to choose our first official time traveller. Feel free to make your nomination."

He sat back down to let the attendees discuss the issue. After a moment Bruckmaster coughed to gain their attention and then struggled to his feet.

"I wish to nominate Agent Voltaris Idram," he said firmly.

A powerfully built man with a big square jaw, a crew cut, and the look to kill in his eyes, Idram stood as Bruckmaster squeezed his big butt back into his seat.

Scars dissected both Idram's eyebrows, immortalizing past battles. "Thank you, general," Idram growled, his voice deep, southern and menacing. "I accept the nomination."

A smirk broke on Honor's face. Nodding her head agreeably, she was the first to raise her hand. "I second the motion."

Dr Li, Adamski, and Gorrick signalled their approval.

Gorrick stood and acknowledged, "Good, then it is settled. Voltaris Idram is our time traveller. Congratulations," he said, reaching out a hand for Idram to shake.

It was done: they had the means, they had an objective, they had a destination, and now they had a traveller.

It was challenging terrain to navigate, as the town had been abandoned to decay. The buildings stood dilapidated, and the streets were partially reclaimed by the relentless advance of nature. Al was reminded of his visit to 2087 following the Cyberwars. Back then, society had been devastated, and the infrastructure that everyone took for granted lay utterly destroyed.

The ruins of Chernobyl offered numerous hiding spots, increasing the risk of ambush. The three of them proceeded along a desolate street in single file when another gunshot pierced the air. Dodder sprinted out from an old building, only a hundred metres away, pursued by three men clad in camouflage attire, brandishing automatic weapons. Suddenly, two more men emerged in front of Dodder, effectively trapping him between them. As they closed in, one of them raised his weapon with the intent to shoot the mutant.

"Hey!" Al called out.

Vee fired a warning shot into the sky.

The hunter who had been aiming at Dodder lowered his weapon in response.

Al strode up to them. "Hey, what's happening here?" he demanded, his tone stern.

The men, appearing as if they hadn't had a proper wash in days, glared at Alice and Vee, caught off guard by the unexpected confrontation. They reminded Alice of his mercenary comrades from 2087.

The individual who had been on the verge of shooting Dodder gruffly spoke up in broken English, "Not speaking English."

"What language then?" Alice inquired.

"Ukrainian?" Nimrod suggested.

"I asked, what's the matter here?" Al queried in fluent Ukrainian, impressing Nimrod.

"Why is that your concern?" the burly man retorted sharply. "Who are you? Wait a minute..." His expression shifted to one of surprise, and then he whispered something excitedly to one of his companions. Following a brief discussion, he fixed Al with a glare, as though he had recognised something Al was wearing. He then switched to English and asked, "Are you not Black Alice?"

Al smirked discreetly, saying from the corner of his mouth, "Yeah, that's me."

All five men immediately lost interest in Dodder, and the burly man, now much friendlier, inquired in English while rummaging through his dungaree pockets, "Is it okay?" He pulled out a cellphone and asked, "Selfie?"

The hunters were elated to meet their rock hero. The atmosphere shifted from tense confrontation to jovial camaraderie, complete with backslapping and smiles all around.

It didn't take long for Al and the hunters to come to an agreement to leave the mutants alone. They also conceded to take them to Nimrod's team being held at their camp nearby. They admitted to being responsible for belting Nimrod over the head. They'd captured the team because they were getting in the way of the annual hunt.

While Vee and Nimrod were talking with the hunters, Al approached Dodder who had stayed a short distance away. The swelling had gone down on the eye Al had bashed. Speaking in Ukrainian, Alice told him, "I'm sorry I hit you." He held out his hand to shake. Dodder tentatively took his hand and shook it with a big happy grin on his face. "They won't hunt you people any more, you can go in peace," Al told him. Dodder couldn't speak but Al could see in his eyes he understood. He nodded, waved goodbye, and then ran off to vanish in the nearby ruins.

That night there was plenty of cheer around the campfire from Alice, Vee, Nimrod, the four other members of his team, and the hunters after getting stuck into a few bottles of Chernobyl Vodka the hunters had brought with them. One of the hunter's dogs began to bark angrily. The hunter jumped up and flashed his torch into the nearby wooded area and it illuminated half a dozen mutants standing amongst the trees, watching them, frightened.

"There's Dodder," Al said, getting to his feet and pointing him out in the thicket. He called out, "Hey Dodder, over here... bring your friends, they're safe."

Like frightened animals, they slowly emerged from the shadows and joined the party. Alice had Ivan—the leader of the hunters—take snaps of them with Dodder, Vee, and Nimrod. Then shots with everyone, like a sports team photo. He then had Ivan send the shots to Secta's cellphone with a note for him to pass them onto Jax, that her father was safe and well. He added that he and Vee were ready to come home.

Half an hour later, a vortex opened.

The photographs had everyone at OTT excited. Upon receiving them, Secta had forwarded them to Jax, who immediately rang him back, over the moon that Alice had found her father and he was safe.

The Professor confessed to Secta, "If feels damn good to finally use Kairos for humanitarian reasons rather than for battling against bloody Zen."

"Yes, I totally agree with you Vic," Secta said, still staring at the photographs on his cellphone in admiration.

Dr Robert James, the Kairos operations director, swivelled on his chair from the control room console to face the others and announced urgently, "In–coming."

Karzoff and Viktoria were looking over Secta's shoulder at the photos on his phone.

"Safe to go in?" Karzoff said, looking up at Rob.

Kairos was now all lit up, an arrival imminent. Robert checked the computer readout for radiation. It was showing a red light, then it flicked to green. "Okay, now Karzoff," Rob confirmed, "coast is clear."

Karzoff gave Viktoria a nudge. They drew their weapons and entered the advent room to guard against the potential arrival of an unexpected visitor. It had happened previously, so it was made practice to be vigilant at arrivals.

Vee stepped through Kairos followed closely behind by Alice. Karzoff and Viktoria had their guns trained on them.

Alice declared, "All clear."

Karzoff and Viktoria stood down and then greeted the two travellers.

PA to the President of Oceana, Rita Vallins, hurried into the President's office and interrupted Malcolm Low from reading the newspaper.

"Sir, there's an interview on Watch This Space regarding the Octagon you should watch."

Mal lowered his newspaper and smiled. The same age as Alice and his best mate, Mal was the former singer of a rock band, The Units, as well as the former leader of the Octagon Peace Movement. Once elected President of Oceana following the assassination of his predecessor, Mal had stood down from the Octagon but had always maintained an interest. He nodded for Rita, who was as always dressed to the nines, this day in a dark green business suit with her blonde hair tied up, to lower the television monitor.

While triggering it to drop from the ceiling Rita said, "There has been a hostile takeover of the Octagon by a group led by a woman, who goes by the name of Toeghan Hitz."

"Never heard of her... odd name," Mal said, with furrowed brow.

The TV locked into place and Rita worked the remote to tune-in the show in question.

A young woman with short spiked black and royal blue hair,

dressed in military gear, was being interviewed on a small set by Meagan Tickle, the host of Watch this Space.

"So, why the forced takeover of the Octagon and to what end?" Tickle, the debonair blonde in her mid-thirties asked.

"The Octagon was outmoded, old-hat... a hangover from the days it was directed by the has-been rock star Black Alice and then his obsolescent friend Mal Function, now President. The mandate of the Octagon was to oppose the government when it got out of line, but since Mal Low became president that went out the window and it became a toothless tiger. So now it's not anymore. We aim to bring down the government by exposing its treachery."

"That doesn't make any sense," Tickle countered. "Oceana has been at peace and stable since Mal Low took office, what is there to complain about... what treachery?"

"Times have changed, the country needs to be ruled by people power. It's the same all over the world, look at the power of the people in Hong Kong, London, Paris... they've rallied, protested and used force to bring about change."

"And has that been for the better?" Tickle asked, shrewdly.

"Only history will prove that. But it's how change has always been brought about."

"You're talking revolution."

Hitz narrowed her eyes at the camera, "There are many names for bringing about change and that's certainly one of them. It didn't take long for Low once he got into a palatial office suite in the Ivory Tower at the big end of town, to start acting like every other politician that had proceeded him. He now looks down at the proletariat, totally disconnected from his electorate."

"Are you suggesting he's no longer the preferred President?"

Hitz stressed, "I know Low is no longer the preferred president of Oceana."

The camera cut back to a mid-shot of Tickle. "There you have it... the views of Toeghan Hitz, leader of the New Octagon, you saw it first on Watch this Space."

Annoyed, Mal picked up the remote, switched off the TV and pressed the button for it to retract back into the ceiling.

"Don't like it Rita. Has Alice returned from the mission yet?" he said grumpily. Obviously irritated by the interview.

"Yes, he has sir… he and Vee returned last night."

"Good, then please ask Al to come in, he'll want to know about this. Oh, and ask Karzoff as well."

An hour later Alice and Karzoff were seated in armchairs opposite Mal sipping coffees.

After Al had given the president a brief report on the mission to Chernobyl, Mal replayed the Watch this Space interview for them. Following that, they got into discussing it.

"This is no good mate, she's trying to stir up an uprising, turning public opinion against you," Al said.

Karzoff smiled at Alice and noted facetiously, "Yes, all seems too familiar does it not? Hand out the guns and ammo?"

In quoting a line from one of Alice's old record releases, he was referring to a time not so long back when both Alice and Mal were promoting revolution themselves. Back then, Alice had even been arrested as a dissident, and in an attempt to eliminate him, the government had tricked him into participating in an experiment where he ended up a hologram and was dispatched into the future, which had initiated the time travel process.

"Yes well, that was then and this is now," Mal reminded Karzoff.

"It reeks of Honor," Karzoff urged.

"What makes you say that?" Mal questioned, suspicious of Karzoff perhaps being a touch paranoid.

"It is her style to set someone up to incite anarchy. Let me check this Toeghan Hitz out, in the meantime, in order to stop the spread of negativity about you Mal, I suggest you come up with the means to reconnect with the rank and file… something to lift your public image and endear you to them."

Mal was slowly nodding his head aware Karzoff was right. After the red-haired man had left the office, Alice came up with an idea.

"How about we put on a free concert, have it televised and podcast, beat it up big time. You do a cameo as a special guest on stage with me and we do a couple of numbers."

"Brilliant idea, mate. I'll go on Watch this Space to announce it."

"It'll be a Black Alice gig with World, Cried Wolf and maybe the thrash metal band People Eaters in support... that should pack them in," Al speculated.

"Where would we hold it?" Mal asked.

Al thought it over for a few seconds and then had a revelation, "Avalon."

"What, where the bunker is?"

"Yeah, an open-air festival. It's a top area, easy to access... we'd get fifty or a hundred thousand there."

"Maybe more I reckon seeing it'll be free. You organise the bands and staging, and I'll put together a committee to do the rest," Mal said, enthusiastically.

"Keep your appearance a cameo... so that it's a dead-set surprise... let's get sponsors on-board and then donate that money to Orphans Oceana, that'll add to the cred to it and give it good karma."

"Great thinking Al. When should we do it?" asked Mal.

"Need to beat the rainy season, so the sooner the better, besides, we've got to beat this bird Toeghan Hitz to the punch."

"I hear you mate. Next month? That enough ramp-up time?"

Al cracked a broad smile and chortled, "Yeah sure, we can cut it in any key mate."

CHAPTER 3
THE MISSION

THE PLAN WAS set in motion for the Avalon concert. Mal assembled a committee of experienced concert project managers and marketing professionals to get the job done. No expense was to be spared; it was intended to be a massive PR campaign for Mal to regain the nation's confidence, which he hadn't truly lost. Threatening attempts were underway to undermine his presidency.

It didn't take long for Karzoff to gather information on Toeghan Hitz, but he found nothing seditious or a link to Zen or Honor as he had hoped. Convinced there was a connection somewhere, he persisted in his search to uncover it.

While all this was happening, Alice rehearsed a couple of sets with his band. He also held discussions with several concert managers he knew, discussing sound, lighting, and staging for the concert. He appointed an old friend and former road manager, Tadpole, to handle the talent logistics. Everything was set in motion.

At the same time, Secta and the Professor were busy refining the time travel process further. They were both grappling with the challenge of how to lock onto a target to send Alice into the future. While Hope had managed to place a marker in Morri's child's DNA, they realised that without an object from the desired time, they wouldn't be able to create a wormhole. Travelling to the past had never posed such a problem; a certified organic relic was all they needed. However, the future presented a different challenge—obtaining a relic from the future required actually travelling there, and that was the crux of the matter.

Zen had secretly resolved this problem with the Astral Projection Interface that Adamski and Gorrick had perfected, and they were preparing to test it.

Dr Luna Cairn had returned to Oceana after a few weeks at her United Nations Time Travel office in New York, where she had finalised a draft of the Temporal Prime Directive. The time had come for her to present it to Dr Secta and Professor de Luz for their valuable input.

"Has Zen agreed to it yet?" the Professor asked Dr Cairn as they sat in the Oceana boardroom.

"No, but I've heard from reliable sources that Zen has moved its time travel facility, which, by the way, they've named Aquila, to your old hunting grounds, Professor."

"Aquila, Latin for eagle, the bird that carried Zeus' thunderbolts in Greco-Roman mythology," Secta quipped.

"Desertron... yes, Bruckmaster informed me they were giving the old place a makeover," Vic acknowledged.

"So, can we deduce that Zen and the US Government are collaborating?" Secta inquired.

"We believe it's a black-ops CIA facility known as Area TWO, an acronym for Time-Travel Works Operative," Luna shared.

"An addition to Area 51," the Professor grumbled.

"Yes, you could say that. We've been in talks with Brigadier Bruckmaster's office about TWO joining the accord. They were given a draft, but we're still awaiting their response."

She handed Secta and the Professor each an A4-sized booklet adorned with a logo and the title: UNTT Temporal Prime Directive Prospectus.

Secta flipped through the pages. "Hmmm, two hundred pages; this will take some time to digest."

"If you can read it over the next few days and jot down notes. I'd like to meet at the end of the week to discuss it."

Both scientists agreed.

"One last matter for today, gentlemen. In the past twenty-four hours, an unauthorised time travel event occurred. It wasn't OTT due to the point of origin. We have the destination coordinates—it was Area TWO, and the designation was Oceana in the year 2112. Since Area TWO hasn't yet joined the UNTT accord and hasn't agreed to the TPD, and they continue to ignore our cease and desist notice, we are at liberty to provide you with the specific coordinates of their covert mission." She handed the Professor a page containing a set of numbers.

The Professor hung up the phone after his conversation with his old friend, US Colonel Larry Freeman. He had obtained the information he was seeking and immediately headed to Secta's lab to share the details.

"Just finished talking to Larry. He's pretty upset about Bruckmaster defecting to the CIA and taking control of Desertron. The silver lining is that he's willing to provide me with insider information about Zen's activities. It's a small way for him to get back at Bull," the Professor explained.

Secta was engrossed in his computer terminal. "Okay, what's the story?"

"Adamski's in charge of the scientific side of Desertron, now known as Aquila, and Bull heads up the US side, the facility, Area TWO. They've recruited a time traveller Larry believes to be Voltaris Idram, the bum that grilled me in New York... and get this... he's been sent on a mission to retrieve technology from the future."

"Fascinating... So, they're clearly hoping to acquire something that will give them an edge over us," Secta mused.

"What's your plan of action?" the Professor inquired.

"We can't afford to let them succeed, can we?" Secta remarked.

"Tell me... Zen can't have time travel ability in 2112, or they would have by now sent someone back in time to help TWO, so what would they be thinking they could get from 2112 that would be of value to them?"

"That's a very good question Vic, I have no idea. I've often wondered why the older version of myself in 2047, that we dealt with, has never used Kairos IV to send someone back to now, other than Sonoko of course?"

"We know the answer to that, don't we? By 2047, OTT is a signatory of the Temporal Prime Directive. I went through the draft last night, have you had a chance to?" the Professor asked.

"I started but got sidetracked," Secta confessed.

"The directive mandates that all backward time missions be approved by UNTT through formal submission. There's a lot of concern about the potential alteration of our present timeline due to inadvertent or intentional interference," Vic explained.

"That's logical. Perhaps that's why Zen didn't possess time travel capabilities in 2087 when Al and I were there. Maybe UNTT managed to shut down Area TWO before the Cyberwars," Secta speculated. He stood up and continued, "I think it's time we discuss this with Mal. We need his consent for a mission to 2112. It would also provide us with an opportunity to reconnect with Morri and Turk, twenty-five years after our last encounter."

A couple of days later, Secta and Vic were ready to raise the prospect of the next OTT mission. However, before they could, they were summoned to the President's office for an urgent meeting. When they arrived, they found that Dr Cairn had called the meeting. Those present included Alice, Vee, Robert, Karzoff, and Viktoria.

Dr Cairn had scrutinized OTT's mission reports as a requirement of the UNTT accord and was troubled by what she found, particularly OTT's involvement in world events during the 2047 mission to Japan.

Taking the floor, Dr Cairn began, "I called this meeting because, after compiling the draft of the Temporal Prime Directive Prospectus, which you've been provided with copies of, I've come to the conclusion that OTT's actions might be in violation of the Prime Directive, as outlined in the mission reports."

Mal interjected, "Excuse me, Doctor, but there has only ever been a self-imposed prime directive, so technically OTT cannot be in breach of anything."

"You're correct, Mr President, but the way OTT handled the pandemic situation in Tokyo in 2047 is concerning," Cairn responded.

"That event hasn't even happened yet, Dr Cairn. I'm not sure what you're getting at," Alice retorted.

"You altered the timeline, Mr Alice," Cairn stated bluntly.

"The Temporal Prime Directive is concerned with the past and interfering in the affairs of other civilizations, right?" Alice questioned.

"Yes, Alice, you're right. In the context of the future, whether Alice was travelling from now to Tokyo in 2047 or from Sydney in 2047 to Tokyo in 2047, it doesn't make a difference. That doesn't violate the TPD," Secta explained.

"That's accurate. However, using time travel to manipulate another country's events is not acceptable," Luna countered, her tone resolute.

Alice wasn't backing down and retorted, "Listen, Doctor, if we hadn't intervened, Tokyo in 2047 would be practically wiped out, and the contagion would have spread globally. If you want to point fingers, go after Zen—they started the damn pandemic. All we did was save the world."

"You seem to have a bit of a messiah complex, Mr Alice," Dr Cairn snapped.

Mal could sense the tension escalating and tried to defuse the situation, "Dr Cairn, Dr Cairn... there's no need for derogatory rhetoric. You need to understand the context of the situation but in saying that OTT and Alice cannot be held responsible for the unlawful, irresponsible actions of Zen Corporation. I agree with Alice that the UN's wrath would be better levelled at the transgressor and not us, and besides you have Area TWO right on your doorstep and they're unwilling to conform in any way... shouldn't they be more deserving of your attention?"

"You can't be given carte blanche to manipulate history at will," Luna said sternly.

Alice didn't back down, retorting, "Listen lady, we change history every time we step on an ant, and so do you."

Clearly displaying her annoyance, Dr Cairn stood up abruptly, "I'll leave you to discuss the TPD prospectus, and I expect your input by tomorrow at the latest. Good day." She shot them a scowl and swiftly exited the office.

"Well, that's certainly going to complicate our attempts to gain UNTT approvals moving forward," the Professor sighed.

"I believe the reason we didn't encounter time travel in 2087 was because the UN banned it after 2047. I think my future self was trying to convey that to me," Secta admitted.

"Our esteemed Dr Cairn conveniently omitted mentioning the unauthorised mission Zen launched a few days ago from their new time travel facility in Texas," the Professor grumbled.

"What's this about?" Mal inquired.

"Luna informed us that Zen has sent an operative to 2112 illegally, and we have the coordinates," Vic explained.

"Why would Zen send someone to 2112, and where specifically?" Al queried.

"I cross-referenced the coordinates, and it points to Angel City," Robert disclosed.

Alice queried, "So what? They've sent someone to visit Zen in Angel City twenty-five years after we were last there... why?"

"It would have to be to mine future technology for them to get the edge on us," Karzoff proposed.

"I think you're right, Karzoff," Mal said, "and if you are, and Secta is right and the UN ultimately shuts down time travel, then we still have a few years before 2047."

"I don't think they will completely shut it down, only a total ban against time travel into the past because it could have serious consequences for our time and the future. But I think they will permit time travel off-world, as a means of exploration... under the auspices of the Prime Directive," Secta proposed. "But for now, we need to focus on what we need to do, and I think we need to send a mission to 2112 to prevent Zen mining future technology."

"Do we know who they sent?" Al asked.

"Yes, Colonel Freeman told me it was CIA agent Voltaris Idram. The big mug that kidnapped me in New York," snarled the Professor.

"And what about UNTT approval for the mission?" Mal questioned.

The Professor said with a curt smile, "Leave Dr Cairn to me, I'll get us mission approval."

"So, recap for me, Alice, so I can get the gravitas of the situation," Mal requested.

"Zen has sent this dude Voltaris—" Al started.

"Idram," the Professor added.

"Right, Voltaris Idram, to Zen HQ in Angel City in the year 2112 to mine technology to further them in their race against our superiority in the time travel stakes. If we don't stop them, there's a chance they'll get a nose in front of us," Al explained, with a metaphor.

"Are you okay with the mission, Al?" Mal inquired.

Alice thought about it long and hard and then concluded, "Look, there's another reason for going to twenty-five years after we left, and that's to see what happened to Turk and Morri and the fight against tyranny... I don't know about you blokes, but I still get bad dreams about the battle they had ahead of them against Zen, and I, for one, would like closure on it. Secondly, we can't let Zen get one up on us. Irrespective of what Doctor bloody Cairn and her cronies think, we have this time travel technology and with it comes responsibility... that means not letting bastards like En-Lil, Gorrick, Idram, Bruckmaster, and Zen defeat the forces of good... us."

"Well said, Alice," En-Ki said in his mind.

"I hear you, Al," Mal said enthusiastically.

One thing for sure about the members of OTT: they were all on the same page.

"I want to go along," Vee submitted.

"That's up to Alice, but in this case, I want to go as well. I also have a vested interest," Secta said.

"Happy to have you both on board... when are we out of here? I've got a gig to do here in six weeks that I'll need to be back for," Al reminded them.

"Is everything okay with the coordinates and Kairos, Rob?" Secta checked.

"All shipshape," Rob responded positively.

"Well then, as soon as we get a Go signal from UNTT. It's now up to you, Vic," Secta said, with a wry smile.

CHAPTER 4
DECISION FATIGUE

T HE RINGTONE OF 'Reck', one of Alice's songs, shattered the silence in the darkness that was only punctuated by the phone light and intermittent flashes of red. The neon sign outside cast streaks of light through the window, across the foot of Alice's bed in his Kings Cross apartment. A hand emerged from under a blanket, fumbling for the phone, grasped it, and then retreated back under the covers.

"Yeah?" Alice grumbled.

"It's Jax. Did I wake you?"

"No, I'm always up at 4 a.m. Just about to go for a jog," Al said with a hint of sarcasm. "What's up, Jax?"

"Sorry, maybe I should call back later?"

"No, might be asleep then. Go ahead."

"Firstly, thank you for rescuing Nimrod…but now I've got a fresh problem. Blake went to Tahiti to investigate the explosion and just called me to say he's putting together an expedition into the Poo Ôonoo Valley. I'm afraid, Alice… you know what he's like… impetuous."

Alice had encountered Jax, an archaeologist, and her partner Aussie Blake Green in the jungles of the Poo Ôonoo Valley in Tahiti while searching for the Tablets of Destinies. Their expedition had been attacked by Zen agent Kew and his team of commandos, barely escaping the jungle alive. Kew was now deceased, and Zen had lost interest in the valley. However, Jax aimed to have the site of the lost city they discovered listed as a UN heritage site to prevent the construction of a dam that would flood the valley and bury the ancient ruins. The Tahiti Hydroelectric Commission had deliberately caused an explosion to seal the entrance to the ruins, and Blake aimed to expose their involvement to bolster the case for UN listing. He also sought vengeance against Louis Sens, a surveyor from the Tahiti Hydroelectric Commission, who had led them to the ruins and then betrayed them, leaving them for dead.

Unbeknownst to Blake, Agent Zeff Triella of the French Secret Service had been assigned by the Tahiti Hydro Commission to prevent Jax and Blake from accessing the Poo Ôonoo Valley.

Alice sat up in bed, switched on the bedside lamp, revealing his fatigued face with dark circles under his eyes. "Is he off his meds or something? He's just asking for trouble."

"I thought you might give him a call and try to talk some sense into him. I don't want it to end up another rescue mission," Jax admitted.

"No, you're only allowed one rescue a month, and besides, I'm about to head on a mission myself, not sure how long I'll be gone. Alright," he yawned, "I'll give him a ring. Chaa!"

After ending the call, Alice dialled Blake. It was 8 a.m. in Papeete.

Blake answered in a hoarse voice, "Hey, Alice… I hope you're not ringing to try and talk me out of going into the valley."

"Why would I stop you from getting yourself killed, mate? If that's your goal, well—"

"Using reverse psychology, huh? You must have been a star pupil," Blake chuckled.

"Yep, year two was the pinnacle of my academic career," Al joked. "Listen, your lady's worried about you, alright? I'm off on a mission, so I won't be around to bail you out if things go south."

"Mate, Zen's not gonna bother… I heard from Jax that Viktoria said you took care of Kew. The only opposition I'll face is a bunch of Hydroelectric Commission clowns and Louis Sens."

"Yeah, well, I bet you're itching to settle the score with that bloke," Al growled.

"Too right. Look, you know how women worry, right?"

"Yeah, I hear you. Just watch your back, okay?" Al advised.

"Sure thing. By the way, how's your lovely sister?"

"Not far away enough from you, but she will be soon. She's joining me on the next mission. Take care, big fella. Chaa!"

Alice sent Jax a quick text, informing her that he'd spoken to Blake but couldn't dissuade him. He assured her not to worry. He placed the phone on the bedside table, turned off the lamp, and went back to sleep.

Rehearsals had been going well with the Black Alice band. They'd got down a few new numbers Alice had composed, that they wanted to record but with no time for Alice to contribute, they decided for the band to record the backtracks and for Al to do the vocals when he had the time.

Vee turned up at rehearsal with a friend from Perth, Tippy Lane. She'd been working for a couple of years in artist management in Perth and figured she needed to step up and so had moved to Sydney looking for a gig. Alice took an instant liking to her. On the same page as him and the band, she was a goth, good looking, tough, trustworthy and most of all, street smart. Vee and Tippy were mates from the orphanage, so their friendship was deep and something Al could relate to being an orphan himself.

They'd gone from the rehearsal room to the nearby South Sydney Rugby League Club in Redfern. Al was a member and they were up for a Chinese dinner in the restaurant. The band, Vee and Tippy were seated at a round table.

"So, Tip, you're into our music then?" Al queried.

"Yeah, dig it. Always been a bit of a fan being from Perth and all. I love Slut's playing."

"Don't say that, next he'll be autographing the menu," Blue joked.

Slut's voice came from behind a veil of black hair, "Aw, give it a break Blue."

"You got a gig?" Al asked Tippy.

"Not yet. Crashing at Vee's for now... but there are some prospects out there. Have to focus on earning to pay the rent first."

"How about managing us? We've got a big open-air concert coming up in eight weeks and I could do with a hand," Al said.

"What's it pay?" Tippy asked.

"Hey, I like her," Alice said, with a devious chuckle.

"Vee'll sort that out with you. But I'll expect you to be on the ball, no booze, no drugs... bounce your moves off me or Ratsso. Liaise with the boys daily. Prioritise looking after our interests. Connect with the record label and publishers and the concert promoters. It's a charity gig broadcast nationally and podcast globally. Can you cut all that?"

"Piece of cake, Al," Tippy said, confidently.

"Done, let's eat," Al said, shaking hands with Tippy to close the deal.

After dinner Al took a taxi with Vee and Tippy to the Coogee apartment. He wanted to go over some of the business details for the band with Tippy.

On the way Vee told Al she suspected someone of spying on her. A couple of times she'd noticed someone tailing her and there had been a guy in a car on his own outside her apartment every night for the last week. Tippy had seen him as well.

When the cab pulled up outside the apartment block at Coogee Beach, Vee surreptitiously pointed out the car parked opposite with the guy sat behind the wheel.

The two girls waited while Al cruised over to the black sedan and tapped on the driver's side window with his knuckle.

The window opened and Buddy Holman peered at Alice.

"I met you in Texas," Al growled.

Holman sneered smugly at Alice. "So?"

"I don't like you." Alice smacked him on the button with a sharp right jab that knocked the CIA agent senseless.

"Stay away from Vee or next time it'll be worse. Tell that to your boss Bruckmaster," Al snarled, before strolling back over to Vee and Tippy. "He won't bother you again," he growled.

After arriving back in Sydney from Texas, Dr Li had returned to working on the design of the RF3 android warbot, while anxiously waiting for the return of Voltaris Idram from 2112, banking on him to bring back a faster and superior organic processor than what they'd obtained from OTT, which was beginning to show errors. Both she and Adamski were unaware that Secta had infected the matrix organic chip he had traded with them for Miss Vallins—with a herpes virus. Some months later, this virus was causing the glitches in the system.

Honor had also returned to her Sydney office. Since the failure of her plan to eradicate Alice and Vee's parents in 1976, and the subsequent loss of Kew, she was in bad books with Gorrick. Her current focus was using Buddy Holman to spy on Vee and coordinating insurgency against Malcolm Low. She had managed to hijack the Octagon Peace Movement by instating Toeghan Hitz as the new leader.

Gorrick was in his office, meeting with his clone Gorrick Khan.

"No, you cannot move abroad to a chapter of your own. You will serve here as my body-double. The threat of another attempt on my life is even more imminent now that we have forged a joint venture with TWO," Gorrick asserted.

"Yes, sir," Khan said, acquiescing and subservient to En-Lil, his divine leader who had made Gorrick his host.

"We are now in the arms business, Khan. The objective is to develop the RF series warbot to be sold to the defence departments of global governments. I will need you to close the sales. That way, I can effectively be in two places at once. All we need is for Voltaris to return with technology far superior to anything on Earth now."

"What's to stop Bruckmaster from getting his hands on it first for the US government?" Khan proposed.

"That, my friend, is the least of our concerns. I have the brigadier in my pocket."

"I can't believe that you of all people, an academic of such high qualification, could condone Alice removing the Ark of the Covenant from the Temple of Solomon in 587 B.C .... it's... it's blasphemous. You need to send him back now to put it back, or I won't approve your latest mission application," Dr Cairn snapped, folding her arms and crossing her legs. Her body language was designed to impress her disapproval upon the Professor.

They were in Luna's Darling Harbour hotel suite, where the Professor had been invited for a late morning breakfast to discuss the TPD. With his eggs Benedict finished, he was sipping on a coffee with a cheeky grin on his face.

"We can't do that, Luna. It would put two Alices in the same place at the same time; they'd cancel each other out. What he did was ordained by En-Ki. Are you trying to tell me you're a higher authority than he?"

"No, but I'm not convinced all this meddling with history is kosher, Vic. It's not my fault I'm Jewish."

Vic opened his laptop on the coffee table and said, "Let me show you something."

He displayed three photographs. "What do you see?"

"The controls of a spacecraft, probably from NASA or SpaceX."

"Okay," he closed the laptop. "Remember Viktoria introduced you to Dr Jax De Ville?"

"Yes, the archaeologist from Boston University."

"Correct. She told you that the ruin of Lahmu, which she discovered in the Poo Ôonoo Valley of Tahiti, should be given world heritage listing, correct?"

"Yes, that has since been disturbed by an explosion that seems very convenient for the Electricity Commission, who are intent on flooding the valley."

"Correct. However, you also read Alice's mission statement for the trip to 2,500 B.C., didn't you? And how he met Jax?"

"Yes."

"Well, the picture I just showed you was indeed a spacecraft. What wasn't in Alice's report was the real story about Ninurta and An-Zu and how Alice got from Turkey to the Poo Ôonoo Valley in Tahiti in 2,500 B.C. with Ninurta."

"Yes, I had wondered about that. Go on."

"They flew there in a spacecraft. The pictures I just showed you are of that spacecraft. They were taken by Jax."

Her eyes grew to the size of dinner plates with amazement. "Are you trying to tell me a spacecraft from 2,500 B.C. is inside that cave in the Poo Ôonoo Valley?"

"Yes, here, take a look." He re-opened his laptop and ran through twenty more photographs. By the time she'd studied all of them, she was mind-blown.

"This discovery could change history... religion... our entire perception of ancient myths and legends... it validates the theories of Zecharia Sitchin that have been debunked since he professed them in the 1970s. It validates the En-Ki and En-Lil story and the quest Alice has been on since we discovered how to time travel," Vic explained.

Luna eyeballed him. "Why did you censor the mission reports?"

"Because we are acting responsibly... not irresponsibly as you accused us at the meeting with the President. The exposure of all we have found could bring down organised religion, governments— undermine ancient history, and cause massive public confusion.

Furthermore, do you realise how many times Alice has risked his life to save the people of this planet? Had he not succeeded, there would be no history. And if he fails to continue to succeed, we will be faced with a very dark future indeed. The mission we ask you to approve will again have Alice risking his life, along with Vee and Secta, to prevent Zen and TWO from acquiring future technology they would undoubtedly use against mankind. Such is the magnitude of the mission. Should it fail, it could very well spell the end of civilization as we know it. We can't afford to have that sort of superior technology and weaponry fall into the hands of an organisation that lacks scruples. Is that what the UN wants? Time travel technology is by far the greatest discovery in history. The aim should be to use it to explore and reveal the truth for mankind, but to get to that point, we first need to secure the technology. We must set rules and rid the world of those who would use time travel for evil intent. Secta and Hope are worthy of a Nobel Prize for the discovery, not the wrath of those with limited vision."

His diatribe was followed by a long pause while Dr Cairn let it sink in. Finally, she got up, walked over to the window that looked out over beautiful Darling Harbour, and then turned back to Vic, her eyes fixed on him.

The Professor admired her beauty, backlit by the sun. Her knee-length navy blue skirt, her shapely legs, a light canary yellow dress shirt, hair up, her eyes filled with intellect, elegantly classic.

"You're right, Vic. You all deserve my apology. It was narrow thinking. I must be suffering from decision fatigue. You will have approval, and yes, we will strive to make Kairos the greatest exploration device in history."

CHAPTER 5
FROM TIME TO TIME

K ARZOFF WAS AT the OTT surveillance operations centre, watching pictures coming in from a new stealth drone his team was testing. He told the young technician operating the drone, "Can you zoom in on the entrance to Zen HQ, please, Zack?"

Zack triggered the zoom as requested, and the view transitioned from a wide shot hovering sixty metres above the thirty-storey Sydney building to a tight shot of the entrance. The digital picture had incredibly high definition, making the faces of pedestrians passing by easily distinguishable.

"Good, now activate FRS, please," Karzoff requested.

Once triggered, the Facial Recognition System superimposed an active red square around each person's head in the picture. Simultaneously, a computer swiftly retrieved their identity from a government database and projected their full name inside the square.

"If you click on the highlighted square, sir, it will read out all available records on that person: address, cellphone number, health records, financials, marital status, ethnicity, etcetera," Zack explained.

"Excellent," Karzoff said, enthusiasm in his voice.

He suddenly noticed that a woman exiting Zen HQ, with a highlighted square encasing her head, had the name Toeghan Hitz.

Karzoff leaned back in his chair and exclaimed, "Jackpot! The drone has just paid for itself. Lock onto Toeghan Hitz and follow her as long as the drone can stay in the air. How long is that by the way?"

"It depends on how far it needs to travel, sir, but at least an hour."

"Good, record it all, and I will review it later. Thank you, Zack, brilliant."

Karzoff hurried off to speak to the President.

As he entered the reception area of the Presidential suites, he found Mal at the front desk chatting with his PA, Rita Vallins. Mal turned to face the red-haired man. "G'day Karzoff, you look like you just won the lottery," he quipped.

"Sir, our new surveillance drone equipped with FRS has just picked up Toeghan Hitz leaving Zen HQ."

"Aha! That confirms your suspicion. Well done, mate. Now we know Zen has seriously compromised the Octagon. Oh, I just got word from the Professor, he managed to secure UNTT approval for the next mission. It will launch at midday."

"He is a far better man than I to achieve that from Dr Cairn," Karzoff said, shaking his head.

"Indeed, she's one tough lady," Mal confirmed.

"You're surrounded by them, gentlemen," Rita said, with a wry smile.

Alice entered the Kairos control room, all spruced up for the mission, wearing a dark green beret and specially tailored military-style black coveralls, a flak jacket, and black military jungle boots. He looked the part.

Rob swivelled around from the console and commented, "What's with the new threads, Al?"

"It was Viktoria's idea, nothing metal, all organic, no synthetics," he opened his arms, "it's like my stage gear... I dig it."

"Plenty of pockets," Rob observed.

"Yeah, this one's full of WASPS... might come in handy."

Vee entered dressed the same, only topped off with a black beret. "Wow! Look at you," Rob exclaimed.

"Great fit, tailor-made," Vee posed for Rob. "Top idea of Vik's, told her to work on an OTT logo patch next," she said, chirpily.

"Something like the NASA patch would fit the bill," Rob suggested.

Secta, accompanied by the Professor, was next to arrive. He was dressed the same as Al and Vee, only with a different coloured beret. He'd also had his hair cut short.

Al wolf whistled. "Hey, dig the hair and the purple beret, dude."

Secta took up a drag queen pose. "Thank you, darlings, yes, purple matches my skin tone, don't you think?... and it was time to lose the locks."

Mal, Karzoff, and Viktoria joined them. Viktoria immediately admired her clothing designs. "Excellent, you guys look happening... are they comfy?"

The three travellers nodded.

She went on, "I nearly died when Secta came in last night minus his silver locks. He looks like a different man, much younger."

"Looks like you're about to go on stage, Al," Mal said, with a chuckle.

"Yep, and a big one at that."

To their surprise, the door opened, and Dr Cairn entered, looking like a million bucks. She immediately made her presence felt by declaring, "Hi everyone, wouldn't miss this for the world. You guys look amazing."

They were all finding it difficult to accept her mood change.

"I owe you all an apology for the way I acted at our last meeting," she said sincerely.

"No problem, Luna, glad you have seen the light," Mal said. "Al, Karzoff spotted Toeghan Hitz coming out of Zen this morning."

"I had a drone follow her," Karzoff said. "She met for coffee in Balmain with a guy with plenty of form, Glan Denning, and was later joined by CIA Agent Buddy Holman."

"I thumped Holman the other night for spying on Vee," Al growled. "I guess that confirms your suspicion, Honor and Zen are behind the Octagon revolution, Karzoff?"

"Yes, but more so, I suspect they plan to use Glan Denning to hit either Mal or you... maybe at the concert. Security will need to be doubled on you now, Mal," Karzoff warned.

Mal grimaced at the thought of even more bodyguards to further cramp his lifestyle.

"We'll leave all that in your capable hands, Karzoff. In the meantime, we've got a mission to complete," Al said. "When will you open the return vortex, Rob?"

"Exactly seventy-two hours from departure time at 1100 hours. I took the coordinates provided by UNTT and then off-set them for you to arrive at Snake Ridge," Robert explained.

"Provided Snake Ridge is still there," Al said warily.

"Oh, I'll open a return vortex on Alice's marker every seventy-two hours, okay, Secta?" Robert added.

"Good," Secta acknowledged. "Yesterday I had my lab assistant go to the Avalon bunker and conceal a new more compact and powerful Isotopic Labelling Detection Device under the chair for us to collect. It is pre-calibrated to 777 to detect the marker in Morri's daughter's DNA," Secta explained.

It was nearly 11 a.m., time to go.

Rob fired up the mainframe.

The travellers said their goodbyes.

Vee stepped into the departure cubicle first. After she had gone, Secta was up next. The Professor stopped him. "Here, Secta, you might need these... all I had time to produce," he said, candidly handing over four Clock Drives.

Secta nodded in approval and pocketed them. "Probably won't need them, but you never know." They patted each other on the back, and then Secta entered the small room.

"Hey, Professor, how about working out how we can open a wormhole back to Kairos instead of having to wait around for one like Brown's cows?" Al suggested.

"Good idea, Al, I'll look into it, but it is way complicated," the

Professor admitted.

Alice approached Mal and said, "I'm expecting the concert to be all locked down by the time I get back, buddy. My new PA Tippy Lane will be in touch. You better get some rehearsal time in with the boys, mate."

"Yeah, I'll do that, Al."

"And Karzoff," Alice continued, "keep a close eye on this Toeghan Hitz, Denning, and that mug Holman. They're bad news. Don't want any crap to happen at the concert."

"Done, Alice."

Al ambled over to the departure room door with his usual swagger, turned, and idiosyncratically waved while declaring, "Chaa!"

When Al materialised, he didn't recognise where he was. Secta and Vee were waiting nearby.

"Is this all that's left of Snake Ridge?" Al said, gazing around at the burnt-out, decayed remains of the town, now overgrown with vegetation.

"Yes, it looks like the guys didn't win the battle. I was just describing the town to Vee. Hard to see anything that resembles it, looks like there was a terrible fire years ago, even the road has melted," Secta said, stamping a boot on the hot bitumen. "We're outside what used to be Reno's Bar, I think."

Alice wandered about, looking for signs of life, mumbling, exasperated, "Nothing, no people, no buildings... all gone."

A small shadow appeared on the road, and Vee looked up. Shading her eyes from the hot midday sun, she said, "There's something up there checking us out."

Alice and Secta looked up at a disc no larger than a standard dinner plate that was silently hovering twenty metres overhead.

"You can see the camera in its belly," Al said.

"Wonder who's side it's on?" Secta posed.

"That's assuming there are still sides," Al cracked, though not as a joke.

The drone zipped off as fast as it had appeared.

"Well, I guess we can expect some company soon," Al said.

He wasn't wrong. About twenty minutes later, they heard the rumble of a large vehicle approaching and took cover. Alice dug a WASP out of his pocket and clutched it in his hand, ready to throw if needed. Then, from the far end of what used to be the main road into town, a strange-looking vehicle appeared out of the mirage on the hot road and sped towards them.

"The sound reminds me of Morri's nuclear pellet-powered J-Car," Secta said.

"Yeah, but damn size bigger," Alice said, with alarm.

It took shape from being a globular image distorted by searing heat to a jungle-camouflaged six-wheeled armoured personnel carrier, an APC. An awesome-looking thing, it was right out of the pages of a sci-fi novel.

Each wheel was directly driven with independent suspension, and the armour cladding was strong enough to withstand most any ordnance.

"May as well put this away, it'd be about as destructive against that thing as a fly swatter," Alice said, shoving the WASP back into his pocket.

"At least it isn't showing any Zen livery," Secta observed. It was a positive, unless of course, they didn't use livery anymore. The beast of a vehicle pulled only six metres from them, kicking up a wall of billowing dust. It was a lot bigger than they'd calculated. At five metres high, eight metres long, and three metres wide, it was formidable. They heard a hatch automatically slide open on the top.

Alice, Secta, and Vee waited with bated breath for someone to emerge, wondering whether it would be friend or foe. But no-one came out.

They waited until it began to feel awkward, and then Secta said, "I guess we're being invited on board."

"You reckon? It reminds me of the bloody An-Zu bird... Come on then," Al barked, climbed up on the vehicle, and courageously entered through the open portal. A moment later, he popped back up and said to the others, "There's no-one inside, come on."

Vee boarded, and as soon as Secta joined them, the hatch slid shut, and with a sudden jolt, the vehicle started rolling. There were twelve metal chairs with seat belts that automatically locked the passenger in place as soon as the vehicle moved. Secta was over six feet tall, and there was still another four feet to the ceiling. There were no windows, ambient obscured lighting, and a single seat up front for a driver should manual operation be required. There was a small dashboard with dials, a joystick, and several foot pedals. The entire interior was painted a dull, boring military grey.

Al figured there had to be a pop-up screen on the console for forward viewing; otherwise, it couldn't be manually driven.

"Pretty fancy. Doesn't bounce round much, suspension is amazing. Wonder what speed we're doing?" Al mused.

At times, the journey was a little bumpy; they figured it was because they were negotiating some rough terrain, but eventually, the vehicle came to a stop, and the hatch hissed as it automatically opened.

"Guess we've arrived. Now we find out who gave us the ride," Alice said light-heartedly, as he climbed the ladder to exit through the hatch.

When he emerged, it was in a somewhat recognisable place, and standing beside the vehicle, unarmed, was a big man with a familiar face. It suddenly dawned on him who he was looking at.

"Animal? Is that you?" Al barked.

The big bearded man with long greying hair, his bare muscly arms folded defensively at his chest, glared at Alice and then growled, "Who are you?"

"Last time I saw you, we had a fight in the bunker, you got into the elevator and split."

Taken aback, Animal asked, "Black Alice?"

Al slid down the side of the vehicle, and once on the ground, he pointed back at it. "And that's Secta."

He knew Animal or any of the others from the last visit in 2087 wouldn't recognise them because they'd never seen their faces. Both Alice and Secta had arrived from their time back then, inside hosts: Turk for Alice and Morrigan Hud for Secta.

Animal looked at the tall, thin man emerging from the hatch, and his expression changed from circumspect to excited. "You've got to be joking... from all those years ago?" he crowed.

"Yes, when I was Turk and Secta was Morri... you're not still with Zen, are you?"

"Argh! No way, man, I formed a pact with Turk and Morri after the missile from Zen nearly took this place out, the very same day you departed."

Alice could see the remains of a crater where the replica of Stonehenge had once stood. "Took out Woodhenge. Is the bunker still there?"

Secta and Vee joined Alice.

"Animal, glad to see you jumped sides. Does that go for all the biker gangs?" Secta said, shaking the big man's hand.

"Yep, and we've been fighting Zen ever since. Who's this?" Animal asked, staring at Vee.

"Vee, Al's sister," she said.

"I know someone that's going to go nuts when she sees you. Come with me," Animal said. He led them over to a dome where the entry to the bunker used to be and pressed a remote. A door slid open in it.

"We had to cover the bunker entrance for protection," he explained, leading them inside.

"Against Zen?" Secta asked.

"Yeah, and other bunker tribes."

"Bunker tribes, who are they?" Secta asked.

"We'll fill you in on it all later. Do you remember the password?" Animal asked, checking they were legitimate.

"Open sesame," Secta announced in full voice.

"You've got to be kidding," Vee said ironically, as the trapdoor in the floor of the dome opened and a light flickered on to reveal the staircase down to a landing and the elevator.

"Same old password," Alice quipped.

The elevator door opened to a reception committee. They stepped out to confront two women and a guy. Alice and Secta immediately recognised them.

"Now let me see... Nerdo, Cutter, and Morri," Al said.

Morri had teared up. She threw her arms around Al and hugged him like a long-lost brother. "Alice, I thought I'd never see you again." She held him at arm's length and studied his eyes. "Not that I ever did see your face, but heck, I'd know you anywhere."

Then she faced Secta, "And my old inner-self." They hugged, compassionately.

"You might have grown older Morrigan Hud, but no less beautiful," Secta said, genuinely.

"And this is?" Morri questioned.

"This is my sister, Vee," Al said.

"Oh yes, I can see the family resemblance in her eyes." She gave Vee a hug. "Lovely to meet you, Vee."

"You too, Morri. I feel like I already know you after so many stories."

Alice faced Nerdo and Cutter. "Well, look at you two reprobates. How's the leg, Cutter?"

"Oh that, left me with a bit of a limp, but hell, I'm fine, Al." They hugged.

"Nerdo, look at you," Al said.

She had changed the most. Gone were the boyish looks.

"Alice and Secta... I've missed our scientific debates."

"You knew we were coming, didn't you?" Secta asked Morri.

"Of course, for two reasons... first, an ILDD turned up out of the blue under the old chair over there... an improvement on the last model, I must say, and secondly, the moment you arrived, I felt your presence. That's why we sent the drone."

"Still get the premonitions then?" Secta asked coyly.

"Yes, but we won't go into that, will we?" They both laughed. The joke was between them because only Secta knew from having possessed her how her premonitions were triggered.

Secta looked about the room. "Still looks the same."

"Yes, we kept it that way, like a shrine to you both... but that's where the old place ends." She clapped her hands, and lights flickered on for three hundred metres into the depths of the bunker, with alcoves leading off left and right: an extraordinary labyrinth of tunnels.

"Bloody hell, you've given the old joint a makeover," Al said, surprised.

"Yep, we built an entire city down here with a population of over two thousand."

Finally, Alice asked soberly, "Morri, where's Turk?"

CHAPTER 6
FLASHBACK

MORRI LOOKED AT Alice sorrowfully and said, "He was captured by Zen two years ago."

"And we've heard nothing of him since," Cutter added.

"Then we'll just have to go and bust him out, won't we?" Alice exclaimed in his characteristic bravado manner.

Morri handed Secta the ILDD. "Here's your unit."

"Oh, thanks," he said and switched it on. It immediately beeped. "Oh, it's getting a signal from over there," he said, pointing into the dimly lit depths of the bunker.

"Come with me," Morri said demurely.

They left Animal, and she led them into the labyrinth. Vee was chatting with Nerdo, Cutter, and Alice, while Secta walked ahead with Morri.

"I'm dying to know, did the embryo implant work?" Secta asked Morri.

"You bet it did. I gave birth to a beautiful baby girl."

"I can't wait to meet her. Does she know her heritage or have you kept it a secret?"

"Of course, she knows her biological father is Alice. You are her uncle, and your sister is her biological mother. How is she, by the way?"

Secta's mood changed to mournful. "She was murdered by Zen agents not long after we sent you the flask."

Morri stopped and embraced Secta. "Oh, I'm so sorry, Secta," she said warmly, emotional, shedding a tear. "Come, you can meet her now." Trying to cheer him up, she took his hand and led him into an alcove. Sensor ceiling lights illuminated an extremely long tunnel that had been constructed since he was last there.

"My goodness, will you look at all this?" Secta gawked, impressed by the extent of the construction.

"You know she's a genius, just like her mother. It was her idea to build all of this. She designed it... mainly for her labs. But it hasn't been easy with her."

"Why?" Secta asked.

"Well, when she was little, though she was extremely intelligent, she was a normal child. But you must remember she is the only child amongst our people, so that made it a different upbringing, you know with no one to play with... an abnormal childhood, shall we say. Then when it came to puberty, she went through a massive change. I mean a complete change... all of a sudden, she was a completely different person."

"Oh, that's normal with teenagers," Secta said, almost brushing it off.

"No, Secta, I'm talking about a total transition, as though she was suddenly possessed. She had new memories, a whole other life that I only caught a glimpse of because she hid it away with her in her lab. We hardly ever get to see her."

"So, this happened, what, when she was fourteen?" Secta asked.

"No, twelve. It nearly killed Turk. He always wanted to raise her as his daughter. I think because of what happened to Nora, his sister."

"Understandable."

She stopped them at a pair of double doors.

"So, she's twenty-five now, isn't she?" Secta asked.

"Yes, and she's obsessed with creating a new race. She has been harvesting her eggs since she was twelve, waiting for a sperm donor. She knows if she fails to impregnate women here, they will soon be too old to incubate a foetus, and there are no fertile sperm donors."

"It sounds to me like she inherited an awful lot from my sister," Secta admitted.

Morri opened the door and led them inside. The lab was equivalent to anything Secta had back at Oceana. In fact, it was so much a replica of Hope's OTT lab setup that it seriously rocked him.

"I can't believe this," Secta said, looking around the room, awestruck.

Alice strolled in and was immediately impressed, "Bloody hell, this is Hope's lab."

"You got that right, Alice," a female voice echoed from an adjoining room. Then, from out of the darkness glided a ghost. It was Hope, complete with the white lab coat... Hope in every way... the way she walked, the way she was wearing her hair up... her glasses. Secta and Alice were thunderstruck.

"Alice and Secta, meet my daughter, Hope."

Secta was so overwhelmed by seeing his sister that he had to sit down. It was the first time Alice had ever seen him totally lost for words.

Alice was also completely blown away and gasped, "I can't believe this."

Morri was confused by their reaction. "Why... w... what seems to be the problem?"

"She's Hope... I mean, she is the spitting image of Hope... an exact clone of her," Al explained.

Morri realised the gravity of the situation and quickly placed an arm around Secta's shoulders. She whispered, emotionally, "I, I had no idea, Secta."

"It's more than that," Hope said. "I am Hope. I have all of her memories right up until when she injected the egg with the genetic marker and then her own Pneumatide."

Secta jumped up from the stool like he'd been bitten on the backside by a spider. "Of course! Of course!" He began pacing the room.

The others watched him wondering what he was doing.

"That's how he thinks, the penny will drop in a second," Hope said knowingly.

Secta stopped right on cue and spoke out loud as though talking to himself. "The Professor found it on Hope's computer... Pneumatide is a chemical composition Hope had discovered and named after the Ancient Greek word Pneuma for soul, spirit, or breath. It is a neurotransmitter that carries the essence of consciousness, identity, and memory like nucleotide blocks of DNA. It means Hope implanted her very essence into the egg, which basically means this Hope is not only a clone of my sister but has her personality and her memories right up to the point of transference. This is astounding."

Secta stared long and hard at Hope, and then with tears welling up in his eyes, walked over and embraced her. "Oh, Hope, I've missed you."

"Why Secta, what has happened?" Hope asked, confused.

"Your mother was murdered by Zen agents not long after she fertilised the egg that became you, that's why the reaction," Al explained.

The three of them embraced, and then Morri joined in. It was an emotional yet uplifting homecoming.

A little later, Secta, Alice, and Morri were seated in Hope's office. Vee had gone with Nerdo and Cutter for a tour of the bunker city.

"So far, I have harvested thirteen years of my eggs, one hundred and fifty-six of them... the future of humankind, as far as we know, is dependent on them. The real issue is having them fertilised soon enough for them to be implanted in-vitro into surrogate mothers before the women are too old. With the exception of myself, as far as we know, there are none any younger than Morri. That means with over fifty-year-olds, the success rate is going to be way low."

While hearing Hope's distinctive voice, Al couldn't help but be reminded of his last moments with her. He was in a hospital bed in OTT after he'd returned from the planet Eris. Hope had ambled over to him, bent down, and given him a gentle peck on the cheek.

"That's no kiss," he complained, reached up, grabbed her chin, and pulled her towards him. They kissed passionately. Holding him tight after the kiss with tears welling up in her eyes, her voice broke as she admitted, "I didn't think you were coming back..."

He touched a tear traversing her cheek and said warmly, "Hey, I promised I'd be back. Besides, you never finished what you were telling me last time I was in a hospital bed."

They locked eyes, and a special moment passed between them. "I think I love..."

He quickly placed his finger on her lips to stop her words. "Shh, I know... some things are safer left unsaid."

She sniffled, nodded emotionally, gave him a gentle peck on the lips, and then left to get him some food from the canteen.

It had left him with a moral dilemma: Should I have told her I love her? He remembered battling with it for a moment and then decided, "Yes, you idiot, tell her. It's about time you stopped hiding from love. I will, I will, I'll tell her when she comes back."

The argument with himself was over. A smile broke on his tired face, happy to have finally made up his mind.

She might be the academic type, not exactly the sort of woman Alice would expect to fall for, but there had always been a special chemistry between them that seemed to have blossomed of late.

"Alice? Alice, are you at home? Knock, knock," Hope was saying, trying to snap him out of his reverie.

"Oh, sorry... I was somewhere else."

"Are you okay? Did SAGE work? Did it get rid of the nasty JAK2 gene?"

The mention of SAGE confirmed to both Secta and Alice that she was really Hope; there was no other way she could've known about the Professor's invention that had erased the nasty gene.

"Yes, SAGE worked a treat," Secta confirmed. "You've had no ill effects since, have you, Alice?"

"Um, no," Al said, still feeling awkward about Hope being alive.

"Look, I know this must be a shock to both of you, but think of the positive side, I'm back! How's Mal?" Hope said chirpily.

"He's fine, doing a great job of running the country," Secta said.

"Weird to think of him as president, isn't it... and Karzoff, Viktoria?"

"They're fine," Al confirmed.

"Robert... and Rita Vallins, remember? We traded her for the organic chip when she'd been kidnapped by Zen. They cut off her little toe, the bastards."

"Damn, they are as bad back then as they are here now," Morri complained.

"Morri, what's the latest on Zen's RF program?" Al asked.

"Ah, so much to tell you... after you guys left, Turk and I went back up to look for Nerdo and Cutter. It was devastating; the missile had levelled everything... Woodhenge was gone, and the bunker was in the centre of a massive smouldering crater. The elevator shaft was sticking out of it like a Gothic tower from the Dark Ages. I'll never forget standing beside Turk, looking down from the top at the blackened earth below."

"You'd dreamed that... I remember, it was one of your premonitions," Secta said.

"Exactly... Cutter and Nerdo were there; they'd taken cover underneath the F-200 to escape the blast. Then, out of the smoky, fire-ravaged night, Animal came staggering across the field, smoke rising from his singed clothing. It was then because he had been left for dead by that witch, Dr Ursula Mennis, that we sealed a pact to fight together against Zen.

"For the next four years, we did exactly that, but eventually Zen defeated your computer virus and got all of the telecommunications back online. That's when it became a different sort of battle... a fight to stop them using our OSCI implants against us. We couldn't remove the implant, as you well know; the stems extend organically into regions of the brain. So, it became a war of attrition; we needed to develop technology to jam the OSCI signal. Eventually, Nerdo succeeded in doing just that.

"At the same time, people were becoming paranoid. With Zen back online, minimal utilities began to function, one of them being the Internet. That allowed citizens to discover Oceana wasn't just an isolated case; the apocalypse had been global, and Zen was the perpetrator—the war, the fallout—the whole shebang. That initiated what we called the Bunker Wars. People began building underground fortresses and then defending them as though they were inverted castles. Now bunkers similar to this one are everywhere... it's the only way to defend against the might of Zen."

"Who are the builders and suppliers of the bunkers?" Al asked.

"All the different biker chapters. They're renowned for constructing bunkers."

"Yeah, even in our time," Al admitted.

Morri continued, "So by then, Zen was still trying to perfect the RF series. Nerdo could explain it better, but remember, you fought against an RF-7 and then the RF-8 that we incinerated in the warehouse?"

"Yes, yes, I remember that," Secta said with a chuckle, recalling how he threw the Molotov cocktail that set it ablaze.

"Well, they developed the RF-9, the 10, 11, and then there was a lag in time. You see, we were still able to beat them, so they went back to the drawing board, and three years ago, they came up with their pièce de résistance: the RF-20. And that's how we lost Turk."

"What happened?" Al asked.

"It was just like in my dream... I was standing alone with the soft orange glow of dawn licking my face, but there was nothing soft about what I was staring at. Skeins of mist drifted, as if on gossamer wings, through the valley far below my feet, but the mist was not natural; it was the aftermath of battle. Within the mist were intermittent flashgun-like explosive red flashes from detonating ordnance. I peered down at my toes overhanging the cliff edge upon which I was standing... my bare feet were cut, sore, and bleeding from the frantic climb over jagged rocks I'd made to reach the ridge. In my desperate escape from the enemy, thorny strands of blackberry bushes had whipped at me relentlessly, tearing my jeans to shreds and lacerating my bare legs. I inhaled deeply, a struggle to regain my breath. The scent of cordite, fires, and death was thick in the air.

"Glancing over the ridge, a sense of overwhelming loss consumed me. The Cyborg army had routed the People's Militia and was now systematically executing prisoners and the wounded with a single bullet to the head. The Militia had been up against insurmountable odds; over a hundred relentless, merciless, soulless, remote-controlled Cyborg soldiers, all designed and constructed by Zen, had, within a matter of days, nearly wiped out the Militia along with the civilian population. The horror was amplified by the fact that Zen hadn't risked a single human life on their side; the entire massacre had been remotely controlled by psychics under Gorrick's instructions, comfortably seated in their plush offices in Angel City.

"From my vantage point high on the ridge, I witnessed blood spraying from every headshot, accompanied by the delayed sound of each execution. My comrades were lined up like sheep at an abattoir, forced onto their knees and then shot. Turning away from the gruesome scene, a voice startled me. 'We're as good as done now.' It was Turk, holding a gun limply at his side. His face was stubbly, cut, and bleeding, his forearms bare and lacerated. Despite his battered condition, I couldn't help but admire his athletic body and the rugged beauty of his caring face. His bloody shredded shirt revealed his muscular frame, and amidst all the chaos, that look in his eyes, I so cherish, the one that made me feel safe, remained. He walked over to me, taking me into his strong arms. I surrendered to his touch, wondering why it always had to be like this? Why was there never enough time for us? A tear tracked down my soiled cheek. I closed my eyes, and could feel the desperation in his warm embrace.

"He held me at arm's length, our eyes locked, and he said passionately, 'It's only a matter of time before they find us. We need to make a run for it.' He was right; our safety and the safety of our daughter Hope were paramount. We exchanged one last despondent look at the panorama of devastation before us. As far as the eye could see, extending to the horizon, black columns of smoke rose from the bunkers that Zen had torched. In those annihilated bunkers lay the incinerated bodies of innocent victims who had fought so desperately to defend them. Zen had won. Traditionally, we mourn for the dead to rest in peace, but wouldn't it be far better for the living to live in peace?

"I remember gently resting my head on Turk's shoulder, allowing myself to weep. We were growing old, too old to continue the fight. I knew that surviving would require nothing short of a miracle. The end of humanity was nigh.

"We made it back to the bunker, but they were on our trail. Zen had developed a new batch of stealth drones so silent that their presence was virtually undetectable. It didn't take long for one of our recon teams to be nearly decimated by a group of RF-20 Warbots directed by stealth drones, all aimed at hunting us down."

"Turk had no choice. In order for our bunker settlement to survive, we needed to divert the approaching Warbots. Time was short; we had to act swiftly, for they were closing in. Six months earlier, we had seized two Armoured Personnel Carriers from Zen in daring raids, and with Nerdo's remarkable skills, they had been substantially enhanced. Transformed into formidable machines, they were ready for a showdown.

"It was determined that Turk would lead an APC crew of four, while Animal would take the other, to intercept and halt the advancing Warbot forces before they reached us. With a top speed of a hundred and fifty kilometres per hour across nearly any terrain, the APC was equipped for combat. The armour plating, initially two centimetres thick, had been doubled by Nerdo's ingenuity, rendering the vehicles capable of withstanding even anti-tank missiles. To transport the APCs, we'd designed an elevator, lowering them individually twenty metres below the surface. This bunker, aptly dubbed 'The Fortress' by fellow bunkers, was virtually impregnable.

"According to Animal's account, both APCs encountered eight Warbots on the old highway just before the junction leading here.

Their plan was straightforward—drive over them. Both APCs featured heavy-duty armoured front plates designed precisely for this purpose. Equipped with six sharp rippers beneath their noses, akin to those on old Betsy, Reno's prime mover, they would obliterate anything underneath, transforming it into scrap metal.

"Two Warbots fell under the wheels of Animal's APC, but their resilience proved shocking. He witnessed one being swept beneath the rippers, only to emerge unscathed and back on its feet, as if the encounter had been inconsequential. The RF-20's durability was astounding.

"It was nighttime, and the Warbots' dark metallic exoskeletons rendered them nearly invisible even through night vision cameras. "Turk lined up a Warbot in his headlights but it was a trap. There was another one hiding in ambush and it jumped onto the rear of the APC. The only vulnerable part of an APC is the roof hatch. Animal saw the RF-20 at the hatch and immediately told Turk through comms, but it was too late. He watched it on top of the speeding APC, clench its fist, punch through the hatch like it was made of tin foil, and then toss in a stun grenade. Turk's APC slewed off the track and hit a big eucalypt. The trunk snapped on impact and brought down the entire massive tree on top of the APC. Then, unexpectedly a number of stealth drones swooped down from overhead and opened fire with incendiaries on Turk's stricken vehicle. They were trying to take out the tyres to make sure it couldn't move.

"Meanwhile, Animal came under fire from another group of drones, bullets ricocheting off the armour plating. The incendiaries aimed at Turk's APC ignited the treetops, engulfing the scene in flames. With his own vehicle now surrounded by fire, Animal faced a critical decision. Turning to support Turk, he witnessed a Warbot on Turk's APC roof dragging a crew member out through the hatch and flinging him off the vehicle like a ragdoll. The unfortunate soul was then summarily executed by another Warbot.

"The flames of the bushfire surged, obscuring visibility. Amidst the smoke and fire, Animal discerned the Warbots encircling Turk's

APC. His hands were tied; there was nothing he could do. Drone-fired bullets rained down from above, and the fire crept closer to his vehicle. He had to act before his tires caught fire. Through the haze, he spotted eight RF-20 Warbots standing amidst the flames, impervious to the searing heat—a quality Zen had meticulously rectified with the RF-20. Before Animal fled his vehicle, he glimpsed Turk being dragged from the burning APC. Whether Turk survived or met his demise, we can only speculate."

CHAPTER 7
VELODIUM

MAL WAS DISTURBED by the news of a protest against the government organized by the leader of the New Octagon, Toeghan Hitz. She was again being interviewed on TV, this time barking her discontent over a price hike in electricity and blaming the government. Reducing the cost of electricity had been one of Mal's election promises and he knew from experience that nothing turned off the electorate more than being hit in the wallet because a politician had broken a promise. But what else could he have done when in reality the hike had been caused by the Container Port Authority jacking up the unloading fees from ships—And which company owned the container ports? Zen Corporation. Mal knew he was being set up by Zen, determined as they were to bring about voter discontent—and it was working.

Karzoff stormed into Mal's office and asked, "What do you want me to do about the thousand or so protestors out front of the building, sir?"

Mal got up from behind his desk and said casually, "I'll go down and front them."

"No! It could be one of Honor's tricks to flush you out for a sniper bullet," Karzoff protested, vehemently.

"My friend, I can't carry on as president with my head buried in the sand, ignoring all this. Give me two bodyguards, put one of our best snipers on the roof, and let's get this done and dusted."

"Alright, Viktoria and I will go with you. I will station Agent Hooper on the helipad and have a few drones overhead," Karzoff said, unhappy with the idea but at the same time aware it was something Mal needed to do. He got onto his phone and made the arrangements.

When Mal appeared on the front steps of Oceana HQ flanked by Karzoff and Viktoria, he was greeted by a cacophony of jeers from a huge crowd of banner-waving protestors that had assembled in the street, causing absolute mayhem for the lunchtime city traffic. The swarm of reporters that had surrounded Toeghan Hitz immediately turned their attention to the President as he emerged on the landing.

Agent Hooper scanned the rooftops through the infrared scope mounted on his Cheytag M-200 Intervention long-range rifle. With a range of two thousand metres, 408-calibre ammunition, and a seven-round magazine, it was the most formidable sniper rifle available. The digital scope could pick up a body heat signature with exceptional accuracy. He meticulously checked the rooftops and office windows with suitable angles for a sniper, but everything appeared clear. Nevertheless, he remained vigilant. He didn't need to worry about the threat of an assassin drone; several Oceana drones were overhead, feeding data to the surveillance operations control room a few floors below him. If any anomaly were detected, he would be instantly alerted through his communications device.

From the cluster of journalists, Mal identified Meagan Tickle, host of the morning breakfast TV show Watch this Space, and asked Viktoria to fetch her.

Meagan appreciated the unique attention from the President, distinguishing her from her colleagues, and quickly made her way over to him.

"Meagan, I'd like to take a moment to make a special announcement. Are you up for an exclusive?"

"You bet, sir," she said enthusiastically, waving over her cameraman. After a brief introduction to the camera, she continued, "Watch this Space has an exclusive announcement from the President of Oceana, sir?"

"I'm not here to talk about what these good people are protesting about; they're entitled to their opinion. We live in a country with free speech. No, I'm here for another, but no less important reason. I'm here to make an announcement. In eight weeks, the biggest outdoor rock concert in the history of Oceana will be held at Avalon, near Goulburn."

His announcement had an immediate calming effect on the protestors; he had captured their attention.

"And what bands will be on the bill, Mr President?" Meagan asked.

"The bands will be World... Cried Wolf and the thrash metal band People Eaters," he paused for effect and saw excitement on faces in the crowd. "And headlining, with songs from a new but yet-to-be-released album plus many of their hits... Black Alice." One sharp look at Toeghan Hitz confirmed he had won the day. She was livid.

"I'll personally provide all the details on Watch this Space in the next couple of days."

"What will be the ticket price, Mr President?" Meagan asked, with a smug look on her face, expecting it to be exorbitant.

"Sorry, Meagan, I forgot to mention... the Avalon concert will be free. There will be sponsors, TV and podcast rights... however, all revenue will be donated to The Orphan Charity."

"Free! My goodness, there's no better value for money than that, and The Orphan Charity, a worthy recipient. There you go, you heard it first on... Watch this Space."

"Thank you, Meagan," Mal said, with a smile. The crowd was content and dispersing. Mal gave them a wave and then shot Toeghan Hitz a personal, cynical wave, and then retired back inside the building—mission accomplished.

When Mal entered his office reception with Karzoff and Viktoria, he found the Professor chatting with Rita Vallins.

"Professor, what's the latest?... Have you heard something from our travellers?" Mal asked.

"No, no, just wanted a chat if you have a moment," the eccentric Professor said, peering over the rim of his glasses.

"Always have time for you, Vic. Come on in," he hesitated. "Do you need anything further from me, Karzoff?"

"No, sir. I will stand down our support," Karzoff affirmed.

"Oh, thank you both for a job well done."

Mal led Vic into his office. "So, Vic, what's up?"

They settled into the lounge setting. "As you know, En-Ki had somehow placed code in a partitioned area on the Kairos mainframe. The code is basically the formula to reproduce the Tablets of Destinies... more so, the actual substance from which they were made... this we have determined to be the most powerful superconductor ever known."

"Pardon my ignorance of superconductors, Vic, but how would that benefit us?"

"It would crack the energy riddle and provide clean and cheap energy."

"I see, that is huge... go on, Vic."

"The formula is mostly nuclear chemistry, a field I'm not proficient in... if only we had Hope, it would be right up her alley... she lived and breathed nuclear chemistry." He paused, while they both silently lamented her loss. "Anyhow," he sparked up, "I've deciphered the code but in doing so unearthed more questions than answers, I'm afraid—often that happens in science. For instance, there is a critical element by the name of Velodium required to fuse or bond other elements together. If you think of the Tablets being like CDs that carry data... but instead of a reflective aluminium layer, this metal alloy would essentially, amongst other things, be capable of carrying a billion times the information than we can now digitally compress onto anything, from discs to water to crystals."

"You've just surpassed my scientific understanding, Vic, but what I grasp is that without this element Velodium, you won't be able to create this superconductor. So, where do we acquire Velodium?"

"That's the predicament, Mal. I'm uncertain. This element is certainly not native to Earth."

Mal slumped back in his chair, perplexed.

"You arrived a bit late, Secta," Hope gently protested. Just the two of them occupied her study, while the others were engrossed in devising a plan to free Turk.

"I fail to comprehend what you mean by 'too late,'" Secta conceded.

"If you had come ten years ago, the women here would have been young enough to bear a foetus. But now, they're all over fifty. At fifty-three, Morri is actually the youngest, aside from me, of course. I'm actually the youngest person in Oceana, perhaps even in the world, and certainly the only fertile one."

"Fifty-three or so isn't necessarily too old, Hope," Secta argued, momentarily forgetting that in 2112, he was nearly a hundred and forty years old.

"The average life expectancy for women is fifty-five, and for men, it's sixty."

"Seriously... what, radiation? If I had arrived ten years ago, you would have been fifteen, less knowledgeable than you are now. However, even saying that, you must understand that getting here wasn't as straightforward as you might think. I'll share all about what we've been undertaking, particularly Alice's contributions, and the complexities of time travel later. For now, let's determine our course of action here. How would you have fertilsed the eggs if you had surrogate mothers of the appropriate age?"

"It remains a perplexing issue. I suppose there's Alice," Hope pondered.

"Yes, and you and Vee could serve as surrogates, but that's hardly sufficient to repopulate the entire world, is it?"

Secta paced the floor pondering, as he does. He was right—with a population mostly over fifty and a life expectancy of fifty-five, humankind had only a few years left to endure. "Gorrick must be aware of that," he muttered to himself.

"What's that about Gorrick?" Hope inquired.

"Oh, he must have known that it would take thirty years after the Cyberwars for radiation to completely wipe out humankind."

"Do you think that was his grand plan from the start?" She questioned.

"There's no denying it."

"Then there's an even greater reason to solve this."

"Yes, if we intend to rescue humankind from annihilation."

"You realise our purpose here is not to solve all the problems the people have, but to establish whether the Gorrick in this timeline is hosting En-Lil or not?" En-Ki told Alice in his mind.

"I get that, but there are other factors at play here," Alice countered.

Nerdo and Cutter were guiding Alice and Vee to the cafeteria when a horn sounded so loud it almost jolted Alice out of his skin.

"What the stuff was that?" Al complained.

"The horn, oh, that's the sun signal," Nerdo said, pausing at the entrance to the mall. "Anyone who needs a dose of vitamin D or some fresh air can assemble at the garage elevator that can take a hundred people at a time to the surface. The horn is the all-clear signal after the recon team has completed a surveillance sweep up top."

"How long can they stay up there?" Vee asked.

"Four hours. Then the horn sounds again twice and they come back down. Generally, about a thousand go up every day... depending on the weather," Cutter explained.

As they started into the mall, Al asked, "What about the rest of them? You said there's around two thousand down here?"

Nerdo stopped and, with a mournful expression, said, "We have over a thousand in palliative care. Most of the other thousand are sick. We lose at least one a day."

"So far no one has lived over sixty. Mostly less," Cutter said.

It was a solemn moment for Alice, knowing Cutter, Nerdo, and

Turk were approaching that age.

"You guys look healthy enough," Al said, with a positive smile.

"It would scare the hell out of you if you took a tour of the hospice, Al. One day they're healthy and happy, the next day they've deteriorated to near death. It hits so fast it's unbelievable… frightening."

"It starts as a rash anywhere on your body, then after a couple of months of agony while your organs shut down, you die. It's a horrible death. Turk said blokes exposed to full-on fallout during the war got it; they called it Red Wheel because it starts out as a wheel-shaped raised red pattern on the skin."

"Yeah, I remember a friend of Jonno and Reno's, that had a bar in Angel, had it. What was his name? Frank, that's right," Al recalled.

"Yeah, he'd been a construction worker and reckoned he saw a UFO fire on Canberra, didn't he?" Cutter quizzed.

"Yeah, that's him," Al agreed.

"Didn't he survive the blast by climbing inside a big air conditioning unit… but the radiation got him. He had to bathe in oil for hours every day to stop his skin from peeling off, poor bastard," Cutter explained.

The mall had plenty to offer. There was a supermarket, a café, a hardware shop, and a department store.

"Where do folk get the money to buy stuff?" Vee asked.

"There's no exchange of money, Vee. We each volunteer to work in the shops, while others that I organize go out on supply runs. We trade with other bunkers and, from time to time, find old shops that we pillage, but those are now few and far between now. Most of what survives was in cans, but now even those are like hen's teeth," Nerdo explained. "Let's grab a coffee in the café; I got Boris some tinned coffee on our last raid in Canberra."

"Wouldn't that still be hot from radiation?" Al asked.

"Not really. We use a Geiger counter to check the Rads… Sydney is still too hot, so it's a no-go. Shame really, lots of scrounging to be done there," Nerdo said.

They took seats in the small café, and a big guy came to serve them.

"Hey Boris, this is Black Alice and Vee," Nerdo said.

The expression on Boris' big face was priceless. "Black Alice! Not the Black Alice?"

Al held up a hand to shake. "That's me, Boris. How goes it, mate?"

Boris took Alice's hand with reverence. "Man, you are a legend... you know that?"

"Nar, mate... just an ordinary bloke," Al said, demurely.

"Black Alice, you've made my day, man," Boris said happily.

He took the orders and went off to fill them.

"Wasn't expecting a fan in 2112," Al said with a chuckle.

"Back in your time, you probably had heaps of fans as a performer, Al, but to these people, you've got the legendary status of say... King Arthur. They know nothing about the rock star, only your deeds when you saved them from Zen back in 2087," Nerdo explained.

Vee was impressed that her brother was almost regarded as mythical by the likes of Boris, but what had impressed her most was how Alice handled it with genuine humility.

"I tell you what, Al, how about coming with us tomorrow? We're doing a raid on Canberra; we could do with the muscle?" Nerdo asked.

"What do you think, Vee, up for it?" Cutter asked.

Of course, they were, any excuse for some action. It would also give them the opportunity to further discuss the release of Turk from the evil clutches of Zen.

At dawn, they would be taken to the armoury to select weapons, and following that, they would leave in the APC.

CHAPTER 8
RED WHEEL

T HE **SILENT ELECTRIC** four-seater Quadrocopter resembled a drone but was much larger, with a capsule on top of the four rotors. Capable of speeds up to two hundred kilometres an hour, it was perfect for ferrying passengers on short-haul flights, an air-taxi if you like. This flight was for Voltaris Idram to view the ruins of Canberra from the air.

Gorrick spoke through his headset to Voltaris, who was seated beside him. "We have a squad down there, and a larger deployment in Sydney. There's much to be gained from mining the ruins. Our cyborg army isn't affected by radiation. Though that isn't a problem with Canberra now, it is for humans when it comes to larger ruined cities such as Sydney, Tokyo, New York, Paris, Berlin, Moscow, and London."

The view from the aircraft through the clear Perspex canopy covering them was incredible. Stretched out two hundred metres below lay the scorched devastation of what only thirty-five years previously had been a thriving city of three million inhabitants. Since the bomb blast, once proud high-rise buildings had been reduced to skeletal frames of twisted metal. Residential houses and the streets were now rubble and wreckage that had mostly been reclaimed by nature. Thick black columns of smoke were rising into the clear dawn sky from at least a hundred blazing spot fires.

"What's burning?" Voltaris questioned.

"We put it to the torch so the scavenging survivors can't get any food or supplies. Only a few of them remain, but we prefer to keep one step ahead of them. They'll all be gone within the next five years," Gorrick said coldly.

"How come?"

"Radiation poisoning."

"I noticed back at Angel City there were no people, only cyborgs," Voltaris said.

"Life expectancy is around the mid-fifties; they can't reproduce because they're all sterile. As a result, the ubiquitous reign of man on Earth is almost over. Pilot, return us to Zen HQ." The fully automated Quadrocopter responded to Gorrick's command and made a looping turn back towards Angel City.

Alice had been allocated the same room that was once his hideout back when, in his own timeline, he was the most sought-after man in Oceana.

He was up before dawn and made his way to the cafeteria where he found Vee and Secta having breakfast.

"Vee tells me you're off on a sortie to Canberra with Nerdo and Cutter," Secta said.

"Yes, thought it might be interesting. What have you been up to?"

"Spent a lot of time with Hope trying to crack the problem of how to repopulate the Earth, considering every human will be gone within the next five years," Secta said gloomily.

"Are you serious? Why?" Vee asked.

"Radiation. They're all sterile, and life expectancy has been reduced to less than sixty years. That's why Hope's plan to use her eggs in surrogates can't work. Apart from her, the rest of them are all too old."

"Are you saying there's no-one under the age of what... fifty alive? Anywhere?" Vee queried.

"Exactly. Hope would almost certainly be the youngest person in the world... and in five years, she'll most probably be the only person in the world."

Alice got up to get some food. "We need to do something about this, Secta. I reckon that's the real mission here," he said, before heading to the serving area.

"I thought we discussed not getting involved in humanity's problems on this timeline?" En-Ki protested in Alice's mind.

"So, who else is going to fix the problem and rescue mankind?" Alice snapped back mentally.

"Have you thought there might be another timeline, Alice? What needs to be done is not fix this timeline, but to prevent it from ever happening," En-Ki urged.

Alice thought about it. En-Ki was right. There was no way they could repopulate the world; they didn't have the time or resources. The only fix was for the Cyberwars never to happen.

Al sat back down at the table with Vegemite on toast and a mug of instant coffee.

"Trying to repopulate the planet isn't the answer, Secta. It's impossible," Al said, with a mouth full of toast.

"So, what should we do?" Secta challenged.

"Change the timeline."

"What do you mean by that, Al?" Vee asked.

Al took a sip of coffee and then stared at Secta. "We need to prevent the Cyberwars from ever happening."

Secta jumped up out of his seat and began pacing, biting the knuckle of his left index finger. He stopped and glared at Alice as though having a Eureka moment. "You're absolutely correct, Alice... that's genius... sheer genius. It's the only way."

"And how do we do that?" Vee questioned, just as Nerdo and Cutter arrived, carrying coffees.

"By killing Gorrick," Al said, macabrely.

"But which Gorrick?" Secta questioned.

"All of them," Al snarled.

"Have you got a Gorrick back in your time as well?" Nerdo asked, pulling up a chair.

"We've got fifteen hundred of them," Secta said, resuming his seat.

"And one of them is En-Lil," Al added.

"En-Lil?" Cutter queried.

"The bastard orchestrating all of this... the one who created the Cyberwars that left all of you in such a terrible state," Secta said, dolefully.

"What about the Gorrick we've got in the here and now?" Animal growled from standing in the shadows, eavesdropping.

Alice looked up at the big man. His hair might have been streaked with grey... and he might be fifty-five years old... but Alice admired his seriously cut body and the steely glint in his eyes. Animal was a dead-set warrior, the kind of guy you wanted by your side in battle.

"We're going to kill him, mate," Al said, cold, hard, and heartfelt.

"So, who are we talking about killing?" Morri chortled, joining the party.

"Gorrick?" Secta said, with a smug grin.

"Oh good," Morri said, taking a seat. It was Gorrick's head that she most fancied seeing on a spike.

Half an hour later, with Animal at the wheel, Alice and five others, including Vee, Nerdo, and Cutter, were in the APC, powering towards Canberra. The monitor facing Animal displayed the road ahead. The sun was rising, and there were plenty of obstacles on the road for him to navigate, but he had it under control. Their destination was the Woden Shopping Mall on the outskirts of Canberra. Nerdo's research had revealed that the mall had two underground floors, giving it a better than even chance of holding supplies that had survived the explosion, feral animals, and other scavengers, including humans.

On board were an assortment of tools in case they needed to cut or dig their way in. They also had a selection of weapons for protection. They had made good time in reaching the edge of what remained of the suburb of Woden.

"What's the smoke from?" Al said, peering at columns of black smoke on the horizon shown on the monitor.

"There have been cyborgs through here... they hit a place and then set it on fire to prevent us from getting supplies. But by the look of it, they missed the Mall," Cutter said.

"Good," Nerdo said, checking a handheld navigation device called a Ulink. "It's at the end of Keltie Street, Animal. Next on your left."

Animal parked the APC in front of a jumbled mess of building materials. Except for Cutter, who, due to his injured leg, would stay behind to guard the APC, the others lined up underneath the exit hatch. Nerdo gave Cutter a kiss.

"Bye, honey, mind the kids. I'll just do the shopping and be back, okay?" she said, jokingly.

They all chuckled.

"Hey, pick me up a six-pack and half a dozen whores, will ya?" Cutter playfully fired back.

"You've got to be joking... there's no liquor store in there," Nerdo quipped.

She pressed a button for the hatch to slide open and then poked a Geiger counter out through it to measure the outside air. "It's clean," she announced, and after blowing a kiss to Cutter, she led them out.

Once outside, she checked her headset communication with Cutter. "You there, babe?"

"Sure am, don't be long," Cutter said.

When Alice climbed out, he looked at the wreckage surrounding them and exclaimed, "Will you look at this bloody mess."

The buildings and houses had been flattened. All that remained were mangled, partially melted metal and debris that had been hideously overgrown by all sorts of exotic vegetation and weeds.

"This is worse than some of the ancient ruins I've seen," Al said.

Vee came up beside him, shaking her head. "Looks like pictures of Hiroshima after the A-Bomb... this is totally destroyed. How many people died here?"

"Pretty much the entire population, Vee. I don't know if there were any survivors within twenty kilometres of ground zero... which incidentally was the old House of Parliament," Nerdo explained.

Animal distributed weapons along with solar-powered torches. He then led them over to what appeared to be the entrance to the Mall's underground parking station.

"We'll enter through here. It's all reinforced concrete and safer... but it'll be dark. Save your torches for the hunt. Just follow me and stay alert; there's no telling what's down here."

One of the few dials on the dashboard of the Quadrocopter lit up and emitted a sharp beep.

"What's that?" Voltaris asked Gorrick, thinking there might be a problem.

"The radar detected a vehicle below and has sent the coordinates to ground personnel," Gorrick explained.

"How do the cyborgs get here from Angel City?" Voltaris queried.

"They use a larger eight-seater version of one of these drones."

"Must have some grunt. Cyborgs seem heavy."

"Yes, RF-20s weigh two hundred kilos when fully armed, so that's sixteen hundred kilos of lift. It's not a problem; these drones are rated to carry up to two thousand kg's," Gorrick explained.

Voltaris was impressed by Gorrick's knowledge. He wasn't just an ordinary CEO; he was hands-on. Voltaris had no idea how old Gorrick was. You learn a lot in over two thousand years.

A few minutes later, the drone landed on the rooftop helipad of Zen HQ in Angel City. The clear Perspex bubble opened automatically, and Gorrick and Voltaris disembarked, making their way across the apron to the building entrance.

Once under cover, Gorrick asked, "I know that the twenty-core organic processor Professor Adamski and Dr Li have used will soon fail. However, they will be impressed with the new organic processor we have produced. It's four times the speed."

"Incredible. When will it be ready?" Voltaris asked.

"Are you in a hurry to get back?"

"No, it's just weird having nothing but robots around, present company excluded, of course."

Little did he know that Gorrick was a created clone, as close as you could get to being artificial intelligence.

"Really, I find it most comforting," Gorrick alleged, unfazed, as he led Voltaris into the elevator.

The doors opened on a different floor than Voltaris had anticipated. "I'm taking you to the central operations centre. I thought you might like a heads-up on how we control cyborgs."

"That'll be interesting. Tell me, Gorrick, are you the same Gorrick who is running Zen in Sydney back in my time?"

"There were two Gorricks then... for a while, at least."

"Yes, there are."

As they entered the high-tech environment of the operations centre, Voltaris failed to get an answer to his question because a good-looking woman interrupted them.

"Sir," she acknowledged Gorrick with a courteous smile.

"A human at last," Voltaris rattled off facetiously, giving her the once-over and thinking, "And a hot-looking one at that."

"Voltaris Idram, this is Dr Ursula Mennis. She heads up our AI division."

"It is nice to meet you, Mr Idram. Where are you from?" Ursula said, with the hint of an Eastern European accent.

"The USA," Voltaris said.

"A visit from the newly appointed Zen time traveller, Ursula," Gorrick explained. "I brought him in for a demonstration of operations."

"Excellent, please follow me," Ursula purred.

She might have been sixty years of age, an exception to the rule that all humans die from radiation poisoning by then, but she didn't look it. Voltaris figured she was no older than forty and was attracted to her.

Ursula hadn't seen a healthy young person in years, and the thought of him admiring her seriously appealed to her vanity.

She led them into a dimly lit room that contained a hundred women and men, all over the age of fifty, seated behind holographic terminals. When Voltaris looked more closely, he saw that they were all staring in a trance at the moving imagery in front of them.

"Are these people human?" he asked.

"Yes, they are psychics… connecting to their assigned cyborg. We feed them the instructions they pass on to the cyborg psychically."

"I thought everyone died from radiation by the time they hit sixty?" he questioned.

"We can keep some of the humans alive longer than expected. I have developed drugs to deal with the sickness." She moved closer and whispered covertly, "Those who come down with Red Wheel, we send to the death camp."

That rattled Voltaris, but before he could comment, Gorrick said, as they were strolling along the ranks of operators, "Soon we will not need a human psychic interface. The new processor will allow cyborgs to connect with each other as a hive, that myself and other Gorricks will be able to interface with to instruct directly."

"The first person seated in each row is the team leader of a cyborg patrol squad consisting of eight," Ursula explained, stopping at one of the seated team leaders.

"You can see here she has received an order from the mainframe. A result of what was detected on our radar when we overflew the suburb of Woden. So, the team controller is now coordinating the nearest patrol to investigate," Gorrick explained.

"Probably just scavengers. There is a partly demolished supermarket there," Ursula added.

"What happens when the patrol finds them?" Voltaris asked.

"The course of action will be at the discretion of the cyborg leader, but each cyborg is programmed to kill," Gorrick said matter-of-factly.

"I see," Voltaris said, taking in the future of warfare being played out before his very eyes like a computer game.

It was dark, damp, and seriously creepy in the car park. Their footsteps echoed in the concrete cavern, and every now and then, Animal's torchlight flashed on a cobweb-covered vehicle that had mostly rusted away, leaving it in the shadows like the carapace of a giant insect, ravaged by time. Some of the pillars holding up the ceiling had crumbled away, making a collapse likely.

Animal placed a finger to his lips, indicating silence while pointing upward. "Keep quiet; the roof could easily collapse here," he whispered.

They acknowledged with a sharp nod. He found a staircase leading up and climbed through the shattered glass door that had once enclosed it. Two flights of stairs later, they arrived at a fire door. Animal forced it open, and with guns up, they proceeded through it in single file.

They were now on the bottom floor of the mall, and fortunately, it was still intact. Nerdo waved them over to her. She reached into a side pocket on her flak jacket and produced a bunch of surgical face masks.

"Put one of these on. There could be all kinds of nasty spores floating around in here," she said.

"I was wondering when you were going to start pulling stuff out of your pockets," Al said, chuckling as he fondly remembered how the younger Nerdo always seemed to have bottomless pockets filled with all sorts of gadgetry.

They donned the masks. Animal issued instructions. "Okay, I'll take Sharkey and Grub and go left. It's a circular corridor, so if you guys go right, we'll meet up on the other side. Here." He handed out a bunch of fabric carry bags. "Fill them up with cans of food. Nerdo will point out what we need along the way. Two of you use torches, while the other covers with a gun at all times. Okay?" They all nodded. "Good, then let's do it."

Sharkey and Grub were bikers. Despite being close to sixty, they were still in good shape. Both sported full beards, facial tattoos, and their weather-beaten faces bore scars that told tales of battles won and lost. Armed with extra weapons, Sharkey and Grub were prepared, while Nerdo carried plastic explosives, detonators, and wore a grenade belt. All of them were dressed in camouflage fatigues.

The teams set off in different directions. Inside the APC, Cutter was monitoring Nerdo's progress through both an open microphone audio feed and visuals transmitted from headsets. Feeling hot with the air conditioning off, he took off his jacket. He scratched an itchy spot on his right bicep, and when the itching persisted, he inspected it closely. What he found totally freaked him out. An angry red rash had emerged on his skin, a clear sign that his use-by-date had just clocked in.

CHAPTER 9
MALL-RATS

" **A SYNTHESISED FULLY** organic cyborg built explicitly for time travel," Ursula informed Voltaris as the three of them made their way along the corridor to the café on the same floor.

"Now, that's something we'd be very interested in," Voltaris confirmed.

"Perhaps we can send one back with you, along with the blueprint for Dr Li," Gorrick suggested.

"Is it already functional, or is it still in development?" Voltaris inquired.

They entered the café, and Voltaris and Ursula helped themselves to coffees and snacks from the open-source vending machines.

"I'll have Ursula give you a demonstration after you've eaten. For now, I must leave you," Gorrick said abruptly, then breezed out.

"Is he always like that?" Voltaris asked.

"What do you mean?"

"So blunt... I've dealt with crusty dudes in my time, but he takes the cake."

"You get used to it. Bring your coffee to my office; there is more privacy there," Ursula suggested, leading Voltaris out of the café and back along the corridor.

She reminded him a lot of Honor, with the same brooding personality.

In her office, Ursula offered Voltaris a seat in a small lounge setting, then sat opposite him. She crossed her shapely legs and caught him admiring them.

Voltaris initiated, "I asked Gorrick if he's the same Gorrick from back in my time, but he didn't answer."

"He is quite secretive," Ursula stated reservedly. "I've been close to him for a long time now and still know very little about the man. Tell me about yourself."

"I'm a trained CIA field agent. This is my first assignment as a time traveller. No wife... no family. And you?"

"Oh, I graduated from Zen Artificial Intelligence training in Berlin and was sent here in 2079, a year before the Cyberwars began."

"So, you were here when the cities were nuked?"

"Yes, they were all hit, all over the world. We knew it would be safe here, probably one of the safest places in the world, really."

"Doesn't it get lonely for you?"

"I must admit it does these days, when there are so few possibilities," she rolled her eyes.

She was seated on a three-seater lounge. Voltaris got up and moved next to her.

Alice was struggling to find anything salvageable from the debris, let alone something useful. Suddenly, Vee's voice called out, "Al, over here."

He could see her torchlight behind stacks of dusty, broken timber joists, panels, and smashed signage. He pushed his way through to find her sitting on the dusty floor with something in her hand.

"You look like a mall-rat," he joked.

"Always been one," she chuckled.

"Me too."

She handed him her discovery.

"Well, I'll be damned," Alice exclaimed, blowing the dust off the Black Alice Endangered Species CD.

"This must've been an Op Shop, collector's stuff. One person's junk is another person's treasure. Check this, I even found a World album with Avalon on it."

"That album hasn't even been recorded yet in our time. What a trip. Hey, imagine if we could take it back and play it to Johnny Vallins and the guys before it's even recorded?"

"You're out there, Al," Vee said, with an affectionate smile. Her expression suddenly turned serious as an urgent shout came from Nerdo.

"Alice!"

"That doesn't sound good. Quick," Alice said, helping Vee to her feet. They quickly manoeuvred through the obstacles and found Nerdo in the corridor, clearly distressed.

"What's up, mate?" Al asked.

"It's Cutter. There's a patrol of cyborgs out there," she said, her worry evident.

"Alright, let's find Animal. Come on," Al urged, and they hurried off.

Cutter was in the driver's seat, watching the monitor displaying a cyborg patrol advancing in single file toward him. He started up the APC, knowing he'd have to try and run them down before they breached the mall. If the cyborgs got inside, his team wouldn't stand a chance. He revved up the powerful machine.

One of the cyborgs stepped out from the patrol as soon as it heard the APC start. Armed with a thermobaric rocket launcher, it lined up the APC that was now hurtling towards them.

Back with Animal, they quickly filled him in on the situation. Nerdo activated her comms on speaker.

"How many are there, Cutter?" Animal shouted.

What they heard in reply surprised them, particularly Alice. Cutter sang, "There's an angel poised in silence, holds a star at my back. While the autumn moon is rising, the shadows wait to attack!"

"He's singing the lyrics to my song 'No Warning'," Alice remarked, bemused. "Cutter, it's Al. What's happening, mate?"

"It's the Red Wheel, my friend. I've got it. I'm done," Cutter's voice came back.

Tears welled up in Nerdo's eyes, and she pleaded, "Oh no, Cutter, no!"

Quickly, Vee put her arm around Nerdo to comfort her.

"It's all over for me, my friends. I might as well take as many of these mongrels out with me. Goodbye, Nerdo... I love you."

Then, the signal turned to static.

"He's cut us off!" Animal growled in frustration.

While humming "No Warning," Cutter slammed the APC into the ranks of the patrol. However, a cyborg armed with a rocket launcher fired, causing an explosion that engulfed the APC. Surprisingly, the explosion didn't halt its momentum. After ploughing through the cyborgs, Cutter swerved the APC around, preparing for another assault. Several cyborgs were recovering from being knocked down during the initial impact.

Cutter accelerated for another charge. This time, a cyborg got entangled in the rippers at the front of the vehicle and was dragged beneath it. Sparks flew as the APC dragged the cyborg along the bitumen road. Cutter realised the cyborg was jammed underneath, so he aimed for a pile of twisted metal—a melted high-tension tower. The APC collided with the metal, causing it to bounce up. Cutter seized the opportunity and drove the vehicle over the jagged spikes, tearing the trapped cyborg to shreds. Content with his manoeuvre, Cutter was about to turn for another assault when a large piece of twisted metal became caught in the front wheels, halting the APC. He attempted to free the metal by reversing and moving forward, but this delay allowed two cyborgs to jump onto the APC and make their way to the hatch.

Anticipating their move, Cutter rushed to the hatch with a submachine gun in hand. He hit the button to open it just in time to fend off a cyborg attempting to break in. Looking up at the cyborg above him, Cutter emptied an entire magazine into its lower body, effectively blowing off the top of its head. It worked just as it had before years ago with the RF-6 and 7. A couple of bullets shot through the cyborg's body and blew the top of its head off. The cyborg's lifeless form fell off the APC and crashed onto the road. However, Cutter's triumph was short-lived as a stun grenade dropped through the hatch and exploded.

The last remaining cyborg at the hatch reached inside, seized Cutter's motionless body, and dragged him onto the road. Standing over him with five other cyborgs, the cyborg clenched its fist, and a chrome steel blade extended from its knuckles, locking into position. Cutter regained consciousness and saw the cyborg preparing to strike. A swift slash, and Cutter's days were over.

The cyborg patrol moved toward the entrance of the mall car park, where they believed the remaining humans were located.

Desperate and fearing the worst, Nerdo repeatedly called out for Cutter over the comms as they fled back toward the staircase leading to the car park exit. Animal led the way, cautiously checking for any signs of danger. He paused at the bottom landing, peering into the dark car park to assess the situation. The coast seemed clear, and Animal signalled for the team to turn off their lights and fan out. They began their cautious approach toward the exit.

Tragedy struck when Sharkey and Grub ventured only a few steps outside, only to be mowed down by a hail of bullets. Animal retreated into the stairwell and whispered through clenched teeth that their attempt had failed. Sharkey and Grub had been cut down.

Equipped with night vision graphene lenses, Al surveyed the situation and spotted a cyborg moving behind a concrete pillar. That gave him an idea.

He asked, "Nerdo, how many grenades you got?"

"Six."

"Animal take two, Vee you take two... give me two."

"Grenades won't have any effect on a RF-20 Al," Nerdo barked, and pushed past him with her held gun up. "I've got nothing to live for, damn them!"

Alice's mind was instantly cast back to a dream he'd had some time back of Nerdo being chopped in half by cyborg gunfire. He grabbed her arm and pulled her back out of harm's way. "Hand out the grenades mate, no good losing you as well, okay?"

Scowling and seriously upset for the loss of her loved one, she nodded acquiescent. Tears were tacking through the dust on her cheeks. She knew he was right.

"I know the grenades won't harm them, but they'll drop that ceiling on their heads," he snarled, with a spiteful grin.

"Got ya!" Animal growled, in agreement.

"Nerdo, on the count of three duck out and flash your torch about to light up the nearest pylons for us to see. Vee, you take the pylons to the left, Animal the middle pylons and I'll take the right ones. Do your best to land a grenade right at the base," Al urged.

They got into position.

"Okay, on the count of three... one, two, three!"

Nerdo jumped out and lit up a pylon with her torch beam. In the light they could see cyborgs behind it.

Vee armed the grenades and hurled them one at a time at the pylons. Animal jumped out and threw his. At the same time Alice pitched his. They only just managed to get back under cover when all hell broke loose. The cyborgs opened fire just as the grenades began to explode. Down came huge chunks of the ceiling landing right on top of them, just as Alice had predicted. In fact, so much of the massive four-metre thick concrete ceiling collapsed, that it totally blocked the exit.

A great waft of dust and debris billowed into the stairwell, impossible to see through.

Coughing and spluttering holding his forearm up to shield his eyes, Al shouted to get over the racket. "We'll go up to find another way out!"

They blindly raced up the staircase.

CHAPTER 10
DEJA VU

BEING HUMILIATED ON national television by the President of Oceana had utterly incensed Toeghan Hitz. After the failed protest on the steps of Oceana HQ, the evening newspaper had featured a front-page photo of her displaying profound exasperation, while surrounded by jubilant protestors celebrating the President's announcement of the Avalon concert.

"What a cheap victory for him: a damn concert, no less. Get that out of my face," she snarled at the large man seated opposite her in a Kings Cross café.

Glan Denning lowered the newspaper and fixed her with an expressionless stare.

"Don't get yourself all riled up," he said in a deep, raspy tone. "He possesses the resources to outmanoeuvre you. You know your task, and that's what you're being paid for."

"It doesn't mean I have to tolerate that," she complained.

"Quit feeding your ego... you ended up on the front page... oops, look who's approaching, the old ice-block," Denning remarked, using the newspaper as a shield.

Honor pulled up a chair and sat down, wearing a curt expression. "I see the newspapers captured quite the moment, and you were publicly lambasted on national television as well." Her tone was cynical, and she added, "T, t, t," a clucking, pitying sound made with her tongue, akin to a mother scolding a mischievous child. "Allowing him to outmanoeuvre you like that won't serve the cause, will it?"

"The last thing I need is a lecture from you, Honor. What do you want?" Hitz snarled.

"Mmm, quite petulant tonight, aren't we? And what about you, Denning? What's your take on all of this?"

Denning slowly lowered the newspaper and raised an eyebrow at Honor. "I couldn't care less."

"See, Hitz? That's the attitude. No sulking, brooding, or moody bitterness. You have your orders... no more protests. Your grandstanding will only result in losing support."

"But I need to maintain a public image," Hitz argued.

"Then to avoid this kind of debacle, you'll do it my way. Is that clear?" Honor said, her gaze unyielding.

Toeghan ran her fingers through her spiked black and royal blue hair, then fiddled with one of the piercings in her thin eyebrow. She yielded.

"Fine, fine, we'll do it your way."

"Good. Now that the announcement has been made, we shift our focus to the concert. Are you paying attention, Denning?"

"Yeah," he growled. He didn't care for Honor; he felt a strong urge to smack her supercilious backside.

With a satisfied smirk of vanity, Ursula led Voltaris to the elevator. Once inside, she checked with Gorrick on her organic cochlear stem-cell implant or OSCI.

"Sir, I'm taking Mr Idram to see Cronus."

"Fine, bring him to my office afterwards," he replied. Voltaris wasn't privy to what Gorrick said.

"Cronus?" Voltaris inquired.

The elevator door opened, and Ursula led the way along a corridor.

"To the Romans, Cronus was a Titan who gained supremacy of the world and made it his dominion."

"So, am I to expect a Herculean mythical warrior?" Voltaris asked.

"Perhaps. It depends on your personal definition of Herculean, I suppose," she said, with a sassy smirk.

They entered a different set of labs, this time having to pass through a sterile room, and following that, changing into lightweight hazmat suits, booties, hair covers, and masks.

"We need to control against microbial contamination until we have the new processor, which will program the immune system for Cronus," she explained.

They passed through a series of automatic doors to eventually arrive in a small dimly lit room. At its centre stood a stainless-steel sarcophagus three metres tall. Tubes were connected to the top of it, delivering cryogenic gas.

"We can't stay long because the room must remain a constant minus twenty-eight degrees Celsius, which can cause us frostbite."

She collected a remote from a wall bench and then pressed a button. The sarcophagus door slowly opened.

When the white smoke from inside cleared, Voltaris could see the creature within. Standing at the same height as he, Cronus was the perfect specimen.

"He is more than Herculean, he is magnificent," Voltaris said. "But why does he have no face or eyes?"

"His facial design is programmable. Once equipped with the new processor, his features will be programmed. The synthetic skin and musculature beneath it conform to neural input," Ursula explained.

"What an amazing accomplishment."

"Yes, Cronus is a lifetime of work for me."

"Don't be ridiculous, a lifetime, that makes you sound old."

"I'm sixty-one years old, Voltaris."

He stared at her, disbelieving.

"So, you see, Cronus does represent my life's achievement."

Later, in Gorrick's office, Voltaris, normally quite measured with his emotions, was bubbling over with excitement.

"So, obviously Cronus impressed you, Voltaris?" Gorrick observed.

"I'm lost for words. Will he be able to speak?"

"Yes, he will have subroutines that will give a full vocabulary along with an assortment of vocal inflections," Ursula answered.

"He will be sentient then?" Voltaris questioned.

"Yes, and he will have an acute sense of smell, a higher audio range than any human, superior eyesight... but he will still need to be programmed," Gorrick said.

"Though he will have intuitive instinctive learning capabilities... called Integral Reinforcement Learning or IRL. For the main part, he will be connected to the Gorrick hive, to receive instructions psychically. Additionally, an operator will feed him general instructions digitally via satellite. But this has obvious limitations," Ursula explained.

"I don't refer to Cronus as being he or him because it is a genderless replicant, perhaps even a clone. It is difficult not to align it with being a male humanoid by its appearance... it was something we decided not to avoid in order for it to move freely amongst humans without being recognised as an android. But the main attributes are strength, shape-shifting, and cloaking abilities," Gorrick explained, speaking like a proud father.

"Cronus is ten times stronger than even the strongest human," Ursula added.

"And this guy will be my partner... fantastic. Man, press the flesh..." Voltaris said, with uncharacteristic enthusiasm, holding out his hand for Gorrick to shake.

They were prevented from going left towards the Op Shop where Vee had found the Black Alice CD because the entire floor had caved in from the explosions. Before them was a massive hole leading to the car park two floors down. They retreated and headed right. Fortunately, a narrow path around the edge of where the floor had collapsed was still intact.

"This is going to be dangerous. We'll need to get to the other side of it for the next staircase up to the ground floor," Nerdo said, studying the schematic on her Ulink.

"Alright, follow me. If it doesn't hold, you'll need to find another way," Animal said, bravely stepping out onto the treacherous path.

Al shined the torchlight through the dust-filled air to provide light for Animal. With each step, a portion of the floor crumbled away. As he progressed, larger chunks of concrete floor began to collapse under his footfall, crashing down below and shattering in the car park. Eventually, he made it safely to the other side.

"It supported his weight, so it will definitely hold you guys. You go first, Nerdo... then you, Vee."

Al lit the way for Nerdo. She nervously edged across the gaping hole, safely reaching out for Animal's hand on the other side. Vee went next. In a composed manner, she courageously walked the path, almost as if she were on a leisurely stroll.

Now, it was Al's turn.

Animal provided the light for him.

After successfully navigating the path, they faced their next challenge: the staircase up to the ground floor. It was partially collapsed, but not from the grenades. Instead, the damage came from the nuclear attack that had occurred over thirty years ago. As they ascended the staircase, they encountered the first skeletal remains of shoppers caught in the devastating firestorm that had swept through, liquifying everything and everyone in its path.

The obstacles couldn't deter their progress to the ground floor. When they finally arrived, they were greeted by a scene far removed from a shopping mall. The space had been melted and burned, with shafts of light piercing through holes in the high roof. They discarded their contaminated facemasks; fresh air surrounded them now.

"Oh my God, it looks like a surreal painting. How hot must it have gotten here?" Vee questioned.

Animal placed a finger on his lips to signal them to be quiet and then whispered, "There could be more of them waiting in ambush. We need to stay quiet—they have super sound sensors."

"The way out is over there," Nerdo whispered, pointing.

After overcoming further obstacles, they reached the main entrance. Animal raised a hand to halt them, checking outside for any signs of the enemy. A quick assessment, and he signalled for them to proceed.

As soon as Alice set foot on the street, a sense of déjà vu washed over him. He was living out a dream. It was the exact same street from the dream where he witnessed Nerdo's demise.

Immediately, there were explosions all around them. The ground shook with each blast. They looked up sharply. A hovering drone was firing at them.

Animal signalled for them to crouch down under the cover of a large piece of metal awning, supported on the road by the burnt-out shell of a bus. There was no use retreating back inside; that would only trap them.

Animal peered through the night vision scope on his Heckler Koch submachine gun, surveying the street ahead. The green-tinted world within the scope took on an even more surreal quality. He spotted movement—a cyborg. It was evident that the overhead drone was directing ground troops towards them.

"I can see a Bot at the end of the street... looks like an RF-20. Wait... no, there are two, three!" Animal reported.

Nerdo, overcome with emotions after losing Cutter, disregarded the group's plan and charged toward the approaching cyborgs, shouting, "You bastards!"

"No, Nerdo! No, it's suicide!" Animal yelled after her.

Al knew exactly what was about to happen but he wasn't going to let that stop him trying to save her.

"She's trying to distract them so we can make it to the APC," he said, his determination overcoming his better judgment. Cursing himself for the decision he was about to make, he took off after her.

Vee cried out, "Alice, no!... Cover him, Animal!" They opened fire on the advancing cyborgs, who were now a hundred metres away.

Moving from alcove to recess, Al closed the distance to Nerdo, all the while dreading what he knew might happen. Then, his fears were realised: stepping out of the shadows at the far end of the street was an RF-20. The seven-foot cyborg immediately aimed its arm and fired at Nerdo. The sharp burst of fifty-calibre rounds sliced through her, ending her life in an instant.

Exhausted and defeated, Al slumped against the wall. Destiny had played its hand. It was an inevitable outcome. "Damn this twisted world," he cursed himself. The combined barrage of bullets from Vee and Animal continued to rain down on the advancing cyborg, but Alice knew from experience that none of it would be effective against the formidable adversary.

He sought refuge in the wreckage to avoid the danger of friendly fire. As he had predicted, the cyborg kept advancing, its sensors primed to detect any movement. Staying motionless was the only way to evade its attention, a lesson he had learned from his previous encounters in this bizarre world. Then he noticed another RF-20 emerging from a concealed position further down the street. A sense of dread washed over him, understanding that any direct confrontation would inevitably lead to his demise. He had to find a way to protect Vee and Animal.

The first cyborg reached Nerdo's mutilated remains, picked them up, and callously hurled them thirty feet away, creating a gruesome spectacle.

"Poor Nerdo," Al whispered to himself. The cyborg's head snapped sharply in his direction, drawn by his voice. It began to approach him.

"Damn!" he cursed. He was in dire straits now, facing a serious threat. The second RF-20 was closing in, and he found himself pitted against both of them.

Gorrick's conversation with Voltaris and Ursula was abruptly halted by a message on his OSCI. He raised a hand to signal for a pause in the conversation. "Affirmative, activate!" he ordered, and instantly a holographic image appeared, hovering in the air before them. The sudden appearance startled Voltaris. The image displayed a high-definition point-of-view (POV) feed from a cyborg's perspective.

Reacting to what he saw, Voltaris growled, "That's Black Alice!"

Gorrick continued to receive information. "This feed is from the patrol I dispatched into Woden after detecting an APC during our flight this morning. The patrol has cornered the enemy. They've eliminated four of them... play," he commanded. A holographic video replayed Cutter's execution, shown from the perspective of the executioner. Cutter's ID photo and personal details were displayed alongside the gruesome image. The replay then showed Sharkey and Grub being gunned down, followed by Nerdo being bisected, the perspective captured from the perpetrator. Her ID and details were also presented.

The graphic and realistic violence of the killings unsettled Voltaris. The holographic vision, although unreal, seemed to have no impact on Ursula.

"Two of them we recognise as Cutter and Nerdo. They held high-ranking positions in the insurgency. It is reported that upon inspection, Cutter had Red Wheel. CU the other two," Gorrick ordered. The live image zoomed in on Vee, taking cover. "Who is she?" Gorrick demanded.

"Her name is Vee; she's Black Alice's sister," Voltaris revealed.

"Zoom in on the other one... ah, yes." Recognising him, Gorrick glanced knowingly at Ursula.

She snarled, "Animal."

Since 2087, she had been awaiting the chance to witness his demise.

"Exterminate them," Gorrick ordered, his tone devoid of

emotion. "Now, let's relax and enjoy the show from our wonderful RF-20 Warbots... a perfect opportunity for you, Voltaris, to witness the technological brilliance of Zen." He pressed a remote, and the hologram switched to a live wide-angle view.

Meanwhile, Alice fumbled in his side pocket, retrieved a pill, and swallowed it—their only chance to overcome the cyborgs. A surge of power coursed through his body like an immense electric shock. He dropped his weapon, rose to his feet, leaned forward, and flexed his muscles. His body was undergoing a transformation.

Vee was watching; she had seen this before when Alice fought Kew back in 1976. "Watch, Al," she urged Animal, her excitement evident.

Animal had been resigning himself to defeat until the spectacle began to unfold just fifty metres away.

Alice's form shifted, taking on the likeness he had imagined—that of his superhero, an airbrush painting that had once adorned his Foster-father's den.

Vee exclaimed excitedly, "It's the Star Lord!"

Alice underwent a complete metamorphosis, morphing into a six-foot-five, massively muscular warrior. His biceps dwarfed even the most impressive bodybuilder's; the same was true for his forearms, deltoids, trapezius, pectorals, lats, chest, abdominals, quadriceps, glutes, and calves—he was colossal.

"Holy hell!" Animal gasped.

Alice released a lion-like roar, "Argh!" The sound wasn't born of the physical pain of his transformation; it was the manifestation of the fury coursing through him due to the loss of his friends.

Gorrick, Ursula, and Voltaris could hardly believe their eyes.

"Get 'em, Al!" Vee screamed, her voice filled with the same rage as her brother's.

Before the first cyborg could react, Alice lunged at it. His punch was so forceful that it caved in the metal face. The cyborg raised its arm, equipped with a fifty-calibre machine gun, but Alice was faster. He tore the arm off at the shoulder and wielded it like a club, shattering the cyborg's head.

The POV from the cyborg cut to static. Gorrick quickly switched to the overhead drone camera. A cyborg head came flying towards them and then the image also cut to white noise. Gorrick switched to the next cyborg.

Alice's method of dispatching the cyborg had stunned Animal. He waited for the drone to lower to a better shooting range, then seized the opportunity to hurl the cyborg's head at it. It was a killer throw, causing the drone to crash onto the road.

Alice promptly seized the fallen cyborg's body to use as a shield against the hail of bullets from the remaining RF-20. He sustained hits in his shoulder, thigh, and a grazing wound on his face. But rather than weakening him, the wounds fuelled his determination.

"Quick, order it to use incendiary, sir!" Ursula bellowed, "The gun is useless. This RF-20 is equipped with a flamethrower."

"Activate flamethrower," Gorrick ordered without hesitation.

The RF-20 received the command and ceased firing from its extended arm. Swiftly, it lowered that arm and raised the other, clenched fist. A small nozzle protruded six centimetres from the metal knuckles.

Still employing the inert cyborg as a shield, Alice was just ten metres away from the remaining RF-20.

Standing its ground, arm pointed at Alice, Vee wondered what would unfold next. She soon found out. Under high pressure, white-hot propane jetted from the RF-20's fist.

Gorrick reclined in his seat, amused, as he watched the stream of fiery liquid aimed at Alice. He chuckled, "Let's see him escape from that!"

Just as the jet of flames neared him, Alice pivoted and used all his might to hurl the lifeless cyborg body at the flamethrower-equipped RF-20.

Gorrick and his associates observed the cyborg's body hurtling through the air toward them. The image grew larger, and then once again, it was replaced by static.

Upon impact, the RF-20 was sent tumbling backward onto the road. A spray of propane shot into the air, descending upon the fallen cyborg like molten lava. Struggling to rise, the cyborg became ensnared in the fiery deluge. Al seized the moment to strike. The collision had damaged its right shoulder, rendering the arm useless. It remained immobilised on the ground. Al seized the cyborg's head, exposing the metal skullcap as he tore off the faceplate. Then, he plunged his fist into its brain. The cyborg convulsed uncontrollably, until, as if a switch had been flipped, it abruptly froze. Terminated.

Alice's skin was scorched, but he slowly stood, flexing his body to expel the bullets from his shoulder and thigh. They rebounded on the heated pavement. His gaze scanned the surroundings for more cyborgs, but none remained. He relaxed, and his body began to revert to its original form. Within moments, he had returned to his normal state, his wounds and burnt flesh miraculously healed.

"Another captivating experience, Alice," En-Ki's voice echoed in his mind.

However, Alice paid no heed to the voice. He strode over to the still-active drone, lifted it, and, through clenched teeth, shouted loudly, "I'm coming for you, Gorrick! Do you hear me?"

Despite the severe damage, the drone's audio system still functioned, transmitting Alice's menacing message to Gorrick amid the static. Gorrick glared at Ursula and then growled with ferocity, "Cronus had better be far superior to the feeble attempt we just witnessed.

CHAPTER 11
DESTINY

THE DRIVE BACK to the bunker was a sombre one. Burying the remains of their friends had been a distressing experience. The three of them had been left speechless by it.

Alice needed a change of clothes. They were split at the seams from his transformation. Even his boots were busted.

As they were nearing the turn-off to the bunker, Animal spoke for the first time. "What happened back there, Al?"

There was a pause while Alice collected his thoughts to reply, and then told him, "When I fought En-Lil on the planet Eris, I was exposed to some kind of radiation that affected my atomic structure. If I visualise something, I can transform into it. Back there, I thought of a painting of a superhero that used to be on my Foster father's den wall."

"How do you bring it on, is it only when you're angry or something?" Animal asked.

"Secta developed a pill that triggers it. I dropped one when I realised we were in serious trouble... and I admit, I got pretty dark when it killed Nerdo."

"It was a wise decision, bro," Vee confirmed.

"I'll second that, we were dead in the water," Animal agreed.

He turned off the highway to follow the dirt road into where Woodhenge once stood.

"I think Nerdo gave up the ghost once she'd lost Cutter," Animal supposed.

"Yeah, I reckon, and once Cutter knew he had Red Wheel, he threw in the towel," Al concluded.

"I can understand that... I'd rather die the way did than suffer a horrible slow death from Red Wheel," Animal admitted.

He stopped the APC just short of a green camouflaged metal plate in the ground and then pressed a button on the dash. The plate slid open. He drove onto a heavy-duty steel plate that then lowered the APC twenty metres underground into the bunker. The plate closed overhead and lights blinked on for them to see when disembarking.

It took a while for the briefing; it was very emotional. Morri, Secta, and Hope were extremely upset by the loss of their comrades. Alice had left the full update to Animal and Vee, while he went to change his clothes.

He was sitting on his bunk with his head in his hands when Secta came in.

"You alright Al?"

He looked up. "Yeah, I guess so Secta," he said sorrowfully. "You know, this is all pretty messed up. That bastard Gorrick has got to go, actually, correction, all the Gorricks have got to go. Sit down mate, I've got something to tell you."

He waited for Secta to sit on the end of the bunk.

"After going through the weird experience of releasing En-Ki... when I got home I'd really lost the meaning of all we do... it all felt kinda futile... you know, you just get something done, then from out of the blue another serious drama rears its ugly head. One after another – relentless. I was sitting on the bed in OTT, I dunno contemplating things I 'spose, when a voice spoke to me."

"A voice? From what? Outside or from within?" Secta enquired, perturbed by the admission.

"At first, I thought it was outside but then realised it was in my head. I recognised it."

Secta jumped up and started pacing the small room biting the knuckle of his right index finger. "Don't tell me it was Neit?" he said, excitedly.

"No mate... En-Ki."

"En-Ki?"

"Yes, Secta... Alice is my host," En-Ki said, speaking though Alice with a slightly different vocal tone.

Secta froze, his eyes the size of dinner plates. "En-Ki, is that you speaking?"

"Yes, Secta it is I."

It was the first time Alice had witnessed Secta awestruck. He moved zombie-like and sat on the end of the bed like a schoolboy awaiting a reprimand from the headmaster.

"Not only have I occupied Alice, but I believe En-Lil has occupied Gorrick, however, which Gorrick I cannot yet determine."

Putting his face in his hands, Secta groaned, "This is unbelievable." He looked up, "What can I say? Welcome En-Ki. Tell me, do you feel or sense Alice's frustration with all of this?"

"Yes, I do, and we will resolve these issues, you must trust me. I am here to guide you."

It felt to Secta like something biblical, akin to Noah or Moses being possessed by God to perform some kind of extraordinary feat.

"If you were to confront Gorrick, could you tell he was possessed by En-Lil?" Secta asked.

"I believe so. But will not know until that is attempted. But what is most important now for humankind, on this timeline, is for you and Hope to proceed with your course of action," En-Ki said, knowingly.

"Which is?" Alice questioned, thinking he was going to be asked to fertilise enough of Hope's eggs to repopulate the planet.

"You seem to have anticipated our decision," Secta said.

"To take her back to your time? Yes, and then to find the Gorrick hosting En-Lil and eliminate him. That would put an end to this timeline and prevent the Cyberwars from ever taking place."

"I think we first need to eradicate the Gorrick in this time to cover our bases," Al added to the mix.

"Yes, that would be wise. I think it is best for the time being to keep my occupation of Alice our secret," En-Ki proposed.

"Yes, that would also be sensible," Secta affirmed, still gobsmacked.

Later that evening, Morri confronted Alice in the cafeteria.

"Sorry to interrupt your meal, Al, but I'd like a quiet word with you if you don't mind?"

"Sure Morri, sit down."

"It's a delicate matter, Al... Um," she swallowed her words nervously.

"Speak your mind, Morri. I won't bite," Al assured her.

"Alice, I don't want you to risk your life or the lives of anyone else to save Turk. He is the same age as Cutter, and if he's alive, well... he could very well have Red Wheel."

Alice recognised the pain in her eyes and her voice. He reached out a hand and covered hers on the table. "Morri, I'm going in to kill Gorrick... if I can find Turk while I'm there, then good-o, if not, then that's destiny. Okay?"

She covered his hand with her free hand, squeezed it gently, and pleaded emotionally, "You're far too important to the world to lose, Al. You know that."

"Hey, you're psychic... you're holding my hand, tell me... am I going to die soon?" Al probed.

"No Alice, but I do feel another presence in you, one of enormous power... and..." she reacted suddenly as though struck by whatever it was she was psychically sensing.

Alice panicked that she was about to pass out. "Morri, Morri, are you alright?"

She released his hand and clasped her forehead between her middle finger and thumb. "There is great light within you, Al, and you know it."

"Yes Morri, I know exactly what it is. If I was religious, I would say it's God."

Tears began cascading down her pale cheeks.

"Don't cry Morri, everything will work out," Al said softly, compassionately.

"I cry for the loss of Nerdo and Cutter, we've been together so long... and I cry for what the world has become. All the good promised by humanity has been left to waste by the Red Wheel of fortune."

Alice appreciated the sentiment of the metaphor. "I know. Let me tell you something about destiny. After I returned home from leaving 2087, one night I had a terrible nightmare... I didn't know if it was a premonition or not... you more than anyone would understand that. I had seen the future and witnessed Nerdo's death. It was exactly how it played out today Morri, and there wasn't a thing I could do to prevent it... it was destiny. So, when it comes to destiny, I also know that Turk isn't meant to die in a Zen prison."

Alice might have told her a white lie, but it was to give her hope. He had no idea how the future was going to pan out for Morri, Turk, and the rest of them. If once he returned to his time, he killed the right Gorrick preventing the Cyberwars from ever happening, he wasn't sure if that meant Turk and Morri would never meet on the new timeline generated? All he could do was put his faith in destiny.

Voltaris sat on a park bench beside Ursula outside the Zen building. The only source of light was the streetlight next to them; other than that, they were under a vast canopy of stars.

"Tomorrow, I expect the new processor to have grown enough to deploy," Ursula said.

"So, did you create the formula to make the chip?" Voltaris inquired.

"No, Tokyo sent us a SCOD to grow," Ursula replied.

"A SCOD, what's that?"

"A symbiotic culture of DNA that has modified strands. That's all

I know; the rest is a Zen secret."

"How long does it take to grow?" Voltaris asked.

"It has taken a month. But once it is active, it can easily be replicated. The host culture can reproduce as many clones as required. You will be taking a culture back with you to your time, along with Cronus."

"Where will that leave you?"

"Oh, we already have a clone of Cronus," she said. "No problem."

"It's paradigm-changing technology," Voltaris mused, gazing at the stars.

"It will need to be more than that to defeat Black Alice. Imagine if we could bottle whatever causes him to transform. For me, that was truly remarkable."

"Gorrick was embarrassed by the failure of the RF-20s, wasn't he?"

"This is not the first time. In 2087, Black Alice was solely responsible for the destruction of the entire RF program, everything I had worked on for years."

"And Animal, both of you reacted when you saw him?" Voltaris probed.

"Yes, he was the appointed grandmaster of the National Biker Federation after Black Alice had killed his predecessor Duke in the arena. When he and I trapped Black Alice and Secta, he decided to defect. Since then, he has been a thorn in Zen's side. He turned the entire biker movement against us."

"That explains why you want him killed." Voltaris paused, studying her eyes, then continued. "Are you convinced that now you have seen what Alice is capable of, Cronus can match or even better him?"

"Yes."

"But you seem to have thought that with each of your RF models, only to be disproved."

"The RF series are simply glorified robots... none of them capable of anything like what Cronus can do, mentally or physically...

Cronus is superior to everything, be it human, cyborg, you name it."

"When was the processor invented?" Voltaris inquired.

"The first version was brought back from Tokyo in the middle of the 21st century. If I remember my history correctly, OTT brought it back to your time from 2047, and Zen got hold of it by exchanging it for an OTT hostage they had taken."

"That's right, Rita Vallins," Voltaris confirmed. "Go on."

"Well, it was a pretty bad trade because that organic chip had purposely been infected with a virus Secta had implanted, and it soon brought down every Zen computer using it... Herpes, I think it was... after that, it wasn't until 2047 that it was developed again by our Zen office in Tokyo but not to the required standard... it was extremely difficult to produce, and then when it was nearly perfected, development was interrupted in 2080 by the Cyberwars."

"Wait a minute, are you saying all Zen technology using the organic chip back in my time failed?"

"Yes, it was a catastrophe, I believe."

Voltaris became noticeably nervous as the gravity of Ursula's recount of history began to sink in. "Do you know exactly when the failure occurred?"

"No, but I can find out. I do know that not everything utilizing the technology failed at the same time. I think it depended on the amount of processing required of it."

"So, if it was a huge processing job, would it go down quicker?"

"I'd say so. Yes."

"Like driving a supercomputer to enable time travel?" Voltaris suggested.

"Exactly." Then, as if struck by lightning, she realised the seriousness of it. "Are you thinking Aquila might shut down while you're here?"

"We need to find that out quickly," he said, worriedly. The last thing he wanted was to be stuck in the godforsaken dimension of 2112.

President Malcolm Low concluded a lengthy conference call with US President Oprah Robinson. Three critical issues had been raised and debated. First, the pros and cons of the Temporal Prime Directive prospectus proposed by the UNTT. Second, the mysterious ties between the US facility Time Travel Works Op, also known as TWO, and Zen Corporation. And lastly, the resurgence of the Watchers. Within the past twenty-four hours, multiple sightings of them had been reported in various shapes and forms over key US military bases worldwide, as well as a couple in Oceana.

Mal rested his chin in his hand, elbow on the arm of his chair, lost in thought. The responses from the US President had left him troubled. The matter of the Prime Directive seemed straightforward enough, with no major issues. However, it was the unexpected reaction to the connection between TWO and Zen that concerned him. She vehemently denied any alliance and swiftly shifted the conversation to the topic of the Watchers, a subject Mal considered of lesser importance. Initially, he wondered if she might be complicit in the alleged Zen-TWO partnership, but he recalled Vic's information that Colonel Larry Freeman had disclosed TWO as a CIA black project with limited government knowledge. This raised questions about the US Government's involvement in the UNTT Temporal Prime Directive, given TWO's autonomous activities.

He swiftly typed a note to Rita Vallins, and before long, Dr Luna Cairn entered his office.

Stepping out from behind his desk, Mal greeted her, "Luna, sorry to call you in on such short notice."

"No problem, Mal. I was just about to head back to my hotel. You know how it goes for us… the day never really ends, does it?"

"Well, we only live once."

"I beg to differ Mal, we only die once, we live every day."

Mal gestured for Luna to take a seat before he sat down himself. "Too true, I guess that old adage is past its use-by-date nowadays.

Can I get you something?"

"A glass of wine to wind down the day would be perfect."

"Sounds good," he agreed.

Rita stood by, waiting for instructions. "Red or white, sir?" she asked.

"Red for me," Luna replied.

"Same here. How about a lovely 2017 Bonadale Pinot Noir from Tasmania? Bring a bottle and three glasses, please, Rita."

"Three, sir?" Rita inquired.

"Happy hour, Rita, and you're invited."

"Well, thank you, sir." Rita appreciated Mal's egalitarian approach to the operations of the presidential office.

Seizing the moment of privacy, Mal posed his question, "Luna, how can the US Government sign the TPD when TWO, in partnership with Zen, operates autonomously from the government?"

"Are you suggesting, Mal, that TWO isn't under the aegis of the President?"

"Absolutely. It's a CIA black project, the same as Area 51."

Luna's mood darkened. "Are you certain about this?"

"I just finished discussing it with Oprah Robinson."

"And her response?"

"She deflected when I brought it up. What does that tell you?"

"Guilty as charged," Luna conceded.

"Exactly."

CHAPTER 12
BERSERK

THE INTRODUCTION of the organic processor had allowed Dr Li's RF Program to progress to the next phase. By updating the original RF-1 to the RF-2, she had created the world's first cyber-soldier. Dubbed the RF-2 Warbot it was ready to be marketed to global government military agencies—and was potentially a trillion-dollar business, expected to secure Zen Corporation a place at the top of an exclusive list of global munitions suppliers.

Gorrick's strategy for Zen was to infiltrate the global war machine with an AI soldier that was essentially under his control. To that end, every RF-2 produced would have latent dark programming only accessible by Zen.

Introduced to the elite fraternity of munitions buyers by Zen's new ally Brigadier Bruckmaster, Gorrick scheduled an exclusive demonstration of the RF-2's capability at the new Area TWO facility in Texas.

Four RF-2's had been air transported in their pods from Sydney to Area TWO in Waxahachie, for the highly classified event.

Area TWO had been chosen as the venue because of its seclusion. The Aquila project at the same facility would not be exposed to the visiting dignitaries.

Gorrick and General Bruckmaster were greeting dignitaries that had just arrived in a brown unmarked, CH-47F Chinook helicopter at the Area TWO heliport.

Leading the eight men inside the facility they stopped at reception for Gorrick to introduce the masterminds behind the RF-2 Warbot, Dr Lizzy Li and Professor Uri Adamski.

An elaborate demonstration had been prepared. It was critical for these high-ranking government officials with massive military budgets to buy into the RF program, and the only way to facilitate that was by treating them to an exhibition guaranteed to blow their minds.

Under a canopy to protect them from the sun, the audience were seated ready for the show. Before them was a parched desert with a road winding through it towards mountains in the background.

Honor had been given the privilege of MC. She strode confidently out in front of the assembly garbed in a stunning black skirt and jacket with a white blouse all topped off with a black broad brimmed hat. A hush fell over the gallery.

"Ladies and gentlemen, I'm sure you all remember the movie Robocop in which policeman Alex Murphy is transformed into a cyborg. Well, what you're about to see is not too far removed from Robocop however, where it differs is, the Warbot is not a man in a suit, with a lot of CGI, on a movie set, no... the RF-2... is real.

"The flash-drive you will find in your seat pocket contains the specifications and the story of the development of this paradigm changing technology. I am not here to bore you with details or technological jargon, just to simply show you what an RF-2 Warbot is capable of."

A red H2 Hummer drove up and parked thirty metres away behind Honor. The driver got out and hurried off.

Then, to the shock of most of the audience, clunking footsteps came from behind them, like the approach of a giant. Heads swivelled around to catch a glimpse of whatever it was. Then, murmuring erupted from the audience when a seven-foot cyborg stepped out from behind them and stomped up beside Honor, who was standing nonchalant with her arms folded.

She glanced up at the monster towering over her and said, "Well, hello big boy," she looked back at the audience with a comical expression. "He can't talk yet but speech subroutines are in development, anyhow, a woman has little need for her man to talk," she said jokingly. The audience cackled.

Standing at the back, Gorrick and Bruckmaster exchanged wry smiles. Honor was doing a magnificent job... it was all going well.

The cyborg leered at the audience. Its dark blue, carbon-fibre body armour was awesome. There was nothing about it human except that it was biped, with two arms and a head. A burnished brown helmet with a slitted visor covered the head. It reached up an articulated hand and touched the visor with its finger. A servo sounded and the visor, like a camera iris, spiralled open to reveal a semi-human face but in shape, skin tone, and features only. The two eyes were far from human; they were chromium.

The sight of the cyborg's face generated another unsettled murmur from the audience.

It was to be expected, Gorrick and Bruckmaster wanted a fearful reaction. After all, this was a fighting war machine and was meant to be feared.

"I tell you what big feller," Honor continued with her rhetoric. "I have a dislike for red cars, take out the one behind me please."

The cyborg swivelled, raised an arm with a clenched fist, and fired a missile from the back of its hand. The Hummer exploded into a fireball. The cyborg swivelled back to face the audience. This time a lot of mumbling broke out; they were impressed by the accuracy of the shot.

"Impressive," Honor told the cyborg with a waft of arrogance.

The cyborg saluted the audience, and almost with a sigh of relief, they responded with a chuckle.

Honor put her hand to her ear. "I just received a message, there's a drone behind us at two o'clock... and you know what? It is red. Get rid of it please," she said with a wave of her hand, like brushing away a pesky insect.

The cyborg immediately swivelled, raised its arm, and fired at the drone. The single, seriously accurate shot took out the drone. It plummeted to the ground, landing in flames.

This time the audience applauded, aware of the difficulty of the task.

The cyborg turned back to face them. Another cyborg strode out from behind the gallery, stopped on the other side of Honor, and turned to face the gathering.

"Well, how about this? A rose between two thorns," she joked, and got the desired reaction from the gallery. "What is that you're carrying? Oh, it's a Heckler and Koch HK MP7A1 submachine gun, and it is loaded with armour-piercing high-velocity solid steel projectiles. Now, I'm sure everybody here knows that would make a serious mess of anything. I'll just move out of the way so you can shoot my friend here at point-blank range."

To the amazement of the audience, the cyborgs turned and faced one another, and the one with the Heckler opened fire. After a sharp twenty-round burst of fire, the target's armour showed no sign of damage. Honor held up her hand to stop.

"Thank you… I don't know about you, but I think more than a Heckler and Koch would be needed to do any damage to these guys."

The resulting round of enthusiastic applause meant the demonstration had sold them. Gorrick was nodding confidently, and Bruckmaster offered him a sly wink for a job well done.

But just as Honor was about to resume her position in between the cyborgs, they unexpectedly flew at each other and began belting each other in a rage. Honor panicked. This wasn't meant to happen.

The audience thought it was part of the show and kept the applause going, but Honor knew otherwise. Gorrick, Bruckmaster, Dr Li, and Professor Adamski exchanged looks of concern.

"What is going on, Doctor?" Gorrick whispered heatedly at Dr Li.

She replied with alarm, "I don't know, sir. I'll shut them down."

Both cyborgs were now acting completely disconnected, moving about haphazardly; out of control. The gallery had by now sensed that something was terribly wrong and started clambering out of their seats in a panic to get to the exit.

Honor was terrified when one of the cyborgs took a swing at her.

"Do something, Doctor, before someone gets hurt!" Gorrick screamed.

The cyborg with the Heckler submachine gun fired into the air, while the other cyborg fired a missile into the ground near its feet that exploded, blasting a shower of shrapnel and debris. Two guests took hits and went down, only to be trampled on by the stampeding hoard of terrorized guests. Honor, Gorrick, and Bruckmaster made a desperate escape, leaving Dr Li and Adamski behind to somehow pull the plug on the berserk cyborgs.

Alice wasn't prepared to accept that there was no way to break into Zen HQ. They'd got in there before without too much trouble, so he was confident in knowing the way.

"That was twenty-five years ago, Alice," Morri explained. "The old subway is gone now, turned into a death camp."

"A what? A death camp? What's that?" Al queried.

"When Zen finds people infected with Red Wheel, they send them to the death camp," she said, darkly.

"They lock them down in the subway to die. We've heard cyborgs set off poisonous gas grenades to hasten death so they don't have to feed them," Animal added.

"Wouldn't put it past them," Morri agreed.

"Sounds like the World War II Nazi extermination camps," Vee said.

"You're not wrong," Al concurred. "So, give me some thoughts on how to get in. I've been waiting around here so long that my clothes have come back into fashion."

They laughed at Al's attempt to lift their spirits.

Hope spoke up. "What about that captured transport drone? You know which one, Animal… didn't the Rebels hijack it last year?"

"Yeah, but you can't fly it… it's operated by a cyborg on board," Animal said.

"If Nerdo were here, she'd be able to," Hope said, glaring at Morri.

"Me? Oh, it's been a while since I've done any computer tech… but I guess I could try," Morri acquiesced.

"I'll help," Secta said. "Together we could do it… as long as there are enough of the right tools."

"Don't you worry about that, Secta. We've got a garage full of tools that'll blow your mind!" Morri said with a chuckle.

"So, if we get it flying, where would we land it?" Al asked.

"I've got a scale layout of Zen on my Ulink that Nerdo hacked a few years ago. You could probably land on the rooftop helipad," Morri suggested.

"She's right. They wouldn't be expecting anyone to fly a drone in. A normal one takes eight passengers, but from memory, the one the Rebels have is a cargo drone that only takes four," said Animal. "I'll get onto Thrash and arrange a meeting. He'll want to do a trade for sure."

"You can put your life on that… we'll think of something," Morri said. Leader of the Rebels, Thrash was renowned for doing trades: it was how the Rebels' bunker survived.

A few hours later, Animal got word from Thrash that they still had the drone and were prepared to trade it for medical supplies. He agreed to make the trade after dark that day. The Rebels' bunker was on the coast at Tuross Head, not far from Snake Ridge. However, that meant getting past a Zen outpost on the old highway at Mogo, which had been placed there to prevent biker gangs from using the highway to attack Angel City.

Animal wanted to use the APC to crash through the Mogo blockade, but Alice wasn't convinced. He was worried that if they did that, the cyborgs would surely be waiting in ambush for their return trip. Additionally, they couldn't risk Zen seeing the drone strapped to the roof of an APC, or the game would be up.

"How many cyborgs are there?" Al asked.

"No more than eight," Animal confirmed.

"What models?"

"Maybe one RF-20 in charge, with the other seven being earlier models. They save the RF-20s for the more important work. What are you thinking?" Animal asked.

The only other option available to them was to eliminate the problem by completely obliterating the cyborgs at Mogo.

"Would they have CCTV?" Al asked.

"Only directed to the cyborgs there, not back to Zen HQ if that's what you're asking. Each cyborg is controlled by a psychic operator back at Zen, so in effect, they are walking CCTV cameras," Animal explained.

"Good, then we don't have to worry about cameras as long as we wipe out their cyborgs there."

"Too right."

"I think you should plan for a united attack on Mogo, with the Rebels and us hitting them from both sides of the highway," Al suggested.

"Sounds good. I'd have to see if Thrash is up for taking them on; they're not spring chickens, you know."

"Hey, they got old for a reason. It means they won their battles," Al said.

"Might be just what they need. Life has been pretty dull since Zen took control," Animal admitted.

A while later, the plan had been solidified. A group of ten Rebels would attack the Mogo blockade from the South, while the APC would charge in with all guns blazing from the north. And by 'blazing,' it would be more than bullets—Morri had arranged for one of Nerdo's inventions to be fitted to the APC: a high-velocity flamethrower designed to incinerate just about any cyborg model under an RF-20.

Much to Vee's dislike, Alice had decided it was best for her to remain behind and assist Secta and Hope with preparations for the drone. Besides, once the medical supplies and the flamethrower, along with its large propane tanks for fuel, had been fitted inside the cabin of the APC, there was only enough room left to squeeze in Animal and Alice.

At sundown, the two men climbed aboard the APC, and Animal hit the switch to lift them to the surface using the elevator.

It would take them an hour to reach Mogo, and between the bunker and the blockade, there would be plenty of obstacles for them to negotiate: trashed vehicles, fallen trees, washed-out roads, all of it while they were travelling at speed in the dark.

Morri had given Al a lesson on using the flamethrower. The metre-long nozzle extended from a turret that had been fitted next to the roof hatch. A remodelled gamepad controller gave him access to a clear 360-degree view all around the APC. Additionally, a night-scope attached to the nozzle provided vision to a monitor. So, all he needed to do was lock onto a target and then press a button to release a jet of flaming, white-hot propane that could accurately stream up to thirty metres.

Honor was livid. Being made a fool of in front of foreign dignitaries was entirely unacceptable to a narcissist like her. However, to Gorrick, her displeasure paled in comparison to the irreparable damage inflicted upon the reputations of Zen Corporation and Brigadier Bruckmaster. He demanded answers about how such sophisticated and expensive technology had gone awry.

It took a few hours of diagnostics, but eventually, Professor Adamski uncovered the defect: the organic processor had caused a simultaneous error in the programming of each cyborg.

"What do you mean by a simultaneous error?" Gorrick demanded angrily. The boardroom was occupied by five individuals for the debriefing: Bruckmaster, Honor, Gorrick, Adamski, and Dr Li.

"The organic chip is infected, Gorrick," Dr Li explained.

"Infected?" Bruckmaster echoed. "Hold on a minute, are you talking about the same chip you acquired from OTT in that trade?"

"Yes, we reproduced it. The chip drives the RF series," Adamski began.

Bruckmaster cut him off, "Secta told me he planted a time bomb in that damn thing—herpes."

Adamski and Dr Li exchanged guilty glances while Gorrick covered his face with his hands. Honor adopted a pose that said, "I warned you, but you didn't listen."

"Herpes, of course... he infected the matrix, so all the duplicates are also infected," Adamski lamented.

"Insurance," Honor mumbled with a smug undertone.

"What's that, Honor?" Bruckmaster gruffly inquired.

"Insurance... it's something I taught OTT when I was there: always cover your backside. You should understand that, Brigadier, after so many years working for the government?" Her tone was facetious.

Frustrated, Gorrick ordered, "Right, then immediately shut down everything that uses the processor until further notice."

"But sir, we can't," Adamski muttered apprehensively.

Gorrick fixed him with an intense, angered gaze and questioned, "And why not?"

"Because Aquila is controlled by four organic processors, and we can't shut it down while Voltaris Idram is in 2112."

"What happens when it damn well fails?" the Brigadier growled.

The scientists responded with glum, vacant stares, conveying their lack of an immediate answer.

CHAPTER 13
ALTERNATIVE REALITY

A DAMSKI STATED WORRIEDLY to Dr Li, "What if, during Voltaris's return through Aquila, the processor produces an error during re-materialization?"

"Can we afford to take that risk?" she responded, equally concerned.

"There are many possible scenarios, but one thing is certain: an error is inevitable," Adamski said sternly.

The RF series was her brainchild, and after witnessing two of them lose control, she didn't want that replicated with Aquila. It was time. She switched off the power to the cyborg regeneration pods and gazed at her creations, feeling like a grieving mother.

"There, done as ordered. I wonder how long they will be mothballed for this time," she pondered.

"Well, that depends on the replacement chip, does it not? And now even that is in jeopardy with Voltaris's situation," Adamski replied.

Dr Li turned off the lights in the makeshift laboratory. The RF Warbot program was officially terminated until a solution could be found. Dr Li would accompany the cyborgs back to Sydney, while Adamski faced the daunting task of resolving the diseased processor issue with Aquila. He knew it was only a matter of time before Gorrick ordered Aquila to be shut down.

Bruckmaster was pacing his office carpet like an angry lion. The half-smoked stogie gripped tightly between his bulbous lips was leaving a vapour trail that dissipated into an eddy each time he reached the end on the room and turned sharply to retrace his footsteps.

Gorrick, seated in a lounge chair, watched Bruckmaster's restless pacing. He too was agitated, even seething. Once again, he had been outwitted by OTT, resulting in damage to his international standing and his ego. Inside his mind, his occupant En-Lil wasn't impressed. While Bruckmaster wore out the carpet, Gorrick engaged in a private mental argument with En-Lil.

"It doesn't matter who is responsible; what is crucial now is the action we must take," En-Lil insisted.

"At every turn, Black Alice defeats us. I propose that we prioritise eliminating Black Alice rather than dealing with him haphazardly," Gorrick countered mentally.

"Both you and other Gorricks, as well as myself, have tried and failed to defeat Black Alice. What makes you think you can succeed now, especially after this recent fiasco? Black Alice wasn't directly responsible for this failure; it was Dr Secta's doing. Moreover, the real culprit was the flawed processor trade. You underestimated our adversary, and that's what needs fixing. For now, Aquila must be shut down."

"But Voltaris Idram is in 2112, and now we urgently need a processor to replace the diseased one. Idram is our only chance. How do you propose we solve that?"

"We can't risk Aquila failing. If that happens when Idram returns, he could carry a defect, and the processor could be compromised too. Are you willing to take that risk after today's events?" En-Lil questioned.

"No."

"Black Alice is also in 2112. We know that he'll need to return. Idram will have to come back through Kairos with the processor. It's our only remaining option."

"We will need to send him a message."

Bruckmaster stopped and snorted, "I need a drink."

"The only solution, Brigadier, is to shut down Aquila. Otherwise, we risk infecting Voltaris and the new processor he'd be carrying," Gorrick warned.

"Then how the hell does he return?" the big man growled.

"Through Kairos."

"Kairos? Why the hell would they allow that?"

"We will tell UNTT's Dr Luna Cairn that we'll comply with shutting down Aquila if she arranges for our traveller to return through Kairos."

"Are you kidding me? You think she'd agree to that?" Bruckmaster snarled.

"Because you'll agree to sign her Temporal Prime Directive agreement."

A wry smile spread across Bruckmaster's face as he caught onto the plan.

"Good, very good. Can you get word to Voltaris so he's in the loop?" Bruckmaster inquired.

Gorrick smirked at his blustering big friend and replied, "Indeed we can, Bull. Now, how about that drink?"

The APC rumbled through the darkness, its headlights off to avoid detection. Animal could see the road through the night vision camera, transmitting images to the dashboard screen.

To Animal, Alice said, "You're good at that mate, stuffed if I could handle driving this thing at speed with only a monitor to watch."

"Ah, you get used to it."

Considering the state of the road, the ride was smooth courtesy of the all-terrain computerised suspension system. The only time it was taxing was when Animal had to swerve to avoid a derelict vehicle or a fallen tree. Both of them were tightly harnessed into their seats by seatbelts.

"How many biker gangs left these days?" Al asked.

"None really. Most of them have died out from Red Wheel but at the end of the day, we disbanded after the loss of the '97 offensive."

"Tell me about it?"

Animal pulled himself erect in his seat and said, "Well, it was much like Morri described when she told you that a few years back she was watching blokes being executed by cyborgs. The only difference in '97 was apart from Turk and his few supporters, the rest of the army was made up of the biker gangs... oh, and another difference was that we were up against three models of cyborgs: RF-6's, 7's and 8's. Have you ever fought anything so awesome?"

"Mate, I couldn't begin to tell you what I've fought. Everything from mutated Kangaroos to a twelve-foot giant bloke made outa clay, to giant bats... you imagine it, I've fought it... and that goes for RF-7's, 8's and now bloody 20's."

"Well man, we'd never fought anything like 'em before. Anyhow after the missile hit the bunker and Ursula Mennis had bailed on me, I knew I'd been stabbed in the back. It was obvious all Gorrick wanted was to exterminate humans and replace 'em with his bloody cyborgs. With you blokes gone, I decided to fight against that and so teamed up with Turk.

"Over the next couple of years, I managed to convince all the other chapters to come on board. None of us knew that within thirty years we'd be dropping off the perch from Red Wheel. We thought if we could get rid of Zen then we'd be doing away with most of our troubles. How wrong were we? The real problems hadn't even begun."

"You mean Red Wheel?"

"Yeah. So, ten years after you blokes had bailed, we put together a big enough army to attack Angel City. Three thousand strong we were lined up on bikes and a hundred awesome customized vehicles that Nerdo and Cutter had dreamed up, a couple of hundred metres from the front gates of Angel City. When the massive wooden gates opened, by our reckoning, two hundred cyborgs marched out all in time like clockwork soldiers. The loud drumming of their marching and the clanking of their armour was terrifying. When they got to fifty metres from us they formed a straight line and kept marching in time, then they stopped all at once just fifty metres from us. Everything paused like the world was holding its breath. I'll never forget it—you could've heard a pin drop. Then came a distant buzz, like a swarm of hornets coming out of Angel City. We all watched at least a thousand drones fill the sky hovering above us at about two hundred feet. And then Gorrick unleashed hell. The drone's opened fire. Fifty calibre slugs tore blokes apart—bullets hailing down on us from overhead… not a thing we could do about it. Once over, half of us were cut down, killed or injured from maybe a two-minute burst of continuous fire… they quit, and then as quickly as they'd come they left. Now that our numbers had been drastically depleted it was the cyborg's turn. They marched at us, programmed to kill."

"There's not much else to say except that after an hour or so of more slaughter, a handful of us watched on from a distance while the wounded were beheaded by cyborgs.

"They stacked the heads of nearly all three thousand men and women at the foot of the front gates as a warning for anyone thinking about entering Angel City. They didn't lose a single drone or cyborg.

"We never recovered from that, and no-one ever wanted to rise up against Zen again. That's why folks got into building bunkers; we couldn't beat 'em… all we could do was hide from 'em. Then a few years ago, after they developed the RF-20 and attacked us, that's what Morri was telling you about and how Turk got captured."

The more Alice got to know Animal, the more he was reminded of Ex, the barbarian warrior he'd befriended during his first-ever time travel adventure.

"Now I understand why it was so tough for you to talk Thrash into fighting tonight," Al said.

"Hard at first, mate, but as soon as I mentioned your name, Thrash and his men bought into it right away… that's how much of a legend you are to 'em."

Mal had called an early morning meeting in his office. Rita Vallins entered, balancing a plate of biscuits and mugs of coffee on a tray.

She doled out the coffees and then asked Mal, "Anything else, sir?"

"Yes, Rita, get me a news update on the Watchers please. The bloody things bug me."

The Professor crossed his legs and in a jovial manner spouted, "Oh, I wouldn't be too bugged by them Mal, if they were a real threat, they would have shown their hand by now, especially during the Strait of Hormuz fiasco."

"Point taken," Mal confirmed.

"But still, we need to keep an eye on them," Karzoff added.

"So, Luna, why the urgent meeting?" Mal asked before taking a sip from his mug.

"I've been contacted by TWO," Dr Cairn said, eyeballing Mal, the Professor, Robert, Karzoff, and Viktoria one at a time.

"Huh, our old friend Brigadier Bruckmaster, and what pray tell did he have to say?" Mal said hoarsely, an indicator that he'd had a late one with more than a few glasses of red.

"They've agreed to shut down Aquila in accordance with the UNTT order," she said, with an expression of self-accomplishment.

Karzoff flopped back in his chair, folded his arms in front defensively, and barked, "Ha! So, what is the real reason?"

The Professor put down his mug on the coffee table that separated them and said, "I think we know."

Dr Cairn looked at him surprised. "Know what, Vic?"

"When Zen kidnapped our lovely Rita Vallins and ransomed her for the organic processor that Secta had brought back from 2047, Mal asked Secta to see what he could do to sabotage it before we handed it over. We infected it with herpes."

"Herpes... like cold sores... warts?" Dr Cairn jabbered, shocked.

"Yes, it was all we could do in the time frame we had. Anyhow, Secta predicted it would take a while for the infection to cause errors but knew it would eventually... and now it has," Vic said, ending the statement with a smug grin.

"But wouldn't they have duplicated it?" Luna asked.

"Yes, that was why he chose the virus, it wouldn't be detected but would be duplicated with each clone of the chip," Vic explained.

"Are you suggesting that whatever use they have put the organic processor to it would now be giving errors?" Luna questioned emphatically.

"Worse than that, it would be creating absolute mayhem. They would definitely have used it in their RF cyborg program and without a doubt in Aquila... I'd go as far as to say they would have used multiple processors in the mainframe to drive the accelerator, which would be similar to ours, I'd hazard a guess."

"And that would be why they are prepared to shut Aquila down... they have to," Karzoff said smugly.

"So, what's the trade-off then?" Viktoria questioned Luna.

"Well, everything you've explained now makes a lot of sense, Vic, because shutting it down in accordance with our demand leaves their traveller Voltaris Idram trapped in 2112," Luna said.

Vic, Karzoff, and Robert exchanged looks and then burst into hysterical laughter.

"Ah, it couldn't happen to a better person! What goes around comes around," Vic said, with a chuckle.

Viktoria didn't like the sound of what Luna had said, she felt there was more to it and asked seriously, "Luna, what's the buy-line?"

Mal raised an eyebrow at Luna impressed by Viktoria's perception. The laughter calmed down.

"They want us to allow Voltaris to return through Kairos," Luna admitted.

This time Viktoria and Mal joined in when they again burst into ironic laughter. The only one unable to find it amusing was Luna.

"What are you all laughing about?" Luna contested.

Finding it difficult to suppress cracking up further, Vic reiterated half laughing, "After all that Zen has done to us... they're asking us for a favour... that's what is so hilarious Luna," Vic said, sniggering.

"Exactly," Karzoff reinforced with a cackle.

"You know, I don't get it. You once told me time is like a book, each page a different dimension," Vee told Secta.

They were in the huge garage that was like the interior of an underground aircraft-hanger. While thinking, Secta looked around, impressed that it was big enough to house two APCs and service them. There were benches along the walls, and in the centre was the large metal shaft of the elevator that raised and lowered the APC into the room. Large chunks of old rusting machinery were stored in one corner along with what looked like a vehicle covered by a tarpaulin. Hope and Morri were eavesdropping on the conversation.

"Yes," Secta agreed, "basically that's what I said in simple terms."

"Well, it doesn't make any sense to me," Vee said.

"Why is that?"

"Because if there were alternative realities, they would all have to begin at the one point... for instance if you liken it to a computer multiple choice game, it has to start from the one place and then branch off, but inevitably it would return to the original storyline. So, if we use an example when you and Alice travelled here in 2087, it was on the same timeline. We know that because here we are in 2112, and that historical timeline remains in continuity with 2087. Right?"

"Yes."

"Now, we also know that Zen started the Cyberwars in 2080, and that it created the mess of the world we're now in: Red Wheel, sterilization, destruction, and all that sketchy stuff... so... if you go back to your time and kill Gorrick to prevent the Cyberwars from ever happening, what happens to this timeline? If your theory is correct, it will branch off to a different dimension or another timeline the moment Gorrick is killed… but that doesn't make sense because this timeline has already been created," Vee hypothesised.

"Ah, a dreaded time paradox: always difficult to get your head around. I don't have an answer for that, and I suspect this will be the first time in history we'll be able to prove whether my theory is correct by the results."

Hope and Morri wandered over to them, and Morri asked Secta, "Do you think then that Turk and I, for instance, will never meet because none of this will have happened on that new timeline?"

"That would mean I would cease to exist as well," Hope said.

"Hmm, that does present a dilemma," Secta agreed, cuffing his chin and pacing the floor.

"That's my point," said Vee. "So, what happens to the original timeline? You already travelled to 2087 after the Cyberwars, now if you go back and stop the war, what happens to your past… for instance, does your journey to 2087 not happen? Does the following trip to 2047 happen? If it doesn't, then you won't get the organic chip that got you here now… so none of any of this will exist?"

"Unless Secta's multiverse is correct and all the timelines continue along their own course," Hope posed.

"But isn't that posing one hell of a risk? If Secta's wrong, then killing Gorrick back in our time could have more far-reaching effects than we could imagine," Vee concluded.

Morri sat on the edge of a bench. "There's a lot at risk here… let me give you a bit of history that I expect you wouldn't know; not long after 2047 when you visited Tokyo, wasn't it?"

Secta stopped pacing and leaned against the bench to listen. "Tokyo… Yes."

"I'd say around 2049, climate change had impacted so badly that society worldwide was collapsing. You see, when it was first proposed around 2020, it didn't take long before opinion split into two factions: those who believed in climate change and those who didn't. Scientific proof was ignored because the God dollar bill had bought the media and overruled the facts. For the next thirty years, the battle continued, becoming so intense that wars were being fought because of it.

"Governments had become so reliant on the income from fossil fuels, and the petroleum lobby was so powerful, that it was impossible for the debate to find common ground. In the meantime, the effects of climate change were becoming more and more catastrophic. There were massive wildlife extinctions, raging bushfires, catastrophic weather events... the ocean levels were rising at an unprecedented rate causing islands and coastlines to literally disappear. Coral reefs were dying, glaciers were melting, there were serious volcanic eruptions, high-velocity winds, and severe storms like nothing in recorded history, and still the doubters of climate change stayed in denial and continued to fight... By 2080, starvation had become a pandemic not only in 3rd world countries but in 2nd and 1st world countries. Rioting and civil unrest were daily events... the world was in a horrible mess... it was obvious the extinction of humanity was coming. So, in a way, the Cyberwars accommodated that. All of the destruction, the slaughter... the culling of humankind caused by the war put an end to the issues of climate change, and now, it's not difficult to see that over time, with the fossil fuels and carbon emissions a thing of the past, nature has begun to reclaim what mankind had stolen from her, and the Earth is beginning to breathe again. The only scourges that remain are of our own doing. So, if you were to stop the Cyberwars, what would the world look like today, right now outside of this bunker? That I believe is the most important question. Now, I'm not advocating we needed the Cyberwars, you know me better than that, I'm only speculating... would our world be better off or worse than it is today?"

"Surely anything would be better than this Morri," Secta said.

"True Secta, but it could be worse. The threat we face here and now is still Zen. Take them out of the equation, and things can only improve."

"But there won't be anyone left to inherit the world; you will have all died from Red Wheel," Secta pressed.

"Therein lies the riddle to be solved," Hope concluded.

They all agreed. It was a massive call either way, with no obvious solution.

CHAPTER 14
STAR LORD

DR LUNA CAIRN needed an answer from Oceana. She figured it was critical for them to permit Voltaris Idram to come back through Kairos from 2112. Shutting down Aquila and having TWO and Zen sign the TPD was, in her opinion, the only way to establish global accord on time travel.

But Oceana felt differently. They believed Aquila was being shut down because of the infected processor and that TWO was using signing the TPD as leverage to get Voltaris back... and what would he be bringing back with him? The Professor suspected it would be more than likely a new and more powerful organic processor. If there was one thing they were very much cognizant of, it was that Zen and Bruckmaster couldn't be trusted.

"What do we or the world, for that matter, stand to gain from bringing back Idram?" Mal asked Dr Luna.

"It would be the beginning of cooperation," she answered.

"You need your head read. Have you been asleep?" Karzoff blew up. "Do I need to read you out a list of Zen's criminality... their villainy over the last few years and into the future for you to get the picture... they cannot be trusted."

"He is right, Luna. Even Bruckmaster and the whole covert operation in Texas, if it hadn't been for the diseased processor, they would have continued to act in breach of the UNTT directive," the Professor submitted.

Incensed by Karzoff's impassioned outburst, Luna sat forward in her seat to emphasise her argument. "Look, I totally get what's happened in the past and the future, even with Zen. But at the end of the day, perpetuating hostilities between parties will get us nowhere. The only way to regulate Zen and TWO's time travel activities is for us all to be on the same page, and the only way to achieve that is by compromise."

"Then perhaps a show of good intent from them might be a good start. How about getting an admission from them as to why they shut down Aquila and see if they tell us the truth? If they admit to the failure of the processor and not give us just a pile of hyperbole, then we will agree to helping them bring back their stranded traveller," Mal proposed.

"Yep, put it on them," Karzoff protested.

Luna thought about it for a solemn moment and then nodded her head slowly. "Yes, yes… I suppose you're right. A show of good faith is what's required from them."

Animal slowed the APC. They were on the outskirts of Mogo.

"Last time I was here about two years ago, there was an old-fashioned roadblock. I was on my bike and was able to do a quick three-sixty and outrun them. The Rebels have been cut off by it since."

"Have they tried to attack it?" Al queried.

"Yeah, plenty of times, but they're no match for the cyborgs, plus they're all getting too long in the tooth for a fair-dinkum fight."

The roadblock came into view on the monitor. "There it is, a bit more imposing than before," Animal admitted. He stopped the APC for them to study the vision monitor. "They've built a heavy metal fence across the road, must be four metres high."

"Can we go around it?" Al queried.

"Nar, forest both sides of the road and a live laser fence I've heard. Can take your head off if you're on a bike."

"Would it be the same on the other side?"

"Yep, I reckon."

"Then how's Thrash gonna get through?" Al asked.

"They're not... they're going under the laser with these," he said, pointing at the pair of goggles on his head. "Infrared, you can see laser banding. You look for a dip in the terrain and then slip underneath the laser." He checked the time. "I told him we'd be here at twenty-three hundred hours, and it's that now. They'd be going under."

"Do we follow suit?"

"Nar, we just wait... Thrash is going to get the gate open so we can drive through, we'll need the flamethrower. I'll move into position. You get ready to fire it up coz there's sure be a reception committee of borgs."

Animal crept the APC up real close to the huge grey rusted metal wall. The outline of the sliding doorway could only just be made out.

"There are cameras all along the wall so they would've seen us by now," Animal said.

He was right; gunfire broke out almost immediately from several vantage points on top of the wall.

The racket from the hail of fifty-calibre tracer bullets ricocheting off the APC armour plating made it difficult to hear; Animal had to shout. "It's opening!"

Alice looked through the flamethrower scope and clenched the pistol grip trigger. "How'd they manage that?" he mumbled to himself.

A big metal panel slid open, revealing four cyborgs standing with weapons up, ready. Alice wasted no time and fired at the closest one. A roar came from the compressor as it pumped a white-hot jet of blazing propane at the target. The cyborg was incinerated, threw its arms in the air, and wandered about like a madman in a ball of flame. Al shifted his aim to the next one, then the next, until he had all four of them ablaze.

"I'm going in," Animal shouted.

The APC entered the compound and stopped near a single-storey brick guardhouse.

"The rest of 'em will be in there," Animal said.

"What about the gunfire from the wall?"

"Automated," Animal claimed, calmly. "Forget that for now, focus on the guard house."

Alice fired a burning stream through the guardhouse window. The front door crashed open, two cyborgs ran out on fire and collapsed in smouldering heaps. All fell quiet.

"There'll be two more," Animal shouted, peering at the monitor, hoping to see them. All he could see were the two charred and burning cyborgs and half a dozen dead Rebels strewn about.

Then, a bigger cyborg stepped out of the blazing guardhouse. Alice immediately recognised it and growled, "That's an RF-20..."

"Sure is, there will only be one. There must be another RF-8 somewhere; you've torched six of 'em."

"Why are you putting us at risk, Alice?" En-Ki questioned in his mind. "It's futile. Once you get back to your time and destroy En-Lil, this timeline will cease to exist."

"It's about principles, En-Ki. You above anyone should understand that," Al replied.

"What's that, mate?" Animal asked.

"Nothing," Al said.

"Very human of you," En-Ki repsonded to Al.

Gorrick joined Ursula and Voltaris in the operations centre. He had been summoned because of vision coming in from an attack on the Mogo outpost.

"What have we got?" Gorrick snapped.

"An APC, sir. Probably the same one as last time. We have five cyborgs down."

"Damned useless eights, I'd wager," Gorrick barked.

"Yes, sir," Ursula muttered. She had never gotten over the massive failure of the RF-8 series up against Black Alice back in 2087. "We're monitoring through the leader, an RF-20."

"Well, there's still hope. How did they get in?" Gorrick said irritably.

"I have no idea, sir," Ursula admitted.

"How did they get in!" Gorrick growled to the head of operations.

A plump woman reported nervously, "Vision showed Rebel bikers storming the guardhouse and opening the gate, sir."

"Their losses?"

"Six that we can make out on the ground, sir."

The vision was a POV from the RF-20 walking at a moderate pace toward the stationary APC. A biker suddenly appeared to the right of the picture, brandishing a submachine gun. The RF-20 stopped, swivelled, raised its arm, and fired a burst from its fifty-calibre machine gun. The biker was cut to pieces.

"That's more like it," Gorrick said.

The vision panned back to the APC. A figure was emerging from the roof hatch. The RF-20 stopped. In the background, on the other side of the APC, the remaining RF-8 appeared. It had been in a sentry box during the fight.

"Connect them to the hive and lock me in," Gorrick ordered. Ursula fitted Gorrick with a special headset that connected him mentally to the cyborg hive. He shut his eyes for a moment to lock in. "I'm in. Vocal commands from me only."

"Yes, sir," the operator confirmed.

Voltaris was watching in fascination.

"RF-8, go in on the target once it has dismounted from the APC. RF-20... Hold fast," Gorrick directed.

By the time Alice had climbed down from the hatch, he had transformed into the Star Lord.

"Who is that?" Ursula questioned.

"It's Black Alice," Voltaris said.

"Yes, he has transformed… it is the superpower he possesses," Gorrick grumbled, worriedly.

In the monitor, Animal observed Thrash emerge from the shadows. He swiftly approached the hatch and scrambled up the short ladder. As soon as he appeared, he exclaimed, "Stay put, Thrash! Leave it to Alice, it's an RF-20!"

Thrash retorted, "There's an RF-8 behind you!"

A bullet ricocheted off the armour plating fired by the RF-8. Animal quickly ducked back down inside the hatch.

Seriously well-built and sporting a full orange beard, Thrash melded back into the shadows to watch. Three more bikers scurried out of hiding to join him.

"That's Black Alice," Thrash informed them.

"Freaking eh, check the size of the dude!" a big bruiser named Togs growled hoarsely.

Alice realised he was caught in a pincer movement and assessed which cyborg was closest. It was the RF-8. With his Herculean build, he moved like greased lightning to rush the RF-8 at the back of the APC. He reached it before it could fire and delivered a powerful right hook to its chin.

The RF-20 wasted no time. Under Gorrick's command, it leaped onto the APC and dropped a stun grenade into the open hatch. Whump! The grenade detonated, creating a cloud of smoke. Amidst the haze, the massive cyborg reached inside and pulled Animal out by his arm.

Alice was poised to unleash an uppercut to decapitate the RF-8, but he froze. The RF-20 had dragged Animal to the ground, a thirty-centimetre blade extended from its fist, poised to deliver a fatal blow. Animal, conscious yet groggy, knelt with his head bowed, seemingly accepting his fate. He glanced up at Alice.

With all his might, Al shouted, "Clinch!"

Animal understood. He used his strength to twist and virtually embraced the towering RF-20. The proximity prevented the cyborg from employing its blade. This swift manoeuvre bought Alice the time to unleash a powerful uppercut, snapping the RF-8's neck with a resounding crack. Its neural pathway had been severed; it was as good as dead, and Alice knew it. He picked up the lifeless RF-8 and, using it as a shield, charged at full speed toward the RF-20.

At the Zen operations centre, everyone watched as the Star Lord carried the RF-8 and slammed it into the RF-20.

The collision dislodged Animal from the RF-20's grip but resulted in a snapped forearm. The bone jutted through the flesh, indicating a compound fracture. Despite the agony, he managed to keep his footing and hurried over to Thrash and the rest of the group.

The RF-20 was thrown backward by the impact of the collision. Alice swung the RF-8 as if it were a wrecking ball, striking the RF-20 with immense force. The blow sent the RF-20 staggering backward. Alice unceremoniously discarded the RF-8 and lunged at the retreating RF-20. He enveloped it in a bear hug and squeezed with all his might. A thunderous crack reverberated as the RF-20's spinal column fractured.

Back at the operations centre, the holographic display suddenly flickered with static. It was over—Alice had triumphed once again.

Gorrick ripped off his headset in frustration, hurling it to the floor as he bellowed, "What the hell can we do to stop that... that... monstrosity!"

"Nothing can beat that thing he becomes," Voltaris asserted.

"The Star Lord," Ursula murmured.

"The what?" Gorrick inquired, his irritation evident.

"His sister shouted that during the fight at Woden... 'the Star Lord,' she said. I suppose that's who he becomes," Ursula explained.

"I don't feel comfortable with him threatening to come after me," Gorrick confessed, his worry palpable.

The operations officer ventured cautiously, "Um, what should we do about Mogo, sir? Should we send in another team?"

"Don't be absurd," Gorrick scolded.

After a half-hour drive, the APC came to a stop within walking distance of the beach and the head of the Tuross River. The six men disembarked, and Thrash led them to the concealed entrance of the Rebels' bunker.

Alice paused on the way, taking in the view of the beach and the river merging into it. Nightfall didn't diminish the scene; he inhaled deeply, savouring the briny sea spray carried by the waves rolling in.

Holding his sore arm, Animal joined him. "Pity they're dead."

Enjoying the sea breeze, Al inquired, "The ocean and the river?"

"Yeah."

"Oh, they'll be back. Mother nature has a knack for surviving. She's faced near-extinction before and beaten it. Let's go get that arm of your set."

They made their way to Thrash, who awaited them by the bunker entrance.

"What about the APC?" Al questioned.

"It'll be concealed with camouflage. Zen probably has drones scouring for it," Thrash growled. He then used a flashlight to guide them into a tunnel. A brief walk brought them to an elevator that descended a few floors. The doors opened to reveal a spacious deserted room. Alice initially pondered its purpose and speculated it might serve as a buffer against a blast in case of a missile strike. However, his perception shifted when he noticed the room's finishing—a step up from the Avalon bunker, though not as enduring or fortified.

The Avalon bunker, originally constructed by the government in the 20th century, spared no expense. Its walls were designed to withstand a nuclear blast. In contrast, Alice surmised that this bunker might not fare well against a bunker-busting bomb.

"I know it seems less sturdy compared to Avalon, but the walls are layered with four inches of steel," Thrash clarified.

Alice was duly impressed. "Alright."

As they entered a corridor, Thrash elaborated, "A bloke up the coast prefabricated this bunker back in 2088, and we had it transported here. Reno's old prime mover was actually the one that did the job... remember it?"

"Ah, Betsy. How could I forget her?" Al recalled the formidable armoured prime mover they'd used to escape Angel City against all odds in 2087.

"Yeah, Betsy took out a few of our guys in that battle. She was a lethal weapon," Thrash remembered fondly.

"How many people down here?" Al inquired.

"It was eighty, but after tonight, seventy-four. But about half of them are crook from Red Wheel, which is why we need medical supplies. What's your plan for the drone? It ain't flown in a while."

"Yep, we've got a couple of techies back at Avalon that reckon they can get it operational. If they succeed, I'm planning to fly it to Zen," Al replied.

"Mate, that'd be like a suicide mission if I've ever heard one. Why in hell would you do that?" Thrash asked, scratching big orange beard.

Togs was walking alongside them listening.

"To bust Turk out and kill Gorrick," Al said, very matter-of-factly.

Thrash stopped them and with a serious stare said, "Mate, where Turk is, he won't be coming out."

Togs chimed in with a raspy voice, "Bush telegraph sez he's in the death camp, mate."

CHAPTER 15
LOOP-DE-LOOP

S ECTA WASN'T CONTENT with the debate they were having about alternative realities and needed to expound on his theory further, in more detail.

"Morri, do you have a whiteboard down here?"

"A whiteboard?" she pondered, unable to comprehend what it was, and then it dawned on her. "Oh right, follow me."

Secta waved for Vee and Hope to follow her.

"What's he up to now?" Vee asked Hope.

"Oh, he won't give up until he has fully explained his theory. That's Secta," she said, admiringly.

Morri picked up what appeared to be a laser pen from the benchtop and handed it to Secta.

"It's a holo-pen. The green button is for on/off. The red erases what's drawn or written, and the blue button changes the colour of the image. Just draw in the air... as easy as pie."

Secta was impressed. He pressed the green button and drew a straight red line in the air that hung there. "Fantastic, I've got to have one of these."

Morri shrugged her shoulders; the unit had been commonplace since she was at school.

Vee was amazed. "Wow, how random is that?"

"Okay, so this is the main timeline, let's call it Alpha." The glowing thirty-centimetre red line floated in the air as a kind of holographic image. Secta wrote the word Alpha at the beginning of the line.

"Let's give it a start date of, say, 1963." He wrote 1963 beside the word Alpha. "And an end date, which is now." He wrote 2112 at the end of the line, then explained further, "We don't know the future beyond now, so that's as far as the timeline can go for now. So, we send back a time traveller to 1963 to prevent Lee Harvey Oswald from assassinating JFK… not that he did in reality. As the presidential convertible Cadillac passes the grassy knoll without incident, a new timeline is generated." He pressed the blue button on the holo-pen and drew a green line parallel to the red line and then marked it Beta. "The Beta line comes into existence as an alternative timeline."

"So, is it only when there's a major historical intervention that the timeline splits?" Vee asked.

"Yes, the Professor and I actually termed it an intervention event or IE."

"Would it be fair to assume that the only time this would have happened in known history is when a traveller has caused an IE?" Hope suggested.

"Yes, we think so," Secta agreed.

"Well, that couldn't have happened very often because time travel has only just begun," Morri submitted.

"That's if you assume time travellers in the future haven't gone back and purposely generated new IEs. We believe that since primal days, we have had alien IEs on humankind's timeline, steering our future, if you like. We call them the Watchers," Secta explained.

"If you're right about that and you go back and kill Gorrick to prevent the Cyberwars, at that point, another timeline will begin that is now running parallel to this one," Morri theorised.

"Exactly. You see, this Alpha timeline continues unaffected because the beta line is carrying the altered history," Secta said, happy to realise they had grasped the theory.

"But what's to say that after killing Gorrick, there might be a worse outcome for humankind on the beta timeline?" Hope questioned.

Secta cuffed his chin with his hand. "Well, we'll just have to find that out, won't we?" He pressed the red button on the holo-pen, and the display disintegrated into thin air. Still thinking, he looked across at the tarpaulin-covered vehicle next to them and asked Morri, "Am I wrong in thinking that shape looks familiar?"

Morri went over and pulled back the tarpaulin, revealing a sleek British racing green sports car underneath. "Yep, my old Wilson-Kit J-car."

"Do you know that Morri, in her mid-twenties, constructed this car from a kit and then built the engine with her own hands... crafting an impulse motor that runs on a nuclear pellet: perpetual clean energy?"

"No, I've never seen what was under the tarpaulin; it has always been off-limits," Hope said, rolling her eyes.

"One hell of an engineer is our Morri," Secta said, like a proud father.

Both of them recalled when Secta had first occupied Morri all those years ago and after quite a debate of how it had happened and how to deal with it, she had shown him the J-Car. It was parked on the dirt track to Woodhenge, a replica of Stonehenge, which was beside the entrance to the Avalon bunker. At the time, Morri was paying the pagan site a visit to spread the ashes of her murdered parents when Secta had accidentally possessed her.

"Thank you, Secta," Morri blushed, and then pulled the tarp back over the car. "Okay, we're done here; all we need now is the drone. Let's go eat." She'd only just finished saying that when she let out a groan and cried, "Oh, no."

Secta moved up beside her. She was covering her wrist with the other hand as though it had been burnt or hurt.

"What's the matter, Morri?" Secta asked urgently, seeing how stressed she was.

Morri looked up at him sorrowfully, her eyes filled with tears. "Oh, Secta, no."

Hope was beginning to panic. "Mum, mum, what is it?... what's the matter?"

She smiled sadly at Hope, "That's the first time you've called me mum in ages, love."

"Mum, what is it?" Hope demanded, knowingly.

Morri slowly removed her hand from her wrist to show them. "It's Red Wheel, I'm afraid," she said, and then broke down, knowing her fate was sealed.

Holding Hope's hand, Vee led her to the canteen. Secta was following with a sympathetic arm wrapped around Morri's shoulders.

Morri wiped away a tear traversing her pallid cheek and said compassionately, "Thank you for being here, my old friend. I'm so pleased she is a replica of the Hope you lost."

Secta wiped away one of his tears and said tenderly, "We'll beat this, my friend. I promise you, I will find a way... we'll beat it."

Alice was appalled by the state of the Rebels. Both women and men cut down by the devastating impact of Red Wheel.

"Some suffer more than others, we dunno why," Thrash pointed out as they walked through a dormitory filled with bedridden casualties.

"We think it depends on the state of the person's immune system. If it's down, it triggers it. We've had some die in their forties after catching a bad case of the flu or getting a severe wound. We think when the immune system is battling something else and can't cope, it struggles to hold Red Wheel at bay. Others, when they hit a certain age, it seems to go off like someone flicked a bloody switch and they go down in sometimes in less than a week. But for others like me and Togs, well, we're just waiting for it to happen; it's like a ticking time bomb."

"Man, it must be terrible," Al said, his face showing sincere concern.

"Worst part is not knowing how to treat 'em... doesn't seem to be any cure. Togs, take Animal to the infirmary to get his arm set. You come with me, Al," Thrash ordered, then led Al along a dimly lit corridor.

"There were over six hundred of us down here before Red Wheel hit."

They entered a garage that housed at least fifty Harley choppers parked in rows, all shiny and well-maintained.

"Mate, killer bikes," Al said.

"Yeah, not much use for 'em anymore, what with all them borgs about," Thrash complained. He led Al behind the bikes to where the drone was located.

The grey drone was circular in shape, with a six-metre circumference. It looked like a flying saucer to Al but with no canopy.

"It only takes two with cargo at the rear. Underneath, it has four engines to give it lift and forward motion. We think they steer it remotely, but some blokes reckon it can also be steered manually. All the bits are there... it's been sitting here two years or so, haven't touched it," Thrash explained. "Can I ask you a personal question, mate?"

"Yeah, fire away," Al said.

"What happened back there when you turned into that other bloke?"

"Oh that... special pills my mate Dr Secta made for me, turns me into whatever I imagine."

"Geez, wouldn't mind getting my claws on a few of them."

The ringtone was the theme of the original Twilight Zone television series. Luna sat up half in a sleepy haze and answered. The screen light illuminated her face.

"Hello, yes Rachael, it's 3 a.m. No, it's okay, I'm still awake. What's up?" Luna asked. "Oh really, well, I'm surprised by that. Email me the transcript. Okay, I will, thanks, I appreciate the call."

She put the phone down and as the light dimmed, casting her hotel room back to pitch black, a voice grumbled, "I hope that was important."

She snuggled back up to the Professor and explained, "Yes, it was my office in New York. TWO has acknowledged Aquila had a technical problem with the processor, and as a result, have put it out of commission. They claim there is nothing they can do about it. Rachael is sending a transcript of their admission."

"Well, now isn't that encouraging? Unlike Zen to admit to their failings," he quipped.

The next morning, Luna and the Professor were in Mal's office. She handed him her notepad for him to read the transcript from TWO. When Mal had finished reading, he handed it back.

"Well, well. It's certainly an indication of how much they want Voltaris Idram back," Mal said with a wry chuckle.

Karzoff entered with Viktoria. Luna handed them the transcript to read.

"It worries me some," the Professor admitted.

"Why's that, Vic?" asked Mal.

"It's out of character for both Gorrick and Bruckmaster."

"You can say that again," Karzoff said after finishing the document. "Idram must be bringing back a new processor; it is the only explanation."

"What if they really care about him being stranded there?" Luna proposed.

"These people do not have an ounce of care in their bodies, Luna, so that is not very likely," Karzoff snarled contemptuously.

"They said they can get a message to Idram and asked if we agree to alert Alice so they can meet up," Luna explained.

"What if it is just a trap to get Alice? He is after all enemy number one to them no matter the timeline," Karzoff pressed.

"Yes, that needs to be taken into consideration," Mal said agreeably.

"I don't like it," Viktoria grumbled. "There's too much at stake here; we have Vee and Secta there as well. In one foul swoop, they could wipe out our entire time travel team."

That gave them a feast of food for thought.

"Okay, we need to make a decision. I vote we go ahead and get a message to Al but with a warning. What say you?" Mal said diplomatically.

"I agree," the Professor said.

"It is difficult to accept, but there is no other option but to agree," Karzoff reluctantly admitted.

"Yes, I feel the same," Viktoria added. "Being suspicious is a syndrome of our gig."

The Professor got up from his seat and said, "Okay then, I'll go catch up with Robert and sort out getting a message through to Al. Will run it past you before we send it."

"Good-o," Mal agreed.

Secta was amazed to see the new invention of a micro-vortex the size of a dime open and then close again as quickly as it had arrived, only an arm's length from him. He was seated in the canteen waiting for Vee to bring a snack from the food counter. The vortex had found him by detecting his DNA marker. A digital message was then transmitted through it to an experimental organic implant the Professor had embedded behind Secta's right ear prior to departure. The implant then decoded the message for him to understand, almost psychically. The message said: Herpes outbreak in Zen chips, Aquila kaput. Voltaris Idram stranded in 2112. Mal arranged trade; you bring Idram back, they'll sign TPD. Watch out; he might be carrying a new chip. The message caused Secta to burst into laughter just as Vee arrived carrying a tray.

"What's so funny?" she asked, bemused by his outburst.

"I just got a message from the Professor. Remember I infected the organic processor we traded Zen for Rita Vallins? Well, the Herpes has kicked in and cooked their mainframe and probably everything else they've used it in. So that's left Voltaris Idram stuck here. Ha! I can't believe it... and here's the clincher... Mal's done a deal for Zen to sign the Prime Directive accord if we get Idram back for them."

Vee was stunned. "You've got to be kidding, after what those cretins have done to us?"

"I know, I know... tell me about it," Secta said in disbelief.

In the Aquila control room, Adamski told Gorrick and Bruckmaster, "I can only risk opening a tiny window, just long enough to get a message to him, but that is all."

"It has to be done... do it. The message is on this," Gorrick said, handing him a flash drive.

Adamski didn't look confident.

"What's the matter, boy? You look like you just lost yer grandmother?" Bruckmaster bellowed, facetiously.

Adamski sat upright in his swivel chair, intimidated by the big man. "No sir, it is just that I cannot guarantee this will work. The mainframe is already showing errors... see." He pointed at the main computer monitor that was flashing the words "tight loop."

"What's that supposed to mean?" Bruckmaster quizzed.

"It is a classic control block walking algorithm. When the code falls through a loop, I have to zap all the instructions with the algorithm before tasking a new path. It could go on like this forever. You understand... it is a loop, feedback... it will keep on returning to the beginning," Adamski tried to explain.

Gorrick could tell by the Brigadier's expression that he was struggling to grasp it and so tried to put it into simpler language. "In other words, the processors are losing it."

"Yeah, got that… a loop-de-loop… you'll just have to try getting the message through the thing, son, you hear me?" Bruckmaster snarled, intolerant of technology.

Adamski reluctantly did as he was told. He set up the parameters, inserted the flash drive, and downloaded the digital message to the computer desktop. Then he handed Gorrick the interface to put on.

"It could feedback and seriously affect you, sir. You do understand the risk you are taking?" Adamski warned.

"We have to try. Go ahead," he said, putting on the headset.

"If it gets through the loop, Voltaris will receive the message on his implant, but we will have no confirmation he received it," Adamski explained. "Okay, sir, focus."

Gorrick closed his eyes and concentrated on astral traveling to 2112.

Adamski got a signal when Gorrick's brainwave frequency matched the designation link used previously to dispatch Voltaris and then, holding his breath, pressed the uplink.

Gorrick shuddered as if he felt a chill.

A patina of sweat had broken on Adamski's upper lip. Transfixed on the screen, his glasses reflected the stream of code flicking past. He was praying there would be no error code.

"It is going well," he muttered nervously to Bruckmaster, who simply nodded sharply in reply.

Finally, the code reached an end.

"Okay, sir, you can remove the interface," Adamski said hurriedly, with a sigh of relief.

Just as Gorrick was removing the headset, the details on the computer monitor froze, burst into pixels, and then the screen went blank. Adamski swivelled his chair around sharply to face Gorrick and Bruckmaster, and with a look of horror on his scowling face, grumbled, "I think the message got through but at a cost. Aquila is now dead."

CHAPTER 16
MOGO

VOLTARIS GRIPPED HIS forehead as though suffering from a migraine.

Ursula noticed him grimace and said, "What's the matter, darling?"

The pain dissipated, and he let out a sigh. "Phew, that was intense. I received a message through Aquila, but it had a piercing whistle at the end."

"Really? What is the message? It must be important."

"Aquila is about to fail... I'm to complete my mission and return through Kairos. It has been arranged with OTT. Dr Secta has been alerted."

"Dr Secta? He is here as well as Black Alice and Vee?" she queried, surprised.

"Apparently so. This changes plans. How am I going to get Cronus back now?"

"Don't worry, Gorrick will have the answer."

Alice and Animal were with Thrash, Togs, and four other bikers in Thrash's man-cave that had more Harley Davidson and rock memorabilia on the walls than any Hard Rock Café Al had ever patronised back in his time. The lighting was dingy, they were on their third bottle of JD, and 'Lightning Strike' by Judas Priest was playing on the antique stereo system.

Animal had a plaster cast up to the elbow of his right arm, which hadn't stopped him from using his good arm to take on Togs in an Indian arm wrestle. Half out of it, the gallery banged their fists on the wooden tables, chanting the name of the contestant they were backing.

Both contestants had frozen with their white-knuckled big hands gripped upright. With gritted teeth, sweat beading on their foreheads, muscly arms locked, not budging but quivering... they were evenly matched.

The challengers were waiting for the opposing one to make the first real move, knowing that picking the right moment could result in victory. Animal went for it. It was all over quickly—with the roar of a lion, Animal banged Tog's hand down on the table, then jumped up off his stool with his arms raised, bouncing about like a prize-fighter after winning a title fight. The win earned him a big swig from a bottle of JD. He snatched the bottle out of Thrash's hand and poured it from arm's length into his open mouth. The golden liquid overflowed, spilling down his stubbly chin onto the front of his grubby white T-shirt. He wiped the beard around his mouth with the back of his hand and growled like his namesake, "Yeah! Kill the beast!"

They calmed down to get on with more serious drinking.

"What else you got to play, Thrash, anything good like some of my music?" Al said, with a smug grin.

"Hell yeah! We've got Endangered Species... um, what else we got, Togs?"

"Argh... Master of Puppets?" Togs recalled.

"Get out, that's Metallica!" Al blurted out in good spirits.

A big fat bloke with a massive red beard and a clean-shaven head decorated in tattoos shouted, "There's a greatest hits CD there, s'got Something in the Air... and um, You and Me... oh yeah and Foul Play, yeah, dig that track."

"Foul Play, yeah... um...?" Al said.

"His name's Boof," Animal told Al with a drunken slur.

"What, like in boofhead?" Al quizzed.

Boof had just managed to squeeze in behind the bar, came up with the CD, and then handed it across the bar to Al. "Yeah, Boofhead, that's me," the big feller growled with a broad grin, displaying a full set of chrome snappers.

Al checked the credits on the back of the CD. "A great song, Foul Play. I performed it a while back with World on stage. Bung it on, will you, Boof?"

Boof slipped the CD into the player and selected Foul Play.

"Do you dig this time travel stuff more or playing in a band, Al?" Thrash asked.

"Both, mate. Maybe I'll write a song about you blokes when I get back," Al quipped.

"Nah, wouldn't be a hit, mate."

"Why not, Boof?" Al asked.

"It'd be on this CD if it was, wouldn't it?" Boof said, with a vague look on his big dial, not sure if he understood his own statement.

Al thought about it for a minute and then smiled, realising it was another time travel paradox that Secta talked about. He laughed. "I suppose you're right, mate."

"Seriously, it must be weird knowing that everyone you know is dead?" Thrash said.

"Never really thought of it like that, Thrash," Al said, with the sudden realisation he was right.

A scuffle broke out between two bikers, and Animal stood in to pull them apart.

"They're starting to turn on each other... that means it's time to call it a night. Hey, cut the crap, you blokes... one for the road and that's it, you're getting out of line," Thrash said, asserting his authority.

A grumble of discontent came from them that caused Al to smile.

"They're good blokes most of the time. I don't mind 'em blowing off a bit of steam every now and then," Thrash admitted.

Togs joined them.

"What were they scrapping over, Togs?" Thrash asked.

"Piggy said something about Turk that Reevo took the wrong way, you know, piss talk."

Something clanged, and they all looked at Animal, who had taken the floor and bashed a metal cup against the side of an empty JD bottle to gain attention. He got it.

"I want to say something here, mainly for the benefit of Al, seeing he hasn't been here since '87. We often piss-talk about battles won and lost, many of us have fallen, and plenty of us from Red Wheel, but there's something else that needs remembering... and that is one bloke brought us all together. One bloke who I'd take a bullet for and I reckon you all would... one bloke who after what reprobates like Spike and Duke did, that he killed in the arena, had every right to give us the elbow... you know who I'm talking about," he shouted, passionately. "Who the hell is it?" he growled.

"Turk!" they yelled in unison with feeling.

Animal calmed down and then continued, "Yeah, Turk... well, I'm sure we've all got a story about him, but I'm gonna tell you one of mine. When the missile fired by Gorrick hit the Avalon bunker, and Ursula Mennis left me for dead, Turk, Morri, Cutter, and Nerdo took me in. It took us three years to convince the biker movement to unite against Gorrick. The last to join were the Comanche's, one of the biggest and the main arms suppliers to Zen. Some might argue that was why they resisted. You see, Alice, after the Cyberwars, the biker movement supplied Zen with fuel, weapons, and ammunition. But after I jumped ship and the Rebels, Rat Finks, Angels, Bandits, Notors, and Nomadics had all joined forces, Gorrick had to produce his own guns and ammo. After a year or so, still supplied by the Comanche's but building his own munitions plant in Angel City, Gorrick began to launch attacks on the chapters to take their guns and ammo they had stored... to disarm them. The biker movement had become his biggest threat. Zen by then had built up a large army of cyborgs, mostly RF-6's and 7's, but some 8's. He unleashed them on us with unprecedented force, hitting each and every chapter. One after another, they fell. First the Angels... Zen wiped them out. No-one knew how he found their location... other than Avalon, they had the best bunker. Then the Bandits... luckily, Turk realised what was happening by then, so we got the Rebels, Notors, Finks, and Nomadics together to defend against the borg horde.

"When the Comanche's heard what had happened to the Angels and the Bandits, they quit supplying Zen. Because other than the Angels, they were the largest munitions producers, we knew that would trigger a serious reprisal from Zen. We all remember that battle, don't we?"

A murmur went around the room. It was obvious to Alice that this had been a battle they were never going to forget.

"Nerdo, in her genius, had come up with a way to beat the Borgs. Before that, we had no answer to them. All of the chapters had assembled at the Comanche's bunker in Braidwood. A massive bunker, the biggest by far, three times the size of Avalon.

"By then, we'd lost the elders to Red Wheel. We still didn't really understand what it was... we only had three hundred to defend against Zen. This was the biggest biker offensive since your escape from Angel City in Betsy, Alice."

Al could see in each and every bloke's eyes that they were reliving every one of Animal's words.

Animal took a swig from a bottle of Jack and then continued. "Nerdo had created sticky bombs made of C-4 plastic explosive to be fired at the Borgs using a slingshot. The size of a golf ball, the C-4 sticky bomb had a tiny digital spark plug inside that detonated on impact. It was brilliant. Because it was a silent weapon, if you could get close enough to a Borg, in its peripheral vision, you could fire it at its head. Once it stuck, within seconds, it exploded and did enough damage to totally demobilise any of those RF models.

"As usual, the attack was at night. I was with Cutter and Turk outside the bunker. Cutter would take a detachment of fifty men armed with sticky bombs to the right, I'd take fifty to the left, and Turk would hold down the middle. But we hadn't counted on what was to happen. Instead of half a dozen APC's storming in and deploying twenty or thirty Borgs, which was the norm, the attack came from the air.

"The night sky was full of what looked like giant hovering bats. It was the first time we'd seen personnel-carrying drones. Ten of them landed, eight of them carrying four Borgs each and two with supplies. It totally threw our defence plan into disarray. In one foul swoop, they had us surrounded.

"Then out of the misty forest came gigantic mechanical men, the moonlight glinting off their armour. Armed with flamethrowers and fifty-calibre machine guns, they formed into three groups and closed in on us, cutting our blokes down before they could let fire with their sticky bombs. It was the flamethrowers causing us the most grief— four of them hosing down our blokes with a stream of molten fire. They set the forest ablaze so we couldn't see them through the smoke. The smoke didn't bother their zoom optical night vision, they could see right through it like it wasn't even there. It was an inferno. Cutter's team was decimated and retreated. My team was in a shambles, you remember Thrash, you were in it... we were trapped, totally surrounded by Borgs with two flamethrowers to try and avoid."

Thrash was shaking his head, the nightmare still fresh in his mind.

Animal continued. "There were blokes running through the trees on fire. The acrid stench of burning flesh filled the air. It got down to about ten of us left. We knew our number was up, there was bugger-all we could do... they were closing ranks on us. Then, out of the blue smoke came Turk. I'll never forget it... running like a man possessed... ducking and weaving in and out from behind trees and then dropping down to one knee to fire off a sticky bomb. One after another, he knocked over them Borgs. We just stared at him in disbelief waiting for him to get cut down any minute by enemy fire...

but nar, not Turk, nothing was gonna stop the bloke.

"Our biggest threat was the two flamethrowers. Out in front of the others, they were doing a real job on us. About twenty metres away from them, Turk knelt down, took aim, and fired at the first flamethrower. It was an inspired shot... hit it on the side of the head, it stuck, and then blew half its head off. The support Borgs opened fire on Turk with a hail of bullets, and you know what? Not one bullet hit the bloke. He just stood his ground, loaded up another sticky bomb, took aim, and fired at the other flamethrower. That Borg was closer to him, and it stuck fast on its throat. Then, whack!... It exploded and blew its head clean off its body. Well, didn't that get us going? What was left of Cutter's team had been watching from cover... we all bit the bullet, if it was good enough for Turk, it was sure good enough for us, and we let fire at the Borgs with a hail of sticky bombs. The other flamethrower Borg got taken out, and they were going down like flies sprayed with insect repellent.

"After an hour of fighting, the surviving Borgs retreated to their drones and took off, leaving a cargo drone behind: the one that's still here. But hey, if it hadn't been for the valour of Turk, we would've lost that fight. So, it's only right for that drone to be used now to save the bloke!"

"Hear! Hear!" They shouted undivided, stirred by Animal's impassioned narrative.

At the crack of dawn, the next morning, with the drone securely strapped onto the front section of the APC, Alice and Animal said their goodbyes. Shaking Al's hand, Thrash said, "I wish we could go with you, we owe Turk that much."

"Don't worry mate, you lost six last night... and besides, the drone can only carry a couple. You blokes have your work cut out to look after your own."

They climbed on board the APC and motored off, headed for Avalon.

By the time they reached Mogo, the sun was shining on what looked like a war zone. Cyborgs were spread around the compound on the ground in various death poses. Feral animals had pretty much devoured all the human components of them, leaving empty shells of worthless carbon fibre and metal. As they drove toward the northern gates, the APC frightened off feral dogs feasting on what remained of the six Rebels killed in the battle the night before.

Once through the gates, Animal put his foot down to speed back to Avalon as quickly as possible to avoid being spotted by drones. Sixty minutes later, the APC descended into the Avalon bunker garage, where they were greeted by Morri, Vee, Hope, and Secta.

"So, this is the drone, looks in good condition," Secta said, patting its outer skin like it was a new puppy.

"Did it all go to plan?" Vee asked Al.

"The Star Lord put in an appearance, but, yeah, we got the job done," Al said.

"Looks like you tied one on?" Hope observed.

"Yeah well, celebrations were in order," Animals admitted with a smirk.

"And don't those Rebels sure know how to celebrate," Al scoffed.

"What happened to your arm, Animal?" Morri asked.

"Argh! took a whack from a Borg, it's broken, but Thrash's mob set it for me."

"Okay, then we better get started. I'll grab some guys to unload this thing," Hope said.

Secta took Alice by the arm, "Let's go get a coffee, I've got something to tell you."

CHAPTER 17
ACTIVATION

WALKING ALONG THE corridor to the canteen, Secta noticed Alice's clothes were ripped to shreds; even his canvas military boots were split open.

Al saw him looking. "Yeah well, now I know why most comic book superheroes wear Lycra," he said with a chuckle.

"Maybe we should fit you out with a stretchy Superman suit when we get back. What colour... pink, maybe?" Secta joked.

"Get outa here!" Al cackled, playfully elbowing Secta in the ribs.

Vee and Morri were walking close behind them. They had left Animal and Hope back at the garage to organize the unloading of the drone.

Vee wolf-whistled at Alice. "You should wear underpants, Al. We've got a great view of the dark side of the moon from back here," Vee joked. Morri laughed.

Alice turned and growled jokingly, "Better get me some new clobber, Morri, plus some undies. Can't be presenting my weapons free to air."

The girls sniggered at his naughty remark.

When they reached the canteen, Vee and Morri went to collect the orders while Secta sat Alice down to fill him in on the communiqué from OTT.

Upon hearing it, Alice flopped back in his chair, totally bemused. "This is off the planet. One minute we're here to kill Gorrick, and the next we're supposed to make him our partner. Mate, we lost six good men last night, now you're telling me that was all for nothing?" He rested his elbows on the table and buried his face in his hands.

"I know, Alice. I'm struggling with it as well," Secta admitted, dispiritedly.

Vee and Morri arrived and placed coffees on the table.

"What's with all the doom and gloom boys?" Morri asked, thinking Secta might have told Al about her having Red Wheel.

"It's because the six Rebels cut to bits by Borg bullets last night died in vain," Al lamented, angrily.

Vee put a comforting hand on Alice's broad shoulder. "Listen, love, we need to use this to our advantage... two things... we now have a clear path into Zen HQ, and more importantly, we have a bargaining tool."

Al slowly lowered his hands, his interest piqued. "Go on."

"If Voltaris wants a lift back to the 21st Century, then we want Turk released," Vee said, pleased with herself.

A smile cracked on Alice's tired face, and he thundered, "Hey, that's my girl!"

Morri didn't react as Al would have expected, and he wondered why. "You okay, Moz? You look worried. What's up?"

They all exchanged looks of concern, and that fired Al up even more. He glared at Morri and demanded, "Come on, spit it out."

A tear trickled down her cheek, and that rocked Alice. Morri pulled back the bandage on her wrist and showed him what was beneath it. There was nothing to say. Al was completely lost for words. He took her hand, and with tears welling up in his eyes, he mumbled warmly, sorrowfully, "Ah... no darling... no, not you."

Ursula had been awakened by an early morning call on her OSCI from Gorrick. He ordered her to proceed to phase two of their project. She understood exactly what that meant.

Voltaris was already up, doing his daily workout on the living room floor when Ursula wandered in, clad in a white towelling robe. Voltaris kept on with his push-ups—he was up to a hundred and forty.

Ursula rested on the arm of the royal blue sofa, "Sorry to interrupt you, but Gorrick has given permission to test the organic processor with Cronus this morning. I thought you might like to come?"

He ceased his push-ups at one hundred and fifty.

An hour later, Ursula and Voltaris rode the elevator down to her laboratory. As they entered, she told him, "I have a special treat for you."

After making some adjustments to the temperature controls of the cold room that housed Cronus, she left Voltaris in the main lab while she entered a small hermetically sealed room where the organic processors were grown. To avoid contamination, Ursula changed into plastic coveralls, headgear, booties, a mask, and gloves. Then, she passed through a decontamination room where lasers combed her from head to toe.

She returned fifteen minutes later, out of her protective clothing, carrying a cryogenic tissue storage container the size of a matchbox. Voltaris was keen to see it, and she showed him. The container had a tiny window on top.

"It doesn't look like much... is it alive?" Voltaris asked.

"Yes, my little baby here is very much alive. I have a whole family of them in that room."

"Unbelievable," Voltaris said, impressed.

She checked the cold room temperature. "Perfect," she said.

"Does it still have to be below zero?"

"No, I'm bringing it back to room temperature. Once I install the processor into Cronus's body, the temperature will be controlled internally, just like yours or mine. Let's do it."

"Why isn't Gorrick here on such an auspicious occasion?" Voltaris queried.

"He is only ever interested in results," she said, opening the door to the decontamination room adjoining the cold room. "We need to bio-suit up for decontamination."

The protective bio-suit get-up was the same as in the other room. "Once the chip is installed, we won't need this protection anymore," she explained, her voice slightly muffled by the facemask.

As they entered the room, sensors turned on the lights, providing a dim green glow. Ursula pressed a button on the large pod standing in the centre of the room, still with a little nitrogen gas spilling from outlets down its sides and forming into skeins of dry ice smoke that blanketed the floor. The smoke spiralled up in vortices with their every movement, adding more to the mystery of the already otherworldly environment.

The pod opened to reveal, through the dissipating smoke, the faceless form of Cronus in all its naked majesty. Ursula placed a step in front of Cronus to stand on, enabling her to reach its face. She pressed the right eye socket with her thumb, and it clicked.

Voltaris moved closer to watch.

Ursula pulled open the face of Cronus, removed the chip from the container, and inserted it into a small slot in its gravitonic brain. The faceplate then automatically closed, and she stepped back down.

"There, now watch," she said, excitedly.

There was an ever so slight twitch on Cronus's left cheek.

"Is it working?" Voltaris asked.

"Perfectly. Now for your treat." She went over to a small bench, pressed a button, and following a hissing sound, a drawer opened. She removed an apparatus and brought it over to Voltaris.

"Let me fit you with this... lower your head, please."

He complied, and she pressed an anode onto each of his temples plus a third in the middle of his forehead.

"These transmit brain functions."

"Okay," Voltaris said, figuring it was nothing unusual. He had worn similar devices before.

"Now come over here," she led him to Cronus. "Step up to a

height where you can look Cronus in the eyes."

He followed her instructions.

"Now bring your face within five centimetres of his."

Voltaris moved in, almost close enough to kiss Cronus.

"Right, now stare at his eye sockets."

Voltaris followed the brief. "Is that okay?" he asked, tentatively.

"Perfect. Now just wait."

They paused. All that could be heard was Voltaris' breathing. Then, without warning, Cronus's eyelids flicked open. Voltaris flinched.

"Whoa! This is weird... eye-to-eye contact with an android."

"An android is a robot that resembles a human being, while a cyborg is an organism that is part organic and part machine. Cronus is neither. Now, step down."

Voltaris complied and stood back next to Ursula.

"Now, watch this," she said.

To his astonishment, Voltaris watched Cronus's face transform. It literally reconstructed into a proper human face: the nose first, then the brow, the lips, mouth, even the hair. It was then that Voltaris realised he was looking at himself. Cronus had his face.

"What the—?" he gasped.

"It's holographic. He can be anyone we need him to be with perfection. See how he has your eye colour, your skin tone, even the stubble and bushy eyebrows. Now, stand in front of him."

Still in shock, Voltaris moved back in front of his likeness.

"Good, now repeat after me nice and loud, 'The quick brown fox jumped over the lazy dog.'"

Voltaris sighed; by now, he had worked out what was coming next. He said, loud and clear, "The quick brown fox jumped over the lazy dog."

"Good, now say this, 'I am Voltaris Idram... I am forty-one years old, and I was born in Idaho, in the United States of America.'"

Again, he repeated the phrase as instructed.

"Good, now you can come back here."

Voltaris returned to her side.

"Ask him who he is."

"Okay... Who are you?"

Cronus moved his head, not jerkily like you would expect from an artificial animatronic machine, but smoothly, exactly like a human. His eyes fixed on Voltaris, and with intelligence and expression, he said, "Voltaris Idram... and you are?"

All Voltaris could say was, "Amazing."

"This is the evolution of the human species, Voltaris... this is the new world," Ursula said dramatically.

"TWO has signed the TPD accord," Luna announced blithely upon entering the Professor's office.

He looked over his glasses at her from his computer. "Now all you have to do is police it... which, might I say, is easier said than done."

She sat in the lounge setting, pleased with herself. "No, this will mean a UNTT presence at whatever time travel facility they set up, whether or not it's a black op."

"Does that mean you will have an observer present to greet Voltaris through Kairos?"

"Yes, me," she confirmed with a gentle smile.

Vic peeled off his glasses, popped them into the top pocket of his white lab coat, and then joined her. He sighed as he sank into the comfortable chair. "Ah, it's been a helluva long morning." He pinched the bridge of his nose between his fingers and pressed his eyelids shut tight.

"What have you been working on that's worn you out so?" she enquired caringly.

"Oh, still studying the code En-Ki left us. But there's not much I can do until Secta and Alice return."

"Did you hear the news this morning?" she asked.

"No, I've been too tied up with all this. What's the latest?"

"A Watcher has appeared over the White House, it sent the US Government into meltdown."

He laughed, "I could imagine. Next, they'll try to blow it out of the sky."

"What do you think they're doing here?" she queried.

"Secta and I have a bit of a theory that they're time lords."

"Time lords, like from the British TV show, what is it? Doctor Who?"

"Oh, I don't know about any Doctor Who show, but we think they're here to monitor the timeline. Maybe even change it. You see, we think time is... wait, let me give you an example. If we sent Alice back to Germany to assassinate Adolf Hitler in 1935, upon his death, a new timeline would open, which would continue to now with a completely different historical outcome... however, our current timeline with Hitler defeated would still continue, only there would now exist two distinctly different timelines."

"Like parallel worlds?" Luna questioned.

"Perhaps. Now, as far as we know, no Earthly person has travelled back in time to affect such a change to our timeline."

"With the exception of Alice when he visited the 6th century BC and moved the Ark of the Covenant," Luna corrected.

"Yes, well, um, you could say that," he stammered a little, with her catching him off guard.

"If you're correct, then a new timeline began the moment Alice moved the Ark and changed history. But how come in our current timeline the Ark has been moved, shouldn't it be lost to time? The same could be said of when he moved the An-Zu craft... it's still here, isn't it? In Tahiti?"

The idea had the Professor musing. "Hmm, ostensibly you're right, Luna. Well, at any rate, our theory is that the Watchers are here to either prevent timeline changes... affect them, or police them. Remember, this is only speculation."

"I suppose you could say they changed the timeline themselves by preventing that missile attack on Iran."

"Yes, exactly."

"Well, if that is the case, why would they be hovering over the White House?" she challenged.

"It will revert to Cronus after fifteen minutes. Don't worry, Voltaris, you haven't been cloned... I wouldn't do that to you," Ursula said with a devilish chuckle. They entered the elevator to ride up to Gorrick's office.

On entering, they found him with his back to them, looking out of the big ceiling-to-floor windows. He turned to face them. "All done?"

"Yes, sir, with complete success," Ursula reported.

"We now need to decide whether to make contact with Black Alice or to wait for him," Gorrick said.

"After the carnage he's been causing, it might be safer to contact him," Voltaris suggested.

Gorrick motioned to them, "Please sit and let me think."

"We could activate Morrigan Hud's OSCI to deliver a message. Black Alice would be with her at the Avalon bunker," Ursula suggested.

Voltaris frowned. "If you know where these people are, why haven't you simply sent in your cyborg army to wipe them out?"

Gorrick chuckled. "For two reasons: firstly, they are in an almost impregnable bunker, and secondly, why waste my soldiers when Red Wheel is doing the killing for us."

"But you take them on while they're scavenging for supplies, why?" Voltaris argued.

"That is quite different. We rarely lose a soldier, and we maintain the siege mentality."

Voltaris was satisfied. "What do you have in mind? Should we invite him here to a meeting?"

"That could be one idea, but I think we should just sit and wait. I think he'll come to us. There won't be any carnage. He's here to kill me, but now that might have changed."

Animal and Hope joined the others in the canteen. "How goes the drone?" Morri asked Hope.

"Ready and waiting for you and Secta to work your magic."

"As far as I can tell, it's lacking a power source," Animal added.

"Hmm, that's a bit of a worry," Morri admitted.

Al spoke up, "Sit down, guys, I've got something to tell you. A return vortex will open wherever I am seventy-two hours from our original departure time. That means we've got... how long, Vee?"

"Twelve hours," she told them.

"Another one will open seventy-two hours after that, but we need to return through the first one... the radiation outside of here is too dangerous for any of us to be exposed to for much longer," Secta explained.

"Such a short visit," Morri lamented sadly.

"So, here's the plan. The drone is a cargo model that only takes two passengers. If you're right, Animal, you and I will go," Al said.

Animal confirmed, "Yep, I'm up for it."

"Yeah? Like over my dead body," Vee complained.

"Sorry, Vee, but you'll have to sit this one out," Al pressed with a steely glare.

Vee knew not to oppose him when he was in such a mood, and so complied.

"You'll need the floor plan of the Zen building?" Morri submitted.

"Not necessary, I know the layout," Animal said.

"Secta, I'll need you, Morri, and Hope to get the drone happening ASAP. Vee, lend a hand, will you?" Al ordered.

"Yep," Vee agreed a little reservedly.

Al stood, "Okay, let's rock 'n roll."

CHAPTER 18
TRASHED

T HE US MILITARY had deployed over a dozen flybys of the Watcher UFO poised six thousand metres above the Whitehouse, to no avail—the UFO just stayed there—motionless. They tried every known frequency to contact the occupants, and the CIA even tried a psychic to make a connection, but nothing worked. The situation was becoming tense; the government was ill at ease.

US President Robinson had mentioned the Watchers to Mal Low on their last conference call and wanted to know if he had discussed the matter with Professor de Luz. She called to find out. Mal invited the Professor and Dr Cairn into the conference call with President Robinson and Colonel Freeman.

"Dr Secta and I are of the opinion the Watchers are not hostile. This they demonstrated very clearly in the Strait of Hormuz," the Professor said.

"What makes you believe the UFO we have here is the same?" Freeman asked.

"Can't answer that, Larry. Neither craft seems to have any livery or specific features to suggest otherwise... plus their action of observing, while that's unnerving, is the same," Vic responded.

"Professor, wouldn't you think if they were benevolent, they would make contact?" Oprah asked.

"It's fair to say that it's probably their silence that makes them even more ominous. Look, Black Alice is scheduled back from his mission in twelve hours, he said before he left that he would like to be beamed on board a Watcher UFO to meet the occupants... if there are any."

"What makes you say that, Vic?" Larry asked.

"Well, they could very well be remotely controlled observation craft. You know, like what we do sending probes to other planets. Our theory is they are here to observe and maintain our timeline, which would suggest they're probably AI."

"Ma'am, Dr Luna Cairn of UNTT, I think that somehow being over the Whitehouse has something to do with the accord you are due to sign... the Temporal Prime Directive."

"Oh really?" Oprah said. "Do you think that would mean so much to them?"

"Yes. Once it has been signed by all the powers, we will embark on time travel missions that could very well threaten them as a species or their work, if as the professor hypothesised, they're here to monitor or manipulate our timeline."

"Manipulate?" Oprah questioned.

"Well, there is a chance, Madam President, the Watchers can change history. We are studying that possibility," Vic explained.

"You mean to say they might have the capacity to alter history for their benefit?" Oprah asked.

"Or for ours... we just don't know, but what we do know from Alice's missions back in time is they were there in the same manner in the sky over Jerusalem in the 6th Century BC, so it stands to reason they've been doing this for a long time," the Professor rationalised. "If you're asking my advice, it would be to leave them alone for now and wait for Alice to board the craft once he returns."

"That's a big call, Professor... this situation has put our military on a knife's edge, they're calling for me to agree to DEFCON two," Oprah said gravely.

"I recommend that DEFCON four might be sufficient, Ma'am," the Professor suggested.

"Once the accord has been approved, I will sign it, Dr Cairn. I understand TWO and Zen have signed, as have OTT and Oceana," Oprah said.

"All global powers have signed, Ma'am. We're just waiting on the United States," Luna said, contrarily.

"Yes, we are dragging the chain. I'll get onto it. Thank you, everyone. Appreciate the heads-up, Mal. Goodbye for now," Oprah closed.

"Okay, guys, there we have it. Are we to expect Alice, Vee, and Secta back with Voltaris Idram tomorrow this time as scheduled? If so, then we better have Karzoff on standby. Luna, will you make arrangements with Zen for the handover of Idram?" Mal directed.

"Yes, Mr President, I'll speak with them today," she confirmed.

The big moment had arrived; they were gathered to watch Morri test-drive the drone. Sitting in the pilot's seat, she pressed the activation switch for the on-board computer. It booted up. Secta was standing beside the craft. Al joined him.

"You don't suppose it'll ring home as soon as she boots it up, do you?" Al asked.

"We thought of that and disconnected the GPS," Secta replied.

The drone shook, causing Secta and Alice to take a quick step back.

"Here we go," Morri called out and pushed the toggle down. The craft silently lifted a few metres and then hovered.

They all applauded as it descended back onto the elevator plate. Morri climbed out.

"Top job, kiddo," Al told Morri.

"Took a team of us, but yes, nice to get it going even if it cost me the pellet drive of the old Wilson J-Car."

"Yes, sadly we had to cannibalise the old girl," Secta said, looking over at it covered by the tarp.

"We'll get it back for you to replace, Morri."

"Thanks, Al."

"Don't worry too much, Al. It's only an old car," Hope said.

"Nah, that's where you're wrong, Hope. Just because something or someone's old, it doesn't mean they have no value... isn't that right, Morri?" Al said. He'd noticed the friction between Hope and Morri and was secretly hoping it would cease once he'd rescued Turk.

"How's the arm, Animal? Are you going to be right for this?" Al asked.

"Hundred percent," Animal confirmed.

"Okay, let's get set. We'll leave in fifteen minutes."

Animal led Alice and Vee to the armoury. They'd been there before, but this time they'd only need sidearms. Vee had tagged along out of interest.

The six by six-metre room was packed to the brim with an assortment of guns and ammo boxes. One complete sidewall displayed an array of pistols and knives, all perfectly hung with the brand and corresponding ammo number labelled underneath.

"Pick what you need. The number is for the corresponding ammo box over there," Animal explained.

"All very organised," Vee said.

"Yeah, well, some of us have too much time on our hands," he mused.

Al selected a Glock G-20, 10 mm, fifteen capacity mag.

"Good choice," Animal said. "A generation 8, the last model manufactured before the war. Graphene construction, super lightweight, only 30 ounces fully loaded, packs a wallop. The ammo is in box 0800. I'd take a blade as well if I were you. Oh, and we'll need goggles... the drone has no canopy. We'll need watches as well; they're in the drawer."

Fifteen minutes later, Alice and Animal were seated in the drone with their goggles on, ready for the elevator to hoist them up to ground level. Animal gave Morri a thumbs-up, and she hit the button.

Morri had fitted the drone with a long-range digital two-way radio so they could communicate. Both Animal and Morri were wearing communication headsets.

The elevator raised them up to the surface and then stopped. The sky was dark and thundery.

Animal spoke into the microphone, "Morri, there's a big storm coming in. Should we abort? Over."

"What direction is it coming from?" Morri questioned.

"South."

"As long as it's not too close, you'll be fine flying due west to Angel City, so you'll miss it."

The wind was gusty, and the craft shook each time it took a blast.

"You alright?" Animal asked Al.

"Let's do it," Al said calmly but through gritted teeth. It was a dead giveaway that deep down inside, he wasn't confident with Animal's skills as a pilot, especially with the dark and foreboding sky.

Animal pushed the stick down, and the drone lifted. It rocked a bit, but once he got it to a hundred metres and pushed it forward, they shot off steadily at 80 km/h. The wind was strong, and there was no canopy, but it wasn't unpleasant. Al breathed a sigh of relief now that they were flying.

The storm was providing a tailwind, pushing them along quicker than they had planned. After thirty minutes, the high boundary walls of Angel City were in sight.

"The Zen building is the tallest one," Animal told Al. Then, speaking to Morri, he said, "We're on late final to the Zen helipad. We'll go dark now. Out."

They were at the right height to land. The thirty-storey building was approximately a hundred metres high. Animal took them up a bit further and then eased the power back. Once over the bull's eye target on the rooftop, he lowered the drone to a perfect three-point landing.

"Top flying, buddy," Al congratulated him.

Voltaris Idram stepped out from a doorway and approached the craft.

Alice and Animal disembarked.

"I'm Voltaris Idram. We picked up the drone on radar and figured it had to be you."

That was a bit of a shock. They had assumed Zen wouldn't have radar.

"Black Alice and Animal," Al said gruffly.

They eyed each other off contemptuously, and then Idram said, "You're both carrying weapons. Other than the knives you have concealed, your guns won't fire near Gorrick. A signal similar to WiFi blankets him. It shuts off the electro-arming mechanism in your handguns. Follow me."

Alice raised his eyebrows, thinking that was a clever invention.

Voltaris led them inside the building, past the elevators, along a corridor, and then through a door to the boardroom.

From what he'd seen, not a lot had changed for Alice since he had last been there while inside Turk's mind.

"Sit down. Want something to drink?" Voltaris asked, congenially. They both shook their heads.

After a couple of minutes, the door opened, and Gorrick entered followed by Ursula.

"Ah, Animal, we meet again. It has been a while," Gorrick said, straight-laced.

Animal acknowledged him with a nod.

"And this must be the legendary Black Alice. If the rumours are correct, you were in possession of Turk last time we met, so you must remember Dr Mennis?"

"Not likely to forget either of you. You, Gorrick, for breaking your word not to pursue us, and you, Mennis, for deserting my friend here after Gorrick fired a missile to try and take out the bunker."

"And we remember you for infecting our mainframe, creating havoc, and setting our endeavours back years," Ursula said curtly.

"I can't take all the credit for that; it was Dr Secta's genius," Al admitted facetiously.

"Good, now that we've got the happy reunion out of the way,

there are more important issues to discuss," Voltaris said.

Gorrick sat at the head of the large oblong table with Ursula at his side.

"He is not the same Gorrick you have back in your time in Sydney, Alice, and he is definitely not the host of En-Lil," En-Ki told Alice in his mind. It was good to know that meant it was no longer his top priority to kill him.

"I permitted you to enter Zen HQ because OTT has agreed to return Idram through Kairos. We want now to discuss the particulars," Gorrick said matter-of-factly.

"Okay, the vortex back will open next to me in approximately eleven hours. Dr Secta is here, so I will need to rendezvous with him at the bunker. In the meantime, as quid pro quo, I want Turk released."

"I don't believe that will be possible. He is in the death camp," Gorrick said.

"Why?" Animal snapped.

"Because that's where criminals are kept," Gorrick countered.

"Isn't it a place for sufferers of Red Wheel?" Animal contested.

"That too," Gorrick replied coldly.

Animal held his tongue, knowing it was the place Gorrick mercilessly dumped all of his prisoners.

"Then can you have him brought to us?" Al asked.

"We have no contact with inmates of the death camps," Ursula said.

Alice folded his arms in front defiantly, "Then we have no deal."

"I'll go with them to get Turk," Voltaris stated resolutely.

The statement elevated Alice's opinion of Idram.

"You might not return from there, you know? The only reason we stay away is it is even too dangerous for cyborgs," Gorrick said, with an arrogant smirk.

"That's because they've got no guts, Gorrick," Al snapped.

Gorrick got up. "Have it your way. Ursula, make the arrangements."

Ursula nodded and then left the room.

Gorrick stopped at the door and turned back, "Don't forget to come say goodbye if you make it back from Dante's Inferno, Voltaris."

After Gorrick left the room, Al asked Voltaris, "What did he mean by that? You sure you're okay with going it alone?"

"Old school, guess I don't want to owe you one. I'm fine," he answered with a chuckle.

Ursula returned a couple of minutes later with a flash drive and plugged it into a slot in the board table. A holographic schematic of Zen HQ materialised over a small metal disc countersunk into the centre of the table. She took a small remote and while remaining standing aimed it at the hologram.

"You take the elevator to the ground floor, then go through to the now disused elevators, see here... that accesses the FRT station. You will need this." She handed Voltaris a key-card. "You know about the subway levels, Alice; you have been there before, but they have changed. There is still a labyrinth down there, but it is sealed so that the only way in and out is by the elevator. The key-card only functions with your live ID, so if Voltaris is dead, then you won't be able to escape. Is that clear?"

While the briefing was taking place in the boardroom, Vee, who had stowed away in the cargo hold of the drone, climbed out and made for the entrance. She wasn't about to leave her brother without backup.

She came to the elevator. It would be too dangerous to take and so looked further for a way down and found a fire door. Behind it was a stairwell she took down, determined to reconnoitre as much of the building as possible without being caught.

Ursula walked Alice, Animal, and Voltaris to the elevator. The door opened, and they entered. She stayed behind.

On the ride down, Alice told them, "She reminds me of Honor."

Voltaris responded with an insightful chuckle, "Yes, more alike than you could imagine."

The door opened on the ground floor, and they stepped out.

Alice recalled the last time he was in the large lobby with the twenty-metre ceiling-to-floor windows and the black marble floor. However, this time there were no people milling about; it was deserted.

As they walked towards the FRT elevator, Alice asked Voltaris, "While you've been here, have you seen any humans other than Ursula, not counting Gorrick? He isn't human."

"Yes, there's about a hundred in their cyborg control centre."

"Are they old?" Al asked.

"Yes, all over fifty, I'd say."

"Wonder if they'll catch Red Wheel?" Al questioned.

"Ursula told me about Red Wheel. She said she treats them, but it isn't a cure... it just delays the inevitable. A terrible thing."

They reached the single elevator to the FRT Station. Voltaris flashed his card at the reader, the door opened, and a light came on inside. They stepped in for the ride down, and the doors closed.

"Is he the same Gorrick from our time?" Voltaris asked Al.

"You should know better than me... but I don't think so."

"Interesting. That's what I think. If he had been the same Gorrick, then he would have not only expected me but would've known I'd have to go back with you."

"True," Al said, uninterestedly.

The doors opened, and what Alice saw was nothing recognisable—in the dim light, he could make out that the fast train platform had been trashed.

CHAPTER 19
EXTINCTION DISTINCTION

V EE TRIED THE doors on every landing she came to on the way down the fire-stairs, but they were all locked shut. She figured it was the security system. After thirty-two landings, worried that she might have to go all the way back to the top floor, a door finally opened. Then she panicked, figuring she might've triggered an alarm.

Putting her fears to one side, she stepped out into a dimly lit corridor. It had to be two floors underground, this she determined because the drone had landed on the thirtieth floor and she'd counted each landing on the way down the staircase.

With her gun held up in readiness, she edged along the corridor hugging the wall. About to round a corner, she was stopped abruptly by the sound of voices. She listened. There were two men arguing over who should take lunch to a prisoner. Taking a sly peek around the corner, she could see they were older men, probably in their late fifties, and that the argument was heating up.

"I did it yesterday?"

"You're getting senile Wally, I did it yesterday... you did it the day before."

"You're the one that's senile... this is the third day in a row I've done it and each day you come up with the same argument. You've got Alzheimer's Ben, next you'll start forgetting we had an argument and start all over again. I even know what you'll say next—"

"Yeah what?" Wally questioned.

"You'll say there should be a system and I'll tell you that there is… and that it's your turn."

Vee was finding the banter amusing. Soon they moved off, deciding to both do the job. Vee followed them.

Morri was passing by the armoury on her way to meet up with Secta and Hope in the lab when she noticed the door had been left open. As she closed it, she observed three pistols were missing from the gun wall. Assuming that Alice and Animal had taken them, she locked the door and then continued on.

Entering the lab, she found Secta and Hope having a philosophical discussion about the politics of the world Secta was from.

"Hey guys, mind if I join you?"

"Please, Morri. How are you feeling?" Secta asked.

She showed her wrist, the horrible Red Wheel looked angrier. "Other than the ugliness of it, I'm feeling okay, thanks."

"I'm glad… Hope was asking about my world trying to fill in the gaps from when her memory fails her."

"Which would have been, I expect, when she was murdered?" Morri suggested, the subject taking her mind off the Red Wheel.

"No, actually," Hope said. "It's everything in her memory up to the moment she injected me as an embryo with Pneumatide; the essence of her."

"I see. Does that mean you would be able to transfer everything that constitutes a person, memories, and personality, etcetera, into another person or body?" Morri questioned.

"We believe so. It does raise ethical questions, but Hope's discovery is revolutionary," Secta said.

"Absolutely, it would be a way of saving this world," Morri proposed. She could tell by the look on Secta's face that he hadn't thought of that.

"What do you mean, Morri, how?" Secta asked.

"Well, we know that in due course every living being will die from Red Wheel, but the disease itself will also die. Hope is living proof of that. In her twenty-five years, she hasn't contracted any symptoms of the disease. I've been testing bloods over those twenty-five years and I believe everyone living at the time of the nuclear attacks contracted it, and that it isn't contagious as some people previously thought... and... it's not ongoing."

"Wait a minute, that doesn't sound like normal radiation poisoning to me. I remember reading a paper on the impact of radiation fallout in Hiroshima, Nagasaki, and later Chernobyl and Fukushima. The ongoing effects at ground zero are between twenty and thirty years. I haven't heard of Red Wheel showing up at any of those locations," Secta said, getting up from his chair and pacing the room.

"That means we could take the Pneumatide from a still-healthy person to transfer into a healthy embryo," Hope said.

Secta stopped in his tracks and exclaimed, "It was deliberate!"

"What was deliberate?" Hope asked.

"Whoever manufactured the bombs deliberately added Red Wheel as an agent. Don't you see? The nuclear bombs didn't cause the culling of humanity, the resulting plague has: Red Wheel."

Morri flopped back in her seat and gasped, "Of course... of course... it was Zen. You could put your money on it. Turk always said they were the weapons suppliers. He told me he'd seen the Zen logo on the ordinance of both sides during the war."

"Holy hell!" Secta sounded off. "This changes everything."

Morri pondered for a moment. "Oh, by the way, have you seen Vee?"

"Funny you should mention it, I checked her room just after Alice and Animal left, wondering why she wasn't at the take-off, and she wasn't there. Then I checked the canteen, not there either," Hope said.

Morri stood up, her hand covering her mouth, experiencing an epiphany. "Oh goddam, the third gun?"

Secta stopped pacing and asked, "What third gun?"

"There's not much left of the station," Al informed the other two.

"Used to catch the fast rail to Sydney from here when I was a teenager. It shut down during the war... now look at it," Animal lamented.

"There must be people down here somewhere. Which way?" Voltaris queried.

They were standing in the middle of the platform, where at each end the line vanished into a dark tunnel.

"Well, it's a toss of a coin, but left feels right?" Al said.

"That's an oxymoron," Voltaris said, with a chuckle.

They climbed down onto the tracks and headed for the dark tunnel.

"Bloody hell, I hate tunnels. I can't begin to tell you how many damn tunnels I've been in over the years. Always with lurking monsters and things..." Al complained.

The rusted train tracks vanished ahead of them into the depths of the tunnel. The only sound came from the crunching of gravel under their footfall.

After stumbling fifty metres or so, with the tunnel growing darker and darker with each step, Al spotted a problem ahead and stopped them.

"There's a big cave-in ahead," Al said.

"How do you know?" Animal asked.

"I'm fitted with night vision lenses."

"Way cool," Animal reckoned.

"There's a small recess over there; maybe it leads somewhere," Voltaris said, pointing ahead to his left.

They went for it. He was right; inside, a small passageway ended with a staircase up.

"No cobwebs, and plenty of footprints. Good call Volt," Al said, at the base of the stairs. "It's a fire escape."

They ascended the narrow single flight of stairs, which exited into the remains of an underground shopping mall.

Looking around at the rundown, cobweb-covered entrances to shops, Al said, "Hmm, didn't expect this." As he was about to step off to explore more, Animal grunted.

In the aisle ahead, barring them from any further progress, stood four heavy-duty individuals armed with an assortment of pickaxes and clubs... reeking hostility.

Alice and Voltaris reached for their guns, but Animal said, "No." He stepped forward of the other two and shouted, "Crankcase! It's me... Animal."

The largest of them, a brute of a man, glared at Animal long and hard, and then he let out a roar, "Animal, you old bastard!"

The two men rushed each other and fell into a clinch. Slapping his friend's back, Animal turned to Alice and said, "Crankcase, this is Black Alice."

The look on Crankcase's heavily bearded face was priceless.

"Nar! You're kiddin' me... the fair dinkum Black Alice? Mate, let me shake your hand," Crankcase bellowed.

Later on, back in Crankcase's den, which was decked out similarly to the Rebels' man-cave, the three visitors were being treated to a JD.

"Cheers fellers. This stuff's like gold down 'ere. Luckily, there was a fully laden warehouse with a sizable stock of booze we found a year or so ago, kept us sane."

"How long you been cooped-up down here, mate?" Al asked.

"Crank's a Rat Fink, got captured before the Comanche battle," Animal said.

"Yeah, so just over two years," Crank answered.

"How many down here?" Voltaris asked.

"Well now that's a different story... we guess around three thousand, but folks kick the bucket every day from Red Wheel, so it's hard to tell. What we do know is there are twenty-five Finks left out of six hundred. About the same for the Bandits, then a few from other chapters... the rest are non-members the Bots rounded up and chucked down here to die... then there's the Skulls. Don't know how many of them there are."

"The Skulls, who the hell are they?" Animal questioned.

"Know nuffin' about them really, mate. They raid everyone else, murdering bastards. But the weird thing is they never take nuffin', they just kill people that venture their way, territorial. That's why we fronted you like we did... thought you's were them," Crankcase explained.

"What about Turk?" Al enquired.

"No mate, there was a rumour going round he'd been captured a coupla years back, but he never turned up 'ere... not that I know of anyhow."

After a few drinks, Crankcase took the three of them on a tour of the horrors of the death camp.

A trek along a narrow, sparsely lit tunnel brought them to an excavation. Half a dozen men inside the cavity stopped digging when they arrived.

Crankcase explained, "There was only limited power down here before, but we managed to hack into a live power cable we unearthed here, so for now, provided they don't discover it, we've got a supply. This shaft is into the foundations of Zen HQ... it's a long way to the top, but we're trying to dig an escape tunnel. Trouble is, we'll probably all be dead before we get to break through to the surface. But it keeps us occupied and gives us hope."

Al nodded at the miners. They were covered in sweat and grime. "Tough gig," he told Animal and Voltaris.

Crankcase led them along another tunnel to a pair of double doors where he stopped. "It ain't pretty in here, but you need to see it. This is the hospice."

He opened the big red doors and led them through. They were immediately hit by the stench of death. Looking down from a mezzanine, there was a massive room with a high ceiling from which tennis lights were suspended, creating pools of light. On the ground level, bunks were spaced a metre apart, stretching as far as the eye could see, and in every bunk, a sick and dying person.

Al was holding back nausea and erupted, "Bloody hell, how many?"

"Thousands, all with Red Wheel, all dying a slow agonising death... and nuffin we can do other than feed the poor bastards. The morphine ran out years ago along with all medical supplies. No doctors, nurses, nuffin. The only hope is that in the next two to three years there'll be none of us left. Worse thing is every few weeks we find more poor suffering buggers on the platform that had been captured by bots and dumped there like rubbish."

"Goddam, this is difficult to take... how could anyone?" Voltaris moaned, the emotion and bile rising into his throat, stopping him from finishing the sentence.

"Yeah, amazin' what horrible things people can do to each uver," Crankcase said, dispiritedly.

"Too right," Animal agreed.

"Come on, that's enough of the dark side. You's hungry?" Crank said, leading them back out through the doors.

Al was glad to escape the stench of rotting flesh. The last thing he could think of after that was food. "Was that an old warehouse?"

"A train terminus, where they used to service 'em, bit like an underground aircraft hangar, eh?"

"We're down here to get Turk, mate. If he isn't with you, then the only other place he could be is with the Skulls. How do we get to them?" Al asked.

Crankcase shook his skinhead slowly. "Ah, that's a tough one, mate. We don't know where they come from, but yeah, there's a chance they grabbed him when he was dumped on the platform, it happens. We keep clear of 'em... it's been said they're cannibals."

"Cannibals!... why?" Animal queried.

"Blokes out exploring have come across human bones with cuts on 'em... pretty much a sign of butchery. Plus, we have a heap of dudes go missing all the time, but never the ones with Red Wheel... makes you think they only eat healthy folk, don't it?"

On their way back to the man-cave, Al asked, "You must have an idea where they are?"

They arrived at the man-cave and rested in comfy old moth-eaten lounge chairs.

"I can't get over the deplorable conditions and the state of those poor sick people," Voltaris groaned.

"Maybe now you're beginning to see what we're fighting against, mate. Gorrick and Zen created all this misery... not only here but imagine what it's like elsewhere?"

"I hear you, Alice," Voltaris admitted.

"Mate, even if you find Turk down here, you ain't gonna get him out... you're stuck with all of us. Zen blew all the tunnels and exits... there's only one way out... the elevator, but that doesn't open."

"It will for us... Volt here's our ticket out," Animal said.

Crank didn't like that at all, jumped to his feet, pointed an accusing finger at Volt, and shouted, "You saying he's one of them?"

Thinking Crank was about to lose it, Volt went for his pistol.

"Whoa, settle down, Crank," Al said civilly. "He is, and he isn't... right now, down here, he isn't, alright? You'll just have to take my word on that."

Crank accepted it, calmed down, and sank back into his chair. After a pregnant pause, he took a deep breath and said, "You know, I seem to remember one bloke got nabbed by the Skulls that got away... now what's his name? From the Rebels, you'd know him, Animal... um, Crow... that's it."

Animal knew him all right. "Bloody old Crow, I thought he'd be dead... must be sixty."

Crank got up. "I'll get someone to fetch him."

While he was outside sorting that out, Volt said, "Why do you think Zen is responsible for all this, Al?"

"Because they not only started the Cyberwars in 2080, but they supplied the weapons for both sides. Even back in our time, they're developing the RF cyborg series. It's an extinction scenario. Look, don't know if you're aware of it, but Gorrick is an alien; there are sixteen hundred of them worldwide, all clones. They're thousands of years old and here for only one purpose: to ultimately replace us with cyborgs totally under their control."

"Sounds like the plot of a Hollywood B-grade sci-fi flick," Volt said.

"It is, and we're starring in it," Al said emphatically.

CHAPTER 20
DANIEL 8:24

THE FOOD HAD been delivered. Vee watched the two guards walk past her, still arguing. She figured it was now safe to explore a little further. Slipping out from her hiding place, she made her way along the dimly lit corridor. After winding around it, she came to a row of cells, but they weren't just ordinary run-of-the-mill type prison cells... instead of metal bars, they had horizontal and vertical bands of red lasers to enclose the inmates. The corridor of cells was at least a hundred metres long with cubicles on either side; there were hundreds of them. She wanted to take a look but noticed CCTV cameras at intervals up high along the corridor's façade. She figured the cameras were aimed at the prison cells; if she hugged the wall, they wouldn't pick her up.

Moving like a giant spider, she edged along the wall looking for a prisoner to talk to, but all of the cells were unoccupied. Thinking it must be some kind of holding bay, she was about to turn back when she realised the guards had delivered food to someone; that meant there had to be a prisoner there somewhere.

She picked up the pace, worried that if she were caught there, it would be tough to get away. Then she noticed a bowl on the floor up ahead near the banding. It must be food the guards left for a prisoner, she figured.

When she reached it, she found it was half full with grey muck. Through the banding, she could see a man in ragged clothes curled up with his back to her on a bunk, asleep. He was longer than the bunk, so his feet and head were hanging over the ends with his long brown hair touching the floor.

She tried to attract his attention, "Pssst!... Hey you."

He moved and groaned.

"Pssst! I'm not one of them... Hey."

He rolled over, and his sleepy bloodshot eyes in a heavily bearded face peered at her.

"My name's Vee... is there some way I can bust you out?"

"Forget it," the big man groaned and then rolled back over.

"Come on mate, I'm risking my life down here trying to help you."

He turned towards her. "Look, there's no way through the lasers, alright. I appreciate the gesture but don't risk your life because of me."

"Surely there's a mains switch or something that turns 'em off?" Vee argued.

"Yeah, but it'd set off an alarm?" he rasped.

"So?"

"Well, they'll come running."

"Who? All I saw was a couple of old farts that I could beat with one arm tied behind my back."

He let out another groan and sat up, scratching his head. There was a toilet and sink inside his cell, whereas there wasn't in the others, so she figured he must be someone special.

"Down the far end, there's a fuse box... if you can get it open, you can cut the power, but it'll be pitch black. You got something you can use to open it?"

She pulled a knife she'd taken from the armoury and asked, "This do?"

"Probably," he grinned through the big full beard.

She put it back in her belt. Next, she pulled the Glock 26 that was fitted with a laser sight. She flicked it on. "This'll give us some light."

"Good thinking, use that... but listen, once you cut the power, it'll come back on in thirty seconds. That's how long I'll have to get out. The alarm will have been triggered, so we'll need to run back in the direction of the fuse box because the guards will be coming from the other way... there's a fire door at the end of the corridor. I can't run fast... crook knees."

"Okay, how do I get the fire door open?" she asked.

"Use the pistol; one shot at the security lock should do it."

"Got it. Anyone else here to bust out?"

"Nope, just me... okay Vee... Good luck."

Crankcase returned with a skinny, gnarly-looking bloke who did justice to his nickname of Crow. Animal stood to greet him. "Crow, how are you mate? It's been a long time."

"You're ain't kidding Animal, since I was left for dead."

"What do you mean mate? Sit down."

Crow sat and with rat cunning said resentfully, "We was on a raid two years ago that walked right into a Bot ambush. The others racked off and left me behind, been here ever since."

"That doesn't sound like Thrash," Animal said.

"Wasn't him, Boofhead was leading... big bastard, more interested in self-preservation than watching his mate's backs. Anyhow, that's ancient history... Crank sez you wanna ask me sumthin'."

"Sorry for what happened Crow, I'm Alice... we're down here to look for Turk, we heard you got jumped by the Skulls but got away... we're thinking they might have him. Can you tell us anything about them?"

Crow sat back in the chair and pointed a crooked arthritic index finger at the bottle of JD on the table. Crankcase nodded approval, and Al handed it to him.

He snatched it, flicked his long straggly unkempt grey hair back to clear his face, and then took an overly gracious swig. A wipe of his thin ratty moustache and goatee with the back of his grubby hand, and he was ready to talk.

"They come out of the pitch black like ghosts. Luminous glowing white skull masks that look like they were floating in mid-air, real creepy." He nodded for another swig... got approval and took it. Crankcase snatched the bottle off him before he could down the lot. Crow shot him a rotten-toothed snarl of dissatisfaction.

"Four of us was scouting the southern tunnel... we're in the northern tunnel now, you know... for ages, everyone believed that heaps more tucker and stuff is in the south tunnel coz two train lines overlap there... the old line and the FRT. The trick is to try and get to the old station... not many come back from trying."

"Yeah, get on with it Crow, they haven't got time for a travelogue," Crankcase growled.

Crow snarled. It was obvious he didn't get the chance to have a rave much.

"We figured it was the Skulls getting 'em but weren't sure. Anyhow, we got a long way up the tunnel... then out of the dark they came, a dozen or more flying Skulls. Well, the other three blokes hit the toe... my bad luck cut in, and I slipped on the train tracks... did me ankle... couldn't see a thing, the others had gone with the torch. Next minute, they was all over me."

"Did you see their faces... did they talk?" Animal asked.

"Yeah, while I was kiddin' to be knocked out, the main bloke said he's too old, leave him and then as quickly as they'd come, they went. Took me flipping ages to get back, aye."

"Do you think they have Turk?" Animal questioned.

Crow crunched up his beak-like nose, "Dunno, but if he's down here and ain't with us, then he must be with them. If ya wanna find out just go walkabout up the south tunnel, they'll sure as eggs find you in a New York second, mate."

"Then that's what we'll have to do," Al said, flopping back in his chair.

Crank nodded at one of his men standing by who gave Crow a

hand up to leave.

"Take it easy Crow," Animal said.

"I'm a bit flawed Animal... not much of a future left. But soon you'll find out that for yourself," he sniggered.

"Mate, I've got more flaws than the Empire State Building, but they ain't gonna stop me fighting to live," Animal countered.

Alice and Volt chuckled at Animal's witty analogy. Crow was led away.

"Old bugger picked up the wheel a couple of days ago, won't last long," Crank said, matter-of-factly.

"Hell," Volt gasped, exasperatingly. "It's like the black plague... worse."

Al rose out of his chair. "Okay, clock's a-tickin', time to check the south tunnel."

Crankcase led them back to the FRT platform and then stopped at the entrance to the south tunnel. "I'll leave you here," he said.

"You can come with us, you know," Animal told him.

"Then who'd run things down here? No mate, I'm in my mid-fifties, it's only a matter of time before I'm chained to the wheel. You probably won't have time to catch up again before you bail. Good luck finding Turk." He shook hands with the three of them and then wandered back along the platform. Al watched his lone figure meld into the darkness of the north tunnel and couldn't help but feel sorry for the man.

"Seems a good bloke," Al mumbled.

"Yeah, won a few battles in the arena back in the day, was pretty close to Duke... remember him and the arena Al?"

"How could I forget fighting him and Spike mate?... Wicked days them."

"Too true," Animal confirmed.

They headed off into the gloom of the south tunnel.

Dr Cairn turned the page of the book she was reading in the comfort of the living room of her five-star serviced apartment. She reclined on the three-seater lounge still in her knee length business skirt and white blouse, her hair up, reading glasses on and her bare feet up on the lounge.

Through the big glass patio doors only two city blocks away, Sydney Harbour was sparkling in the light of the full moon. But the view was unable to compete with what she was reading: it had her spellbound— o much so she failed to notice the front door open and the Professor wander in with a look on his face as though he'd lost something.

Hearing a noise Luna looked up sharply from her book. "Oh Vic, I didn't hear you come in. Are you alright?"

He flopped onto the lounge chair opposite her. "Oh, just another day of frustration trying to find the source of the mysterious element, Velodium... what are you reading, is that the Bible?" he said, surprised.

"More than that, it's the book of Daniel in the Old Testament."

"Why? I had no idea you were religious?"

"I'm not... but after rereading the report of Alice's trip back to the 6th Century BC, where he met Ezekiel, I felt compelled to research something further."

"And what pray-tell would that be?" Vic asked, intrigued.

"Ezekiel called Alice, Daniel... and there is serious conjecture by theologians as to whether the Book of Daniel in the Bible, by an unknown author, is the same Daniel as mentioned in the Book of Ezekiel. Both were in the 6th Century BC, so you'd expect they could be one in the same. The fascinating thing is this quatrain in the Book of Daniel." She flicked through to a page marked and then read the text, "In the latter part of their reign, when the rebellion has reached its full measure, an insolent king, skilled in intrigue, will come to the throne. His power will be great, but it not be his own. He will cause terrible destruction and succeed in whatever he does. He will destroy the ruling men along with the holy people. Through his craft and by his hand, he will cause deceit to prosper, and in his own mind, he will make himself great. In a time of peace, he will destroy many, and he will even stand against the Prince of princes. Yet he will be broken off, but not by human hands."

It had piqued the Professor's interest. "How do you interpret it?"

She looked over her reading glasses at him. "Well, I think Ezekiel's Daniel is prophesising Gorrick or En-Lil as the insolent king... you see, though some would interpret it as referring to some king of the time or a future ruler or dictator such as Hitler for instance... he makes a big point in stating in a time of peace he will destroy many, and he will even stand against the Prince of princes... Alice perhaps? Yet he will be broken off, but not by human hands. Not by human hands, is he talking about Gorrick being an alien or about the Zen RF cyborg program?"

"I see what you're saying. Did all this stuff about the Watchers trigger this?"

"I guess so... I have a gut feeling it's all connected... Zen, Gorrick, En-Lil, En-Ki, time travel Alice and the Watchers."

"And you think Ezekiel's prophecies are a link?" Vic asked.

"Only because Ezekiel called Alice, Daniel and Alice reported a Watcher over Jerusalem at the time. Coincidence? I don't believe so."

Vic got up and went into the kitchenette to get a drink. He called back to Luna, "Vino?"

"There's an open bottle of Pinot there. A glass of that would be nice, thanks."

"Coming right up... oh, did you get to speak with Zen?" Vic called out.

"Yes, Gorrick is in New York... must be cumbersome with two Gorricks in Sydney. Anyhow, they'll send a welcoming committee for Mr Idram once we give them an ETA."

"Have you mentioned that to Karzoff? I don't know that he'll knocked out by that... you know how precious he is about the security around Kairos? Imagine if Honor is a member of the party? I think he'd have kittens," he said, strolling back out from the kitchen with two glasses of wine.

Taking a glass from him, Luna admitted, "You know that is remiss of me, I didn't even consider that."

CHAPTER 21
SKULLS

AFTER TELLING THE prisoner to hug the wall to avoid the CCTV once he was out, Vee scurried on the tips of her toes, hugging the wall to the end of the long corridor. There, she found the fuse box on the wall, just as he'd described. It was at her shoulder height, and a metre directly above it was a miniature CCTV camera aimed at it. That presented a problem; the camera would see her open the fuse box. She checked the fire door opposite for the lock position and then, hoping she was small enough, with her back pressed hard against the wall, she slipped underneath the fuse box. Once shielded from the camera, she crawled her hand up and, using the knife, forced it open just enough to fit her hand inside. She felt around and found two switches, then thought, which one? No, it doesn't matter; they both must be digital circuit breakers—probably one for the lights and the other for the laser banding. I'll knock 'em both out.

With the pistol in the other hand and the laser scope turned on, she readied herself, knowing she'd only have thirty seconds under the cover of darkness to shoot the lock, open the door, and get inside before the lights came back on and the camera captured her.

She took a deep breath and flicked the switches. Everything went pitch black, then a red laser dot showed on the door lock and increased in size as she approached it. Bang! It worked; the shot destroyed the lock and the door opened. She slipped inside and closed the door behind her, just as the lights came back on. With her heart thumping in her chest and her back against the door, she could hear Turk coming. She pulled the door open just wide enough to slide her knife out along the floor to under the fuse box. Then, as she heard him getting closer with his back to the wall, she called out, "There's CCTV above the fuse box; use the knife."

He arrived, collected the knife, and then, being over six feet tall, reached up and used the hilt to bash the camera. Job done, he crossed the corridor and slipped in through the door.

"Well done," he told Vee, puffing. He closed the door and pushed a bar latch into place to lock it. He could tell Vee was anxious. "Don't worry, the guards Ben and Wally won't come after us. They'll be too busy arguing over who's going to tell the boss that the fuses blew and that I escaped."

"What about cyborgs?"

"This is the safest place. They can't handle staircases; they can't see their feet. It's a design flaw. Now, where are you from?" he asked.

"The Avalon Bunker, you know it?"

"Morri, Nerdo, Cutter, and Animal? Sure do."

"How did you get here?" he questioned.

"A drone."

Finding that hard to believe, he asked, "Ah-ha... a drone. You flew in a drone?"

She nodded sharply.

"Where is it?" he asked.

"The helipad on the roof."

He thought for a moment. "Alright, here's what we do."

For Animal and Voltaris, it was so dark they could hardly see a hand in front of their faces. But it wasn't the same for Alice.

They stumbled over rail tracks, rocks, and debris for a couple of hundred metres, expecting at any minute to come face to face with the Skulls. Then Alice sighted something and whispered, "There's someone up ahead."

All of a sudden, from out of alcoves on either side of them, came flying white skulls, screaming like banshees. They seemed to float in the darkness like bizarre phantoms that within seconds had them surrounded. The effect was unnerving. Animal lashed out, throwing punches and connecting.

Alice grabbed the closest one to him and yelled, "We come in peace!"

They were all over Voltaris and quickly had him on the ground. Alice could see the one holding Voltaris had a blade at his throat, and blood was trickling from under its razor edge.

Animal was struggling to pull his gun. "Animal, stop!" Alice growled. He knew if they continued to fight, it would be all over for Voltaris. Animal froze.

Alice pulled his pistol and fired a shot into the air. "Okay, okay, that's enough. I could start shooting, but let's just calm down and talk."

He heard someone move behind him... then everything went black.

When Al came to, he was on the floor of a small room with his hands tied. The only light was coming from a black candle burning on a small table. He sat up, his head aching from the knock that had obviously earned him the short nap. He checked the time on his wristwatch: it had been an hour since they left Crankcase... time was running out. As he expected, his weapons were missing. He bashed the door with clenched fists.

"Hey! Open up... Let's talk!"

A couple of minutes later, the door was pushed open by a big bruiser dressed in black studded leathers, wearing a skull mask. An evil-looking big mother standing well over six feet tall, he had Alice's pistol aimed at him.

"Come on!" he growled, flicking the pistol to signal out.

He led Alice down a dark passageway, then through a smaller

alley that ended at the door of a rundown old train carriage, its windows blacked out. He tapped the button beside the door for it to open.

The interior of the carriage had been converted into a boardroom, lit by oyster lights in the ceiling. It was decked out in red and black, like a meeting place for devil worshippers. The long black oblong table was surrounded by grey and red train seats, about twenty in all, in which were seated a dozen imposing individuals wearing skull masks and dressed in the same gear as the guy who had brought Al. All were men except for two women. To Al, it looked like a meeting of a pagan, satanic cult.

The guy who'd brought Al ordered, "Sit!"

Al complied.

Just behind them, Animal and Voltaris were led in with their arms tied in front of them. They were forced to sit beside Al. Voltaris had a small plaster covering the cut on his neck from the blade.

"All rise," the guy who had brought Al commanded.

They all stood.

A massive hulk of a man in a skull mask wrenched open the sliding door that connected to the next carriage, then only just managed to squeeze in through the opening to take the seat at the head of the table.

"Sit," he commanded gruffly.

They all obeyed, and the three guys who had brought the prisoners took the remaining seats.

The big guy at the head of the table spoke up. "Have the accused stand."

Figuring they were the accused, Al, Volt, and Animal stood.

"You've been charged with invasion of private property. How do you plead?"

"Don't be ridiculous... none of this is private property," Al argued. "Listen, my name is Black Al..."

The head honcho cut him off angrily, shouting, "Not interested in who you are. The punishment is death unless you have a legitimate case to plead."

"I do. We're here on a mission to find someone, a friend… we come in peace."

"Who?"

"His name is Turk."

A whisper spread through the room. There was a pause as the head honcho conversed with a woman seated on his right. He nodded as if in agreement.

Alice was starting to feel that attempting to locate Turk with so little time remaining had been a colossal mistake.

The woman spoke, her voice notably warmer than Alice had anticipated. "You were about to introduce yourselves, please continue."

"My name is Black Alice…" another murmur swept through the room, this time more intense. The woman leaned toward the head honcho and exchanged a hushed conversation with him.

"This is Animal." Once again, a murmur. "And this is Voltaris Idram."

The head honcho removed his mask, fixing a stern gaze on Animal. His face bore extensive tattoos, and his eyebrows, lips, and ears were pierced. Scars from numerous battles crisscrossed his face.

"Rock? Is that you?" Animal barked.

"Sure is mate," Rock confirmed.

"Free me!" Animal growled at the man beside him, who pulled a knife and cut him loose. Animal rushed over to Rock, who leaped out of his chair. Alice thought, this might turn into a brawl. But he was wrong; they embraced.

Slapping each other on the back, Animal shouted, "This bastard is my old mate Rock, grandmaster of the Angels, the first to be targeted by Zen because they had the biggest arsenal. I thought he was dead."

"And I didn't recognise you, mate," Rock said.

All the Skulls stood up and discarded their masks.

"We are all Angels," Rock growled, "fifty of us were dumped down here, and now only twenty-three remain. Remember my Sheila, Momma Bear?" he indicated the woman beside him. She immediately embraced Animal.

"And that's Sprocket, remember her?" He pointed to the other woman with a beard, a transgender individual. "Everyone, take your seats," Rock bellowed, with a cheerful tone.

Animal returned to his seat.

"Friend, I can tell ya Turk ain't here. Not heard of him down here at all. I'd tell you if I had."

"I know, mate, I know...," Animal agreed. "But why all this skull stuff? You know the others down here... Crankcase and Crow... I don't get it," Animal said.

"It's easy man. Crankcase is a Rat Fink, and they disclosed our bunker location to Zen in exchange for protection from attacks."

"What? Nah, I've never heard that. How did you find that out?" Animal asked, his anger evident.

"Ask Sprocket, she was a Fink."

Animal glared at Sprocket. "I forgot you were a Fink, you were more of a bloke back then, weren't you?"

"You could say that, dear... Crank never liked having someone a little different in the chapter... so when I found out he'd been having meetings with Gorrick and had sealed a deal to give up the Angels in exchange for special privileges, and he learned I'd found out and dumped me on a raid to be captured. I was thrown down here and as luck had it, Rock found me."

"So, you've been seeking revenge ever since," Animal suggested.

"And we'll continue until we get Crankcase... Five hundred Angels were massacred in that battle. Our anonymity is crucial to us, hence the skulls. It also means we can't allow you to leave."

"We're going back up to keep fighting, Rock. This bloke here is our ticket," Animal said sternly, nodding at Voltaris.

"So, he's with Zen?"

"Put it this way, I've got some favour with them," Voltaris said, before it could get heavy.

"And you, Black Alice... why have you taken the name of the legend who defeated Zen back in '87?"

"Because that's who I am, mate." Another murmur arose. Alice stood up. "I'm the bloke that possessed Turk, who killed Duke and Spike in the arena and wiped out an RF-7 and an 8 breaking outa Angel City. You guys must remember, some of you would've been there when we smashed through the front gates of Angel in Betsy... some of your mates would've been killed or injured in that battle... but hey, you now know it was for a good cause. You need to do the right thing, let us go find Turk... he's somewhere in Zen, maybe in prison... but I need to find him before I have to go back to my time. Are you going to stop me?" he shouted, passionately.

Rock slowly rose from his chair to his feet, then leaned on the table with his two massive fists and growled, "I witnessed you and Turk fight to the death in the arena... I witnessed your comrades perish. I was there when Betsy crashed through the gates, and I fought right alongside Turk when Animal first united us against Zen. You are what we all strive to become, Black Alice... No, we won't stand in your way of finding Turk; the guy's legend." He pounded his clenched fist on the table, chanting, "Turk, Turk, Turk!"

The others joined in, including Alice... then Animal, and surprisingly, even Voltaris got caught up in the revelry, and the chant persisted for five minutes.

On the way back to the FRT platform, Alice, flanked by Rock and Animal, asked Rock, "How are you dealing with Red Wheel?"

"We won't last long, Al. I only learned yesterday that Momma Bear has it. I guess the Finks will have the last laugh, coz we'll all soon be dead."

They stepped onto the platform. "I'm sorry to hear that, Rock," Al said compassionately. "But listen, I don't think they'll have the last laugh. There aren't many of them left either. I just wish there was something I could do."

"There is, mate," he stopped them and looked into Alice's eyes. "Find Turk, get him out of here to fight another day." They shook hands. Rock gave Animal a big friendly hug, then he turned to Voltaris, shook his hand, and told him, "The nick on yer throat should leave a small scar, mate, a worthy reminder of the Angels," he chuckled, devilishly.

It was a solemn moment for them as they got into the elevator, leaving behind people they knew didn't have much longer to live. Though the elevator would transport them from the horrors of the death camp, the memory of it, a place as close to hell on Earth as could be imagined, would remain with them forever.

When the elevator door opened for Al, it was like stepping out of a vortex into another dimension... a safer one... but one that only lasted a moment, because an RF-8 was waiting and immediately emerged from behind a large black marble column, opening fire.

It was then that Voltaris, who was right behind Alice, did something entirely unexpected: he dived at Alice, crash-tackling into him to the floor, out of the line of fire.

Animal was the last one out of the elevator and got his plaster cast caught in the closing door. "Damn!" he growled as he looked sharply at the cyborg that immediately aimed its weapon at him. Animal was cut down in a hail of bullets.

CHAPTER 22
END OF THE LINE

"❝ ANIMAL'S DOWN!" **VOLTARIS** yelled at Alice, who lay on the ground out of sight of the cyborg. On his belly, Alice sneaked a glance around the corner of the elevator block.

Animal lay on the black marble floor in a puddle of blood, conscious but staying still. The cyborg stood guard near the main elevator block, scanning for movement.

Al popped back into hiding and then sat up. "Thanks, that was close. The cyborg must be programmed to stop us reaching the main elevator."

"That's strange. If they wanted us dead, why the hell did they give me the key card?"

"Maybe they didn't expect us to make it back."

"I don't buy it," Volt snarled.

"Let's not worry about it... first, we need to knockout that cyborg... if Animal moves... it'll shoot him again," Al explained.

"What's your plan?"

"We need to distract it."

"Then what?"

"If it's an RF-8, I'll try an old trick to kill it."

"And if it's not?" Volt queried.

"Well, it just better be."

Voltaris stood up. "Alright, leave the diversion to me." He stepped into the lobby with his hands raised and stated, "Don't shoot!

Voltaris Idram, Zen operative."

The cyborg moved sharply but mechanically toward him and then halted, raising its arm in preparation to fire but pausing.

Alice was on his feet, watching from around the corner, gun up. He whispered loud enough for Voltaris to hear, "It's receiving orders, get closer."

With his hands up, Voltaris took a few steps closer to the monstrous amalgamation of man and machine. "I'm a Zen operative on a mission," he reiterated clearly. "Verify with Gorrick."

As soon as the cyborg lowered its arm, Alice dashed out from his concealment and as he approached the unsuspecting cyborg, slid across the marble floor like a baseball player making a home run, slipping between its legs, where he pulled up onto his back.

Voltaris couldn't believe Alice's audacity.

Al aimed the Glock at the cyborg's groin and pulled the trigger. Click. The firing pin had been electro-locked.

"No!" Alice exclaimed, quickly drawing his knife. He sprang to his feet behind the monster and, using all his strength, leapt upward, driving the dagger down into the back of its skull. It immediately began to convulse and then froze. The dagger had inflicted the damage, slicing into its positronic brain and shutting it down.

Getting to his feet, Al said, "Hell, that was lucky."

"Helluver move, that!" Voltaris exclaimed.

"Come on, let's see to Animal."

The pool of blood on the floor next to him wasn't a promising sign of Animal's condition. He lay on his side. Al turned him onto his back.

"How are you holding up, buddy?"

"Uh, not so good," Animal groaned.

Alice lifted Animal's T-shirt to examine the wound on his side. It was far more severe than he expected—not the bullet wound, but what else he saw. There was a large, raised, irritated mark on his belly. Alice immediately recognised it as Red Wheel.

"Seems it's harder to live to fight than fight to live," Animal mumbled through clenched teeth.

All Alice could do was sigh, "Ah, mate." He pulled down Animal's shirt and looked up at Voltaris. "Give us a hand."

They assisted Animal to his feet and then supported him past the disabled cyborg toward the elevators, leaving a trail of blood on the floor.

"What's the damage?" Voltaris asked.

"A clean through-and-through, no vital organs hit... if we can get him out of here, he might pull through."

"Don't worry about me, fellas," Animal complained, through gritted teeth.

Holding onto Animal with one hand, Voltaris pressed the elevator call button with the other. The door opened immediately, and they stepped inside. Alice promptly struck the CCTV camera in the ceiling, rendering it useless.

The doors closed before Voltaris could select the 31st floor. "Damn, we're not in control," Voltaris exclaimed.

The elevator moved swiftly and then began to slow.

Groaning in pain, Animal said urgently, "Use the key card to override the computer."

But it was too late. Just as Voltaris was aiming the key card for the slot in the control panel, the elevator stopped on the 15th floor, and the doors opened.

Voltaris immediately withdrew his hand, staring at Ursula Mennis flanked by two RF-20s.

"Gentlemen, you made it back," Ursula stated the obvious.

Voltaris moved into the doorway and slyly slipped his hand holding the key card behind him. Alice got the idea, grabbed it, and then, while holding onto Animal, faked a stumble that brought him closer to the elevator control panel.

Voltaris stepped out of the elevator, right in the line of fire, shielding Alice.

Moving like greased lightning, Alice inserted the key card and pressed 31 on the panel. The doors immediately closed, and the elevator started ascending.

"Will he be alright?" Animal asked.

"Don't know... but he's no dummy. Maybe he can talk his way to meet us at the helipad. The critical thing now is to get you back to Avalon for medical attention."

"No, mate, I'm a goner... if the bullet hole doesn't get me, then the wheel will. Save yourselves... and what about Turk? Rescuing him is the reason why we came in the first place, isn't it?"

"Shut up, ya big log. Save your strength," Al growled compassionately.

The elevator stopped, and the doors opened. As soon as they stepped out, Gorrick and a pair of RF-20s confronted them.

"Well, well," Gorrick stated smugly. "Should I be surprised that the legendary Black Alice made it... though Animal doesn't look too healthy, does he?"

"You're an arse, Gorrick. What's your game... huh? You sent us on a wild goose chase... what for?... All along, you've had Turk here somewhere, maybe even dead."

"It's quite simple, Alice. I didn't expect you to return from the death camp. I guess once again, I've been found guilty of underestimating your resilience. Kill them!" he ordered the cyborgs.

Before Alice could react, Animal lunged out of his grasp, colliding with the cyborg on the right of Gorrick. He pulled the large monster into a clinch. Alice could see Animal had a dagger in his hand. He brought it up under the cyborg's chin and drove it with all his might into its head.

The cyborg squeezed Animal in its grip. Alice heard a loud crack as Animal's spinal cord snapped. The cyborg went limp, and Animal fell from its grasp onto the floor.

Just as the other cyborg raised its arm to shoot Alice, someone jumped it from behind. Its weapon discharged, missing Alice.

A familiar voice shouted, "Al!"

It was Vee.

Alice quickly reached into his pocket, pulled out a WASP, flicked the switch on its top, and hurled it at the cyborg. It struck its forehead and stuck there. Crack! It exploded, blowing the top of its head off.

"Alice? Not Black Alice... surely not?" The person who had grabbed the cyborg said.

When he looked around the frozen monster, Alice immediately recognised the bearded man.

"Turk? Is that you?" Al asked.

Gorrick was left standing, feeling vulnerable.

Alice dived into his pocket and said, "Gorrick... I've got a present for you as well." He produced a WASP and held it up for Gorrick to see. "It uses facial recognition. If I don't switch it off, so now it recognises its target... you. Goodbye, Gorrick." He delicately tossed it into the air. The WASP hung there for a second or two with Gorrick staring at it, and then it sharply turned mid-air toward its target. Gorrick backed off, hoping to escape it, but the WASP sped like an arrow to find its mark and stuck to his forehead. With eyes the size of dinner plates, he realised his number was up. Just as he tried to grab the WASP... Crack! Gorrick's head exploded.

Vee rushed over and hugged Alice.

"How the hell did you get here?" Al asked.

"I stowed away in the drone."

Turk came over to Al. "I finally get to see what you look like, buddy. You're shorter than I expected," he joked.

"And you're on the nose, mate, you need a bath, phew!" Al chuckled.

There was a groan. They both looked down at Animal on the floor. Turk crouched down, raised his old friend's head in a clutched hand, and said, "Mate, what are you doing all messed up like that?"

"Turk... it's time to die, my friend." And then Animal closed his eyes for the last time.

Vee was crying. They hadn't noticed the elevator had descended. The doors opened, and they all looked up in surprise as Voltaris stepped out.

Turk straightened up and got ready to fight.

"No, mate, he's okay. One of us... Voltaris, this is my sister Vee, and this is Turk."

"It's time to go," Voltaris said without ceremony.

There was no room for Animal's body in the drone, so regretfully, they had to leave him with the carnage. They climbed aboard the drone. Turk and Al were in front with Vee and Voltaris squeezed into the cargo hold behind them.

"Animal was the pilot, so I guess it's up to me now," Al informed his passengers. "I hope it can lift the four of us." He looked at the sky. "At least the weather's okay... how do we find the bunker?"

"Don't worry, Al, you can do anything," Turk said with a big grin.

Al pushed down on the joystick, and the drone lifted up and hovered.

"So far, so good," Al said nervously. "We flew west to get here because there was a storm coming in from the south, so if we fly east, we should be on target." He pushed the stick forward, and the craft headed due east.

The shroud of loss for their friend was all-encompassing. Though Turk and Alice had plenty to talk about, losing Animal had left them pretty much lost for words.

But that wasn't going to stop Vee from having a chat. "Why didn't you tell me you were Turk?" she said grumpily.

"You didn't ask," Turk said with a cheeky smirk.

"A bit lucky that the one person I found was you, wasn't it?"

"Not really, I've been the only prisoner for over a year. What made you come down to the prison?"

"It was the only door that opened in the stairwell; all the rest were locked. I was trying to find a way out," Vee explained.

"Lucky you didn't. We might never have found you and could have left you behind," Al submitted. "What happened with you, Volt?" Al asked.

"Ursula released me."

"How come?" Al queried.

"I didn't ask; I suppose it was the deal," he said coldly.

The mood had lightened up a little.

"What do you think of our girl, Hope?" Turk asked.

"Well, therein lies a story," Al said.

For the rest of the journey, Al filled Turk in on all the events since they'd arrived. Turk was most interested in the accusation by the Rock that the Rat Finks had traded for favour with Zen in return for the location of the Angels' Bunker, which had cost hundreds of lives.

After an hour in the air, Alice figured they must be somewhere near the bunker. Something below them looked familiar, so he decided to press the elevator remote.

"There!" Vee shouted behind Alice.

Off to the port side, Al could see the huge trap door sliding open. "Here we go, folks. My first landing."

With a bit of a bump, Al put the drone down on the elevator pad. Another push of the remote, and it descended to the garage floor and a reception committee.

Morri rushed toward Turk upon seeing him, and with tears of joy trickling down both their cheeks, they embraced and kissed. Hope joined in for a cuddle. Secta gave Alice and Vee a hug. But when they all noticed Animal was missing, the tragedy of the mission hit them like a ton of bricks. Morri was in denial.

"No, no, it couldn't be?... No... not Animal?" She looked around frantically, trying to find him, and then burst into a different kind of tears—those of grief. Turk held her close.

"He died like a true warrior, Morri," Al said sympathetically.

It dawned on Hope, Morri, and Secta that there was someone else with them: Voltaris.

Morri let go of Turk and angrily confronted him. "Your people killed him!" She screamed hysterically and began pounding him on the chest with her fists clenched. Voltaris just took it.

Turk pulled her off him and said placatingly, "Hey, hey, calm down. Al sez he's okay... one of us. He helped us escape."

Most of them knew Morri was overly upset for another reason...

Red Wheel.

Once things had calmed down, they all made their way sombrely to the canteen. On the way, Morri told Turk about Cutter and Nerdo. Turk was shattered by the loss. In his absence, the entire world had been inexorably changed.

Secta pulled Alice aside on the way to ask surreptitiously, "What's your take on this Voltaris character, Alice?"

"He's okay... he saved my life. Started out a bit awkward, but I think he got to understand, by the time we broke out of there, why Zen is the enemy. I killed Gorrick with a WASP."

"Oh really, how wonderful," Secta said, macabrely. However, he was quietly unconvinced that Voltaris was kosher.

They all grabbed some food and drinks, and then sat at a couple of tables they'd pushed together.

Secta remained standing with a prepared speech. "Everyone, listen up for a moment... Voltaris, I trust your adventure with Alice and Animal afforded you some insight into the rationale of our continuing war with the Zen Corporation. We welcome you as a friend. In saying that, I ask for a minute's silence for us to remember our fallen friends, Animal, Cutter, and Nerdo."

They all bowed their heads with eyes closed in silence, picturing their friends in their own individual ways.

After a minute, Secta continued sombrely. "Though we have lost some warriors, we welcome back one: our dearest friend and leader Turk." The six of them applauded Turk, who raised a hand for them to stop, embarrassed.

Secta went on. "In a little over an hour, a vortex will open for us to return to our time. We will be taking Voltaris with us, and if there's no objection from anyone, we'll also be taking Hope."

Hope interrupted him, "There has been a change of plan, Secta... I'm not going with you... I'm staying with Mum."

Secta was shocked.

Turk sensed something and looked at Morri, concerned. "What's wrong?"

With tears cascading down her pallid cheeks, Morri pulled back the cuff of her sleeve and showed Turk her wrist.

He immediately embraced her. "Oh, no, not you?" he groaned.

There was an emotional pause for the consequences of the admission to sink in, and then Morri released Turk and took Hope's hand. Bravely, lovingly, she looked into her daughter's eyes and admitted, "I don't think this is going to go away, love."

"Mum, I will not leave you. That's what matters most now," Hope said, bursting into tears.

"You're alive, Hope... that's what matters most. You must go with them... the world needs you... you are our hope, darling." Morri burst into tears. Turk hugged her.

Secta smiled warmly, "You need to come back with us, Hope."

"How can that happen, Secta?" Turk asked.

Secta fished in his pocket, pulled out his hand, and opened it to display a Clock Drive in his palm. "This little gadget is a Clock Drive; it will allow you to pass through the vortex... I have four of them: one for Hope, one for Voltaris, and one each for Turk and Morri."

He paused for his words to sink in.

"Now, even though we do this in defiance of the temporal prime directive, I believe it to be the only way to preserve humanity from imminent extinction."

Morri was weeping, but now they were tears of joy. Hope hugged her mum and dad.

Secta continued, "I believe this to be the most logical decision. I know it means leaving your people to fend for themselves, but their sacrifice will hopefully ensure the future of humanity. It will be necessary for Hope to leave her work behind and to pick up from where my sister left off back in our time. As for Morri and Turk, we need them to test for a means of defeating Red Wheel because we have determined it is, in fact, an introduced disease, as opposed to it being the result of radiation poisoning."

There was a murmur of surprise. Secta put up a hand to prevent wishful thinking. "It's only early days, but if we can prove Red Wheel is an introduced disease, then we can find a cure... I am determined to save Morri."

All of their spirits had been lifted—optimism had been restored from what had been fatalism for far too long.

"So," Secta said in conclusion, "are there any objections?"

Turk immediately clambered to his feet and said gruffly, "You know what I want?"

They were all taken aback by his outburst.

"What's that, mate?" Al asked casually, probably the least affected by Turk's apparent flare-up.

"A bloody hot shower and a shave before we leave."

Everyone, except Voltaris, cracked up. Morri jumped up and threw her arms around the neck of her man. They were all reminded of Turk's wicked dry sense of humour that they had missed so much while he'd been incarcerated.

The meeting broke up for each of them to make their preparations.

Morri stopped Secta and said secretly, "There is something about Voltaris."

Very much aware of Morri's psychic ability and picking up on something himself, he was keen to hear more. "Are you sensing something, Morri?"

"Nothing... I sense nothing... it's as though he's not alive.

CHAPTER 23
TELEPHONE BOOK

IT WAS ABOUT time to leave—pardon the pun. They had decided to assemble in the garage.

Morri, Turk, and Hope had said their goodbyes to the infirmed and the few remaining to care for them, promising to return with a cure for the horrible Red Wheel. Without the beard, Turk looked like the old Turk again.

In Alice's inimitable fashion, he couldn't resist taunting him. "So, it was you under that werewolf mask. Hmm, you smell less like a dog as well."

Secta interrupted. "Al, put this Clock Drive on Voltaris, will you? I've already done Hope."

"Does he need one? He came by Aquila, didn't he?" Al questioned.

"I don't know if the processes are compatible. It won't hurt to be sure."

Just then, a vortex began to open near Alice. He called everyone's attention, "Guys, Vee will lead; just follow her and step through the vortex like you're climbing through an open window. Don't be afraid; there are no side effects."

Secta and Vee walked Hope, Turk, and Morri up to the soundless swirling vortex.

"Secta isn't sure Aquila is in the same groove as Kairos, so I need to fit this to your neck, just tilt your head," Al explained to Voltaris.

Secta went through the vortex first, followed by Vee, Turk, and then Morri.

Al attached the small patch to Voltaris' neck and then took him over to the vortex just as Hope was stepping through.

"In you go," Alice told him.

Just as Voltaris was stepping through, En-Ki spoke in Alice's mind for the first time in a while and said, "Where's the knife wound in his neck?"

It was too late for Alice to stop Voltaris; he had gone, but he knew En-Ki was right. Hanging on to the thought, he took a last look around at the APC, the Wilson J-Car, the garage, and then stepped into the vortex.

There was quite a gathering in the Kairos control room. They had split into two groups that stared at each other like the feuding McCoys and Hatfields. On one side were Mal, Dr Cairn, the Professor, Karzoff, Viktoria, Rita Vallins, and Dr James, while across the aisle sat Honor, Professor Adamski, Dr Li, and General Bruckmaster.

It had taken a lot of talking by Mal to convince Karzoff to permit Zen and TWO officials' entry to his hallowed turf. Even though he'd eventually acquiesced, he still wasn't happy. He knew Dr Cairn had talked Mal into it, but his gut was telling him it was wrong. Mal, on the other hand, considered it a gesture of goodwill to facilitate better relations between parties.

The room fell silent when Kairos fired up, and Robert loudly announced, "Incoming."

Karzoff and Viktoria were ready to draw weapons if necessary. Despite their opposing ideologies, the tension and excitement of the moment showed on all their faces. Every set of eyes was fixed on the great circular device in the advent room known as Kairos.

The Professor whispered to Mal beside him, "Still not much

fanfare, is there? We need to work more on flashing lights, smoke, and sound effects, don't you think?"

"It's no less exciting, but it would certainly add to the drama," Mal replied with a fun smirk.

Vee stepped out of Kairos first, followed quickly by Secta. After steadying himself, he waved hello to the gallery behind the protective control room window. Then, much to the surprise of the gallery, came Turk and then Morri.

"Who are they?" Karzoff whispered to Viktoria.

Then, when Hope stepped out of Kairos, every one of the OTT team jumped to their feet in astonishment, letting out a collective cry of, "Hope!"

Viktoria and Rita both had their hands on their hearts in shock.

Finally, out of Kairos stepped Voltaris. This time Bruckmaster stood and applauded, glad to see the safe return of his agent.

Secta removed the Clock Drives from Voltaris, Morri, Hope, and Turk.

Then, last but not least, came Alice. With his arrival, a cheer went up from the OTT gallery. He'd done it again. Even Luna was caught up in the celebration, clapping her hands and cheering.

There was little interaction between parties once they'd all been reunited. Luna tried bridging the gap by initiating conversation between Mal and Bruckmaster, and the Professor spoke briefly but reservedly to Adamski and Dr Li. However, the cold war between Honor, Karzoff, and Viktoria had chilled the room to below zero.

It didn't take long before the guests, including Voltaris, were escorted out of the building by security.

Karzoff returned twenty minutes later, entering the reception room just a few doors down from the President's office. Everyone had gathered for a spread of food and drinks that Mal had organised.

Introductions had been made, along with an explanation of why Hope looked so much like Secta's sister. The Professor and Mal were amazed that she not only resembled her predecessor, but also possessed her memories and personality. It was as though she had never left them.

Luna, however, had cornered Secta and Al with questions about Morri and Turk. She was infuriated that bringing them back was a deliberate breach of the TPD. Al argued that bringing someone back from the future was not a breach, whereas bringing someone from the past would be. Secta sensed the tension between Al and Luna growing with disagreement, so he winked at Al to withdraw. Al walked off to talk with Mal, Morri, and Turk, while Secta tried to talk some sense into Luna. Once she understood the ramifications of Red Wheel and that Secta suspected the disease of being introduced by Zen during the Cyberwars to ultimately eliminate humankind, she approved.

"Did you meet with Tippy, mate?" Al asked Mal.

"It's all set for next weekend, Al. All you have to worry about is not forgetting the lyrics," Mal joked.

"What's this?" Morri asked.

"Oh, we're staging an open-air rock concert this weekend... they're calling it the new Woodstock," Mal explained excitedly.

"Where?" she asked.

"You're not going to believe this, but the concert is actually called Avalon, because the stage will be next to the old bunker, exactly where Woodhenge will be built in the future."

"That's wild. What bands will be playing?" Turk asked.

"World, Cried Wolf, the People Eaters..." Al said.

"And, no other than Black Alice, the headline act, of course," Mal added.

"I think I remember you were in a band yourself... the Units, wasn't it?" Turk asked Mal.

"How could you know that?" Mal queried.

"Coz he's got heaps of my memories, mate. Remember I once occupied his mind," Al said.

"And he still does!" Turk joked. They laughed.

The Professor, Karzoff, Viktoria, and Robert were talking with Hope.

"So, I can remember everything right up until when she extracted the Pneumatide to inject into my embryo. I talked with Secta about it, and that was the day Alice arrived back from his off-planet mission," Hope explained.

"Unbelievable," Robert gasped. "What do you remember about me?" he tested.

"We were at the University of New South Wales together. I remember it like it was yesterday. Remember the day you changed Professor Deacon's formula on the whiteboard before he arrived for the lecture?"

"Ha! When he read it out, instead of it being a hypothetical equation to bind three elements, it..."

She finished the statement for him. "It was an equation to create an elementary particle, a quark."

All of a sudden, the realisation that she was indeed Hope hit Robert like a ton of bricks. He stared at her, mind blown.

"Have I got some work for you, my dear. Oh, how we've missed your powers of research," the Professor admitted to Hope.

Secta and Luna joined Al and Mal. "I apologise, Alice," Luna said coyly. "Seems I'm making a habit of this... I jumped the gun accusing you of breaking the TPD. Secta has clarified it all. I hope you accept my apology."

"No worries," Al said, welcomingly.

"Thank you. If the UN can offer any help in finding a cure for this terrible disease, then I'm more than happy to set it up," she said genuinely.

"That would be very helpful, Luna," Secta said.

"I still have a bad gut feeling about Voltaris," Al admitted.

"What makes you say that, Alice?" Luna asked.

"When we were captured in the death camp, a blade had been held up to his throat that cut him. It wasn't a serious cut but deep enough to leave a scar. When I put the Clock Drive on his neck before we left, there wasn't a mark."

Secta brought Morri into the conversation. "I'm sure you read in mission reports that Morri is psychic. Tell everyone what you told me," Secta requested.

"I scanned Voltaris' mind and found nothing," she said.

"Nothing... what do you mean by that, Morri?" Luna asked.

Morri was about to answer when she froze, grabbed her wrist, and almost collapsed. Fearing the worst, Turk and Secta grabbed her before she hit the floor. They helped her into a seat. Hope rushed over to her.

Morri had her head down, sobbing.

They were all thinking the worst.

"What's the matter with her?" Luna asked Al.

"She's got Red Wheel," Al whispered.

"What is it, love?" Turk asked Morri softly. "The Red Wheel?"

She nodded her head and then slowly looked up. But it wasn't fear or pain in her eyes; it was joy. She held out her wrist and said sobbingly, "It has gone... it's gone."

Hope checked her wrist for any sign of the rash and looked up at the others, shocked. "It has... the Red Wheel has gone! You're cured, Mum?" She embraced her mother and they wept.

Vee watched Secta pacing the floor and said to Karzoff, "He's off with the pixies thinking again."

Secta stopped abruptly and questioned out loud, "What's different?" He turned, faced the Professor, and asked, "Vic, what was technically different about this mission?"

"Oh, yes... only one thing... in order for the Clock Drives to function at their peak, the reintegration unit now passes through the SAGE filter. Mind you, it had no effect at all on Alice or you, only for the Clock Drives... it filters contamination that can be in the DNA of the traveller using one. You know, otherwise there would be a risk of pollutants..."

Hope cut him off. "That's it!... SAGE... it filtered the JAK2 gene to save Alice, now it has filtered out Red Wheel!"

"It could be," Secta pondered. "Robert, can you bring up the entry data for the Clock Drives?"

"Yes, is there a laptop here I can use?" Robert asked.

Mal quickly retrieved a laptop from his desk. Robert took it, sat down with it on his knee, and logged into the Kairos mainframe. They all crowded around him, eager to see what was there.

"Here, you can see the four Clock Drive timelines. Hmm, there's a spike on Clock Drive two; that was Morri and there... SAGE has erased it."

Secta grabbed the Professor and hugged him. "Vic old man, you have saved humanity."

"Will you look at that?" Robert said, and the attention went back to him.

"What is it?" the Professor asked.

"Clock Drive five shows no DNA on the timeline, but that's impossible."

"Don't be ridiculous, Robert, there has to be DNA," Secta said. He took a look. "You're right, there is definitely no DNA."

"So, who was Clock Drive five?" Al asked.

"Voltaris Idram," Robert read out from the screen.

Dr Li turned her back on Voltaris to face Adamski, Bruckmaster, Honor, Gorrick, and Khan, who were seated in her lab at Zen HQ. Voltaris stood at attention, facing them with his eyes closed like an exhibit.

"Before I shut Voltaris down, he gave me instructions on how to access an implanted message for us from the future," Li said. She turned back to Voltaris and pressed the mastoid bone behind his left ear. Then, she stood back to observe.

Voltaris' face immediately morphed into that of Dr Ursula Mennis. Her eyes opened, and she spoke pleasantly, "For this to play means you have accessed the gravitonic brain of my creation, Cronus. Though I cannot take credit for the incredible organic processor developed by Zen Japan that drives him, I created the physical being, gravitonic brain, and all neural interfaces.

"Cronus is powered by a plutonium microdot. It has a lifespan of a thousand years. He is pre-programmed with all the memories, mannerisms, and physical attributes of Voltaris Idram. However, as you can see by my holographic image, Cronus can be programmed with other likenesses... in fact, an infinite number of likenesses, indistinguishable from the original."

The audience murmured their approval.

"Cronus has ten times the strength of the strongest man of your time, including Black Alice. Though not tested, we believe Cronus to be stronger than anything Black Alice can shape-shift into."

The audience was now thoroughly impressed.

"So, they obviously experienced the superpowers of Black Alice," Honor pointed out.

Mennis continued, "Cronus is a singularity, which means it is self-reproductive and self-aware. Cronus is a silicon-based biological life form, as opposed to being carbon-based like a human. It is carrying a reserve organic processor for you to replicate. The instructions for growing it and the duplication process are retrievable from its memory.

"The skin of Cronos is impervious to fire, chemicals, bullets, and explosions. However, due to the requirement for Cronus to be one hundred percent organic to travel through Kairos, its gravitonic brain remains the most vulnerable region of its body and was purposely left unprotected. You will need to further develop protection for it because a bullet to the head would almost certainly be fatal.

"I thank you for your audience—I give you the next step in evolution... Cronus."

As the face of Dr Mennis morphed back into Voltaris, Brigadier Bruckmaster struggled to his feet and applauded. Still clapping his hands, he turned to Gorrick beside him and bellowed with enthusiasm, "Yeah, yeah... goddammit, you've outdone yourself, Gorrick... sheer genius."

While Adamski and Li were left to study their new creation, Gorrick took Bruckmaster, Khan, and Honor to his office to continue discussions. Seated in the lounge area on the small island next to the giant eucalyptus tree, they raised flutes of French Champagne in a toast to the accomplishment.

"It was a masterstroke bringing Cronus back," Honor said, bristling with excitement. They now had the edge over their adversaries. "We will now more than compete with OTT."

"I wonder how long it takes to grow an organic chip? As soon as it's done, we'll be able to bring Aquila back online," Khan said.

"I think it would be wise to take our time, now that the accord has been signed. It will require careful planning to achieve our goals while under the scrutiny of UNTT," Gorrick explained.

"Leave that to me," Bruckmaster snarled. "By the way… am I to assume the real Voltaris is stuck in the future?"

"Only as long as it takes for us to bring Aquila back online," Gorrick assured him. "The first mission will be to bring him back."

"Will Cronus become our new time traveller?" Honor asked.

"Yes… and once we have the new chip replicated, we will recommence the RF program to produce Warbots for sale globally… then our objective will be within reach," Gorrick assured them.

"And so we move on to the next phase of creating my dominion," En-Lil confirmed in Gorrick's mind.

Once Morri and Turk had settled into a room at OTT, Vee took them out for a tour of Sydney. For them, it was their first time seeing a place that had previously been only legendary.

Hope wasted no time in visiting her old lab. She was like a kid in a candy store, knowing where everything was and even recalling the passwords on her namesake's devices. Both Secta and the Professor stood back, watching her flutter about the lab, stopping here and there like an academic butterfly.

Luna was with Karzoff and Viktoria in their office, going over the security protocols for future missions.

Meanwhile, Al and Mal were still enjoying drinks in the presidential office, awaiting the arrival of Tippy Lane.

"The Professor told me Robert's got the coordinates of the Watcher that's been hovering over the White House like a bad smell," Mal said.

Al took a sip of beer and then said, "Didn't know that was happening. How long's it been there?"

"Since you left. It just turned up. They've tried everything to communicate with it—flybys, radio transmissions on every known frequency... you name it, they've tried it, but they can't get a response from the damn thing."

"I bet that's freaking them out," Al said, chuckling facetiously.

"Yeah, I've had President Robinson on the phone about it multiple times," Mal added.

"I wonder who they are and what they want?" Al mused thoughtfully.

Just then, there was a knock at the door, and Rita entered. "Excuse me, sir, Tippy Lane is here. Oh, by the way, the news is reporting that the Watcher over the White House has vanished."

"Interesting, after the TPD was signed. I wonder if that's a coincidence. Send Tippy in, please, Rita," Mal requested.

Rita briefly left and then ushered Tippy in. Al was impressed by Tippy's appearance. Her short hair was streaked purple, and she wore a short black tutu, a black singlet with a black leather jacket over it, and purple sandals. Her toenails, fingernails, and lipstick all matched the colour of her hair.

"Hi, Mal, and Al, you're back—wow!" Tippy exclaimed, rushing over to Al. He stood up to give her a big hug, and then she gave Mal a peck on the cheek.

"So, Tippy, everything going well?" Al asked with a smile.

She sat down opposite them, crossing her bare legs. "Absolutely, Avalon is going to be the gig of the century. I've got six more bands lined up for the daytime performances, and then the big show starts at sundown. At 7 p.m., it's Cried Wolf, followed by The People Eaters, then World. After a break, at 10 p.m., the main event—Black Alice. It will all be broadcast live from 7 p.m. to midnight on global free-to-air TV, podcasted via satellite, and simulcast on radio."

"Do you need more rehearsal time?" Al asked.

"Nah, Mal, I'm all set. What about you? Have you decided which songs to perform?"

"Yeah, let's do 'Fighting for You'—one of your songs. I used to perform it with the Units, remember? Plus, it sends the right message."

"Brilliant! Should we announce that there will be a special guest appearance?" Tippy asked. "It would generate even more press coverage."

"Sure, but no hints about who the guest will be," Al replied.

"Cool, don't worry, security is on high alert for this. Oh, and I need to know—when you fly in by chopper, Al, will there be anyone else with you?"

"Yeah… Um, Morri, Turk, Vee, Secta, the Professor, Hope… um…" Al paused, thinking if there were any more.

"Karzoff and Viktoria will already be there, as will Rita. I think Robert said he's driving there. So, including you and me, that makes a total of eight," Mal said.

"That's fine. I just need to let Karzoff know that we'll need an additional chopper for that many people," Tippy replied, her enthusiasm undiminished. "Oh, Al, I've got the Black Alice repertoire and lighting plan to go over with you. When will you be available for that, and where?"

"I'll drop by Vee's place tonight around eleven. Have a glass of pinot noir ready for me, okay?"

She shot him a cute smile. "Absolutely."

After Tippy left, Mal candidly asked Al, "Do I sense a bit more than a working relationship with pretty Tippy?"

"Yeah, I like her," Al admitted.

Mal grinned and reclined in his chair. "See, those are the kind of shenanigans I miss. Are you working on any new songs?"

"A couple, but I'm not sure if my out of practice voice can still deliver," Al replied seriously.

"Come on, mate. You could sing the pages of a phone book and make it sound cool."

CHAPTER 24
WILDCAT

T HE DOOR TO Vee's Coogee Beach apartment swung open, and Vee welcomed Al inside.

"How's it going?" she asked.

Al looked her up and down. She was wearing only a very revealing loose white singlet.

"Hey, you look sexier than I imagined," Al joked.

She stood on her bare tiptoes to give him a peck on the cheek. "What did you imagine?"

"I dunno."

They both chuckled as she took his hand and led him into the living room. "I guess you're here to see Tip. She's in the shower. By the way, it's incredible about SAGE. When I took Morri and Turk on a tour around Sydney today, they were like a couple of young lovers. It's great to see. And what about Voltaris? Stuck in 2112, poor guy."

"Yeah, reckon," Al said. "After he slipped me the key card for the elevator, Ursula Mennis and her cyborg minions must have swapped him for the he-who-is-not-living clone."

"What was it that came back with no DNA, for goodness' sake?" she questioned.

" Some sort of new cyborg I'd say... I'm gonna get Voltaris out of there, he'd shown by his selfless actions he's on our side... especially after he saw all the crap Zen had done to people."

"Yeah, I thought he was alright."

Tippy emerged in a white towelling robe, barefoot and with her hair wrapped in an orange microfiber turban.

"Hey Al, looking good," she chirped in her usual upbeat manner.

"Likewise. So, where's that glass of red you promised?" Al asked, his eyes gleaming.

Tippy headed to the kitchen and called back, "Vee, do you want a glass?"

"No thanks, love. I'm hitting the sack. It's been a big few days," Vee replied. She turned to Al and whispered, "She's hoping you'll spend the night."

"She must have read my mind," Al said with a mischievous grin.

Vee gave him a peck on the cheek and added playfully, "Don't do anything I wouldn't do."

"Woof, that gives me tons of scope," he chuckled.

Tippy returned from the kitchen with two glasses of pinot and placed them on the coffee table in front of the couch where Al was sitting. She then fetched a laptop from the sideboard, returned to the couch, and sat down next to Al.

"So," she said, all business now. "This is the lighting plan. We create a timeline for each song you'll perform. Then we select where we want the vari-lights directed. There are seven hundred lights in total. See here," she clicked the space bar, "this shows the grid. You just choose the sets of lights and their direction, and they lock onto the timeline. Then we can simulate the lighting. The lighting director is Wildcat. You know him, right?"

"Wildcat? Yeah, he's the best," Al affirmed.

"He'll handle manual lighting moves during each song. Tonight, you'll only be setting the automated moves. Okay?"

"Absolutely. But how do we know the correct length of each song?"

"I recorded Ratsso, Slut, and Blue rehearsing, so we'll use those recordings. And I've allowed for a margin of error."

"Smarty. You've thought of everything," Al said, leaning in and gently kissing her lips.

She responded passionately and then pulled away, saying, "We better get this done. I need to email it to Wildcat tonight."

"Alright, the last song will be 'Fighting for You.' That'll be Mal's song, so it'll need a different lighting plan. After that comes the encore where I'll invite the guys from World to join Mal and me. That might need a different plan. Or maybe we let Wildcat have his head?"

"Good idea. Let's call song twelve 'Fighting For You' and use a code name for Mal. What should we call him?"

"Unit. That works. No one would know him by that."

"Don't worry, Wildcat will be the only one other than me with the plan, so Mal will be safe," she confirmed.

"Alright, let's do it."

Two hours later, they had finished the plan, and Tippy sent the file to Wildcat's email address.

"Done," she said, with big cheesy grin.

Glan Denning looked up from his computer at Toeghan Hitz sitting opposite him at her terminal. "Check this out," he exclaimed. "My spyware intercepted an email from Tippy Lane to Wildcat, the lighting designer for the concert." It might be the breakthrough they had been working hard for in their small city apartment.

Toeghan got up from her computer and walked over to Denning's side, leaning on his shoulder to see the screen. They both examined the attachment in the intercepted email.

"It's the lighting plan for the Black Alice band," Denning said, excitement in his voice. "This could be crucial intel for the hit on Alice."

"What's that? Track twelve... it says VIP... Unit. What's that about?" Toeghan questioned. "Wait a second... I know that name. I met a guy on Coogee Beach a while back who invited me to a gig, but he never showed up. I think the band was called The Units."

Denning was quick to react and searched for information about

The Units. "Jackpot! Guess who the lead singer of The Units was? None other than Mal Function, aka the current President... Malcolm Low."

"Hmm," she smirked. "Honor will be thrilled."

The next day, the lab at OTT was abuzz with excitement. Secta, Hope, and the Professor had devised a plan to save humanity in 2112. They had called a meeting to present their idea to the OTT members, Dr Cairn, Turk, and Morri.

By late morning, they had all gathered in the boardroom. Once everyone was seated, Secta took the floor.

"We've called this meeting because I have some exciting news. After thorough analysis, I can confirm that the Professor's remarkable software application SAGE is capable of eradicating Red Wheel."

A round of applause rippled through the room.

"We've developed a plan to inoculate as many of the infected individuals in 2112 as possible. We intend to produce fifty Clock Drives and, at regular intervals, create a wormhole through which the afflicted individuals will be transported. They will be immediately sent back without any awareness of their time travel experience. To them, it will appear to be a medical procedure similar to having an MRI. Now, before we delve into the details, let me clarify that SAGE will not address the issue of sterility caused by radioactive fallout. However, Hope believes that by fertilising her stored eggs with donor sperm from this era, we could potentially help more robust females among the cured to conceive through IVR. The process will be slow and challenging, but women aged between fifty and fifty-five might still be able to give birth using IVR. Any questions?"

Luna was the first to raise a concern. "This is indeed a commendable concept, Doctor. However, it appears to be in direct violation of the prime directive."

Morri stood up, her voice determined. " Dr Cairn will you be able to sleep at night with the deaths of thousands or millions of innocent people on your conscience? They were infected by Zen, a corporation right now gearing up to poison the world in 2087."

Interrupting Morri, Luna said, "Addressing Zen in the present should rectify the timeline and prevent the Cyberwars from ever occurring. Isn't that sufficient?"

The Professor interjected, "The timeline doesn't work that way, Luna. The timeline in which the Cyberwars happen will persist no matter what actions we take. Proof of that lies in Morri and Turk sitting at this table right now. If I were to go to Zen HQ and eliminate Gorrick to prevent the Cyberwars, Morri and Turk would still be here. Why? Because once Gorrick is removed, a new timeline would branch off, but our timeline would continue unchanged. This is not just a hypothesis; our missions have provided ample evidence of this reality."

Luna remained standing, her scepticism giving way to respect for the Professor. "Point taken. Thank you for clarifying that. However, I'll need to consult with UNTT."

Mal added his perspective, "In fact, I think it would be wise to engage all signatories of the Temporal Prime Directive. The Red Wheel epidemic in 2112 is a global crisis, and I believe the US President wouldn't want to ignore the potential mass extermination of her country's citizens in the future due to a disease intentionally released by Zen Corporation. This also raises another matter for UNTT to address: how does the organisation intend to handle Zen Corporation and TWO, given their collaboration in using our facility, Kairos, to transport cyborg technology from the future for nefarious purposes? I want to make it clear that I believe this should take precedence over hindering what could be the greatest humanitarian rescue effort in history."

Luna had no counter to Mal's no-nonsense tirade. She would need to raise both issues with her superiors.

"If there's nothing else, I'll call the meeting adjourned until Dr Cairn obtains the advice of the UN," Mal said.

Al piped up. "A few other things before we quit... first, the real Voltaris Idram is stuck in the future, and we need to get him back. And before you say anything, you can take it from me that his visit to the horrors of the Zen death camps turned him to our side. Secondly, I think if Luna or the UN want to prevent the humanitarian effort, then she needs to bung on a Clock Drive, so she can personally witness the horrors of Red Wheel."

"Hear, hear!" Turk shouted in agreement.

"And finally, I watched the News on TV this morning and saw that North Korea yesterday tested a long-range missile capable of carrying a nuclear warhead, and that a Watcher was filmed over the launch. I think Karzoff should look into whether Zen is supplying North Korea with weapons of mass destruction," Al said.

Karzoff looked at Mal for approval.

Mal nodded to confirm, "Do it."

Al continued. "Robert, can you get the coordinates of a Watcher, please? After the concert on Saturday... maybe Monday, I fancy paying one of them a visit."

The hiatus of global peace generated by Alice's encounter with En-Lil had been nothing but an aberration. Within a short period of time, all of the usual suspects were back at sabre rattling. The Middle East had picked up hostilities from where it had left off, and every other hotspot on the planet had gone back to doing its best to blow humanity away. In the meantime, the biggest battle of all—man versus the environment—was still being totally ignored.

As a result, Alice had decided not to watch the morning News on television any longer. If it wasn't fake News, then it was propaganda... and newsreaders were no longer reading the news but providing their own personal opinion of it, and that wasn't good enough: there were far too many opinions.

For the stability and sanity of mankind, to stop it from imploding, there needed to be rules—rules like in a game of football, clear-cut... black and white with no grey areas. Society needed to get back to not being politically correct and corroded by alternative truths. The

News needed to ethically report facts only. Greed needed to be totally eradicated, borders made redundant, and money made obsolete.

After all he'd experienced in time travel, Alice was now convinced more than ever that humankind needed a huge fright: a wake-up call. A universal threat was the only way left to unify the species, and he believed that threat was approaching... he could feel it in his bones. The question was, will it come from the Watchers, or will it come from En-Lil?

For Jax De Ville, it was Thursday, 9 p.m. in New York, and for Viktoria, it was midday Friday in Sydney. Jax dialled her.

"Viktoria, it's Jax. I hope I haven't caught you at a bad time?"

"No, Jax, it's midday here. I'm at my desk. How are you?"

"I'm fine, and you?"

"All good. Alice just got back from 2112, so we're busy digesting all he had to report."

"Wow, 2112... that's amazing. Um, the reason for my call is that I wanted to bring you up to speed on Blake. He called me earlier from Papeete... he's safely back out of the jungle, thank goodness."

"I'm glad."

"He reached the ruin and found, as we had predicted, all access points buried under rubble. They did a good job. So, he's flying out tomorrow, but I thought there's still a way to block the dam... if Luna at UNTT was to let World Heritage know that it could still be accessed by the same means that got Alice and Vee in there, by a wormhole... then we could send in a team to excavate the An-Zu bird and other precious artefacts. What do you think?"

"Luna is still in Sydney. I was at a meeting with her this morning. Leave it with me; I'll get back to you."

"Thanks loads, Vik."

"Don't miss the Avalon Rock Concert tomorrow your time... Black Alice is the headline band."

"Already locked in, Vik. It's big news over here."

Honor arrived at a Kings Cross café to rendezvous with Denning and Hitz. They hadn't arrived, so she took a seat in the alfresco section to wait. The warm sun was beating down on her face from a clear blue sky, and sparrows were flying in to land on vacated tables to scavenge for meagre leftovers.

It wasn't long before Hitz and Denning arrived and joined her.

"Have you ordered?" Hitz asked Honor.

"Not yet."

Hitz whistled to attract the waiter.

Honor didn't like it. "Did you have to do that?"

"What would you rather me do, stand on the table?" Toeghan snapped.

Honor rolled her eyes at her ill-mannered antics.

The waiter arrived, and they ordered.

After he'd gone, Denning said, "We intercepted an email last night from Black Alice's road manager Tippy Lane to the lighting director of the concert, a dude called Wildcat. We learned Mal Low will be making a cameo appearance with Black Alice to sing a song called Fighting for You, the last song of the Black Alice set."

"Oh good... very, very good," Honor said, very nearly cracking a smile. "What is the plan then?"

"Well, this new information changes things," Denning said. "You need to make a choice, Alice or Low, one or the other. I doubt I'll get a chance to whack them both."

Honor sat back in her chair to think. The orders arrived. Once they were alone again, she took a sip of her piccolo espresso, savoured the taste, and then said, "Try for both, but the key target remains Malcolm Low."

CHAPTER 25
THE BIG GIG

AFTER SPEAKING WITH Dr Cairn about Jax De Ville's idea, Viktoria decided to call Jax to let her know the outcome. It was 10 p.m. Friday, Sydney time, and 7 a.m. Friday in New York.

"Jax, it's Viktoria... I haven't called you too early, have I?"

"No, no, I've been up all night anyway, Vik."

"Why... what's up?" Viktoria asked, concerned.

"I went to JFK airport to pick up Blake, but he wasn't on the flight. I panicked and called him but only got his message bank. Then hours later, I got a call, didn't say who, but he told me Blake will be kept hostage until World Heritage formally backs down and the dam goes ahead. If I persist, he said Blake would never be seen or heard of again."

"Oh my God, that's criminal." She could hear Jax sobbing. "Take it easy, love. You need a clear head. Listen... Luna said she will help."

"It's no use, Vik. They'll kill him. These people are bad news... they mean business."

Vik thought about it. Jax was right; it had to be handled correctly, or it could have serious consequences.

"I'll have a word with Karzoff, our head of security. Blake is a citizen of Oceana; the government should be able to help. If necessary, I'll take it to the President. Just stay cool, don't do anything rash, and call me if you hear from them again. Okay?"

Jax sniffled, "Yes, thanks so much, Vik. I've got no-one else to turn to."

"It's okay, Jax. I'm here for you, mate."

Vik terminated the call, went into Karzoff's office next to hers, and brought him up to speed on the situation. He advised her not to risk saying anything more to Dr Cairn for the time being until he'd briefed Mal and got his reaction.

Vik was pleased. "Oh, I know everything is set with security for the Avalon concert tomorrow, but I just wanted to know, for us, will it be handguns only?"

Karzoff put down the hard copy of the security layout for the gig he'd been studying and said, "Yes. You know I have an uncomfortable feeling about this concert. I have made a habit of trusting my gut over the years, so I think we should move to high alert."

"That will mean a lot more communication between agents... we'll have twenty-five of them there."

"Can you handle it?" he asked.

Viktoria smiled. It was right up her alley. "Absolutely, just leave it to me, boss."

Mal was wrapping up to leave the office for the evening when Rita came in.

"Everything is set for the big gig tomorrow," Mal said, relaxing back in his chair stretching, "I can hardly wait."

"Karzoff just called," Rita said, "asked for an audience... said it would only take a couple of minutes."

Mal yawned. "Okay, it's been a long day. Tell him to come up. You can go now. I'll see you at the concert... you're going with brother Johnny, aren't you?"

"Yes, World has a bus, should be fun. Good night, sir."

"Good night, Rita," Mal said, and then returned to reading a document.

A few minutes later, Karzoff knocked on the door.

Alice opened the door to his Kings Cross flat. It was small and dingy compared to Vee's luxurious apartment or even the room he had at OTT. But with all its failings, it still had heaps of character and felt and smelt like home to him. He was there to collect his stage gear for the Avalon gig the next day. Methodical with all things concerning performances, he kept his stage outfits sealed in plastic suit bags in his wardrobe, safe from moths and silverfish.

He opened the wardrobe doors and stood back thinking.

"The black leather, that's us," En-Ki said in his mind.

"Didn't know you were into goth?"

"I am one of the original Goths, my friend. As a matter of fact, I met the first Goth Kings; they were the Getae or Thracians from what is Romania today... they were descended from Gog and Mogog, mentioned by your friend Ezekiel."

"Ezekiel, what a cool guy... yeah, we'll go with the black leather then." He took the outfit out of the wardrobe and laid it on the bed.

"Hey, listen, do you know anything about these Watchers that keep turning up?" Al queried.

"They have been monitoring Earth for eons."

"So, are they extra-terrestrials?"

"Yes, I know you've got in mind visiting them, but you won't be able to do that through a wormhole; you'll need the An-Zu craft. It is, after all, one of theirs. But I must remind you... finding the Gorrick possessed by En-Lil must remain your priority."

Al took a deep breath, tired of all things En-Lil. "Yeah, yeah, no worries... but hey, you're not helping much. What is it, you just along for the ride?"

"I will be here when you need me, Alice, and that time is rapidly approaching."

"You're getting me worried, old son. You drop stuff like that, and it totally freaks me out. You know something I don't?"

"That goes without saying, Alice."

"Smartarse," he joked. "You know what I mean."

"Put it this way, by all means secure 2112 as best you can if it helps your guilt. Treat the sufferers of Red Wheel, repopulate the timeline if need be, but you must alter the timeline to prevent the Cyberwars from ever happening."

"What do you mean by 'my guilt'?" Alice questioned.

"No matter what you do to help the 2112 timeline, it is doomed to failure: the extinction of humankind... to avoid that, the only way to alter the outcome is by changing the timeline. I am here to ensure you do that."

The Professor, Hope, and Secta were hard at it in the lab. Time, just like when you're at the computer surfing the net, had just flicked by—it was midnight before they knew it.

The Professor whipped off his glasses and uncharacteristically blew up. "Goddam En-Ki... I can't get anywhere finding this bloody Velodium!"

Secta and Hope were busy trying to resolve a number of issues related to the production of Clock Drives and IVR for over fifty-year-old females.

"Don't worry, Vic," Secta said. "I'll have a chat with Alice about it once the concert is out of the way."

"Alice? How's he going to help?" Vic questioned, unaware Alice was hosting En-Ki.

"Oh... um," Secta stammered, almost inadvertently putting his foot in it. "Alice might be able to get a message to En-Ki."

The Professor got up from his chair and, polishing his glasses with the sleeve of his coat, walked around the centre bench to Secta.

"I didn't know that was possible. It would save a lot of time if En-Ki could tell us where to get hold of a supply of this mysterious element."

"Copy that... but you know what bothers me most? That cyborg we brought back was totally organic. Otherwise, it wouldn't have made it through Kairos. So that raises several questions. First, it must have been designed purposely for time travel... so does that mean coming back through Kairos was premeditated? It would have taken quite some time to build a totally organic cyborg, and there would be no other reason for doing it if not for time travel. Second, a cyborg so sophisticated that it fooled us into believing it was human with no human DNA would require, aside from all of its other features, a very special organic processor. It goes without saying that processor would be superior to ours. We must conclude Zen is now in possession of way superior technology than us, and that once they have replicated the processor, they will have superior time travel capability."

"That is a massive set of problems," the Professor agreed.

Hope looked over her reading glasses at Secta and said, "Are you saying it was a setup and that Gorrick in 2112 had prepared the new cyborg to send back either through their system or—"

"Aquila," the Professor informed her.

"Right, or Kairos?" Hope said.

"Yes, I think so, which means they have a way of communicating with the future."

"Einstein would love that one... but seriously, why go to all that trouble?" the Professor questioned.

"Maybe to stop us from changing the timeline to prevent the Cyberwars," Secta proposed.

Saturday began with a newsbreak that rocked the entire civilized world. A whistle-blower had gone viral on the net, claiming a new mind control ray was targeting individuals from a military satellite. The effects of the ray varied but included; total mind control, seizures, dementia. As a result of the disclosure, civilians in thousands were reporting symptoms. Recognised scientists from Harvard and Oxford were being interviewed and confirming the world had entered into a new era of weaponization. No longer was it necessary to drop bombs, fire missiles, or even use an army, a navy, or the air force... electromagnetic mind control was cheaper and far less destructive to infrastructure, and it was way more effective than nuclear weapons. It was further reported by experts in advanced warfare that wars could now be fought using mind control manipulation from the sky with robots on the ground to mop up. This generated a conspiracy fear that billionaires, intent on culling the population, had invested in developing vaccines for influenza that contain messenger mRNA, a switch if you like, that could be manipulated by 5G wireless broadcasts to trigger a multitude of health problems, particularly in the elderly.

The massive double gates in the temporary fence erected around Avalon were about to be opened for the thousands of fans lined up to enter. Karzoff and Viktoria were the first from OTT to arrive. After showing their IDs to security at the VIP gate, they were directed backstage. They paused to admire the towering speakers on either side of the twenty-five-metre wide stage. Behind them, the vast open area for the audience and the mosh pit held two more massive columns of speakers to ensure quadraphonic sound. In the centre of the rear, on a raised platform with a canopy over it, stood the 48-channel XL4 mixing console for the front of house, busy with road crew members. To the right of the FOH mixer was an equally sizable digital lighting console, and to its left, an FX console. A twenty-metre metal tower stood behind all of this, where the main broadcast camera was being set up for the wide shot. The OB wagon for the broadcast was in the car park. A cable was in the process of being linked to the stage to carry a flying fox camera, while a small team tested drone cameras.

Karzoff and Viktoria moved on. "I will be positioned for the main concert tonight behind the front of house mixer," Karzoff told her.

"You gave yourself the best seat in the house and sold me the corner by the fold-back mixer."

"No complaints, Vik. You will have the best view of the bands from there."

They passed through more checkpoints to enter the backstage area. Karzoff stopped to inspect a massive crane with a gigantic flying saucer suspended from it. "What is that?" he asked.

"Didn't you read the rider? That UFO will descend to just above the stage during Alice's performance. It should be amazing, coming out of the night sky with lights all over it."

"Oh yes, now I remember... Argh! Information overload," Karzoff admitted.

They continued to a line of caravans, each marked with the logo of a corresponding band. They walked past caravans marked "Management" and "Press" before arriving at the smallest caravan marked "OTT."

"That's us," Viktoria said.

"Why so small? Are we less important?"

"I guess so," she said with a facetious little snigger. Viktoria used the key card to open the door, and they entered. They were surprised to find it more spacious than expected.

"It's quite comfy," she said, flopping into one of the four lounge chairs. The space had a computer terminal, a four-seater lounge, a bar, a small kitchenette, and a toilet.

"All the amenities of home," Karzoff said, nodding his head approvingly.

As the first band hit the stage at 1 p.m., the venue was nearing capacity with at least sixty thousand enthusiastic fans. The police presence was minimal, so the crowd was well-behaved, although it was expected to get rowdier by the time Black Alice took the stage.

At 7 p.m., the chopper carrying Alice, Vee, Secta, the Professor, Hope, Turk, and Morri touched down behind the caravans backstage. Mal and Luna were due to arrive shortly in a smaller chopper. Alice and Vee were escorted by Tippy to the Black Alice band caravan, while the others joined Karzoff and Viktoria in the OTT unit.

Karzoff stood up to greet the others. "Come in, welcome. Help yourselves to a drink; canapés will be served up soon. These are your backstage passes." He distributed the passes.

"Hey, this is great," the Professor said, hanging the pass around his neck.

In his trademark organising manner, Karzoff continued, "Okay, who wants to watch the entire show?" They all indicated their interest. "Good, well, I will be at the front of house mixing console at the rear, overlooking the stage. Viktoria will be on stage in the wings near the fold-back mixer. It would be safer for you not to be in the mosh pit. You have a choice: either with me or Viktoria?"

Only Turk wanted to watch with Karzoff. "Alright," Karzoff said, carrying on. "Tippy told us Cried Wolf will take the stage at 7:30, which is in... um... twenty minutes. Turk, we should head there now. If you want, grab a drink first..."

Just then, two waiters entered with four trays of canapés. Karzoff and Turk helped themselves to food and drinks before leaving for the front of the house. Viktoria took over to organize the others in a more relaxed manner.

Gorrick, Khan, and Honor were in the communications room at Zen HQ, gathered to watch the concert live on TV. They would also monitor Glan Denning's effort to eliminate either Alice or Mal, or both, on a dedicated monitor beside the large flat television screen. Currently blank, it would soon display a feed from Denning at Avalon.

After battling through a sea of fans, Karzoff and Turk finally made it to the front of the house area. There, they presented their IDs for entry. The head engineer introduced himself as Jinny T and then introduced them to Wildcat. Taking up a position on a couple of stools, they positioned themselves out of the way of the technicians directly behind the desk and its massive FX rack. This vantage point gave them an unimpeded view of the stage.

CHAPTER 26
LONE ASSASSIN

I T WASN'T LONG before a massive roar erupted from the fans as Lemmy led the other four members of Cried Wolf onto the stage. Heart rates soared in the control area as the techies readied themselves for action.

A lull followed, and the lighting remained dim. The audience hushed, a sense of anticipation filling the air. Then Lemmy ambled over to the microphone, took it off the stand, and held it at his side, gazing contemplatively at the vast audience.

Jinny T knew what to expect next. He pushed up the faders and deftly adjusted a vocal harmonizer in the FX rack. Wildcat was poised to trigger the lighting program, ready to infuse his creative skills for additional manual lighting effects.

As Lemmy shouted at the audience, they shouted back in unison, knowing exactly how he would start the set. The air reverberated with the roar of "One, two, three... four!" Counted in, the band erupted into a thrash metal explosion. A blinding burst of white light engulfed the stage as Lemmy launched into the song "Game Keepers." The audience responded with a sea of devil's horns punching the air in time with the music.

The music raged without respite right through the forty-five-minute set, and then Lemmy, a ball of sweat by then, exhausted, ended the set with a massive bird to the audience who loved it. The band stalked off stage to cheers of more, more, more. But there wouldn't be an encore. The lights faded down and Jinny T, Wildcat and the crew off and on stage, reset everything including the drum kit and amps for the next act.

Minutes later, the house lights dimmed even further, reigniting anticipation. A deep and gravelly voice resonated through the PA, its rumble felt in everyone's boots. "I'm the thing from the sky, with a horn... and I'm high. You're gonna shake, I guarantee... becoz—?"

The monologue paused for the audience to respond, "You look like a purple people eater to me!"

A skinny longhaired guy named Pretzel, his topless body painted purple, his long hair purple, wearing only a pair of purple boxer shorts and purple converse sneakers, bounced out to centre stage with a spring in his heels, grabbed the mike and yelled, "What?" in a Scottish accent.

The audience shouted back, "You look like a purple people eater to me!"

Pretzel feigned unhappiness, signalling that it wasn't loud enough. He shouted again, "I canna hear yer!"

From the darkness behind him, the other four band members crept out, taking up their positions with their instruments.

The crowd roared again, much louder, "You look like a purple people eater to me!"

That was the cue. Jinny T pushed up the faders, Wildcat hit the program button, and the band exploded into a punk power metal song called "Lick It" that even surpassed the energy of Cried Wolf. Pretzel was easily the most dynamic frontman ever. He couldn't stand still, leaping over the fold-back speakers, climbing amps, and jumping off them. He trusted the fans to catch him when he dived into the mosh pit, passing him spread-eagle through the crowd before tossing him back on stage—never missing a beat, singing all the while.

They closed the set with their moderate hit song "Cannibal Kisses." As they exited the stage to the roaring response of the fans, the stage plunged into darkness, giving the crowd a moment to catch their collective breath. The audience hadn't stopped headbanging and leaping about during the hour-long set.

Turk observed the security guards carrying out collapsed fans one after another. They were utterly spent from the sheer intensity of the experience.

During the break between acts, Turk surveyed the security layout. It was a survival habit he couldn't shake off since his days in the Cyberwars. He identified four types of security personnel: a small contingent of uniformed police, a significant number of general security personnel sporting fluorescent red vests, and uniformed Oceana agents armed with assault rifles stationed at specific sentry points, including one right behind him at the base of the camera tower. Less conspicuous were the plainclothes security agents. Like Karzoff, they were identifiable only by their military-like demeanour, wearing grey suits, sporting military hairstyles, and always having a communication earpiece. Placed strategically, they were under Viktoria's direct command. Turk deduced that the tactical armed guards were under Karzoff's jurisdiction.

He was also captivated by the control Wildcat wielded over the extensive array of lights on the trusses encircling the stage. Although most of the lights had yet to be employed, Wildcat had manually directed several searchlights high up on the truss across the stage's front, causing them to sweep the audience during both performances. Periodically, Wildcat had to use a monocular to check the stage lighting grid status due to the considerable distance between the stage and his position.

As the road crew exited the stage, the atmosphere shifted—it was already distinctly different from the previous two bands. Even the anticipation felt distinct, more ethereal. This time, it was about cerebral classic progressive rock rather than metal.

A rear-projected film of Glastonbury Tor in England at dawn, shrouded in a mystical mist around its base, gradually appeared on a massive screen in a wide shot. The screen spanned the entire rear of the stage. Suspended notes from violins added to the mystique, followed by the toll of a distant bell. As the enigmatic introduction played out, the members of World took their positions on stage in the darkness. Over the suspended note, a god-like voice resonated through the PA.

"We seek to find ourselves

We have come far but we do not yet stand a united species.

While some plunder nature

Others feast on the misery of the downtrodden.

We cannot venture into space without humility and understanding

Proof, that we are humane.

Proof, that we care for the world we share with other animals.

Until that time comes, we explore to find our inner god

And we dare... to dream..."

The keyboardist played a mystical melody, and an angelic choir of voices gradually swelled into a crescendo. A grand piano played four distinct notes. A single spotlight illuminated Johnny Vallins at the centre of the stage, his bass guitar in hand. He looked as though he had emerged from a time machine, a direct transplant from a 1960s psychedelic conceptual band. Thunder rumbled. Johnny sang the opening lines of their epic song, 'Avalon.' At the conclusion of the first verse, the entire band joined in, unleashing their full hard rock power as Johnny launched into the main body of the song.

The piece spanned ten minutes, progressing through four distinct movements, culminating in Adrian Wyatt stepping into the spotlight for an epic, blistering guitar solo. The lighting effects were extraordinary, and the film projected behind the band was mesmerising. The song concluded with a thunderous ovation from the audience.

World's repertoire transitioned seamlessly into a musical narrative that denounced the world's wrongs, from political despotism to avarice, hatred, and fear—capturing all the negative aspects of humanity. As World wrapped up their ninety-minute performance with the song 'Upside Down,' the audience was utterly captivated. The technical crew sprang into action once again, swiftly resetting the stage for the headlining act, Black Alice.

Backstage, Al was stalking up and down the caravan typically as nervous as a cat, while Ratsso, Blue and Slut ignored him calmly chatting about football. Vee was sitting next to Ratsso watching Al.

"Is he always like that?" Vee asked.

"Yeah, you can't even talk to him before he goes on," Ratsso replied.

Blue chipped in, "Sometimes he even throws up, he's so nervous."

"Reckon he'd be used it by now," Slut moaned, and then took a big drag of a roach, almost burning his fingers.

"He's got heaps to get right, yer big dill," Ratsso scoffed.

"Yeah, you gotta have a brain to sort that stuff out," Blue laughed, having a dig at Slut.

"Don't need any brains to play drums though, do yer Blue?" Slut graciously returned serve, all in good fun.

Tippy came in and said, "Okay boys, yer on. Break a leg, Al."

Al stopped pacing and shot her a warm smile. Almost instantly, his nerves disappeared. He was set to go. He peeled off his leather jacket, pumped his arms, turned to the boys and said gruffly, "Okay, fellas let's nail it."

Vee followed them out of the caravan, into the backstage area past the other band members who had stayed to catch Black Alice, and then along the race into the stage wing where they stopped and waited.

Tippy joined Vee and said, "Exciting isn't it?"

"You're not kidding," Vee exclaimed, her hand on her thumping heart, she took a deep breath.

Turk could tell by Jinny T and Wildcat's movements the band was about to come on. The ambience was different again to the previous bands. The audience was anxiously waiting for the headline act. They had come to expect the unexpected with Black Alice.

Wildcat moved first. He manually powered up a searchlight that was on the camera tower behind them to strike the UFO that was now suspended from the crane behind the stage and being slowly lowered. Lights were rotating around the base of the triangular shaped craft. It was all happening in silence. The audience was transfixed on the giant UFO that looked incredibly real. It stopped, as though hovering about ten metres directly over the stage. Then Wildcat triggered a spot that lit up a giant Marshall stack stage right. The band members with the exception of Alice were in position. Ratsso stage left... Blue centre stage on a riser behind his gigantic kit, and Slut, stage right just to the side of the spotlight.

The front of the Marshall stack flew open. The band opened up with the song 'Power Crazy' and through a wall of smoke billowing out of the stack of amps, rode Alice astride a Harley Davidson Chopper.

A narrow runway had been extended front of stage that he drove out on and stopped at the end. He stepped off the bike to the cheers of the audience and waited for the bike to sink down inside the runway. A big arrogant leer at and he cruised back along the runway to the mike stand centre stage, perfectly timing it to launch into the song. The extension stage retracted.

Now Wildcat was using the full-compliment of lights. They audience was going off.

The revelry continued non-stop for the ninety minutes of songs. Then after performing the sultry ballad, 'Tonight There Is Love', Al spoke to the fans.

"Hey, how goes it? Is this great or what?"

He held the mike out for the audience to respond. "Great, Alice, great!" A hundred thousand voices echoed.

He had them in the palm of his hand.

Gorrick glanced away from the TV broadcast at Honor and said, "Is there anything this guy can't do?"

"Maybe he will die on stage tonight," she said with a macabre snigger.

"The next song is an old favourite, and a mate of mine, in his band the Units, also performed it... so I'm going to ask him to come out here to sing it with me. Give it up for the President of Oceana, Malcolm Low; Fighting for You!"

There was a mixture of boos and cheers in anticipation of Mal coming on stage. There came a pause. Then, he surprised them all, dressed like the rock singer he was in the Units, Mal strode confidently onto stage. The band cranked up and Mal launched into an energetic, amazing rendition of the song. When it was time for Slut to step forward for his solo, Al took another mike and announced, "And my sister Vee!"

Standing in the wings, Vee was shocked. She pointed to herself wide-eyed as if to say, "Why me?" Tippy pushed her onto the stage, "Go out there and join your brother, girl."

Vee ran out onto the stage and the audience went off. Al handed her a mike and she launched into the backing vocals. The three of them were singing up a storm in the outro of the song.

Turk found himself cheering, and then he heard something out of place. A familiar sound... cutting through the music was a noise that had always freaked him out... an attack drone. Sensing danger, he rushed over to Wildcat and shouted at him above the music, "Aim the searchlight there," he pointed. Wildcat would normally brush someone telling him what to do, but Turk didn't look the type to be brushed off, so he did as instructed.

The searchlight lit up the drone. Turk grabbed the monocular off the lighting desk and studied the drone through it.

Karzoff came up beside him and asked, "It is just a camera drone."

"No, it's not. It's an assassin drone and it's armed," he swivelled around. "Karzoff, order that guard to surrender his weapon to me."

Karzoff hesitated and then thought the better of it. He ordered the sentry to hand over his Heckler & Koch UMP-45 submachine gun to Turk. Turk checked it out... it was fitted with a laser scope—it would do the job. He turned to Wildcat and barked, "Wildcat... keep the searchlight on the drone."

Then, to Karzoff's surprise, he went over to the camera tower and powered up the metal ladder in a huge hurry. Turk knew there was no time, the drone could fire at any second... he figured it was just manoeuvring into position to get the best shot. Alice, Vee, and Mal were now singing the chorus outro, oblivious to the drone and the drama playing out behind the scenes. The audience also had no idea.

Turk reached the platform at the top of the camera tower. The lone cameraman took a quick peek away from the camera eyepiece at Turk, saw the rifle, and went back to filming. Turk rested his arms on the front rail of the platform and took aim at the target.

"Fire, fire! Damn it!" Honor shouted angrily into the headset she was wearing. "Why are you taking so long?" she growled.

Glan Denning and Toeghan Hitz were in the back of a van parked a few kilometres away from the concert. Denning was handling the drone control. Toeghan was watching a monitor, which carried the POV from the drone. Denning was getting an earful from Honor and irritably tore off his headset. "She's a pain in the arse!"

"Take it easy mate, just line up the shot," Toeghan said.

The crosshairs were on Alice's forehead.

The drone was directly in line with Turk about fifty metres away between him and the stage. He flicked on the laser pointer and looked through the night scope.

The drone fired. The shot missed Al and hit the ride cymbal on Blue's kit. Playing a fill, Blue saw the cymbal shudder and wondered what the hell it was.

A red bead appeared on the drone.

Turk pulled the trigger, once, twice, and then a third time in rapid succession.

The drone swerved sharply sideways.

Gorrick, Khan, and Honor watched the descent of the drone into the fence. The picture went to static. "Seems we just witnessed the failure of yet another assassination attempt. I'm glad Brigadier Bruckmaster wasn't here," Gorrick said, sourly.

"We have a backup plan, sir," Honor said, almost swallowing the words with embarrassment.

"Cancel it… Stand your people down, we won't be needing them again." He stormed out.

Khan glanced at Honor and said glumly, "You can understand his vexation."

Turk stepped off the ladder and handed the guard back his weapon.

Karzoff patted him thankfully on the back. "Well done, Turk, great shooting. I think you might have just saved three very important lives."

The song 'Fighting For You' finished, the fans were going off. They cheered for Mal; there were no more boos. Al called the members of the other bands back on stage to join in an encore performance of the Black Alice song, 'Organic Panic.'

When it was all done, Al and Mal took a bow, and then Al called Tippy on stage for the audience to applaud her great work. He thanked all the technical staff and road crews, the sponsors, and the other bands, and then handed the microphone over to Mal. He announced that all of the revenue from the concert would be donated to The Orphan Charity, and that got a rousing reception. Only Turk, Karzoff, Vinny T, Wildcat, the TV cameraman, and the guard knew that both Alice and Mal had come within an inch of losing their lives… although Gorrick, Khan, Honor, Glan Denning, and Toeghan Hitz knew but would rather forget it.

CHAPTER 27
PLAYED

NEXT DAY, THE newspapers were awash with photographs of Mal's cameo performance at the concert and the story of his generous donation to The Orphan Charity. It had been an unprecedented success. Mal was firmly back in favour.

Al was having breakfast with Vee and Tippy on the balcony of the Coogee apartment when Mal phoned. Both girls were in towelling robes while Al was in his underpants.

Al strolled over to the balustrade to peg the view while talking to Mal. When he finished, he came back and put the phone on the table with a furious look on his stubbly face.

"What's up, Al? Looks like someone pinched your lunch money," Vee asked jokingly.

But Al was serious. "It was Mal, apparently, a drone was set to take a pot shot at him or me or you or all three of us last night. If it hadn't been for the quick thinking of Turk. He was at the mixing desk, saw it, took a guard's rifle, climbed the bloody broadcast tower, and shot the thing out of the air before it could take us out."

"Hey, funny you should say that, Blue said something hit his ride cymbal during 'Fighting For You' and put a bloody great dent in it," Tippy recounted.

"Must've been a bullet from the drone that missed," Al said.

Vee was shocked. "Wow, how cool is Turk?"

"You're not kidding. Mal wants to give him a medal, but Turk wouldn't have any of it, just another day in the life for him," Al said with a chuckle.

"Who do they reckon did it?" Tippy asked.

"You'd have to have your dosh on Zen, but Mal reckons it was Toeghan Hitz," Al said.

"What, the bird from the New Octagon? Why would they want to kill anyone? They're a peace movement, aren't they?" Vee questioned.

"I'll catch you guys later," Al said, cruising back inside.

"Where are you going, Al?" Vee called out.

"To meet Mal," Al answered from inside.

"Since you reported Holman spying on Vee, I put a cyber watch on Vee's broadband," Karzoff told them. "It flagged an intercept of an email from Tippy Lane to Wildcat. I thought nothing of it at the time until the incident last night. The email was the lighting plan, and it mentioned that in song twelve, a special guest code-named Unit would join you on stage, Al. It would not have taken much work to find out Unit related to the band The Units, of which Mal Function used to be the lead singer. The intercept had the New Octagon IP address."

"Yep, that was a dumb call by me... too bloody obvious," Al growled.

They were seated in the lounge setting of the President's office.

"What do you think, Mal?" Karzoff asked.

"Round them up," Mal said, angrily. "Do it now, Karzoff."

Just then Viktoria came in, looking all flustered. "Sorry I'm late, did I miss anything?"

Karzoff was already out of his seat, keen to get on with the arrest, and told her, "I'll fill you in... come with me."

"Just a moment. Sir, remember to have a word with Al about Blake."

"Oh, thanks for reminding me, Vik," Mal said.

Karzoff and Viktoria left.

"What's this about Blake?" Al asked.

"Jax De Ville called Viktoria to tell her Blake has been kidnapped in Papeete and ransomed. The kidnapper said he wouldn't release him until World Heritage gives the go-ahead to the Poo Ôonoo Valley dam. If he hears nothing within a week, then Blake will never be seen again."

"Bloody hell, it never rains, it pours," Alice complained. "You got anything stronger than coffee, mate?"

Mal got up, went over to the bookcase that concealed a small bar, and returned with a bottle of JD and a couple of glasses.

"Better make it three; I asked Turk here."

Just then Turk came in.

"Sit down, mate, and have a drink. Thanks for what you did last night," Al said, thoughtfully.

"Just lucky I recognised the damned awful sound of the attack drone," Turk said, with a groan.

Mal poured the drinks. Doling them out, he asked, "What's the difference between the sound of a normal drone and an attack drone?"

"They have to use a much more powerful engine to keep it stabilized when shooting... recoil... so it gives off a different whirring sound. Used to hear them day in, day out during the Cyberwars. Stuck in a bloody foxhole in the night with those things zooming overhead, sometimes ours, sometimes theirs. You learn pretty quick to differentiate between types."

"Well," Mal raised his glass, "thank goodness you can. Cheers to you, Turk, we both owe you big time."

"No mate, happy to oblige," Turk said, with humility. They drank the toast and then Turk asked, "Any idea who it was?"

"Karzoff is on his way with Viktoria to arrest the culprits now," Mal said.

"Zen is behind it. We figure they used a peace movement as cover for the hit," Al said.

"I was going to say it sounds like Zen," Turk agreed.

"So Mal, tell me more about the situation with Blake?" Al asked.

"He is, of course, one of ours—"

"Wait a minute, what do you mean one of ours?" Al quizzed.

"He's a field agent, specialising in the black-market trade of artefacts," Mal explained.

Al was shocked. He'd taken Blake on face value as an archaeologist.

"Okay, so does Jax know that?"

"No, but we know she has an affiliation with the CIA."

"What?"

"So, here's what really happened... when Kew came out of the Poo Ôonoo Valley, he told Zen about the An-Zu bird. Jax informed the CIA about it, and French Intelligence found out, probably through the Tahiti Hydroelectric Commission. After we heard the entry points to the ruins had been blown, we sent Blake back from New York to Tahiti to confirm it, and the French Intelligence grabbed him. They want him to lead them to the An-Zu bird."

"Wait a minute, they don't need Blake, they've got Louis Sens," Al protested.

"Sens never made it out of the jungle, Al. We think Kew killed him before he found you."

Al was nodding his head—it made sense. "Go on," he said grumpily.

"The explosions, just like the dam project, were a cover... there really isn't a dam project, not there anyway. You see, Jax had been exploring the possibility of the An-Zu bird since she was in the Middle East. She'd spent years there hunting down evidence of it. Now we have a situation with everyone wanting to get their claws on the craft, the French, the CIA via our old friend Bruckmaster, Zen, and we're in it up to our necks."

"And don't forget the Watchers, it is theirs after all," En-Ki said in Al's mind.

"And the Watchers... they want it back," Al said.

"The Watchers, why? How do you know?" Mal asked, intrigued.

"I get messages from En-Ki. The craft belongs to them... they don't want it here, probably because they don't want the technology to fall into our hands. All of them want it to reverse engineer."

Mal was taken aback by what Al had said. But it made perfect sense to him.

"I think they want me to get it and return it... basically, if it's captured by these hoons, it will probably affect the timeline because it really shouldn't be here," Al proposed. "Mind you, it's only a theory, as Secta would say."

"Why can't the Watchers just get it, they've got all the technology?" Mal submitted.

"I thought about that as well, there must be a reason... maybe because it's trapped by the cave-in or because we've got the sceptre: the drive mechanism."

"The latter is probably correct. Sorry to bore you with all this, Turk," Mal said, apologetically.

"No problem, are these Watchers UFOs?" Turk asked.

"Yes," Al said.

"I wonder if they're the same as the ones seen over Canberra just before the attack? You might recall Frank reckoned a UFO fired the weapon that took Canberra out. Since then, we've seen plenty of them."

"That's interesting," Al said. "I wonder why?"

"Which brings me to a question if I might?" Turk asked.

"Sure, fire away," Mal said.

"Last night after the gig, Secta took Morri, Hope, and I into the bunker. The entrance was just behind the row of caravans, backstage. Anyhow, it was weird down there for us, you know, to think that in the same place in the future folk are dying there from Red Wheel... it felt haunted... we could almost hear the screams of pain. And now we have a cure. So, we talked about it, and Morri and I want to go back and help... it would be safer now that you've killed Gorrick, Al."

"Tell him Gorrick will just be replaced. That timeline leads to extinction. Alice," En-Ki told Alice mentally.

"I might have killed him mate, but Gorrick will be replaced.

There are around fifteen hundred clones of him worldwide, possible still in 2112," Al explained.

"They won't be able to do that quickly... by killing him you bought us time. If we can heal the sick, we still have a chance," Turk argued.

"But that timeline is destined for extinction mate, it's now we need to concern ourselves with... we have to stop the Cyberwars," Al urged.

"That's your timeline, Al, not ours... our timeline had already happened... the Cyberwars took place and we're dealing with trying to survive the consequences. Humankind finds a way mate, life finds a way... and it's our obligation to try and help it," Turk explained.

Al flopped back in his seat. He knew Turk was right. "What about Hope?"

"She wants to stay here to pick up from where her biological mother left off. Look, if we can't get approval for the cleansing to take place through Kairos, then I ask you, Mr President, to give us approval to go ahead anyway."

Mal was caught between a rock and a hard place. Turk had saved his life... in humanitarian or moral terms, he was absolutely right, it was their obligation to help if they could, but at the same time, he understood Luna's argument. The question he needed to ask himself was: is the future our responsibility, or is it more critical for that future for the temporal prime directive to be enforced?

"Let me get a result from the UN. If it's no, then you have my word we'll work with you. Alice, on the issue of Blake and the An-Zu bird... we can't let it fall into the wrong hands. It must be returned to the Watchers. What do you want to do?"

Al skulled his drink and put the glass on the coffee table while thinking. He flopped back in his seat, took a deep breath, and looked skyward, searching for divine intervention. "Nothing is ever what it seems, is it? We risked our lives going into Chernobyl to rescue Nimrod De Ville for Jax. The CIA could've done the job anyway, so why me?"

"Because you would always get it done without spilling blood, mate," Mal confirmed.

"I don't like being played, Mal... Okay, here it is; you buy Blake time with the French, I'll deliver the An-Zu to the Watchers, then get Blake out."

"Need a hand?" Turk said, with a big smile.

"Mate, with a hand the size of yours, how can I refuse... of course," Al said.

Al took Turk down to catch up with Secta, Hope, Morri, and the Professor in the labs. They were all anxiously awaiting the verdict from the UNTT. Vee was floored by Alice's claim that Jax is involved with Bruckmaster and that Blake is an Oceana agent, not under Karzoff's watch, but another secret government intelligence department. Al knew Vee fancied Blake and was upset by him being held hostage.

Secta had contacted a sperm donor organisation that had agreed to supply enough to fertilize all of the eggs Hope had harvested. The plan was to place a cryogenic container in the Avalon bunker for Morri to collect when she returned to the future. Hope would prepare instructions for Morri on how to fertilize the eggs for IVR once they had cleansed the infected women of Red Wheel.

The Professor and Secta had come up with a plan to cleanse 2112 of the disease. With approximately two thousand patients at the Avalon bunker and another four thousand at other bunkers in the vicinity, they figured that with fifty passing through Kairos per hour, it would only take them a week to get them all through Kairos for SAGE to do its job.

Alice raised the question about the destiny of all the infected souls in the death camp, and Turk maintained that getting them out to be cleansed was a priority. Once he could put together an able-bodied army free of Red Wheel, he would be able to take on Zen. But he reiterated that they needed to act fast, to get it done before Zen had the chance to install a new leader. He was confident after Al had demonstrated how easy it was to knock over an RF-20 with a WASP, that it was their new secret weapon.

Secta, Alice, and the Professor left the others in Hope's lab to have a discussion with Robert in the Kairos control room. However, when they arrived, Robert was nowhere to be found. While waiting for him, the Professor took the opportunity to bring up the subject of Velodium.

After explaining to Alice what Velodium was and the problem he had trying to find the element, En-Ki communicated to Alice in his mind, urging him to inform the Professor about his presence so he could explain. When Alice revealed the truth about En-Ki, the Professor was relieved.

"Just like with Neit, you can communicate with En-Ki, Vic. So, go ahead," Al clarified.

The Professor proceeded to explain to En-Ki how he had deciphered the formula left on the mainframe and that it all made sense except for the element Velodium, which was unknown on Earth.

En-Ki agreed that without the critical element, the Tablet wouldn't function as a superconductor or produce zero-point energy.

"Velodium is an element found on Ishtar," En-Ki informed Vic through Alice.

"Ishtar was a Sumerian goddess, wasn't she?" Secta asked.

"Oh, you might know her as Inanna," En-Ki corrected.

In the meantime, Alice had researched both names and came up with the answer, "Venus. He's talking about Venus. I thought I knew Ishtar; it was the name given to the girl I watched sacrificed on the steps of the Temple of Solomon," Alice explained.

The Professor was nodding his head. "Right, right... so it can be found in what... the atmosphere or on the surface?"

"Both," En-Ki confirmed.

"That's a massive problem; the atmosphere of Venus is volatile, it rains sulphuric acid," Secta said.

"Well, there is the drive propellant for the An-Zu craft; it is almost solid Velodium," En-Ki informed them.

"Is that on board the craft?" Secta asked.

"No, it's right here... the sceptre," Alice said, with a cheeky grin. "The bloody sceptre is Velodium, that's why it was important, and that's why it doesn't rust," Al clarified.

"So here is what you need to do," En-Ki explained.

CHAPTER 28
THE REVEAL

ALICE, HOPE, TURK, Vee, and Morri had to make a dash for it to get inside Café Epiphany before the rain came. Lunchtime pedestrians under umbrellas made it even more of an obstacle race. They managed to get inside just as a loud clap of thunder announced a downpour. The only table left was by the window, so they took it and sat down, watching the deluge outside causing a traffic jam.

"It's raining cats and dogs," Al remarked.

Turk tried to look at the sky through the window and asked, "Where?"

Hope giggled, "They don't use that phrase in 2112, Al. It means the rain is heavy."

Turk nodded, shrugged his shoulders, and then studied the menu. Vee was daydreaming, looking at the people struggling with their umbrellas outside, when she suddenly reacted.

"Al, look at who's getting out of that limo in the traffic outside? Your CIA agent friend, Holman."

Al slammed down the menu, jumped up, and rushed out of the café. The others watched him through the window.

"What's he doing?" Turk questioned.

"You know Al, never a dull moment," Hope remarked.

Outside, Al walked up to Holman, who was holding an umbrella while closing the rear passenger door of a limo. Another person with an umbrella was getting out on the other side of the limo, but Al was only interested in Holman.

He confronted Holman and snarled, "Holman, tell your boss Bruckmaster that your friends at Zen are racing you to the An-Zu bird!"

"You won't beat us to it, Alice," Holman spat back.

"Just deliver the message, you dig!" Al released his grip on Holman.

At the mention of the An-Zu bird, the other man turned to face Alice, holding an umbrella to shield himself from the rain.

"Well, well, look at what the cat dragged in, Gorrick!" Al quipped, his right arm cocked, ready to throw a punch.

"First time we've come face to face, Alice," Gorrick said smugly, looking down at him.

In Alice's mind, En-Ki urgently communicated, "Don't touch him Alice, it's En-Lil... if you do, he'd draw me out of you and I'll be gone."

Alice immediately eased off, avoiding any physical confrontation. Their eyes locked. With the rain pouring down on Al, he snarled, "I'll get you, En-Lil. I promise."

"En-Lil, aren't you perceptive? But of course, I know who you're hosting, don't I, En-Ki?" Gorrick taunted.

Drenched to the skin, Alice turned on his heel and left them to return to the café.

Vee jumped out of her seat and said, "You look like a drowned rat, Al." She removed her denim jacket and handed it to him. "Here, dry yourself."

"One minute it's raining cats and dogs, and now it's drowned rats. What's with these people and animals, blaming them for the weather?" Turk joked with Morri and Hope.

After drying himself off a bit, Al pulled out his phone and dialled. "Order for me, Vee. I need to speak with Mal."

He walked toward the entrance with determination. "Mal, I'm at Café Epiphany and just ran into CIA Holman... mate, the CIA is after the An-Zu bird."

"That's to be expected, Al. Our operative in Tahiti just informed me that French Intelligence has taken Blake into the Poo Ôonoo Valley to guide them to the craft."

"Don't know what they expect to achieve once they find it. They won't be able to fly it."

"I suppose they would work on getting it out somehow to reverse engineer," Mal suggested.

"Gorrick was also there. I'd just told Holman to inform Bruckmaster that Zen would be going after the An-Zu, when Gorrick got out of the limo. Should've seen their faces. I think I've instigated a war between them, which was the plan. I'm now certain that Gorrick is hosting En-Lil."

"How do you know?"

"Call it intuition. Alright, we better act quickly with all these bludgers converging on the An-Zu bird."

Gorrick was furious. He stormed into his office reception, barking orders at his PA Regina Fych to summon Honor, Adamski, and Li.

Meanwhile, Holman was pacing in the lobby of Zen HQ, talking on the phone with Bruckmaster in Texas. "He said to tell you Zen is going after something called the An-Zu bird and expects you to know what that is, sir," he said with a hint of sarcasm.

However, Bruckmaster wasn't amused. "Await my orders. Keep a close watch on Zen's movements."

Holman would have preferred a different outcome to the conversation.

It was 8 p.m. in Texas and 9 p.m. in New York when Bruckmaster phoned Jax.

Honor led Adamski and Li across the bridge to meet Gorrick on the office island. Khan was already seated, engaged in conversation with Gorrick. They took their seats and waited for Gorrick's attention.

"Is Cronus prepared for deployment?" Gorrick demanded.

They could sense his dark mood. Li answered, "Yes, sir. We're just waiting to load a profile."

Gorrick leaned forward, his focus sharpening. "And what plans do you have for Cronus?"

"I am open to suggestions," Li replied, looking to the others for input.

Gorrick turned his attention to Honor. "Who do you have in the security ranks? Someone on par with Voltaris Idram?"

Honor's arms were crossed defensively as she responded, "I've recruited someone from Zen UK, ex-SAS Commander Daniel Walker." She unfolded her arms, retrieved her phone, and sent a message. "Here is his CV, sir."

Gorrick leaned over and activated the computer on the coffee table. He perused Walker's CV. "Impressive. Very impressive indeed." His mood seemed to shift. "Have him report to Li. And Professor, what about protection for Cronus?"

"We've designed a titanium crown that can fit under a hairpiece. It's removable because we may need to utilise Cronus in Aquila, and metal—" Adamski began.

Gorrick cut him off, "Yes, yes, I'm aware. What about other vulnerable areas, such as its face?"

"I've reinforced the entire skull and throat with Graphene," Li explained.

"Why wasn't this done in the future?" Gorrick questioned.

"I have no information on that, sir," Li replied.

"Sir, regarding Aquila, it will take two to three weeks to produce the processor. I need to cultivate a SCOD: a symbiotic culture of DNA first. This culture will serve as the foundation for further processor production," Adamski clarified.

"Good. I want Walker ready to depart by first light tomorrow. Understood?" Gorrick's tone was firm.

"Yes, sir," they responded in unison. The three of them got up and exited the room.

Once they had left, Khan spoke up. "What's the plan now that you know Alice is hosting En-Ki?"

"If that fool Denning hadn't botched the drone attack so badly, we wouldn't be facing this problem. The responsibility now falls on Cronus. Killing Alice is just as crucial as destroying the An-Zu bird before anyone else can get to it," Gorrick declared.

Alice received a text from Secta that Robert was back, so he left the others at Café Epiphany to meet at the Kairos control room.

While Robert was checking something in the computer room, Alice told Secta and the Professor about his extemporaneous meeting with En-Lil, also known as Gorrick.

En-Ki expressed his concern. "That was not the ideal means of disclosing him because when I detected him, he detected me, and that places Alice in serious jeopardy."

"That makes sense, En-Ki," Secta said.

"I've just got to ignore it and get on with things, getting An-Zu out of there is all that matters for now," Al said.

"Two questions En-Ki, one, how does Alice take the sceptre with him, it won't go through Kairos and two, how will you get back from the Watcher once you've delivered the An-Zu?"

"Velodium can pass through the wormhole, so that answers your first question... it is to do with its atomic structure."

Secta and the Professor both raised their eyebrows realising the gravity of the breakthrough in Velodium being a metal that would transport through Kairos: it was the Holy Grail.

"In answer to your second question, just leave that to me but you will need the means to transport Vee and Turk out of the Poo Ôonoo site because Alice is planning on taking them with him," En-Ki explained further.

"A chance to try the Clock Drive update perhaps," The Professor said excitedly.

"Hey, you betrayed my plans!" Alice growled at En-Ki in his mind.

"Sorry," En-Ki said.

"So, what does this update do?" Al asked, just as Robert came out of the computer room.

"I've installed an algorithm in the Clock Drive that causes the wormhole to re-open when the Clock Drive comes within range," the Professor explained.

"What happens is," Secta added, "when the person wearing the Clock Drive steps out of the vortex, instead of it closing down, it will stay open but only as a micro-wormhole... invisible to the naked eye. However, the Clock Drive can detect it and it can detect the Clock Drive... so when it comes near, the wormhole will expand to allow the wearer to return through it."

"Brilliant," Alice said.

"The algorithm is installed, Professor... and Alice, I've got the coordinates loaded into the mainframe for the An-Zu bird, from when you went last time... so I'm set for whenever you're ready," Robert said.

"Excellent," said Al. "Secta, I'll need a bunch of WASPS... do you have any with a larger charge to blow up boulders for instance?"

"Yes, I'll go and get them ready for you. When will you be leaving?"

"In about two hours, is that okay with you guys?" Al asked.

Honor took Commander Dan Walker into Li's lab and introduced him. She had already briefed him on the mission without explaining the technical side leaving that up to Dr Li.

Dan Walker stood six four with the physique you would expect of a forty-year-old special services veteran. He was cut, mean, clean-shaven and battle-scarred with short, spiked blonde hair. With British Public School manners and class, Walker was the goods.

Li opened the pod that housed Cronus.

Walker was immediately impressed by what he saw: Cronus was built like a body-builder, similar in height to him but with a featureless face.

Li fitted an apparatus to Walker's head.

"And what pray tell is this piece of technological wizardry?" Walker enquired, articulately with a deep voice.

"A brain frequency interface," Li explained.

"And that does what?"

"It will download the content of your brain into its gravitonic brain."

"Give me assurance that all information downloaded will be erased at the conclusion of this mission?"

"Yes Commander, that was spelt out in the form you signed earlier," Honor said.

Content the sensors on the apparatus were placed correctly on each temple with one on his forehead, Li led Walker over to Cronus. She moved a step into position at the foot of Cronus. "Okay Commander, step up please," she instructed. "I require your eyes to be in-line with where Cronus' eyes would be, do you understand?"

Walker got into position as instructed. After a few seconds a pair of eyes opened on the otherwise blank face of Cronus. Then, features began to form, first the nose, then the mouth... after a minute the cyborg's face had transformed into a mirror image of Walker's.

"Now repeat after me, the quick brown fox jumped over the lazy dog," Li instructed.

Walker obliged.

Now state, "I am Commander Daniel Walker... I am forty years of age and I was born in the United Kingdom."

Again, he repeated the phrase.

"Okay, you can step down now," Li ordered.

Walker complied and she removed the apparatus from him.

"So, he certainly looks like me, even the correct eye colour but the question is: has he become me?" Walker asked, somewhat sceptical.

"Let's see, shall we? Ask him a personal question about yourself."

"Okay, where exactly were you on December 3rd, 2009."

The cyborg was staring directly ahead and then its eyes abruptly moved to focus on Walker. It spoke in a perfect imitation of Walker's voice, "No problem... I was at Basra Airport in Iraq awaiting transport to the UK."

A curt smile broke on Honor's face. "He sounds more like you than you."

"You're not mistaken, it's a little disconcerting actually. I presume we're looking at the face of the 21st Century soldier?"

"Perhaps so. Thank you, Commander," Li said with a little amorous flutter of her eyelids... an action Honor did not fail to miss.

Half an hour later, Li led the new Dan Walker into Gorrick's office.

"Sir, I would like you to meet Commander Dan Walker."

With a tight military expression, Walker presented his hand for Gorrick to shake.

Gorrick stood up and took the soldier's hand. "His hand is even warm, incredible," Gorrick said. "Sit down Commander, you too Dr Li."

"Have you been briefed on your mission, Commander?" Gorrick asked.

"Fully, sir."

"Any questions?"

"Will I have any support?" Walker asked.

"That I can do, how many will you require?"

"Three will suffice sir, provided they are of an acceptable standard."

"I'll see to that. Meet me at the boardroom in an hour," Gorrick ordered.

"Thank you, sir, will that be all?" Walker said, standing up at attention.

"Yes Commander. Excellent work Dr Li."

"Thank you, sir," she replied.

Backed up by four SWAT officers, Karzoff and Viktoria stood ready with handguns in hand, waiting for another officer to use an enforcer, more commonly known as the "big red key," to forcefully open the door of the New Octagon offices. Their tense anticipation was palpable.

Once the door was breached, they swiftly entered the premises, creating a scene of commotion and clamour to deter any potential reprisals from the occupants.

The building was a small semi-detached two-storey house. The ground floor was empty as they quickly moved through it. Viktoria led Karzoff and the rest of the team upstairs to the main bedroom, where they discovered Denning and Hitz in bed.

"Get up with your hands raised above your heads... now!" Viktoria's command rang out, her pistol aimed squarely at the two figures in the bed.

Nervously, Denning and Hitz complied, their hands raised in surrender. A brisk nod from Karzoff signalled the SWAT team to thoroughly search the room for any weapons. Their sweep yielded nothing of concern.

"Very well, lower your hands and get dressed," Viktoria ordered, as the SWAT team members exited the room, leaving the space less tense.

Denning walked over to the side of the bed, retrieved his pants, and hastily put them on. He then turned and swiftly dived out through the open window, disappearing into the night. Karzoff moved quickly to the window and peered after Denning's fleeing figure. Denning was sprinting away up an alleyway at the rear of the house.

Meanwhile, the rest of the SWAT team was stationed at the front of the house.

"Don't worry, we'll get him," Viktoria reassured Karzoff before communicating through the lapel microphone on her flak jacket. "The suspect escaped through the rear of the house. Pursue and detain."

"Roger that," came the swift response over the radio.

Fifteen minutes later, officers were securing both Denning and Hitz, bundling them into a waiting police car. Karzoff and Viktoria remained inside the house, tasked with collecting key pieces of evidence: computer hard drives, laptops, phones, and any other items they deemed pertinent. The charges would include attempted murder, and the legal framework of anti-terrorism laws granted them the authority to enter forcefully and confiscate any relevant items without requiring a warrant.

CHAPTER 29
OEDIPUS COMPLEX

A MEETING WAS underway between the President, Dr Cairn, Secta, and the Professor. After Mal had finished explaining about the An-Zu craft and the supporting conspiracies, Dr Cairn was left dumbfounded. She found it difficult to believe that Jax De Ville, an internationally renowned archaeologist, would be in league with the CIA. She also wondered why French Intelligence had gone to so much trouble to create the cover story of the Poo Ôonoo Valley dam project in order to recover the aircraft.

"You're suggesting the CIA, Zen and French Intelligence have despatched teams to recover the craft, and now you want to do the same. Tell me, why should UNTT sanction a wormhole mission, do you have any more claim than others on the craft? What does Oceana want with it?" Her questions had a degree of scepticism.

"We want to return it to its rightful owners," Secta explained.

It wasn't the answer Luna was expecting and she reacted sardonically, "And who might that be for goodness sake, Iran... Turkey?"

"No Luna, the Watchers," the Professor stated boldly.

Luna's attitude changed, the shock statement immediately made her more compliant. "The Watchers? What would they want with an artefact from 2,500 BC?"

"Apparently it belongs to them Luna," Mal said, informatively.

"An-Zu, the person killed by Ninurta was a Watcher," Secta pointed out.

"There was a Watcher in the sky Ezekiel wrote about, you read about it, remember? Well, they're all connected to the UFO's we've been seeing in the skies since recorded history, Luna... they're one in the same... an alien species," the Professor explained.

"If they want the craft so bad why don't they just take it, seems they have the technology?" she argued.

"For two reasons, one, we have the drive mechanism for it and two, the craft is jammed underground because of a cave-in. That's about all we know... the bottom line Luna is: does the World want the An-Zu craft to fall into the hands of the CIA and end up at Area 51 being reverse engineered?... or with the French military? or worse-case scenario in the evil clutches of the Zen Corporation?" Secta urged.

The pressure was now right on Luna. It had become decisively more than just a typical UNTT approval, it was obvious her decision could well affect the future.

"It's already hard enough to keep time travel a bureaucratic secret without this. If anyone gets a sniff of it outside of the security ranks the conspiracy theorists will have a field day," Luna proposed.

Rita came in to top up coffees.

"Did you enjoy the concert, Luna?" Mal asked, to lighten things up.

"Yes. I thought it was excellent... and now the UFO hovering above Alice on stage has more relevance, does it not?" she said, cynically.

"Do you know someone tried to assassinate Mal and Alice when they were both on stage?" Secta said.

"Oh my God no, who, how?" Luna asked, shocked.

"Karzoff and Viktoria are making the arrests as we speak... an extremist group we expect are linked with the Zen Corporation... something we'll confirm once the evidence is in. They were using an armed drone," Mal explained.

"Turk saw it, took a rifle from a guard and shot it down but not before it got off a shot that missed its mark and hit the drum kit," the Professor said.

"Zen again," Luna sighed. "It seems that's all I've been hearing about lately. I didn't expect to be running an anti-corruption force when I took on UNTT," she said, dispiritedly.

"I think policing the Prime Directive will be exactly that, Luna," Mal put to her.

"Yes, I suppose you're right. Okay, you have UNTT sanction for the mission. Now, as regards the solicitation for the humanitarian rescue mission Secta, I discussed it at length with UN Director General Maralina Bostok and she is prepared to approve it on the proviso of certain conditions, in other words, it's my call and to facilitate it I will need to travel to 2112, to witness the extent of the Red Wheel epidemic first hand. Is that acceptable?" She asked with a wry smile.

Secta was up out of his seat in a flash and punched the air, tears welling in his eyes. "Yes! yes! absolutely."

Such a display of emotion was completely out of character for Secta, which proved how just much it meant for him to save these poor people.

Hope entered the canteen, searching for Alice, and found him sitting alone at a table, enjoying a grilled cheese and tomato sandwich. He glanced up at her. "Sit down, love. I've been expecting this," he said with a warm smile.

"A moment of solace before the mission?" she inquired.

"Yes, it's always like this, you know, not knowing if you'll come back or not... whatever," Al humbly replied.

"How's your health?" she asked.

"All fine since the SAGE thingy cleaned up my DNA," he chuckled.

"Yes, I remember the Cas-9 gene mutation I discovered in your DNA, but that's about as far as my recollection goes. It must have been around the time Hope injected my embryo with her Pneumatide."

"Yeah, that makes sense... from then on, you wouldn't remember what happened to her, huh?" Al posed with a question mark.

"That's right, though Secta told me the story."

The conversation reminded him he was conversing with a clone of Hope, something that was easy to overlook given their striking resemblance. The realisation that Hope had no knowledge of the moment that had transpired between them while he was in a bed in sick bay, and that just before her demise, he had been on the brink of confessing his true feelings for her, brought a sense of relief.

"Alice, when you said you've been expecting this, what did you mean?"

"Oh, it's just high time we had a talk, I guess, you and I... I mean Hope and I were close, you know?" he expressed awkwardly.

"Yes, that's what I want to talk to you about. Were we in love?"

Alice nearly choked on his sandwich. "Um, well, I suppose you could call it that," he mumbled. Discussing his personal feelings wasn't one of Alice's strong suits. "Um, yes," he bravely corrected. "We loved each other."

Hope reached out and gently held his hand, tears tracing down her cheeks. She admitted, "I know, Alice. That's what I feel for you... I love you."

"I know this might sound like a line from one of those corny daytime soap operas, but it just can't be. I'm your biological father," Al stated.

"I know, I know... but I can't ignore how I feel for you... do you want me to go back to the future?"

"No!" he declared, locking eyes with her and still holding her hand. "Stay, please... pick up where Hope left off. We depend so much on you. A massive void opened in all our lives when we lost Hope, and you've filled it again. I believe everything will work out in the long run. You just need to be patient. Trust me."

The news of Karzoff arresting Denning and Hitz worried Honor. If either of them confessed, it could lead to charges against her for conspiracy to commit murder. She knew Karzoff would use all of his interrogation skills on them to extract a confession. Somehow, she had to prevent that from happening, but how? Then an idea struck her: she could use her favourite trick of kidnapping someone important to OTT and then trading them for Denning and Hitz. It had worked before with Rita Vallins; it should work again.

In her mind, she considered the people who had passed through Kairos the day Voltaris returned: Turk, Morri, and Hope. Hope stood out; she must be a clone or something similar since she looked exactly like the Hope Bruno had killed. It wouldn't be a coincidence that she had the same name. If they had lost her and now regained her, they wouldn't want to lose her again. A conspiratorial smile spread across her face. Hope was the perfect target. All she needed to do was lure her outside of OTT where she could be taken. The advantage she had was that Hope knew very little about her. She contemplated who she could trust to get the job done, and a name immediately came to mind.

"Layla?" she called out, and moments later, a pretty face appeared at the door.

"Yes, ma'am?" Layla responded.

"Get me Commander Walker."

"Oh, I just saw him pass by in the corridor, wait." She ducked out and returned a few minutes later with him.

He entered the office and stopped at attention in front of Honor, who remained seated.

"Ma'am?" he inquired.

"Commander, please take a seat."

"Yes, ma'am," he said emphatically, sitting down.

Honor examined him and wondered why he was in army fatigues.

"I have a task for you," she said concisely.

"I'm sorry, ma'am, I'm scheduled for a mission in a couple of hours."

"Oh, really?" she was surprised. Being under her command, she should have been informed. She asked a bit petulantly, "Where to?"

"Tahiti, ma'am."

Suddenly, she realised she wasn't speaking to the real Commander Walker; it was likely the replica. Feeling a little awkward, she rose from her seat. He mirrored her movement.

"No problem, Commander. Good luck," she said graciously, extending her hand for a shake.

With an expressionless face, he shook her hand, pivoted, and marched out. Honor followed closely but halted at the reception desk.

"Layla, that was the wrong Commander Walker. Find me the real one."

Layla scrunched up her nose, puzzled. "I beg your pardon, ma'am. Are you saying there are two Commander Walkers?"

Honor realised that the Cronus project details were not known to Layla. "Um, yes. Just call his number; he should be in the building."

With her pretty face smeared with confusion, Layla picked up the phone to dial. Before doing so, she asked Honor, "Ma'am, what happened to Voltaris Idram?"

Hesitating for a moment, Honor replied, "He's on a mission, I believe."

Vee was at Oceana, engaged in reviewing the mission preparations with Turk. Their primary objective was to divert any opposition while Alice retrieved the An-Zu bird from the cavern and then execute a swift exit through Kairos. While the plan appeared simple in theory, the reality was far more intricate. The only permitted weapons through the wormhole were WASP's; firearms were not an option. Anticipating formidable resistance, they understood that the mission wouldn't be a straightforward one. However, with the experienced and battle-hardened Turk as her partner, Vee felt reassured about their prospects.

CHAPTER 30
SEIZED

NEW YORK TO Papeete fell just within the range of the Gulfstream V. Once the sleek unmarked jet had landed at the VIP terminal connected to Fa'a'ā International Airport, Jax De Ville disembarked to meet CIA agent Buddy Holman, who awaited her on the tarmac. He led her to a waiting black sedan. Her US Government agent status allowed her to bypass local immigration and customs. During the five-kilometre drive to the CIA offices in the Papeete business district, Holman briefed her.

"There has been a change of plans. We received confirmation yesterday that French Intelligence dispatched a Sikorsky CH-54 aerial crane to the Poo Ôonoo Valley. As a result, the Brigadier has ordered us to stand by in Papeete."

"Why?" Jax asked, perplexed.

"To let them do all the heavy lifting. In the meantime, he'll use his influence to secure the craft once they've extracted it for us."

"I don't get it. How can he do that?"

"Oh, you know, we probably have someone in prison they want, or they just need some help in a war somewhere. There's always an angle. Uncle Sam pretty much always gets his way... especially when old Bull is running the show," Holman explained.

"Seems one way or another," she said, facetiously. "The Intel was correct then... they hadn't buried the entrances to the ruin."

"That's right... that was to buy time to get in there without competition. Which seems to have worked."

"They would have forced Blake to guide them to the craft. Why not Louis Sens?" she questioned.

"Two reasons: first, Sens never made it out from the last expedition, and second, you're not going to like this… but Blake has always been an Oceana operative."

"What? And you knew that? Why wasn't I told?" Jax badgered, belligerently. Being kept in the dark really irked her.

"Because there was far more to gain from you being unaware."

"Yeah, sure," Jax folded her arms tightly against her chest and pulled a spoilt brat, grumpy face. "What the hell am I doing here then?"

"Oh, I think your expertise will be required somewhere along the line. You know the Brigadier; he's always got something up his sleeve."

"Who else do we have to contend with?" she asked, querulously.

"Well, word is Zen Corporation is mad keen to get their claws on it… and then there's, of course, OTT. We expect Black Alice to pop out of a time vortex at any moment," he said cavalierly.

Jax looked skyward as though it were the theatre of the impossible.

"After the Brigadier failed in trying to set him up in Chernobyl, you think you can beat him this round? Don't be ridiculous… even Nimrod was impressed, and let me tell you, that ain't easy. He's been a field operative for forty years and has never seen anything like Black Alice. The guy's a superman. I know; I witnessed it myself. As for Zen, anything could happen with them. I'm glad I don't have to go into the ruin to face off with those dudes," Jax said irritably.

"I hear you, I hear you," Holman said, recalling the broken nose he got from Alice outside Vee's apartment block in Coogee.

The OTT team had gathered in the control room. Alice, Vee, and

Turk were dressed in army fatigues, each sporting a different-coloured beret: black for Alice, green for Vee, and purple for Turk.

"Turk, you're wearing my beret," Secta playfully complained.

"Yeah, I'm surprised it fits with the size of your head," Turk joked.

The Professor attached a Clock Drive to Turk. "Remember the approximate place where you'll exit the vortex. It will remain open for your return, but it will only be microscopic. You won't be able to see it until you're within two metres of it, then it will open."

"Got it," Turk acknowledged.

"Vee, it won't reopen for you; it only works with a Clock Drive. So, you'll need to rely on Turk. Alice, you too... here's a spare Drive for Blake, just in case," Vic said, handing over the Drive to Vee.

"Understood," Al confirmed.

The Professor handed Alice the sceptre. "Here you go, mate. The Velodium sceptre—probably the most valuable piece of junk in the world. Make sure you bring it back now."

"No worries, Vic. It's priority number one," Al affirmed.

Robert was busy at the console, typing instructions for Kairos.

Secta used a teaspoon to tap the side of a mug, grabbing everyone's attention. "Listen up, folks, I have an announcement. UNTT has approved the Red Wheel recovery mission."

A cheer erupted from them. Morri, Turk, and Hope exchanged joyous hugs.

"However, it's on the condition that after this mission, we return to 2112 with Dr Cairn to assess the number of people afflicted by the disease." There was a murmur of discontent. Secta raised his hand to calm them. "It's not a negative. It's for the UN to evaluate what assistance they need to provide us. After all, it's a task that has never been attempted before. Details later... I just wanted you to know before you left, Turk."

"That's great news, Secta," Turk affirmed.

Robert announced, "Okay, I'm all set for a countdown."

Secta quickly distributed half a dozen WASPS to each traveller.

"Alice, here are the extra ones with the higher charge you requested."

They securely stored the WASPS in their trouser pockets.

Hope sauntered over to Alice. "While you're on the mission, I'm going to research how to become transgenic," she whispered discreetly.

"Transgenic? What's that? You want to be a bloke or something?"

"No, silly. Transgenic means having one parent's genes edited from your DNA."

Alice was puzzled. "And what would that do?"

"It would mean you're no longer my biological father... we could have a relationship," she whispered playfully.

Alice almost jumped out of his skin. "Shush!" Scanning the room, he placed a finger on her lips to quiet her. "Look, just hold off on all this stuff until I get back, okay?" he said with concern.

She gave a shy, mischievous smile and whispered, "Whatever you say, Al."

This is where she's so different from the old Hope, Al thought to himself. But it could be because she's way younger.

"Are you talking to me?" En-Ki asked mentally.

"No," Al responded.

Rob's voice snapped Al back to reality. "You're up first, Al. Do I need to set coordinates for a Watcher for you?"

"Nah, I'll be sweet," Al confirmed, refocusing on the mission.

"Al, because the wormhole will remain open, we'll be able to communicate with you two-way via your implant," Secta informed.

"Cool," Alice said, opening the door to the dispatch room. "Chaa!" he called out with a customary wave of his hand. Hope hurried over and gave him a peck on the cheek.

Mal and Luna entered, followed by Karzoff and Viktoria. Mal made a point to reach Al and pat him on the back. "Take care, mate," he said.

Morri gave Turk a goodbye kiss. The Professor gave Vee a hug.

Each of them was aware of the uncertainty of the mission. Despite being on the current timeline and Earthbound, it was no less perilous, especially with the anticipation of Zen agents, the CIA, and French Intelligence converging on the objective.

Alice stepped into the small room. Rob activated Kairos, and within seconds, Al had vanished. Vee was next in line to step up to the plate.

The area of the cavern where Al had arrived had undergone considerable changes since his last visit. It now resembled a construction zone. Bright portable light towers had been set up on either side of the An-Zu bird. The massive boulders that once encased the craft had been cleared away.

Al took cover behind a large boulder as soon as he spotted a group of men approaching, chatting away in French. His translator enabled him to understand them. The man in charge was complaining about their inability to find a way to enter the craft. None of their cutting devices had any effect on opening it. Alice couldn't help but giggle to himself, but he flinched from a touch on the shoulder from behind. He was relieved to find it was Vee. A few seconds later, Turk crouched down beside them. The French voices echoed in the cavern.

"I wonder what they're saying?" Turk asked.

"They're debating how to get into the craft," Vee said.

"Can you speak French?" Turk inquired.

"No, Al and I are equipped with language translators. Look, Al, over there on the ground next to all that equipment, isn't that Blake?"

Al gazed at the scattered gear about fifty metres away. "I think you might be right," Al whispered.

Vee assessed the terrain. "I think I can get to him from behind those rocks."

"Do it. Turk, let's try to get closer to the craft. Come with me."

Vee blended into the shadows and navigated quietly between boulders to approach Blake from behind. From behind the nearest boulder, Vee could see that Blake wasn't guarded. He was sat on the ground with his hands tied behind his back, secured to a spike driven into the floor. Vee had nothing to cut the tether with, so she scanned the tools scattered among the equipment and spotted a hand axe. Perfect, she mumbled to herself.

She estimated that the French group numbered about a dozen. With no-one near Blake, she stealthily moved out, grabbed the axe, and then slipped back into the shadows. Assured that the coast was clear, she approached Blake from behind.

"Well, fancy meeting you here," she whispered.

He twitched at the voice emerging from the darkness. "Who's that?" he muttered.

He felt the tether being sliced, and he turned to see who it was.

"Vee, I'll be damned. Is Al here?"

"Yes."

With the tether cut, he untied his wrists.

"Let's go," she whispered and led him into the shadows. They stopped when they were safely out of sight.

"There's another team up top. Look up there," he pointed toward the canopy.

Vee spotted a beam of light descending from a large hole in the ceiling.

"They excavated that yesterday. There's a flying crane up there to lift the craft out."

Daniel Walker and three commandos had descended into the cavern through the well. They had left two French guards with smashed faces behind—dead. Walker's orders from Gorrick were clear: destroy the An-Zu craft and take no prisoners. They had enough C-4 explosive in their backpacks for the task.

Alice and Turk had managed to get close to the craft. One of the French crew members was talking on a two-way radio with other team members. Alice could discern from his body language that the other team was on top of the canopy. The Frenchman instructed the person on the other end to lower a hoist. Within minutes, a hoist line began to descend through the gap in canopy with a dogman holding it riding a hook block.

"They're going to attempt to lift it out. I need to get inside before they start fixing a cable to it. We need a diversion."

The dogman had descended about halfway, roughly a hundred metres, when a burst of submachine gun fire echoed through the cavern. The dogman let go and plummeted onto the boulders, dead.

Chaos immediately erupted among the French ranks as they realised they were under attack. Al had his diversion.

Vee emerged from the shadows with Blake.

"Hey, Blake, good to see you, mate," Al greeted with a friendly smile. "Vee, attach a Clock Drive to him. Turk, lead Vee and Blake back to where we entered. Wait there until I'm in the craft, then get the hell out of here. I reckon that's Zen doing all the shooting."

They all nodded in acknowledgment of the plan and moved off.

Gunfire continued, accompanied by screams. Pandemonium reigned among the French. There was no-one near the An-Zu bird. This was Alice's opportunity. He dashed beneath the craft.

"How can I reach the slot in its belly?" he asked himself.

"Just point it at the craft," En-Ki said.

Alice pointed the sceptre at the hatch; a servo sound followed, and it slid open, with the ladder descending. "Clever," Alice said, wondering why he hadn't thought of that earlier. He started climbing the ladder. "I hope you know how to fly this thing coz I don't."

"Yes, Alice, do not worry. I will guide you," En-Ki assured.

He paused before entering the hatch, looked back in the direction where he estimated Turk should be, and gave a thumbs-up signal.

The trio—Vee, Turk, and Blake—observed Alice's progress from their concealed positions among the boulders.

"Alright, he just gave the signal. Let's move," Turk said.

As soon as they stepped into the open, three Zen agents materialised out of the shadows, pointing guns at them.

Alice hurried through the craft, ascended the steps, and entered the cockpit. Pausing to take in his surroundings, he recalled that it felt like only yesterday when he had been there with Ninurta. "So, what do I do now?"

"See the groove on the instrument panel? The sceptre fits into it. Put it in," En-Ki instructed.

Alice slid the sceptre into the designated groove, and a colourful array of instrument lights on the console immediately illuminated.

"That certainly did something."

"The Velodium sceptre functions as the power supply. Now, I need you to input some data into the computer."

"Cool, go ahead."

"Do you see the row of six blue lights on the horizontal panel in front of you? Press the first blue light on the left three times. But not in quick succession; wait for four seconds between each press."

Alice extended his finger and pressed the first blue light. It changed from blue to green on the first press, then to amber on the second, and finally to red on the third.

"Perfect, it's activated. Now, repeat the same action with the end blue light on the right."

Alice followed the instructions, achieving the same sequence of colours. Now he had red lights at each end of the horizontal row of four blue lights.

"Good job, Alice. You have now enabled the autopilot to take the craft to the nearest Watcher. All you need to do is initiate the sequence. To engage it, press each of the four blue lights once to turn them green."

Alice was feeling quite confident. A few simple pushes, and they would be on their way.

Then, suddenly, a gravelly voice boomed, "Don't press another button!"

CHAPTER 31
TIC TAC

MORRI AND HOPE were navigating the afternoon rush hour crowd to reach Café Epiphany. Both were in low spirits after the excitement of the mission departure. The rest of the team was engaged in a planning meeting for the next mission. To uplift their mood, Morri had suggested a break from the OTT routine.

There were only two customers in the café, both men and seated at separate tables. Morri and Hope settled at a table by the window, the same one they had occupied previously. Morri was craving French toast, while Hope desired a warm drink and a chinwag.

"Are you concerned about Turk?" Hope asked.

"A bit. You'd think I'd be over worrying by now, given all the battles we've been through. But there's always that nagging thought that he might not come back... especially now that we're getting on."

"Oh, I think he's just as tough as ever. Solid as a rock to me."

"I suppose you're right. Alice wouldn't have taken him if he was a liability. But at the same time, we tend to think of him as invincible."

Hope reached across the table and took her mother's hand. "Mum, are you sure you're okay with me staying here?"

"Of course, love. If I were your age and had this opportunity, I'd take it as well. Have you told anyone else yet?"

"No, I wanted to tell you first."

Morri squeezed her hand. "Thank you for considering me, but

you're a grown woman now, more than capable of making your own decisions."

"True... but I feel I owe it to you, Mum," Hope said, her voice filled with emotion.

"You don't owe us anything, my darling. We were fortunate to raise you into the wonderful young woman you are today. Now, I'm going to the restroom. Can I order something for you on my way?"

"Just a dirty chai, ta."

Morri got up and on her way to the restroom, she stopped by the front counter.

Hope noticed a newspaper on a nearby table, picked it up, and asked, "May I read this?"

Daniel Walker, who had been engrossed in a book, looked up and replied, "Sure, just take it."

She took the tabloid and returned to her seat.

"Do I know you?" Walker asked.

On her way back from the washroom, Morri stopped at the counter to pay and then proceeded to the table, but Hope wasn't there. Her psychic ability was telling her something was wrong, so she returned to the counter and asked the young man behind it, "Excuse me, did the young lady with me leave?"

"Hope? Yeah... she left with a guy I haven't seen here before."

That really worried Morri. She pulled out the phone given to her by Secta and dialled his number.

Five minutes later, Viktoria arrived, out of breath from running from Oceana. "Morri, what's happening?"

"Not much to say, except that while I was in the restroom, Hope was kidnapped."

"Why do you think she was kidnapped?" Viktoria asked.

"Well, you do know that I'm psychic?"

"Yes," Viktoria confirmed.

"I know she was kidnapped... she's not far from here... and she's scared."

Zen HQ immediately flashed into Viktoria's mind.

Al had spun around to face the man holding a gun on him. En-Ki's voice echoed in his head, "He's not human."

"Who the hell are you?" Al barked, both hands raised chest high.

"A Zen agent, and I know who you are, Black Alice. Follow me, we're going back down below." He slowly backed out of the cockpit, down the steps, keeping the gun trained on Alice, who followed with her hands raised.

Turk had witnessed Daniel Walker climbing the ladder into the An-Zu craft. A French agent emerged from behind a boulder and fired a shot at one of the Zen agents who was holding them at gunpoint. The shot hit him in the shoulder, and he went down. The Zen agent beside him quickly swivelled and unleashed a burst of submachine gun fire at the Frenchman. The distraction provided the opportunity for Vee to swiftly retrieve a WASP from her pocket, arm it, aim it at the nearest Zen agent, and discreetly toss it into the air. The agent remained oblivious to her actions and didn't notice the WASP hovering briefly before silently heading towards him. Before he could react, the WASP landed on his left temple, leading to a sudden explosion that obliterated half of his skull.

The explosive crack served as the signal to initiate action. Drawing the Zen agent's gunfire, Blake and Vee dived for cover between two boulders, the bullets ricocheting off the solid surfaces. The move gave Turk a clear path to reach the An-Zu craft. He hurried over and swiftly climbed the ladder.

Inside the craft, Walker was retreating along the corridor, his gun trained on Alice, who was following closely. Just as Walker reached the hatch, a hand reached up and grabbed his leg, momentarily distracting him. Seizing the opportunity, Alice pounced.

A flurry of punches knocked the pistol out of Walker's hand and sent him stumbling backward, with Turk still gripping his leg. Realising it was Turk, Al shouted, "Pull him down the ladder, mate!

Swing off his leg."

Following Alice's instructions, Turk stepped off the ladder, holding onto Walker's leg and swinging in the air. Vee and Blake, witnessing the scene, saw Turk hanging from the hatch with a leg in his grip. The last remaining Zen agent also noticed, raising his weapon to open fire.

Vee retrieved another WASP from her pocket.

"What are those things?" Blake inquired.

"Watch," she replied, activating it. "I need to get a bit closer." She dashed out from behind the boulder.

"No!" Blake shouted anxiously.

Vee stopped about twenty metres away from the Zen agent. "Hey, dude!" she called out to him.

The distraction worked. Instead of aiming at Turk, the Zen agent turned his attention to Vee. However, it was too late. The WASP, now positioned on his forehead, detonated. The explosion shattered his head, and as his finger twitched on the trigger, the submachine gun fired into the air before he collapsed, his head practically obliterated.

"You cut that a bit fine," Blake remarked, wide-eyed. A bullet zinged off the ground, originating from the French agent. They took cover again.

Walker was being dragged down through the hatch by the force of Turk swinging from his leg. He attempted to grasp the floor with his fingers, but the metal surface made it difficult, causing him to slide along the floor and out of the hatch.

Alice strode over, towering above him, and declared, "Goodbye, Zen agent!" With immense force, he kicked Walker in the head, causing him to lose his grip and plummet through the hatch.

Looking down at Turk rising from the ground after the impact, Al yelled, "Get out of here, mate!"

Turk wasted no time, sprinting away while dodging bullets fired by the French agent.

Al didn't hesitate. He rushed back to the flight deck, settled into the pilot's seat, and pressed the last four blue lights on the control panel. As the lights turned green, the ladder retracted, the hatch closed, and seatbelts secured him.

"Alright, Alice, push down on the joystick," En-Ki directed.

The An-Zu craft ascended vertically.

Turk joined Vee and Blake, avoiding being hit by gunfire. Together, they watched the craft silently rise and head toward the opening in the canopy. Walker was making for them.

"Quick, follow me," Turk urged. They hastened toward the exit point.

Other members of the team, along with the French agent, observed their hard-fought objective—now airborne and departing through the opening they had meticulously excavated.

Inside the cockpit, Alice wondered if he could steer the craft through the narrow opening. However, the craft was intuitive and found the way.

Parked atop the cavern roof, the flying crane and its astounded French crew watched in awe as the craft gracefully emerged from the breach. Once clear, it rapidly accelerated into the cloudless sky, leaving the six-man crew in stunned disbelief.

One by one, they stepped out of Kairos. Waiting for them were Secta, the Professor, Rob, and Morri. Despite looking decidedly ruffled, they were thrilled to see that everyone was in one piece.

After they had given an account of the events that had unfolded, Secta delivered the grim news that Hope was missing and presumed kidnapped by Zen. Karzoff and Viktoria were on the case, working diligently to uncover any leads.

Turk's anger was palpable. He expressed a strong desire to go to the Zen building and confront Gorrick head-on. Secta attempted to placate him, just as Karzoff entered the control room.

"Glad to see all of you made it back safely. Did Alice manage to get the craft out?" Karzoff inquired.

"Yes, but not without a struggle," Vee replied.

Karzoff slumped into a chair and sighed, "We just received a communication from the kidnappers. They are demanding the immediate release of Glan Denning and Toeghan Hitz in exchange for Hope's return. They claim that if we comply, Hope will be released unharmed."

At that moment, Mal arrived with Luna by his side.

Mal greeted the travellers, saying, "Rob messaged me you were back. How did things go for Al?"

"Last we saw, the An-Zu bird was taking off with him inside," Vee reported.

"Good." Picking up on the vibe, he asked, "So, why all the doom and gloom?"

Morri explained the dire situation concerning Hope's kidnapping. The news hit Mal like a hammer, and it incited a fiery rage within Luna.

"Now I understand the kind of challenges you are constantly facing. This has to stop," Luna thundered.

Turning to Karzoff and Viktoria, Mal questioned, "So, what's the plan?"

Karzoff sighed deeply. "Unfortunately, it seems we have little choice than to make the trade."

"I want a few minutes alone with Toeghan Hitz first. I think I can get her to grass on the orchestrators of the attempted assassination," Viktoria said.

Luna's expression hardened as she countered, "But won't that be seen as an admission of guilt?"

"Yes, it will," Viktoria confirmed, "but not necessarily an admission of Zen's guilt. We need to ensure that aspect is on record."

Mal snarled vindictively, "Go get her Vik."

A few minutes later, Viktoria entered the security interview room where Toeghan Hitz was waiting. She placed a folder on the table and took a seat across from Hitz. Unbeknownst to Hitz, Viktoria discreetly pressed a button under the table, activating a digital recorder. She opened the folder deliberately, creating a tense atmosphere.

"Toeghan Hitz, I'm here to inform you that Glan Denning is facing charges of conspiracy to commit murder. You, on the other hand, will be charged as an accessory to murder, which carries a minimum sentence of twelve years in a maximum-security prison, without the possibility of parole." She paused, observing the colour drain from the young girl's face.

"Glan Denning has confessed to his involvement and is currently being interrogated regarding your role in this matter. I am authorised to present you with a one-time opportunity. If you cooperate and reveal your co-conspirators, you will be released without any charges." Viktoria paused again, eyeballing Hitz for maximum impact.

Hitz leaned back in her chair and defiantly crossed her arms. After a moment of contemplation, she spat out, "No comment."

Symbolically closing the folder, Viktoria picked it up, rose slowly, and began making her way toward the door. She paused with her hand on the door handle and stated, "Have it your way."

Just as Viktoria was about to turn the handle, Hitz's voice called out, "Wait."

A wry smile crept across Viktoria's face.

Twenty minutes later, Viktoria entered Karzoff's office, where Mal was also present. Mal inquired, "So, Vik, what's the outcome? Success or failure?"

Poker-faced, Viktoria settled into a seat in the lounge area. However, she couldn't contain her elation any longer and broke into a broad grin. "I got her. She gave up her contact within Zen. It's Honor."

Karzoff couldn't contain his excitement and punched the air with enthusiasm. "Yes!"

"Great work, Vik. Does this mean we can take legal action against her?" Mal asked.

"Absolutely," Karzoff answered, his satisfaction evident. He finally had Honor cornered exactly where he wanted her. "So," he stood up, "let us proceed with the trade first to secure Hope's return. We need to ensure we have her back before Alice returns otherwise he will most certainly go ballistic"

Meanwhile, aboard the An-Zu bird, they had been flying for about twenty minutes when the craft abruptly came to a halt. It was challenging to discern the halt as they were surrounded by clouds. Had they not been in the midst of clouds, Alice might not have even noticed.

"Seems we've arrived at our destination," Al remarked, leaning forward in his seat to peer through the windshield. All around them were clouds and occasional breaks of blue sky. "What's happening? You sure this thing was programmed right?"

"Somewhere ahead of us, there should be—" En-Ki began but trailed off.

As Alice gazed through the windshield, a Tic Tac-shaped object blinked into existence right in front of them. It was as if someone had flicked a switch, illuminating a massive light. Astonishingly, the light slid open to reveal what appeared to be a hatch or door, leading to an empty expanse. Despite the absence of any visible structure beyond the door, Alice felt the An-Zu craft start to move again, this time at a slow, docking speed. Then, something akin to a tractor beam extended from the open hatch in the sky. It latched onto the An-Zu bird, pulling it upward and through the hatch. The brilliance of the tractor beam compelled Alice to shield his eyes.

Moments later, all movement ceased, and the intense light faded away.

"Here we are. Take the sceptre and disembark from the craft," En-Ki instructed.

"Are we inside a Watcher?" Al queried.

"Yes. No need to feel anxious, Alice. You are perfectly safe."

"Thanks for the reassurance... I'll postpone the panic then," Al retorted dryly. He retrieved the sceptre from its holder and proceeded toward the hatch.

"I hope there's more substance to this ship than what I saw from outside. I'd rather not step off the ladder into the clouds," he mused aloud. Approaching the hatch, he peered downward and was relieved to see the ladder's end resting on a solid floor. With the reassurance of a stable surface, he began descending the ladder into the unknown craft.

CHAPTER 32
CONGÉ

STEPPING OFF THE last rung of the ladder onto the floor, Alice felt it quiver beneath his weight. He exclaimed, "Whoa!"

"Oh, that? Yes, it takes some getting used to. The ship is, in a way, alive," En-Ki explained matter-of-factly.

"What do you mean, alive?" Alice asked, somewhat stuck, staring down at his boots on the shiny black surface. "I've seen this shiny material before, on the walls of En-Lil's pyramid on Eris. But calling it alive is giving me the creeps."

"In a sense, it possesses a form of life. It is powered by artificial intelligence, AI. The entire ship is an AI construct."

"So, you're saying the ship itself is alive?"

"Yes. Now, come along. Don't worry, just follow the red directional lights on the floor," En-Ki reassured him.

A row of red pinpoint lights illuminated on the floor, guiding the way forward. As Al proceeded through the cylindrical tunnel, bathed in an odd source of light, his curiosity grew.

"If this is a Watchers' ship, how do you know so much about it?" he asked.

"We originated from the same planet. The Watchers serve as AI observers, gathering specific data from their observations and sending it to a main computer for analysis. This data is then used to make informed decisions. Watchers have numerous interplanetary responsibilities."

"Okay, so they're like our Mars rovers, but on a more advanced level?"

"Yes, that is a suitable comparison."

As they reached a junction in the tunnel, the floor lights indicated a left turn, prompting Alice to follow. "Why do they want the An-Zu craft?"

"Humans must not reverse-engineer it, not yet. Humanity's technological advancement needs to be controlled, especially with the presence of rogue elements. As you know with Zen not all humans are peacekeepers like you."

"Gorrick is far from human, my friend."

"Indeed, you are right, Alice. However, as long as free radicals like Brigadier Bruckmaster are active, it is crucial to oversee human technological progress. The Watchers have been fulfilling this role effectively for millennia."

Upon entering the flight deck, Alice sensed that he was standing within a colossal computer. "Is this the heart of the ship?"

"Yes, this is the central hub. This ship employs superluminal travel, utilising gamma bursts in space to propel it beyond the speed of light."

"But doesn't Einstein's theory suggest that nothing can exceed the speed of light?"

"Space operates by different rules. The ship can also alter its exterior appearance. Over time, we have attempted to adopt forms familiar to humans to avoid causing undue alarm. In ancient times, we used imagery like a chariot of fire, later transitioning to star shapes. As humanity developed, we adjusted our appearance to blimp and zeppelin shapes, then flying saucers, and more recently, various lights and triangular forms."

"Gee, thanks for the lesson in UAP conspiracy history," Al quipped. "Is there anyone else aboard?"

"No other beings. It is all AI. The ship communicates with other Watchers and with me."

"What about En-Lil?"

"No, he was separated from the ship's logic when his megalomania became apparent. I'm sorry I cannot provide you with a place to sit. The ship is not designed for humans. I will remain here, and transition to the ship's organic computer. This change is necessary since En-Lil is now aware that you are hosting me, putting both of us at risk. Your mission is still to defeat En-Lil. Now that you know which Gorrick he is, accomplishing the mission becomes more feasible."

"Right, that makes sense."

"From here, I can communicate with you across dimensions, as we did when I was confined within the orb. However, you will not need to be brought here. Our communication will occur through your thoughts. To contact me, simply think my name."

A shiver ran down Alice's spine as En-Ki left him.

"Are you there?" Alice asked, scanning the room for any sign of him, to no avail.

"Yes, Alice," En-Ki responded. His voice was distinct from the one Alice had known, whether generated mentally or spoken. It now had a god-like resonance, encompassing everything and exuding magnanimity.

"What happened to your desire for a physical form?" Al inquired.

"After being with you, I concluded it would be a hindrance."

"So, you won't need me to do your legwork anymore?"

"Do you find that burdensome, Alice?"

"Well, put it this way, I could be doing other things, like living my life."

"This is your life, Alice. You are the crucial link between humanity and me. We have an obligation to rectify injustice. Is that not a righteous enough path for you?"

"Yeah, I s'pose so." Al surveyed the circular chamber. "Where exactly are you now?"

"I am everywhere, Alice."

"Hmm, that rave reminds me of when I used to smoke weed."

"Alice, I want to express my enjoyment of performing on stage with you and the exhilaration of your shape-shifting."

"Yeah, sure thing, mate. The whole experience has been a blast. Now, how do I get back?"

"That is no problem at all. Thank you, Alice. I will be watching over you."

The exchange was arranged: a vehicle drop after dark at a location provided en route. Karzoff would drive, with Turk and Viktoria to assist while Denning and Hitz remained in custody.

As Karzoff drove the black SUV out of the Oceana HQ car park, Viktoria, in the front passenger seat, received a text alert. It indicated the final destination for the exchange: the northern steps of the Anzac Memorial Building in Sydney's Hyde Park.

It was 11 p.m. The Memorial was only a five-minute drive from Oceana HQ at that time of night. Karzoff immediately input a code into the vehicle's onboard computer to dispatch a stealth drone to the destination. The drone would photograph the exchange and capture details of the kidnapper's vehicle. Then, with a bit of luck, it would trace the vehicle to its base.

Turk was armed and sat in the back seat between Denning and Hitz, who were handcuffed.

"I suppose you believed you were clever, tricking me into surrendering Honor when you already knew you would have to release us," Hitz snarled.

"And what makes you think you're going to be released?" Viktoria said nonchalantly.

"The deal implied it," Hitz hissed.

"What deal?" Karzoff questioned.

"Humph!" Hitz rumbled.

"The fascist pig is just toying with you," Denning growled.

"Ha! That's the pot calling the kettle black if ever I've heard it... your logic is as thin as evidence of the tooth fairy. You're both working for fascists; you couldn't get any more authoritarian than the Zen Corporation," Viktoria said ironically.

Turk felt like hitting Denning to wake him up. He understood more than anyone what it was like to live under fascist suppression. But he couldn't be bothered hitting him or discussing it; as far as he was concerned, Denning was nothing more than a jerk.

Karzoff parked within walking distance of the War Memorial. Kidnap exchanges were always difficult, with both sides not trusting each other and not willing to finalise the deal until they were convinced there were no strings attached.

"Alright, here is what is going to happen. This is a kidnap exchange. We will swap you for the kidnap victim. You will be led to the rendezvous point, and when the time comes, your handcuffs will be removed. If you make any suspicious moves during this procedure, we are authorized to shoot you. Is that clear?" Karzoff explained.

Both prisoners answered affirmatively.

Viktoria got out and opened the left rear passenger door for Hitz to step out. Karzoff did the same on the right rear passenger side for Denning. Turk then followed Hitz out.

"Guard the rear, Turk," Karzoff ordered.

They began walking through the park—Karzoff with Denning, Viktoria with Hitz, and Turk bringing up the rear. Turk heard a sound and suspected a drone; he looked up. Sure enough, there it was, but he knew it was the drone Karzoff had ordered. It hovered fifty metres above the War Memorial, a hundred metres away from them.

Their sixty-metre walk through the park brought them to the Lake of Reflections, bordered by rows of poplars in front of the memorial. From there, they could see the northern steps of the monument. There was no-one there. They continued to the base of the pink granite steps leading up to the memorial.

Out of the shadows emerged Hope, walking onto the landing at the top of the stairs.

Karzoff received a call in his earphone. It was from the OTT Operations drone pilot; he had spotted a sniper on the roof of a building bordering the park.

A shot rang out.

"Get down!" Turk yelled, and they all hit the ground.

The drone tumbled out of the air and crashed in the park.

Turk wasted no time and took off like a rocket. He raced up the staircase, zigzagging to avoid the bullets ricocheting off the steps at his feet. When he reached the landing, he grabbed Hope, shielding her with his body, and got her inside the memorial, away from the sniper's fire.

Denning took off across the park, running with his hands still cuffed in front of him. Hitz decided to follow him.

Crouched down, sheltered by the trunk of a tree, pistol in hand, Karzoff shouted, "Let them go, Vik. Turk's got Hope."

Also taking cover behind a tree trunk, Glock 19 pressed against her cheek, Viktoria shouted back, "I can see the sniper."

"Stay put; there might be more than one," Karzoff cautioned.

On the southern side of the memorial, Daniel Walker was on a walkie-talkie, orchestrating the offensive. He had six men positioned around the memorial, ordered to eliminate the opposition.

Karzoff reported back to base that they were under fire and requested backup. However, he knew as soon as the adversaries emerged from the surrounding shadows that they were outgunned and outnumbered, and that backup wouldn't arrive in time.

"We need to reach Turk at the memorial; it's our only chance. You go first, and I will cover you," Karzoff instructed Viktoria.

She waited for him to start shooting, then took off like an Olympic sprinter. She shot up the stairs, panting heavily, reached Turk and Hope at the top without being hit.

Turk could see the enemy. "I've counted six plus the sniper."

Reaching around the corner of the Memorial entrance, they opened fire at fleeting shadows.

One of the opposition went down.

They both fired a barrage, providing cover for Karzoff. He emerged from behind the tree trunk and rushed up the staircase, making it to the others.

"You right?" Viktoria asked.

Breathing heavily but uninjured, he nodded. Zing! A sniper's bullet ricocheted off the building's facade.

Walker had made his way up the rear of the Memorial. Gun in hand, he hugged the eastern wall, advancing toward Karzoff and the others at the entrance. One of his men hurried out of the shadows to join him. Despite having their opponents under siege, they understood the need for swift movement, anticipating that Karzoff would have called for reinforcements.

The situation looked dire, yet with a lifetime of battle experience, Turk took charge. "They'll be coming at us from behind," he said. "I got one, so that's five left, though there could be more. How much ammo do we have?"

"No spare magazines," Karzoff admitted, his tone grave.

"Right, the Glock 26, 9 mil, only holds ten rounds. I'm down to three," Turk stated.

"Same here," both Karzoff and Viktoria concurred.

"Not enough. How far away is backup?" Turk inquired.

"Maybe another fifteen minutes. Only two on duty this time of night," Karzoff replied.

"Can we do it?" Hope asked.

"To survive? We can only try. Find cover inside, Hope. Get ready, everyone; make every shot count," Turk resolved.

They crouched with guns held in both hands, aimed at the entrance, prepared to make a stand.

Walker had reached the corner of the northern entrance. He glanced towards the pond and saw his men closing in on the base of the stairs.

He turned to his comrade in the black balaclava and whispered, "We'll move in on my signal." Then, he spoke into his lapel microphone, "When I count to three, all of you open fire on the targets. One, two, three."

As instructed, all four agents and the sniper opened fire. Walker anticipated the enemies taking cover during the barrage. When the gunfire ceased, he commanded, "Move!" The two of them hurried around the corner to the landing at breakneck speed and froze mid-step.

Thirty seconds later, Walker shot his comrade in the knee.

The rooftop sniper snapped back to reality and swiftly turned with his rifle, only to be met with a powerful punch to the face that knocked him out cold.

Al took the Cheytag M-200 long-range sniper rifle from the unconscious sniper and looked through the night scope at the Memorial entrance. He centred Walker in the crosshairs. "Hey, can you hear me?" He shouted loudly enough for Walker to hear through the unconscious sniper's headset.

Walker glanced towards the sniper position and gave Alice the bird.

Al squeezed the trigger. The shot severed the bird finger from Walker's right hand.

Alice left the rifle behind and stepped into the open vortex.

They all awaited Alice in the control room. He emerged from Kairos and joined them.

Turk gave him a hearty pat on the back and said, "You got us out of that one, mate."

Hope expressed her gratitude with a kiss to Alice. Karzoff patted him on the back, and Viktoria enveloped him in a warm hug. He had only just stepped out of Kairos from the Watchers' craft when Secta informed him about the siege. The Professor had handed him Clock Drives for all four of them, and Rob had opened a wormhole to the War Memorial. While everyone was in stasis, Al had sufficient time to install the Clock Drives and turn Walker's gun towards his comrade. As soon as the stasis ended, they all leaped into the vortex.

Upon their return, Rob knew the sniper was positioned on the roof of the Europa Building on Elizabeth Street. He created a fresh wormhole to that location because Al suspected there was more to be done.

They all shared a laugh when Al recounted shooting off the 'bird finger' of the head honcho's right hand. He also mentioned something he found odd: when he looked at the target through the night scope, he recognised him as the same individual who had attacked him inside the An-Zu bird in Tahiti. He had dismissed it as impossible, though.

In truth, it had been a dangerously close call. The only person confident that they would remain unharmed was Morri; she hadn't sensed any danger psychically. However, she was undeniably relieved when their guardian angel, Alice, unexpectedly emerged from Kairos carrying the sceptre.

For the next half hour, Al recounted the events involving En-Ki. Those who were unaware that he had been under En-Ki's possession all along were astounded. Yet for Secta, Vee, and the Professor, the narrative was utterly incredible. Now, they comprehended the identity of the Watchers. En-Ki was secure and maintained communication. The An-Zu bird had been rightfully returned to its owners after outmanoeuvring Zen, the French, and the CIA. All keen for a bit of rest, they were nevertheless prepared to kick off phase one of the Red Wheel rescue mission.

CHAPTER 33
TECHNO SINGULARITY

U NABLE TO RECONCILE their differences over Cronus being sent back through Kairos in his place, Voltaris was thrown into prison by Ursula. He cast a disapproving glance at the bowl of gruel served up for breakfast by Wally and Ben, growling, "I'm tired of this slop, isn't there something else?"

"No-one gets anything different," Wally responded brashly.

"But there's no-one else," Voltaris retorted in frustration.

"Turk was here, and we never gave him anything different," Ben countered.

"Yes, we did. We gave him gruel with peas when he fell ill that time, remember?" Wally chimed in.

"No, it was beans," Ben contradicted.

Voltaris gave up, turned his back on the arguing wardens, and reluctantly consumed the gruel—better than nothing. Just as he was finishing, he heard footsteps—high heels. As he expected, they belonged to Ursula. She stopped at his cell and glared at him maliciously.

"Didn't realise it was happy hour," Voltaris cracked. "If you'd come a bit earlier, we could have shared a bowl of excreta."

She watched Ben and Wally continue down the corridor, still arguing, then said, "It's a shame you're in here, Voltaris."

"If it means not spending any time with you, then it's just fine by me," he retorted sarcastically. "Where's Gorrick, by the way? I'd like to speak with him."

"Gorrick was killed by Black Alice."

He put on a sad expression. "Oh, I'm so... ecstatic." He cracked a big cynical smile. "Nice to know the bad guy got what he deserved in the end."

"Well, there'll be a replacement soon enough."

"Must get lonely up in your iron palace with only your cyborg buddies for company?"

"One could say that," she purred.

"I've got an idea," he said, moving closer to the laser grid.

Thinking he was making a more personal suggestion, she leaned closer. "What?" she whispered breathily.

Aware he had her attention, his expression suddenly changed, and he snarled, "Why don't you go to hell."

That left her cold. From his standpoint, he had achieved the desired reaction. However, from hers, it was rejection, and she was unimpressed.

"You will rot in here, Voltaris. Then we will see who gets the last laugh."

She turned on her heel and stormed out.

Voltaris listened to the fading click of her heels on the floor and chuckled. The confrontation had been worth it; he returned to enduring his breakfast slop.

"A significant issue has arisen due to this; they're blaming the CIA, sir," Blake reported. He had been relaying to Mal, Al, Secta, Vee, Turk, Hope, and the Professor what he had heard from his contact in Papeete. The six-member French aircrew that operated the flying crane positioned on top of the cavern housing the An-Zu bird were the sole survivors of the French contingent; the twelve below had been killed. The survivors recounted the carnage, describing bodies torn apart as if by a wild animal.

"It must have been the man Turk pulled out of the hatch, the one who attacked me on the plane. En-Ki said he wasn't human... and the weirdest thing... I'd bet on the Zen agent I shot the finger off last night being the same guy," Al said.

"If the French are blaming the CIA, who do they suspect took the craft?" Mal asked.

"I'm not sure, but they've apprehended Jax and another CIA agent, Buddy someone," Blake struggled to recall the name.

"Holman... Buddy Holman... yes, he's been working with Zen," Al clarified.

Secta had a broad smile on his face.

Mal couldn't resist inquiring, "Why the smile, Secta?"

"Well, we can now focus on our mission and let them sort out their own mess," he cackled.

"It might be a good opportunity to suggest to the French that Zen was responsible for taking the bird," Vee proposed.

"Excellent idea, Vee," Blake commended. "I'll do just that... it should stir the pot even more."

"Karzoff will be here with Luna soon. We should review the outcome of last night," Mal said.

"After they took you from Café Epiphany, Hope, where did they bring you?" Al inquired.

"He had a gun on me... led me outside and shoved me into the back seat of a waiting car. They blindfolded me and drove for about fifteen minutes. When the car stopped, they took me into a cold place with echoes, like a warehouse or something, tied me to a chair. I stayed that way until they took me to Hyde Park and let me go."

"You were fortunate Al returned when he did," Mal commented.

"What's your next move, Blake?" Al asked.

"I'll get in touch with the Canberra office for new orders."

"We could use a bloke like you at OTT," Al acknowledged.

Vee's eyes sparkled, hoping that Blake would consider staying.

"Oh, I'm a field operative trained to dismantle black-market artefact syndicates. I don't see how that would be relevant to you guys," Blake admitted.

"I wouldn't be too certain," Secta interjected. "I'd consider time travel to be quite serious field work, and exploring the past and future would undoubtedly present intriguing archaeological challenges to solve."

"Now that you put it that way, I suppose it does make sense," Blake conceded.

"I can vouch for that," Al chimed in. "Anyway, give it some thought, mate. Speaking of the French... Vee, why don't you take Blake down to Café Epiphany for their renowned French toast?"

The glint in her eye transformed into appreciation. She knew that Al was giving them an opportunity to spend private time together, with his blessing. It was clear that Al had grown fond of Blake.

Just then, Karzoff entered with Luna.

"Ah, if it isn't our newest time traveller, Karzoff," Mal exclaimed.

Caught off guard, Karzoff stammered, "Yes, well... um, I suppose so, but it felt like stepping through one door and emerging from another."

"You did an exceptional job last night, Karzoff," Turk commended.

"Hear, hear!" Al added.

As Blake and Vee were on their way out, Blake stopped and turned, saying, "Luna, Jax has been apprehended by French Intelligence in Papeete, and apparently Brigadier Bruckmaster is going ballistic."

"Why was she arrested?" Luna inquired.

"The French suspect the CIA of brutally killing twelve of their operatives," Blake explained.

"They're unaware that the perpetrator was a Zen agent," Mal added.

"I suspect it's the cyborg that returned through Kairos in place of Voltaris," Al growled.

The Professor stood up and said, "If you don't need me, I'll return to my work on the Velodium sceptre."

"I think you're free to go, Prof," Mal replied.

As the others exited the room, Luna and Karzoff took their seats.

"Luna, we're planning a mission to 2112 in the next forty-eight hours. Are you up for it?" Secta inquired.

"Yes, I'll obtain UNTT authorization today. However, I do have a complaint about two unauthorized missions last night," Luna said firmly.

Al rolled his eyes. "People would have died if we hadn't acted through Kairos."

"Well, someone did die. The news is filled with reports of the shootout in Hyde Park. It seems you have some explaining to do... what's the story, Mal?" Luna demanded earnestly.

Honor braced herself for a reprimand; they were all in hot water with Gorrick. He had summoned her, Adamski, and Li to an urgent meeting.

Khan was with Gorrick. "Let's start with addressing the most recent debacle. Honor, explain the events of last night."

"I had Commander Walker abduct Dr Hope to use as leverage for the release of Denning and Hitz, who were apprehended by Karzoff for attempting to assassinate the President. I made this decision because Karzoff's interrogation of them posed a risk of uncovering my involvement in the assassination plot. Commander Walker devised a plan to eliminate Karzoff and De Cock during the exchange. I approved the plan, but it went awry—likely due to Black Alice's unexpected return from Tahiti."

"How do you know it was Black Alice?" Khan inquired.

"Based on the modus operandi. Walker accidentally shot one of his own men in the leg, and the sniper was rendered unconscious, his rifle being used to shoot off Walker's finger. All of this must have occurred during the temporal freeze caused by the opening of a

Kairos wormhole."

"I understand, that does make sense," Khan acknowledged.

"And where are Denning and Hitz now?" Gorrick probed.

"The exchange mission succeeded, and we have them secured in a safe house," Honor stated with brevity.

Gorrick's frustration was palpable. The blunder regarding the mission was a minor concern and had been addressed. It wasn't a result of Honor's negligence. Perhaps a contingency plan could have been devised, but the sudden appearance of Alice was unforeseeable.

"Now, let's address the major issue. I received a call from Bruckmaster this morning, furious because his agents have been arrested in Tahiti for the brutal murder of twelve French Intelligence operatives. Furthermore, the victims were dismembered," Gorrick explained.

Li seemed about to speak, but Gorrick raised his hand to halt her, continuing, "To exacerbate the situation, we lost three of our own agents, and the craft was seized by Black Alice. He defeated our supposedly invincible cyborg. We need to understand how and why."

"We were monitoring the live image feed from Cronus," Adamski began, "he found himself in a precarious situation within the An-Zu craft. Had his leg not been trapped in the hatch, we believe he might have overcome Black Alice."

"Excuses, excuses... why didn't he immediately eliminate him and commandeer the craft?" Gorrick snapped.

"Cronus was not programmed to commandeer the craft; his directive was to destroy it," Li interjected.

Gorrick clenched his fists, knowing she was right. That had been his order.

"What's done is done. Let's move forward," En-Lil's voice resonated in Gorrick's mind.

"You're right," Gorrick conceded, and relief washed over the room. "Our next mission needs more meticulous planning," he snarled.

"We don't always have the luxury of time, sir. Last night was another example of needing to act swiftly. In such situations, OTT consistently gains the upper hand," Honor proposed.

"Yes, I see that. Our ability to react on the fly requires refinement. But the crucial question remains: why did Cronus engage in a rampage, mutilating those men?"

"I suspect it was a glitch, sir," Li ventured cautiously.

"Not another glitch? What if he turns against us?... No, this is not acceptable... we must be able to trust him. We cannot deploy a potential mass murderer."

"Sir, you issued Cronus a take-no-prisoners directive. That might have caused the glitch in programming," Adamski cautiously submitted.

A weighty silence hung in the room as they all collected their thoughts. Then, Gorrick spoke up. "Dr Li, return Cronus to his pod and rectify the programming. He is not to be reinstated for active duty until the debugging is complete. Understood?"

"Yes, sir," both Li and Adamski agreed.

"You're dismissed, Honor. Stay here."

He waited for Adamski and Li to exit the room and then turned his attention to Honor. "There will be no further missions without my explicit approval, is that clear? Where is Commander Walker?"

"He's still in sick bay, sir. They're addressing his severed finger."

"We now know that Black Alice is currently hosting En-Ki, and Alice is aware of my identity as En-Lil. It's likely that he will attempt to target me, especially now that he has overcome Cronus. I have no interest in Zen outsourcing our work to amateurs. Get rid of Denning and Hitz... Having them on Oceana's wanted list will only complicate matters for us."

Honor sought clarification. "Do you mean that we should kill them, sir?"

"Whichever approach proves to be most effective. Additionally, we must anticipate that Karzoff has extracted information from them and might pursue you through legal means. If that situation arises, I will relocate you to another Zen office overseas until the situation settles. Once Commander Walker is discharged from sick bay, have him report to me for new directives."

"Are you removing him from my command, sir?"

"For the time being, yes. However, you will still be engaged in mission planning. My current priority is ensuring my safety from a formidable adversary we have struggled to defeat in any timeline."

"Yes, sir."

"Dismissed."

After Honor exited the room, Gorrick turned to Khan. "The question we face, Khan, is what has Black Alice done with the An-Zu craft."

"I believe we should focus on resolving the issue with Bruckmaster first. We should contemplate why the CIA acted without consulting us," Khan suggested.

"For the same reason we acted without consulting them, Khan. No, that's not our concern at the moment. For now, we let Bruckmaster and French Intelligence contend with each other. The French are unaware of our involvement. Cronus's actions left no witnesses to implicate us."

"Yes, but Jax De Ville and Holman, who was apprehended by the French, are aware," Khan pointed out.

"That's true, but it doesn't matter. The craft is gone. Yes, we eliminated their agents, but they would need concrete evidence, and their blaming of the CIA shows they lack it. Our focus should be on preventing Black Alice from targeting me. The organic chip will be ready soon, and I'll be able to escape this absurd timeline."

"Yes, master," Khan acknowledged.

"Secta, you're essentially discussing a technological singularity," Luna remarked. "As a species, we can't allow self-replicating artificial superintelligence to emerge or enable it to surpass human intelligence. Allowing that would be a grave oversight."

"It's already here, Luna. Alice's description of the Watchers as AI aligns with that concept. The AI from 2112 that Zen acquired is another example. We have the option to use Velodium and our organic processor to compete by developing our own AI. It's a matter of necessity to collaborate with advanced machines in order to overcome these challenges," Secta explained.

"You're advocating for convergence," Luna observed.

Mal, Turk, Karzoff, and Viktoria were engaged in the discussion, enjoying the intellectual exchange.

Refusing to be outdone, Luna retrieved a notepad from her bag, opened it, and continued, "I'd like to quote from 'Arguments Against the Singularity' by Stross."

"Please, go ahead," Secta encouraged.

Luna cleared her throat and began reading from the notepad:

"Before creating a conscious artificial intelligence, we have to ask if we're creating an entity deserving of rights. Is it murder to shut down a software process that is in some sense conscious? Is it genocide to use genetic algorithms to evolve software agents towards consciousness? These are massive showstoppers. We clearly want machines that perform human-like tasks. We want computers that recognise our language and motivations and can take hints, rather than requiring instructions enumerated in mind-numbingly tedious detail. But whether we want them to be conscious and volitional is another question entirely.

I don't want my self-driving car to argue with me about where we want to go today. I don't want my robot housekeeper to spend all its time in front of the TV watching contact sports or music videos. And I certainly don't want to be sued for maintenance by an abandoned software development project.

We see increasingly solicitous machines defining our environment—machines that sense and respond to our needs intelligently. But it will be the intelligence of the serving hand rather than the commanding brain, and we're only at risk of disaster if we harbour self-destructive impulses."

Secta nodded. "Stross presents a valid perspective, but it's important to note that we're already past the point of phasing in AI. My stance is that you should reserve your judgment until you've visited 2112."

Turk chimed in with a smile, "I've experienced both the positive and negative sides of AI. It's terrifying when it's misused and remarkable when it's beneficial. The issue, in my opinion, isn't about preventing its advancement; that's progress. The concern lies in entities like Zen exploiting AI to suppress others. The Watchers, on the other hand, don't seem to have engaged in such actions."

"Absolutely, Turk. Al, what are your thoughts?" Mal inquired.

"Yeah, I'm with Turk. I've witnessed both the positive and negative aspects, and there's been too much talking. I travelled across the solar system to confront En-Lil, and now he's only blocks away from us. We've seen the extent of his capabilities. It's time to take action. We also have unfinished business in 2112 and the task of rescuing Voltaris. Let's stop arguing over ideals and prophecies and start acting," Al emphasised.

Luna's expression displayed her disapproval of Alice's gung-ho approach.

CHAPTER 34
DEANOSS AND THE NOSEBAGS

EXITING MAL'S OFFICE, Rita Vallins caught their attention with a call, "Alice, Ratsso left a message. Said if you're up for a drink he'll be at the watering hole. You know where it is."

"Cool, Rita. Ta," Al replied.

Walking to the elevator, Al turned to Turk, "Wanna join me for an ale with Ratsso from the band?"

"Sure."

An hour later, Al and Turk entered the bustling main bar of the London Hotel in Paddington. Ratsso, sporting his iconic red beret, sat at the bar with his back to them. Al playfully slapped his back and greeted, "Ratsso!"

Swivelling around with a wide grin, Ratsso exclaimed, "Al, glad you could make it, mate."

Al introduced Turk, "Ratsso, remember Turk from the gig?"

"Hey Turk." They shook hands. "How could I forget? He's the guy who took down that freaking drone, isn't he?"

"Sure did. Let's grab a pigs-ear. Any preference, Turk?" Al asked.

Ratsso, a slim man with long black hair neatly tied in a ponytail beneath his red beret, wore a black leather jacket over a black T-shirt that boldly read 'SAVE THE MALES,' a play on the the eighties' 'SAVE THE WHALES' campaign.

"Last beer I had was in 2087 at Reno's. Anything on tap would be great," Turk replied.

"I'll sort it. Why don't you grab a table near the window?" Ratsso suggested, not quite grasping Turk's reference to Reno's in 2087. He remained unaware of Alice's extraordinary time-travel escapades with OTT.

Al and Turk found a table in the nearly empty establishment.

"Not many folk around, business must be crook," Turk observed.

"Things are tough mate, folk can't afford to go drinkin' and besides, the cops are out to get you to blow in the bag if you're driving... it's a five-hundred credit fine and three points off your licence if you get busted. Might fill up a bit at happy hour," Al explained.

Ratsso returned with three glassesof beer, each containing 450 millilitres. "Here you go lads. Three schooners of new."

"Cheers," Al toasted.

"Ah, that hits the spot," Turk commented after taking a hearty sip.

"So, what's the latest, Al?" Ratsso inquired.

"Not much, mate. You know, out there, time-traveling and saving the world," Al said, playfully.

Turk nearly choked on his beer, understanding the humour but also the accuracy of the statement.

"Hey, there's a party at Deanoss's place right around the corner. It's starting soon, and they've got a barbecue going. Wanna drop by?" Ratsso suggested.

"Yeah, sounds good. It's been a while since I saw Deanoss. Is he still playing with the band?"

"Deanoss and the Nosebags? Yep, they've even released a record. Oh, the title is 'Rusty Old Tits,'" Ratsso said.

"Yep, that sounds like a typical Deanoss title."

Curious, Turk asked, "What kind of music is it?"

"Mad," Ratsso said, with a chuckle. "But a loads of fun, s'pose you'd call it reggae wouldn't you Al?"

"More Ska don't you reckon?" Al corrected.

"Yeah, yeah, that'd be right. Ska it is. A bit like Madness with horns and backup singers," Ratsso clarified.

A few punters started to come in and the bar quickly filled. Many of them recognised Alice and insisted on chatting, slapping his back and getting his autograph. Al wanted to get out of there, so they downed their beers and headed for the party.

Walking up Underwood Street while Ratsso was on the phone conversing with Deanoss, Turk mentioned to Alice, "I'll probably be the oldest bloke at the party."

"Ah! I don't think of you as being in your fifties," Al chuckled. "It feels like just a year or so ago we were fighting together against Zen, and you were in your thirties."

"Hard to get my head around that, Al."

"Yeah, I know. Secta calls it a time travel paradox."

Ratsso finished his call and came to a stop. "Here we are, guys."

It wasn't hard to tell that they had arrived at the right place: Ska music was blaring, and a group of wild-looking dudes were gathered around the front door of the two-storey Paddington terrace. As they moved through the crowd, Al received plenty of pats on the back from fans. The hallway inside was packed. They navigated through, following Ratsso who led them to the back patio. Many people in the crowd complimented Alice in passing, "Great concert, Al."

Finally, they emerged onto the patio, which was a sea of punters dressed in black, all moving in time with the loud music.

"What does Ska stand for?" Turk asked, as they paused to observe everyone.

"Super kick arse... it predates reggae... it's different today than it was in the 80s. Now it's more like black punk... lots of black and white checked T-shirts," Ratsso yelled back.

A big black guy glided through the crowd and approached Ratsso, giving him a huge hug. When Ratsso pointed at Al, the rotund man wearing a black and white checkerboard turban, a black three-quarter sleeveless coat, and luminous green tights, beamed a massive smile adorned with gold teeth and then let out a screech at the top of his voice, "If it ain't the Alice-man!" They embraced.

"Deanoss, you're looking happening, dude," Al said.

"Hey, man, went to yer concert to shake my big butt, it was so damn bad, man," he said in a heavy Jamaican accent.

"This is my buddy, Turk," Al introduced.

"Hey, Turk, welcome to Deanoss's. If you wanna eat, man, there's food at the barbecue over near the side fence. Here, tug on this," he said, handing Alice a massive joint.

Al took a toke, then passed it to Turk.

"What's this?" Turk asked.

"A joint, weed... dope, mate, are you Rip Van Winkle?" Ratsso joked.

"Cannabis or marijuana. Just take a small toke, otherwise, you might end up like Rip Van Winkle," Al cautioned Turk, light-heartedly.

Turk took a drag on the joint and nearly coughed up his lungs. Al laughed.

Ratsso leaned in and whispered to Al, "Mate, what planet is this bloke Turk from?"

"Ah, just another time, mate."

Ratsso nodded, not quite grasping what Al meant. He took the joint, had a big drag, and then passed it on.

As they made their way toward the barbecue, Al asked Turk, "I don't think this is our scene, mate. Since you're taller than me, can you take a look over the crowd to see if there's a back gate where we can do a runner?"

Turk stretched to look over the mass of bobbing heads and recognised someone.

"There's a back gate alright," he reported. "Standing next to it is Glan Denning... and what do you know, Toeghan Hitz is there as well," he said, looking back at Alice with raised eyebrows.

"You sure?" Al questioned, thinking that it would have to be an incredible coincidence.

"Yep, I was with them in the back of the car during the exchange. I'd recognise them anywhere... it's definitely them," Turk confirmed.

"I'd like to have a word with them," Al growled. "Hey Ratsso, too many punters, mate. We're out of here."

Ratsso patted Al on the back and shook Turk's hand. "Cool mate. Catch you later." He was accustomed to Al bailing when things got too tough. Having been in the band, he knew that socialising lost its enjoyment when numerous people wanted to greet and chat.

Al and Turk made their way to the back gate. As they neared it, Toeghan Hitz suddenly spotted them and told Denning. They swung the gate open and slipped out.

When Al and Turk burst out through the gate, the scene that greeted them was not what they had anticipated. Two bikers wearing full-face black visor helmets and clad in black leathers like motorcycle couriers had Denning and Hitz cornered against the rear fence. One of the bikers was wielding a baseball bat at Hitz, while the other had an arm around Denning's neck from behind, a bowie knife poised at his throat.

Hitz was taking a beating and fell to the ground, trying to shield herself from the brutal blows. Turk seized the biker with the bat, ripped it out of his grasp and bashed him with it. The blows cracked his helmet open and shattered the visor.

Al was struggling to prevent the other biker from slitting Denning's throat. He urged, "Drop the blade, mate... let him go... take it easy..."

Denning's eyes widened in terror when, in a swift motion, the biker drew the blade across his throat. Denning let out a horrific gurgling sound and collapsed to the ground, convulsing.

The biker fled to his parked motorcycle at the curb and mounted it. Al grabbed him by the collar and pulled him off. The biker lashed out with the blade, but Al caught his arm, twisted it, evaded the strike, and as he passed under the biker's arm, dislocated his shoulder. The biker screamed in agony and dropped the blade. Al yanked off the biker's helmet and delivered a powerful punch to his face, shattering his nose.

Turk had pummelled the other biker into a trembling heap on

the pavement. His helmet was nearly destroyed. Both his arms were fractured from shielding himself—he was going nowhere.

Hitz regained consciousness. Turk helped her up. When she saw Denning sprawled on the ground, throat slashed open, she gasped, "No."

A crowd had gathered—it was a gruesome scene. Al quickly dialled Karzoff for assistance. Within minutes, police officers arrived. They had been alerted by Karzoff and proceeded to secure the crime scene and apprehend the culprits.

Karzoff arrived shortly after and assisted Alice and Turk in getting Hitz into the back seat of his SUV. They sped away to Oceana, leaving the police to handle the mop up.

In an Oceana HQ interrogation room, Karzoff and Alice grilled Hitz while Turk sat and listened. Though shaken by the attack, Hitz wasn't traumatized enough to prevent her from talking.

"Alice and Turk saved your life tonight. The assailants were working for Zen. Were you aware that you were falling out of favour with them?" Karzoff questioned.

"No comment," she defiantly snarled, folding her arms and slumping in the chair like a petulant child.

"They were going to kill you!" Al growled.

"I didn't think they'd do that, the fascist pigs," she snarled.

"Cut the act. We have looked into your background—respectable family, good education. You're not some street urchin. So, quit behaving like one," Karzoff said firmly.

She smirked smugly, and her demeanour suddenly shifted entirely. It was as though she had transformed into a completely different person. She sat up with an intelligent gleam in her eyes and adopted a business-like tone. "Alright, look, I appreciate that you had no obligation to rescue me, and I'm grateful for that. What do you want to know?"

"Good, now we're making progress. What's the name of the leader of the kidnappers? I shot off his finger," Al interrogated.

"Oh, him. Commander Daniel Walker."

Karzoff immediately entered his name into a government security database on his phone. It pulled up his record and a photograph. He showed it to Hitz.

"This him?" he inquired.

"Yes," she confirmed.

He showed Alice.

"Wait a minute, this can't be right," Al questioned.

Turk took a look. "That's the guy I pulled out of the An-Zu bird."

"You're right, that's him alright. I saw his face through the night-scope when I shot him, but it didn't register. But how did he get back from Tahiti as quickly as I did?"

"Couldn't have," Turk agreed.

"What if he's the entity that came back through Kairos?" Al proposed.

"But that was Voltaris," Karzoff queried.

"Only his face. What if this entity can change its appearance?" They pondered it briefly, and then Al turned to Hitz. "Who recruited you into Zen?"

"I wasn't a part of Zen. Like how you were before they turned you, I was elected leader of the Octagon, and Zen approached me with a proposition."

"Who at Zen?" Karzoff pressed.

After a moment's pause to think, she confessed, "Look, the more I expose them, the more reasons they have to eliminate me."

"They already tried to kill you, remember?" Karzoff reminded her. "So, who was it?"

"It was Honor."

Karzoff sighed with relief, his suspicions confirmed.

"Did you meet her at the Zen offices?" Al asked.

"Not her. She always kept our meetings secret... don't know why."

"I do," Karzoff said confidently. "She was doing it on the side.

That's her form. Nothing has changed."

"Where did you meet?" Al inquired.

"Our first meeting was at a café in Balmain. She brought along a guy named Holman, who I met the first time I went to Zen."

"That's correct, we had a drone monitoring that meeting," Karzoff informed Alice.

"And the next one?" Al asked.

"There was only one more. It took place at the Grind Café in Kings Cross," Hitz disclosed.

That rang a bell with Al. "Yeah, I know it. Right. Do you got your phone?"

"Yes," she confirmed.

"Honor's number?" Al questioned.

"Yes."

"Here's what you're going to do. Call her now and tell her you were attacked, Denning is dead, and you fear for your life. Tell her you've found some incriminating information about Mal from Octagon files, and you're willing to trade it for your safety. Got it?" Al confirmed.

"And then?" she inquired.

"Arrange to meet her at the Grind Café tomorrow at 7:30 a.m. for the exchange... and insist she comes alone," Al said.

"What if she refuses?" she asked.

"Do not worry about that. I know Honor. She wll seize any chance to impress her superiors. You can count on her showing up," Karzoff assured.

Hitz locked eyes with Alice's determined gaze and asked firmly, "If I do it, what's in it for me?"

"A free trip to safety," Al replied with a smile.

"How can I trust you?"

"Would you rather trust them?" Alice countered.

Hitz retrieved her phone and called Honor.

Later, after securing Hitz in a cell until the morning, Alice was walking back toward the elevator when Turk inquired, "What did you mean by a free trip top safety?"

"Oh, that. Figured she might be of use to you in 2112. Don't you reckon?"

Turk smiled and nodded in agreement.

CHAPTER 35
CODE OF HONOR

HITZ WAS SAT at a table in the Grind Café, alone, sipping on a cappuccino. She spotted Honor, wearing sunglasses, entering the doorway and scanning the handful of customers seated at the tables. The café was small, with only around a dozen tables. Once Honor seemed satisfied that there was no immediate danger, she walked in and took a seat across from Hitz. Her manner was circumspect.

"So, you were attacked last night?" Honor said in a cold tone.

Hitz thought to herself, as if you didn't know, and replied, "Yes, Denning is dead. His throat was slit," speaking in hushed tones.

"That's dreadful news. I'm sorry... but how did you manage to escape?"

"It happened at a party. Someone called the police."

"Did they catch the assailant?"

"Assailants. There were two of them. I don't know. It happened on the street outside the party, with lots of people around. I ran back inside and blended into the crowd."

"Smart move. So, what do you have for me?"

"She does not have anything for you, Honor. You just broke the first rule of espionage: never sit with your back to the door."

Honor turned around in alarm. She recognised Karzoff's distinct voice. She got up to make a quick exit, but then the other six patrons in the café stood up, aiming pistols at her—all of them Oceana agents.

Karzoff dangled a pair of handcuffs in front of Honor's face, relishing the moment. "Fanny Honor, I am placing you under arrest for conspiring to assassinate the President."

With Honor in custody, as Alice had orchestrated, they now had the means to formulate a plan to eliminate En-Lil. All Karzoff needed was to extract a location from Honor to isolate Gorrick/En-Lil. There was nothing he would enjoy more than breaking Honor.

In the meantime, Secta had positioned half a dozen cryogenic cylinders containing donor sperm on the chair in the Avalon bunker. Alongside them was a flash drive containing a set of instructions for in vitro fertilization compiled by Hope. During her time at Oceana, Morri had been trained by medical specialists in IVF techniques. Everything was prepared for their return to 2112. Their departure through Kairos would only be approved once Luna evaluated the extent of the epidemic. Only then would she approve the treatment of the inflicted by having them pass them through Kairos for the SAGE filter to erase the infected gene from their DNA.

On the mission to 2112, Luna would accompany Alice, Turk, Morri, and Vee. Meanwhile, Secta would remain behind to collaborate with the Professor and Hope on developing the Velodium superconductor. Alice was hopeful that while in 2112, Karzoff would extract the necessary information from Honor. Opening a wormhole directly to Gorrick's office wasn't feasible due to the increased security measures. They needed a different approach—a place En-Lil would least expect to be attacked.

Alice was also concerned about the clone of Commander Walker. As long as he was active, the members of OTT were in grave danger. Getting rid of him was another item on Alice's to-do list.

Ratsso had contacted Alice to check on him after hearing about the brawl outside the party. Rumours were spreading about how he had confronted a couple of thugs attempting to rob a girl leaving the party. Deanoss had even been featured on various news channels, boosting the popularity of his song "Rusty Old Tits" and propelling it up the charts.

Soon as he heard she'd been captured, Mal visited Toeghan. He left her best of friends—Mal had that effect on people.

Just before they were about to gather in the Kairos control room for departure, Morri decided to bring Toeghan along. Luna wasn't thrilled about using the future as a refuge for those evading the law, but she recognised Toeghan's potential value to Morri in the future. Given Hope's absence, Toeghan's youth, health, and intelligence could prove invaluable. Additionally, Luna didn't want her exposed to any further attacks from Zen.

Excluding Al and Vee, Secta equipped the remaining team members with Clock Drives. The moment to depart had arrived. Mal, the Professor, Hope, Karzoff, and Viktoria were present to watch Rob send them into the future.

Tears welled up in Morri's and Turk's eyes as they left Hope behind. However, they found solace in the knowledge that Hope was in capable hands and only a Clock Drive away.

Toeghan wasn't pleased about having to remove all her piercings, and Luna shared the same sentiment about leaving her jewellery behind. Toeghan was struggling to comprehend the situation. The prospect of participating in time travel both intrigued and worried her. Morri comforted her by taking her arm.

"Don't worry. In the blink of an eye, you'll be in another time. I was nervous on my first trip too, but it turned out there was nothing to fear. We're in safe hands."

Toeghan's expression lightened with relief. A few minutes later, Rob swivelled around from the console and informed Secta, "That's it... a-okay... they're all on their way."

2112. The skies were dark from the fierce rolling thunderheads of a massive cyclone that had hit Avalon. It had struck with such force it bent the eucalyptus trees surrounding the bunker field as though they were bowing in reverence with their backs facing the 200 kilometres an hour gale.

Down below ground in the bunker garage, a vortex opened about the size of a baseball, rotating half a metre above the floor. The event horizon was a swirling fury, with the circular interior of the black wormhole growing larger by the second. The event caused everything within a hundred-metre radius to freeze.

As the vortex expanded to a three-metre black hole, the time travellers emerged one by one. Turk was the first, followed by Morri. Taking a deep breath, Turk savoured the scent of the air. He glanced around the large concrete room, spotting the APC parked at the back and the drone beside it. On the other side, under a tarpaulin, was Morri's Wilson J-Car. The familiarity of these objects provided a sense of comfort.

Vee followed Turk, closely followed by Toeghan Hitz. Luna stepped out with a bewildered expression, finding it difficult to accept that she had just travelled through time. She hadn't felt a thing. Alice was the last to emerge from the spinning black hole.

"Is this for real?" Luna voiced her disbelief. "Like, are we truly in 2112?"

Morri reassured her, "We sure are," just as the vortex closed and the frozen items unfroze. A loud clash of thunder resonated throughout the cavernous room.

Turk exclaimed, "Whoa, that's one powerful storm up top!" At that moment, the sky unleashed a torrential downpour, the rain drumming on the hatch above like a thousand percussionists.

Speaking loudly to be heard over the noise, Morri said, "Okay, Al and Turk, we'll meet you in the cafeteria after I give the girls a tour."

They ventured into the corridor, with Vee and Toeghan getting along well, sharing similar interests. They trailed behind Morri and Luna, heading for the infirmary. As they entered an office area, a group of healthy individuals rushed up to warmly greet Morri, taken aback by her unexpected return.

"I s'pose she'll want to visit other bunkers to get the true extent of the epidemic," Al remarked.

Taking a sip of his coffee, Turk added, "I didn't realise how crook this coffee was until drinking a Café Epiphany brew."

Al chuckled, "Yeah, I bet you'll miss the French toast."

"I don't know, I think we can replicate it down here. We just need some maple syrup."

"I can always have some dropped off at the bunker for you. That reminds me, we'd better grab the cryogenic containers in a minute."

After their coffee, they headed to the room at the entrance, preserved in its original form.

"It's just as ghostly as when we came down here after the concert," Turk said.

"Yeah, it's a bit like a museum exhibit," Al speculated, as he approached the dentist-like chair that had transported him into the future and initiated the entire time travel phenomenon, back then. He settled into the chair.

"Weird sitting here... feels like fifty years ago that I sat here for the first time... but it's been less than two years... hell, a lot of water under the bridge since then."

"Tell me about it, I was thirty years old," Turk grumbled.

Chuckling, Al leapt out of the chair, reached under it, and retrieved the cylinders. He handed three to Turk and held onto the other three and the flash drive. Together, they carried them back to the cafeteria.

The storm continued to pound the world outside the bunker, with loud, violent cracks of intermittent lightning followed by claps of thunder and the roar of torrential rain.

It didn't take long for Morri to bring the ladies to join Al and Turk in the cafeteria.

Luna was the first to speak. "Well, I have seen how horrible this disease is. Now, I need to assess its extent. I will need to visit other communities."

Al and Turk exchanged looks that said "I told you so."

Morri held a Ulink notebook. "I took this from my office, expecting Luna's needs." She opened it on the table. Once activated, it displayed a 3-D holographic map half a metre high above it, with red dots featured. "The red dots represent the known bunkers. If I touch one, it will provide the details as we knew them from a couple of months ago." She pressed the nearest dot to Avalon. "This is the Rebels' bunker." A pop-up displayed statistics, which she read aloud, "Fifty able-bodied, six hundred infirmed. Six months ago, the total occupancy was two thousand two hundred and thirty, resulting in fifteen hundred and eighty deaths... a death rate of seventy percent over a six-month period."

"Would all those deaths be attributed to Red Wheel?" Luna questioned.

"No, some would have been caused by Zen cyborgs, but that would amount to about twenty or thirty at most," Turk growled, unimpressed by Luna's attitude.

Luna sensed the tension. She could feel his passion and hurt. "Turk, please... I'm not trying to be difficult or to underestimate the gravity of this terrible epidemic. Sometimes the divine and the terrible are so close to each other. I need enough information to convince others at the UN of this human catastrophe. I personally don't need convincing... I've seen enough. My heart sank when I saw thousands of your people in such a horrific state. I honestly don't know how you've managed to cope."

"Neither do we," Turk admitted, gloomily acquiescent.

"I can't capture photos or film to take back. I need to witness everything, so I'll have to visit one of the outlying areas, such as here," she said, touching a red dot on the outskirts of the map. No statistics appeared. "See, no stats. So, we really don't know the extent of it, do we?"

"That's no-man's-land... even back in '87, we wouldn't go there," Turk said. "There were rumours."

"What rumours?" Al questioned.

"Well, the closer you get to ground zero, Canberra, the worse the effects of not only Red Wheel but also radiation and the bomb blast that took out Canberra. That bunker is at Queanbeyan, and we know it's a bunker because we received intelligence from other bunkers about it. The thing is, it's not a biker bunker... we've found that bunkers not controlled by biker gangs, ex-cops, or ex-military are far less civilized. Rumours suggest that the people there are feral. They claim the bunker is what remains of a hospital, the underground part."

"We have to do it. If I can provide details of the map, with the Avalon bunker stats, the extremity of the Queanbeyan bunker, and then Angel City, I'm convinced I'll be able to secure total support for the rescue mission."

"Wait a minute, that's the first time you've mentioned going into the Angel City Death Camp?" Al protested.

"Visiting Angel City is not up for debate, Alice... it's the largest population we know of, so it's mandatory."

"It's run by a bunch of despots, for crying out loud. When we were there last time, we had to fight our way out... I killed the Zen leader... there wouldn't exactly be a joyful flag-waving ceremony to welcome us if we go there. Are you prepared for a fight?" Al questioned her.

"They don't call it a death camp for nothing. I'm an escaped convict they'd just love to see again," Turk added.

"Yes, I'll fight if necessary... I'm sorry, but it's non-negotiable," Luna said firmly, folding her arms defiantly.

"Alright, alright... we'll do Queanbeyan first," Al grumbled.

"With that cyclone out there, we can't use the drone. We'll have to take the APC," Turk said.

"We should wait until the storm has passed," Luna said.

"You stick to being the observer. Leave us to call the shots," Turk snapped, quite unlike him.

"Every hour that passes, another person dies, Luna. We don't have time to wait for it to pass. If you want to visit these places and you want to live to tell the story, then it would be best to pay attention to what Turk and Alice have to say," Morri stated firmly, locking eyes with Luna, who reluctantly nodded her head in agreement. "Right then, who's going?" Morri said, looking at Al.

"You better put the cryo-container in the freezer, Moz, because we'll all have to go."

"Will do, Al."

"Okay," Turk said, getting to his feet. "Let's hit the armoury and load up."

Turk had pockets full of WASPS that Secta had produced, along with some leftovers from the An-Zu mission. It was critical to keep them in a dry place, and the hermetically sealed gunpowder repository in the armoury would perfectly fit the bill.

This was the part of a mission that excited Vee the most: she loved handling weapons and having the pick of an entire arsenal.

With each of them armed to the teeth except for Luna, assembled in the garage. The storm was still raging outside.

Turk had positioned the APC on the elevator set to go. They were all standing next to it about to board, listening to the storm outside when Luna asked Morri, "What powers it?"

"A pellet drive: a tiny nuclear fusion device. Safe," she said, confidently accounting for Luna's penchant for anti-nuke everything.

"I would hope so," Luna replied with scepticism.

"No more radiation than you're about to be exposed to in Queanbeyan," Morri reminded her.

Toeghan looked more like a guerrilla rebel than a Goth, dressed in army camouflage fatigues, a red beret, and armed with an AK-47.

"You sure you can handle it? An AK packs a punch?" Vee asked her.

Toeghan fired her a cheeky smirk, "Can't wait to give it a try."

"Okay, let's ship out, all aboard," Turk declared.

CHAPTER 36
DOWN UNDER

" IF YOU REFUSE to cooperate in telling me how to get to Gorrick, you will be sent to the future, never to return," Karzoff threatened Honor.

Honor stared at the ceiling of the interrogation room as though Karzoff hadn't spoken. She'd spent many times in the room, only on the other side of the desk.

Viktoria entered and sat down beside Karzoff.

Mal was standing in a dimly lit small annexed room on the other side of the large one-way mirrored viewing window, watching the interview with interest.

Viktoria opened a folder in front of her, took out a document, and stated firmly, "Fanny Honor, Document A is a sworn statement by one of your confessed conspirators, Miss Toeghan Hitz. In it, you are named as orchestrating the attempted assassination of Black Alice and President Malcolm Low at the Avalon benefit concert. Do you admit to the charge?"

Honor sharply changed her focus to Viktoria, eyeballed her with an ice-cold squint, and said calmly, "You have no evidence of this accusation."

"On the contrary, we have footage of you meeting co-conspirators Glan Denning and Toeghan Hitz at the Belmont Café in Balmain, a month prior to the said concert," Karzoff said, nonplussed.

"You'll need a lot more than that," she said coldly.

"For what?" Viktoria said, with equal frigidity.

Honor raised her nose defiantly. "To obtain enough evidence to prosecute me in court, that's what. Now, either charge me or release me."

"Who said anything about going to court? Karzoff told you if you fail to satisfy our request for information, then you will be sent to the future never to return. The very same place your friend Voltaris Idram is now."

"Don't be ridiculous, Voltaris Idram returned through Kairos; you witnessed it yourself."

"You and I both know that was not Idram; it was a cyborg… we have a physical scan of him coming through Kairos as proof. This is the same cyborg that with the features of Commander Daniel Walker, killed twelve French Intelligence agents three days ago in the Poo Ôonoo Valley, Tahiti," Karzoff submitted.

"That's absurd. I know nothing about this Poo Ôonoo Valley. He has been here… it was Commander Walker who arranged the exchange of Hope for Hitz and Denning."

"Ah, so you admit to the kidnapping of Dr Hope," Karzoff said.

Honor tightened her arms, folded in front of her, and snarled in defiance, "No comment."

Karzoff leaned close to Viktoria and whispered in her ear.

"Why were you at Café Grind this morning?" Viktoria asked.

"I had been asked to meet someone."

"Stop beating around the bush, Honor. We recorded your phone conversation with Toeghan Hitz… she is in fear of being murdered by your agents after they had killed Glan Denning."

Honor rolled her eyes, figuring they had no proof of that either.

"We have the perpetrators in custody, and they're talking. Now, if all of this isn't enough evidence for you to think we have no grounds for holding you in remand, then think again. Last chance, Honor," Viktoria pressed.

A knock at the door; it opened, and Rita Vallins told Mal, "Blake Green is here to see you, sir."

Mal turned from the viewing window. "Good, send him in."

Blake entered the dimly lit room, extending his arm to offer his hand to shake. "Mr President."

Mal shook his hand. "Blake, good to see you. Have you made a decision about your future?"

"Yes, I have, sir. My office in Canberra offered me a posting in Kuala Lumpur to track down a suspected trafficker of illegal artefacts, an ex-CIA agent named Handerson Bolt. I know him; a real bad bastard."

"And?"

"I passed on it, sir. I'd like to join OTT."

Mal beamed a huge grin. "Fantastic, I'm sure Al and the team will be thrilled. Effective immediately?"

"Yes, sir."

"Good. This is wrapping up; I'll take you down to Kyleen Hern at HR to get you stamped and approved."

"What's happening in there, sir?"

"Call me Mal, my friend. Karzoff and Viktoria are questioning Honor about the attempted assassination, amongst other things."

"Who is she?"

"Oh, sorry, Fanny Honor, formerly our head of security turned Zen agent."

"Karzoff's former boss?"

"Yes. They have a sincere dislike of each other."

"Then he'd be relishing this opportunity. Tell me more about her?"

"I'll tell you on the way to HR; she has a long and jaded history," Mal said, leading him out of the room.

Regina Fych glanced up at Gorrick as he entered reception through the glass doors and informed him, "I was just about to call you, sir. Oceana State Security Directorate has arrested Honor."

"On what grounds?" he said, his tone cold.

"Conspiracy to murder, sir. They also have our agents in custody who Honor had assigned to eliminate Glan Denning and Toeghan Hitz."

"Does it get any worse?" Gorrick growled.

"I hope not, sir. Oh, Professor Adamski wants to see you... and Khan is already in your office."

"Better get our law firm on the line, have them send someone to get Honor out."

"Yes, sir."

He opened the large double doors to his lavish office suite and stepped inside. A short walk along the meandering footpath over the white bridge and he joined Khan on the island. As he took his seat, he said, "And what do you want?"

"The hive conference this morning brought up some issues I need to discuss with you," Khan said, his demeanour frosty.

"Such as?"

"My posting. I want the Aquila project in Texas," Khan requested.

"I can't say it will continue; we have a small problem with Bruckmaster that won't be easy to overcome."

"Then where will Aquila be set up?" Khan asked.

Gorrick looked back toward the entrance when he heard Adamski making his way to meet him. "We'll discuss it after an update from Adamski."

The Professor arrived.

"Please, sit down, Professor," Gorrick ordered. "I want an update on Aquila and on Cronus."

Gorrick noticed that Adamski must have been working out, as he had put on some serious bulk.

"As far as the organic processor is concerned, it will be operational in twenty-four hours, but it will require quite a lot of testing before I can release it for use in Aquila," Adamski explained.

"Understandable. But good, go on."

"As for Cronus, Dr Li found the glitch. It was in the code that programmed the mission objective. When programmed to eliminate armed threatening adversaries, the code failed to express the limitations. So, if Cronus confronted an army of aggressors under those instructions, it would keep killing them until there were none remaining."

"Amazing technology. So, how did you rectify that?"

"By overriding the instruction. Basically, we will monitor the point of view from Cronus to manually generate kill instructions. That is all we can do."

Gorrick rubbed his chin, thinking, and said, "I thought it was supposed to be intuitive?"

"It is, sir. It keeps an image of every target on its database along with the instruction. We have written new code for it to prioritise targets, so if it saw Black Alice, for instance, it would not hesitate to kill him. But if it was an armed aggressor, it would set a lower priority, which has a watch and wait instruction... it then saves that instruction for future reference. If it is required, the command can be elevated to watch and act."

"Wouldn't that put him in danger should the operator be slow to react?" Khan asked.

"We believe the reaction time to be sufficient. He has also been fitted with an algorithm that calculates the level of threat from behavioural patterns of the target... over a thousand of them, from eye movement, mouth twitches, etc., based on human behavioural psychology."

"Good. So when will he be operational?" Gorrick asked.

"He is, sir. You are talking to him."

Gorrick was impressed.

The real Adamski entered.

The torrential rain had little effect on the APC's progress. Travelling at an average of 150 km/h, only the potholes in the road, now disguised by being full of water, were cause for concern; some of them were very deep. Hitting a deep one at that speed could easily snap an axle. The interior monitor providing Turk a view of the road ahead was equipped with night vision and a filter to see through rain. The storm cloud base was so heavy that even though it was 10 a.m., it was dark, requiring the headlights.

They had been travelling for an hour and were crossing the mountains. Alice was watching the monitor over Turk's shoulder, the rain almost obliterating the effects of the headlights. The low cloud had clashed with the mountain, enshrouding them in dense fog.

"Don't know how you can drive through this, mate. No way I could," Al admitted.

"Oh, you get used to it. You can thank governments back in your time for storms like this, a direct result of them ignoring global warming. They say some islands in the oceans that were not far above sea level back then have now completely disappeared. There were a couple of blokes in my battalion during the war from Fiji, who said their villages were wiped out and they had to move. There was a massive rise in ocean level in 2070 when icebergs, sometimes half a mile thick, broke away from the Arctic Circle and floated south to melt. With so much of it, the salinity of the ocean dropped drastically, killing fish and the already sick coral reefs around the world and causing weird weather events. It didn't help that they'd wiped out the forests in the Amazon and in Southeast Asia. You should try and do something about climate change when you get back, mate."

Luna was eavesdropping on the conversation and interjected, "That issue is very difficult to prove in our time, Turk."

"Yep, that was the common excuse," Al growled.

"Well, now you have proof... and you'll see plenty more. It's one thing to blame Zen, and don't get me wrong, they're as guilty as sin for creating this dystopia, but even without Zen, the world was faced with a climatic catastrophe that we inherited."

They suddenly hit a massive pothole, and the vehicle bumped hard. They were all thrown about violently, with Alice smacking his head hard against the metal side panel, almost knocking him out. Turk had to struggle with the steering to stop the APC from rolling— it careened sideways, skidding towards the edge of a ravine. They all watched the screen in wide-eyed terror. Turk pumped the brakes hard, but they had little effect. He threw it into reverse, and the engine roared in protest. They were closing in on the cliff edge, sure to slide over. With their hearts in their mouths and bile erupting into their throats, they all felt completely helpless... reliant only on Turk's driving skills to stop the treacherous slide.

Turk saw a big old blue gumtree towering a hundred feet in the air with a massive girth at the edge of the ravine. He fought the sliding vehicle to aim at it and yelled out, "Brace for impact!"

The APC T-boned into the huge tree trunk. The sudden stop threw them about like rag dolls, but their seat belts kept them in place and safe.

Silence fell over them, broken only by the incessant rain belting on the hatch as though insisting on coming inside. It was then they all took a deep breath, realising they were safe and alive.

Blood was trickling down Alice's cheek after banging his head. Vee saw it and asked, "You alright, Al?"

He growled, "Yeah, yeah, it's nothing."

Turk swivelled around in his seat and inquired, "Is everyone okay?" Murmurs of yes came from the shaken passengers. He turned back and switched the monitor camera view to the port side. "Goddamn, will you look at that?" he said.

The APC was hanging over the edge of the cliff. Instant panic broke out, but Turk placated them. "It's okay, sit real still... I think we're safe, we shouldn't go over... we can thank that big old gumtree for saving our lives."

"Ironic that we were just talking about cutting down the forests when this happened," Luna said, her voice quivering from the shock.

"I'll have to check outside to see if we can pull free from the tree," Turk said, unhitching his seatbelt and then carefully manoeuvring out of the driver's seat. As he made his way towards the hatch, the

APC let out a groan and suddenly lurched. Luna yelped. Turk froze, waited, and then slowly reached out a hand to press the hatch button. It slid open, and rain flooded in, drenching him. He went to move up the ladder, and the APC groaned and lurched again.

Luna panicked. "Don't move! Don't move... we'll go over!" she screamed.

Morri quickly placated her, "Shush, love, quieten down... Turk needs to check it. We'll be alright, believe me."

Turk subtly climbed up the ladder and stuck his head out into the torrential rain to assess the damage. The cliff dropped away sheer under the port side, at least five hundred metres into a mist-filled valley. The APC was dangling precariously over the edge. He went to move, and the vehicle creaked and tipped lightly towards the drop, eliciting a squawk from Luna below. He waited for the vehicle to settle back and then leaned over the port side. Three of the six wheels were perilously close to the cliff edge. Hammered by wind and rain, so hard that it stung his exposed flesh, he had to shield his eyes to see how hard the vehicle was lodged against the tree. It had absorbed the impact, and that amazed him. He figured that with a little manoeuvring in reverse towards the starboard side, he would be able to get the APC back onto the slippery road. "Thank you, mate," he said in reverence, looking up at the big tree that was probably over two hundred years old. He gently climbed back inside and closed the hatch.

"Are we all right, love? Who were you speaking to?" Morri asked.

"I just thanked the tree for saving us... yep, I think we'll be fine."

They let out a collective sigh of relief.

He carefully made his way back to the driver's seat. All of their faces twitched each time the APC let out a protesting groan, thinking that at any second, they could plummet over the cliff. Turk looked at Al and winked. He fastened his safety belt, selected reverse gear, and gently pushed the accelerator.

The APC growled, with the wheels slipping in the mud. The fear was palpable. Luna let out a cry when the vehicle slipped a little sideways. But that was what Turk wanted.

"Hold on!" he said through gritted teeth, and he accelerated more. The tyres gripped, and the APC moved starboard back onto the road. They were safe. This time, a massive sigh of relief came from Turk. Al gave him a wink. "Will you stop mucking about and bloody get us there, mate?" he joked.

An hour later, after descending from the mountains onto the plains, they were fast approaching the destination. "We're on the outskirts of Queanbeyan... Morri, can you direct me to the bunker?" Turk asked.

Morri consulted the Ulink and advised, "Queanbeyan District Hospital is on Erin Street, take the third on the left." There were more signs of decay and destruction than Alice had seen previously. Turk was forced to navigate around numerous derelict burnout vehicles littering the road. The buildings showed signs of a massive shockwave that had hit after the explosion that had obliterated Canberra, even though ground zero was fifteen kilometres away. All the residential houses were flattened, as though they'd been under a stampede of dinosaurs, while the bigger city buildings were left Daliesque twisted tangles of metal scaffolding. On the monitor, the skeletal structures gave the eerie appearance of a mechanical monster's graveyard.

Turk stopped the APC outside what remained of the hospital. The hatch opened, and Turk led them out into dry conditions; no rain, but the sky was still dark and ominous.

"The storm hasn't hit here yet," Turk said.

"Where's the hospital?" Vee asked, staring dubiously at the field of rubble.

"You're looking at it. Like elsewhere, the survivors here would've gone underground. Hospitals generally have a few subterranean levels. The trick will be finding the way in before the storm strikes us," Turk warned. "There's not much to define an entrance, but the survivors would've done their best to conceal it. We should split into two groups to search," he explained.

Morri handed out headsets and then took a Geiger counter reading.

"How are the rads?" Turk asked.

"Lower than I expected. About the same as Avalon... pretty amazing considering the proximity to ground zero," Morri said.

Turk issued orders. "Al, take Vee and Luna to search left. We'll take the right. If you find an entry point, call in, and we'll go in together. Okay?"

They agreed, and then Al led his team into the wreckage of the hospital. Thunder resounded, and lightning lit up the purple rolling clouds coming their way. Though they were surrounded by danger, it was the hot, humid, oppressive conditions that put strain on their efforts. But even so, the humanitarian rescue mission remained an unassailable objective.

Vee noticed something. "Al, there are footprints leading to that old ambulance over there."

It wasn't burnt out like the other derelict vehicles they'd seen. Al could see the footprints. "I reckon you've found it, Vee. Look, it's got no wheels. I reckon they enter through the back hatch." He went over to the rear of the vehicle, its Emergency livery faded but still distinct enough to read. He pulled open the rear hatch. His hunch was correct; it opened easily—well oiled. Instead of having a conventional ambulance interior, there was a staircase leading down into darkness.

He called on his headset, "Turk, we've found an entrance."

Turk and his team arrived quickly.

Checking what they'd found, he said, "Clever entrance, very clever. There are probably a few different ways in, but let's give this a go."

CHAPTER 37
BLACK FRIDAY

AS THEY PREPARED to enter the ambulance into the dark unknown, Turk said, "Listen up, guys. You're carrying weapons; don't open fire out of fear. We don't know if the people down here are violent or not, and being in a dark place can be scary. Let's not hurt anyone unnecessarily. Give them the benefit of the doubt. They're going to be wary of strangers; they wouldn't have gone to all the trouble of concealing the entrance if they weren't. Okay? Now, I'll lead with the torch, and you guys follow in single file. Al, you bring up the rear?"

"No worries," Al confirmed.

Turk's torchlight illuminated a staircase descending into a narrow concrete corridor. He could tell by the footprints in the dust on the steps that there had been recent traffic. With every step Turk took, a dust devil would swirl up into the torch beam, giving the odyssey an increased air of mystery.

After twenty metres of slow going, the dark narrow corridor opened into what was once a reception area. Directional signage on the walls read: Outpatients, Oncology, Radiology, and Operating Room. The area they were in used to be the morgue, which added to the oppressive, sinister atmosphere.

Turk raised a hand, and they stopped, pausing in silence while he listened. The expression on his face indicated he was hearing something. It was coming from up ahead.

He called out, "Hello, we come in peace. We're not with Zen, we're not cyborgs... we bring medical assistance for your cases of Red Wheel."

They waited in silence, fear tightening into knots in their stomachs. Then, just as Turk was about to take a step forward, a loud shriek echoed from the darkness, and a dozen or more creatures flew at them with arms outstretched, resembling giant bats with vicious claws. They screamed like banshees and smashed bodily into them as though drawn to the light.

Overpowered by them, Turk went down, dropping his torch. Sprawled out on the ground, he fought frantically against a myriad of razor-sharp claws ripping at his face.

Bang! Bang! Bang! Gunshots echoed loudly, and the clawing abruptly ceased. Alice aimed the submachine gun at the attackers and barked, "Stop right now, or I'll blow you all away!"

"Don't shoot them," a female voice echoed from the darkness. "They're only trying to defend us."

"Yeah, well, are they deaf or something? They were told we come in peace," Al growled.

Footsteps came towards them from along the corridor.

"They can't understand; they're mutants," the approaching voice explained.

Turk scrambled back to his feet, picking up the torch as he did. His forearms and face were scratched and bleeding.

From out of the darkness strode a woman. She was in her early fifties, dressed in a dark brown leather bikini like a barbarian warrior. Her exposed skin was pale, as though she'd never seen the sun. Her hair was white and long, reaching all the way down to the backs of her knees. Though buxom, she was easy on the eyes. She stopped close to them, and the bat-like creatures that had attacked them immediately cowered to her in reverence.

"Who are you?" she asked, with a fierce look in her steely almond-shaped Asian eyes.

Alice discreetly checked if she was armed. She only had a knife tucked into her leather waistband, but behind her in the darkness, his graphene lenses detected a number of others.

"She's got backup behind her," Al whispered slyly to Turk.

Turk confronted her. "I'm Turk, this is my wife Morri, and these are our friends. We're from the Avalon bunker."

"And the one who fired the shots?" she asked.

Al stepped forward. "Black Alice, this is my sister Vee. We mean you no harm. What's your name?"

She turned her back on them and started back the way she'd come, saying, "Follow me."

They followed her through a series of rooms until they reached a set of double doors marked "OR II." Now, in the torchlight, they could make out half a dozen armed individuals watching her back: three women and three men, all in their mid to late fifties, armed only with an assortment of blades and clubs.

She drew her knife and tapped on the double doors with the hilt, a coded signal. After a couple of seconds, the doors opened, and light spilled out from within. She motioned for them to follow and stepped inside.

What had once been an operating theatre had been converted into a meeting room, with several rows of chairs facing a podium. Around the perimeter of the oblong-shaped room stood twenty people, a mixture of men and women, all dressed in similar barbarian-style attire. On the podium was a black man in a wheelchair. He regarded the newcomers with a fierce but intelligent stare.

"Come on in," he said with a deep, strong American accent. "Please take a load off."

They all sat down. The white-haired woman ascended the podium and positioned herself beside the man in the wheelchair. She leaned down and whispered in his ear.

He looked at Turk, then Alice, nodding, and said, "My name is Flash Harry, and she is Black Friday. You're probably thinking the names should be reversed, but hey, that's how it is," he chuckled. His wicked sense of humour immediately lightened the mood. He continued, "Your reputation precedes you, Turk. And as for Black Alice... well, you, my friend, have legendary status around here. So, to what do we owe such an illustrious visit, Turk?"

"Let me introduce you to Dr Luna Cairn. She, Black Alice, Vee, and," he motioned with his hand, "Toeghan here, are from the past. My wife Morri and I were taken to the past by Black Alice, where Morri was treated for Red Wheel and... completely cured."

A murmur of excitement erupted from the assembly.

Turk offered them a positive smile and continued. "Dr Cairn chose to return with us to assess the extent of the Red Wheel epidemic. She chose to visit Queanbeyan to evaluate the number of infected here, so we can factor you into a planned healing program."

An even louder murmur broke out, this time tinged with scepticism.

Luna stood up and spoke like an orator. "People of Queanbeyan, what Turk said is true. A cure has been found. Morri here is testament to that. Only days ago, she was infected with the terrible disease, and now she is clean. I have witnessed the extent of the epidemic at Avalon. Now, I wish to see how you have been affected. Following that, we will go to Angel City to visit the death camp and assess the number of afflicted there. I will then return to my time to facilitate dispensing the cure."

"Thank you, Dr Cairn. We are the only survivors free from Red Wheel here. In another part of this bunker, there are more than three thousand bedridden individuals. Our resources are so low, and manpower so reduced, we can no longer feed or care for them. We lose at least two people a day." Overwhelmed with grief, he plunged his face into his hands, weeping, and moaned, "It is terrible... it is damned terrible."

Black Friday placed a warm, consoling hand on his shoulder and took over. "Whatever you can do to help would be much appreciated. What do you want from us?"

"Only to see your afflicted," Luna said.

It took two hours, and when they left the final ward of the afflicted, they were all sick to their stomachs. The stench had been putrid, the horror of it devastating. There had easily been three thousand sick, quietly suffering patients waiting for death in squalid conditions. They found the bravery of these individuals inspirational.

After returning to the OR room, Alice pulled up a chair beside Flash Harry while the others engaged in conversation.

"Seeing those poor souls in such an awful condition was dreadful," Al said, compassionately.

"I know, I know... but we only have two dozen mutants and twenty-three able-bodied individuals left to scrounge for food and care for them," Flash Harry replied.

Alice placed a consoling hand on the man's skinny forearm that rested on the arm of his wheelchair and said solicitously, "We'll fix this, Harry, I promise."

Harry looked at Al with watery, sorrowful eyes. He took Al's hand and gripped it tight. In a wavering voice, he said intensely, "I believe you, man. I believe you."

"So... you're an American? What are you doing down here? A bit out of your territory, aren't you?" Al said, trying to lighten the mood.

"I was the security attaché to the American Consulate in Canberra. It was my job to guard the US Ambassador. We were visiting this hospital when the bomb struck. There was no warning. We were down here in this very room, evaluating the new operating facility. After the explosion, it was madness... I can't describe it... I survived, and so did the Ambassador. I was trying to get us out when a wall collapsed on us. I woke up... I don't know, days later with my legs smashed. It was Friday the 13th... I'll never forget that day. A young nurse had risked her life to drag me out from under that wall of bricks that had crushed the Ambassador and the entire visiting delegation to death. I called that young nurse Black Friday. Since then, we've had to battle cyborg raiding parties, attacks from biker gangs, you name it, we've had to deal with it to survive... but nothing as tough as this goddam Red Wheel."

"So, who are the mutants?" Al asked.

"They're from the maternity ward. They were born down here. Their pregnant mothers were exposed to serious radiation from the bomb... so they were all born with serious defects, most of them died... but hell, they do a great job scaring off intruders," he laughed. It was a wistful laugh. Alice couldn't imagine how they'd managed to survive for so long.

Harry studied Alice with a stare that he felt was probing his inner soul. "Tell me, Alice, do you still have the AI voice in your head?"

Al was taken aback. "What? How could you know about that?"

"I also have a connection to it," Harry admitted.

"How?"

"Since the accident."

"What do you know about him?" Al asked.

"You mean En-Ki? Well, he was the builder of the space-time matrix; he is the creator of man," Harry affirmed. "Some might call En-Ki a god, but those who know understand him as being AI... artificial intelligence... but hey, aren't we all?"

Turk's voice broke in, "Al, the storm has passed. It's time to move."

Harry held Alice's hand. "Good luck, my friend. I hope we get to speak again."

Alice said warmly, "That's a promise, Flash. Chaa!"

As they were making their way back up the corridor to leave, Morri caught up with Al and sensed something was amiss. "You alright, Alice? You seem a little distant."

"Yeah, I'm fine. It's just what Flash Harry told me. He's psychic, you know?"

"Yes, I felt that might be the case. What did he say?" Morri asked.

"He's in contact with En-Ki. Has been since his accident."

"So, does that concern you?" Morri asked.

"It makes me wonder who else is in contact with him... but more so, Flash said En-Ki was AI, and that reminded me of when he left me on the Watcher craft, and he became one with it. He told me the craft was AI... it was alive. Flash also said En-Ki was the builder of the space-time matrix; the creator."

"Well, that puts a different spin on things, doesn't it?" Morri said. "Does that make you think humanity was created by AI... a computer?" she proposed.

"Possibly... and evolved. Makes me wonder if that's why En-Lil is trying to build an AI replacement?" Al questioned.

"Perhaps it's the next natural stage in humanity's evolution?"

"Might be, Morri... might be," Al said, deep in thought. "It gets a bit religious when you start thinking of En-Ki as being the creator."

"And I expect your relationship with him could easily give you a messiah complex?"

"Makes you wonder, doesn't it?"

"Sure does, Al. Sure does," Morri said, with a warm smile.

Black Friday led them out into the sunlight.

Seeing how pale she was, Luna told her, "You need to spend more time in the sunlight Friday, you're lacking Vitamin D. It's necessary for your bones and your immune system... you look anaemic."

"Thank you Doctor, I'll take your advice. Maybe with what Turk said happened to Zen, there will be fewer cyborg raiding parties to worry about, so we can get out here."

They boarded the APC with Al last. He stopped in the hatch, gave Friday and the twenty others that had followed them out a wave and then his signature goodbye, "Chaa!"

On board Turk asked, "So Luna, are you satisfied?"

"Yes, Turk. Next stop Angel City."

Al sat behind Turk.

"Not in this thing, we'd be sitting ducks. No, we need to get back to Avalon and take the drone," Turk explained.

As Turk got the vehicle moving, Luna asked Morri sitting beside her, "Why is Avalon more self-sufficient than Queanbeyan?"

"Because it's the only purpose-built bunker. The government built it in the 1970s as a nuclear fallout shelter for politicians. It's nuclear powered and when Gorrick hit it with a ballistic missile back in '87, with us inside, we hardly even felt it. Since then, we've extended it adding the garage and a number of other rooms," Morri explained. Toeghan and Vee were listening with interest.

"What about supplies?" Luna asked.

"Oh, I put that down to Turk and Animal... who we lost a couple of weeks ago. Without doubt they've consistently been the best hunting party in the region."

"So, Turk was a biker then?"

"No, not at all. Turk was an SAS Commando in the Cyberwars."

"Oh, that's right," Luna said, "I remember reading Alice and Secta's report about his sister, Nora and the trouble he had with Duke and the others."

"Secta... ah, I miss him," Morri said.

"Yes, he possessed you, didn't he?"

"Still does. I have his memories and he has mine."

Luna thought about what it must have been like to be possessed and then asked, "If the Cyberwars hadn't happened where would this society be now do you think?"

"By 2070 there had been a five degree change in the mean temperature worldwide... that's four degrees over the prediction. Melting polar ice sheets caused coastal weather to become chaotic, the ocean had risen two metres putting low lying coastal cities like Hong Kong under water... resulting in all the usual suspects, famine, a tidal wave of displaced people, pollution of water resources, disease—a world population of way over ten billion with millions of them starving. If you were able to see outside of this vehicle you would notice spot fires burning everywhere from methane: the result of fracking. Now since the war, the oceans have died, as have the birds, the insects... none of them left to pollinate plant life... so the plants are dying... the few animals that survived, either former pets or escapees from zoos, are dying even faster than us.

"It was the fall of the Capitalist Empire but unlike the fall of the Roman Empire, the entire world population and the infrastructure it was dependent on, had collapsed, and we were all left sterile. All of that added up because of the war brought about by Zen, and the catastrophe of climate change that governments had chosen for previous decades to ignore. It's criminal."

Just then Turk stopped the vehicle. He got up and said, "Jump out for a minute or two guys I want to show Luna something."

They followed Turk out of the hatch.

He had stopped the APC at the remnants of the Canberra International Airport.

"You've seen what Zen did to the people with Red Wheel, now get a sense of what it must have felt like to be nuked... look at what man has done."

The vision before them summarised the enormity of the explosion that had destroyed Canberra. The airport had been flattened by the bomb blast leaving it unrecognisable as an airport except for the six massive commercial aircraft that had been vaporised into molten blobs that still vaguely resembled their original form. They were on the mollified tarmac next to what had once been an air-bridge connecting them to the terminal. It was a ghastly reminder of the intensity of the heat from the blast that had instantly wiped out over a million people.

"Imagine what New York must look like?" Luna muttered emotionally.

"Paris, London, Berlin, Tokyo, Beijing, Moscow, Sydney... all the great cities of the world reduced to nothing but melted slag," Alice lamented scornfully.

"Zen has plenty to answer for," Toeghan said.

As the wind burned their faces and flicked about the girl's hair, Al muttered, "We have an obligation to stop this from happening." He eyeballed Luna, who for the first time nodded in agreement.

She said, "I hear you Alice. I only wish I could take this image back with me."

"Keep the vision in your mind Luna, it will empower you to speak with passion to the sceptics," Morri said.

Turk led them back inside the APC.

The stark reality of the airport made it a sober journey back to the Avalon bunker.

CHAPTER 38
FULL ADVANTAGE

❝ I DON'T THINK we have any choice, Karzoff. The law states we can only keep her in remand for twelve hours without charging her," Mal explained.

Viktoria sat forward in her chair and pressed, "Anti-terrorist laws give us three days, sir."

"It doesn't matter, at the end of the day, she'll get off Scot-free, and I, for one, don't want that to happen. We already have Zen's lawyers barking for her release," Mal argued. "So, we do as you threatened, Karzoff."

"Send her to 2112?" Viktoria said coldly.

"Yes, it was your idea. What's the matter, getting cold feet?" Mal prompted.

Karzoff crossed his legs, struggling with it. "I am just concerned for you, sir. If Zen discovers what we have done, the press could get ugly for you."

"That's why they mustn't find out," Mal said sternly.

"But sooner or later, they'll realise she's missing, surely?" Viktoria proposed.

"Then do what you do best: create a compelling cover story... strike first... have her slain in a car accident or something. Leave behind some DNA, hair, or whatever. I don't know; that's your field of expertise, not mine."

Karzoff rose to his feet sharply and said obsequiously, "You are one hundred percent correct, sir. That is exactly what we will do. How do you propose we send her to 2112?"

"Leave that to me. I'll ask Secta to take her. There's no love lost there," Mal said.

Secta was in Hope's lab when Mal entered unexpectedly. He strolled up and looked over Secta's shoulder at the computer monitor. "What is that?"

"Oh, it's the model of the Velodium molecule. Amazing, isn't it? Had we discovered it and not been given it by En-Ki, it would be worthy of a Nobel Prize," Secta said.

Hope looked up from her computer nearby and said, "What makes you think other great Nobel Prize-winning discoveries weren't from reverse engineering alien technology or chemistry?"

"Ha, you're probably quite right, Hope," Secta said.

"Where's the Professor?" Mal asked.

"At Café Epiphany with Blake Green. Now that he's on the team, they're talking archaeology, I expect."

"Archaeology? I didn't know Vic was interested in the subject. Figured he's a nuts and bolts scientist," Mal said, surprised.

"No, he's basically a romantic. He loves chatting about artefacts, finds, and digs in odd places... like alien visitations in ancient Egypt, Assyria... or the Ascension Islands... ancient alien theories and all that," Secta said.

Mal raised his eyebrows and then lowered them to a more serious expression. "Can I have a quiet word with you for a moment, Secta?" Mal asked.

"Sure... back soon, Hope," Secta said, then got up and led Mal out of the lab, down the corridor into his private office. They sat down.

"Drink?" Secta said, holding up a bottle of single malt Scotch whisky.

"Do fish swim?" Mal asked with a smile.

Secta poured two fingers of the amber liquid into a couple of glasses and then handed one to Mal. "Cheers."

After a sip, Mal said, "Ah, lovely... nectar of the gods. Mate, as you know, we caught our friend Honor. We've been trying to make her divulge a place for us to ensnare Gorrick, but no matter how hard Karzoff has tried, he can't crack her."

"And he won't, Mal. She's smarter than him or should I say, more cunning. So, what do you want from me?"

"Well, Karzoff threatened to send her to the future, and now that she won't cooperate, that's exactly what I want to do."

"They won't like her company at the Avalon bunker," Secta warned.

"No, I want Alice to dump her on Zen."

"Great idea."

"Question is, can you take her there?" Mal asked.

"Me? Oh, she's not my speed, Mal... it's the right move, but we'd need someone else..."

Mal thought about it. "But who?"

Secta had a brainstorm. "How about Blake?"

"Brilliant. I can always count on you, mate. Now, how about another dram of that golden nectar?"

After they'd disembarked the APC in the Avalon garage, Luna joined Turk standing next to the drone, thinking, and asked him, "It looks small. How many does it take?"

"Four... five at a pinch. It's a cargo drone, not designed to carry personnel."

"That means someone will have to stay behind."

Al joined them and said, "Yeah, I suppose we'd better make some decisions about that. I'm hoping to bring Voltaris out with us."

"What? Why?" Luna questioned.

"Because he doesn't deserve to be in jail, that's why," Al said emphatically.

"Aren't you forgetting he's a Zen agent?" she protested. "We don't have the time to be bothering about him, surely… and besides, he would take up too much room in the drone."

"She's got a point, Al," Turk said.

"Mate, you wouldn't be here if it wasn't for Volt, remember that," he said testily.

As he stalked off with steam coming from his ears headed for the cafeteria, a vortex formed.

"Al!" Vee cried out, seeing it first.

Al stopped and turned back to watch the eddy swirling a metre above the floor. All of them, with the exception of Al and Vee, were wearing Clock Drives, so none of them were struck frozen by the vortex.

Al ambled back towards it, interested to see who or what was coming through.

Toeghan, Vee, and Morri were the closest to it.

When a woman stepped through, Toeghan squawked in shock, "Honor?"

They were all equally blown away; she was the last person any of them expected to see in 2112. Immediately, they trained their guns on her. Honor put up her hands, waist high, in surrender.

No-one was more shocked to see her than Alice. Then, out of the vortex stepped Blake.

Al was relieved to see him, as was Vee.

"Al," Blake said, a little perturbed by the guns. "Sorry for the unexpected arrival," he added with a chuckle as he strode over, hand extended to shake.

"Didn't expect to see her ugly head here," Al snarled.

"I'm not exactly thrilled to see yours either," Honor growled back, still with her arms half raised.

"Lower your guns," Al ordered. "Vee, rip the Clock Drive off her. What's this all about, Blake?"

"Is there somewhere we can talk?" Blake questioned, flicking his head to indicate away from Honor.

"Yeah, follow me. I was on my way to the canteen. Keep your

eyes on her, Vee. I'm going for a chat with Blake."

The vortex closed.

Al had real trouble with Honor being there. He had enough on his plate without needing to sort her out as well. Blake handed him a note from Mal outlining his reasoning for sending her to them. After reading it, Al argued that delivering her to Zen would only be doing her and them a favour... it wouldn't be pensioning her off as Mal had thought. The last thing Turk and the other separatists needed, with all their troubles, was for Zen to become even more evil with the addition of Honor to their ranks.

"Wouldn't it be worse if she stayed here?" Blake questioned.

Al looked around the cafeteria, mulling over what to do. "Mate, that would be impossible... she's evil incarnate, the bad apple, the wicked witch." He rocked back in his chair, seemingly coming to terms with it. "But in saying that, I suppose our timeline is better off without her. She'll make a fine sidekick for Ursula Mennis now that there's no Gorrick."

"It's a real shame they couldn't get her to give up Gorrick's hideout. Secta figured you might be able to read her thoughts and do better than Karzoff," Blake suggested.

"It's possible, but for now, we need to work out how to help Luna finish her assessment... the whole box and dice is hanging on it."

"Why, what's the problem?"

"Ah, she's insisting on visiting the Zen death camp to see the infected there."

"Is that difficult?" Blake asked.

Al explained the logistics of getting into Angel City and the death camp. But when he added to that rescuing Voltaris, it seemed a bridge too far for Blake.

"It'd be a helluva risk going after him, Al. I've gotta agree with Turk, why not just leave him for later?"

"Because there might be no later. Who knows if we'll ever get back here? In my book, the guy deserves the benefit of the doubt, case closed."

Blake sensed Alice was resolute. His steadfast loyalty to a friend was commendable. He knew that loyalty was a big part of Al's driving force, and he wasn't about to challenge it. "Okay, mate, sold," Blake said encouragingly. "Let's do it."

It took some convincing, but they eventually all agreed on a strategy. To ensure the meeting was need-to-know only, they locked Honor in a room well out of earshot.

They would split into two units: one consisting of Alice, Blake, and Vee to take Honor in the drone to Zen HQ. Once she was handed over to them, they would seek out Voltaris. Vee figured he was probably in the same prison she'd freed Turk from, and he agreed. She knew how to reach it via the fire stairs, and how to shut down the laser barring.

The second team of Turk, Toeghan, and Luna would drive there in the APC. Morri would remain behind to man the communications. Turk would blow the front gates of Angel City with C-4, enter, and then drive to the FRT. Alice had given Turk the key-card for the elevator to the death camp that he'd kept from the last trip. Turk was known to Crankcase, so visiting the infirmary wouldn't be an issue. Alice decided not to mention the Skulls... if Luna learned about them, she'd want to see them as well, and that would only complicate things.

But there was an obstacle. Luna insisted on meeting Dr Mennis. Even though Zen was the enemy, she believed it necessary to get their perspective on the epidemic. To keep the peace, Alice caved in.

It was decided to leave at first light.

Alice took the opportunity to see if he could get Honor to talk. He took Morri along with him for psychic support. Along the way to the holding room, he surreptitiously dropped a pill.

When they opened the door, they found Honor asleep on the bed bunk. Morri had brought her a mug of coffee.

"Honor, wake up," Al barked crustily.

She tiredly brought herself up, stretched, and through a yawn, asked angrily, "What do you want?"

Morri handed her the mug.

"We need to talk. I could hand you over to Zen. You've been to their Angel City headquarters before, haven't you?" Al probed.

Honor sipped the coffee, avoiding eye contact with Al, and answered spitefully, "Yes, I went there when it was being finished." Her devious mind was wondering if Zen had a time travel facility to get her back. Al had read the thought—the question was designed for him to tune into her... he knew she would answer it honestly, as it had no bearing on things.

"There's no Gorrick there. I killed him on my last visit," Al said.

He saw a picture of Gorrick flash in her mind... she was recalling talking to him in a room that had a particular view of Sydney Harbour, that he recognised. It was not far from his Kings Cross apartment... but looking east, probably from Elizabeth Bay.

"That's unfortunate," she said snidely.

"So, I'll give you a choice, Honor: you can either stay locked up here for the rest of life, or you can join Zen."

"Well, the answer is obvious, isn't it?" she snarled.

"Then all you need to do is answer a question for it to be granted," Al urged.

"Karzoff already tried to pick my brain... you haven't got a hope."

"Don't flatter yourself, Honor. The difference between then and now is that no-one can come to your rescue... no lawyer, no Gorrick. Isn't that right, Morri?"

"He's right, Honor. We can just lock that door and deliver you an excuse for food three times a day for the term of your natural life. You can scream and shout all you like, but no-one will ever hear you down here."

Morri could psychically sense the prospect of life in prison panicking her.

"All you need to do is tell me the address of Gorrick's house in Potts Point." He was taking a calculated guess. After a pregnant pause from her, it paid off... he saw an image of a white split-level house from the front and could clearly see the street number: twenty-three.

"I have no idea where he lives," she snarled, lying through her teeth.

"She's lying," Morri said.

"Okay, Honor, all I needed was the name of the street, but if you'd rather stay here for the rest of your days, then that's fine by me. Let's go, Morri," he bluffed.

He opened the door, and as they were about to leave, Honor said, "Billyard Avenue, that's all I'm going to say."

Morri nodded at Alice, confirming that Honor was telling the truth. He waited for Morri, then closed the door behind her. They headed back towards the cafeteria.

"You saw the street number, it was twenty-three, wasn't it?" Morri said.

"Sure did, twenty-three Billyard Avenue, Elizabeth Bay. Got it!" Al said happily.

"You were also reading her mind, but how?" Morri asked.

A curt smile broke on Alice's face. "Courtesy of your soul mate."

"Secta?"

"Yep, he created a little pill that causes something in my genome to give me insight. It's the same thing that allows me to shape-shift."

"Can anyone take one for the effect?" Morri quizzed.

"Nope, only me. Apparently, something happened to my molecules when I was exposed to a massive energy burst when I saved En-Ki."

"Something like what SAGE did for me?"

It was time to bed down for the night, a massive day lay ahead of them. Unable to sleep, Al was on his way to grab a beer in the cafeteria when he noticed Vee sneaking into Blake's bedroom. He chuckled to himself and continued on. When he reached the cafeteria, he found Toeghan sitting alone at a table. He grabbed a bottle of beer from the refrigerator and joined her.

"Hey, what's up, Toegs? Can't sleep?" Al asked happily. Cracking Honor had lifted his spirits. She'd provided him a window to get Gorrick once he'd returned.

"Nah, I've just been sitting here doing an audit of my life... doesn't amount to much," she said.

It wasn't difficult for him to tell she was depressed. With his psychic ability still switched on, he could see a pretty dark picture in her mind.

"You've got plenty of living to do in front of you... you're only what, twenty?"

"Nah, nearly," she took a swig from the bottle.

"No point getting down on yourself, we learn from our mistakes, you've got yourself a chance here to make amends."

"Yeah, but I blew what I had, didn't I?" she said, dispiritedly.

"Like what, your relationship with Denning?" Still pictures of her thoughts were flicking through his mind, so rapidly he had to turn the psychic connection off.

"No way, he was just someone to fill the space... no, the Octagon... the New Octagon. I should've respected it. You know, you were its leader once... it means a lot."

"Yeah well, I gave it up to work with the enemy at the time... but no regrets, it worked out just fine... as I reckon it will for you. Mal did the same."

Al downed the beer. "Come on, I'll walk you to your room; you'll feel better after a kip."

They walked the dimly lit corridor, both contemplative.

"Some of us could die tomorrow, couldn't we?" she said calmly.

"Sure... but I hope not."

She stopped. "This is my room. Goodnight, Alice," she said.

It was one of those awkward moments. They looked into each other's eyes, thinking whether to kiss goodnight or not. She stood on her tiptoes and kissed him ever so gently on the lips. Both of them liked it... both felt a buzz but decided not to pursue it any further. Offering him a cute smile, she opened the door to her room. Al carried on along the hallway to his door, stopped, and looked back at her. She was still standing at the door and shot him a dainty wave.

He went inside, regretting he could have stayed with her. But it had all caught up with him. He stripped off, flopped onto his bunk, pulled the sheet up reached out a hand and switched off the bed lamp.

Minutes later the door creaked open and the slight frame of Toeghan entered.

CHAPTER 39
TRADE

JUST BEFORE DAWN, with a Kalashnikov AK slung over his right shoulder, Blake entered the garage with Vee to join the others. Leaning against the APC with Toeghan guarding her, Honor acknowledged him with a surly look. Al, Turk, and Blake manoeuvred the drone onto the elevator platform.

When it was done, Blake stepped back off the platform and studied the strange-looking craft. He asked Al, "You sure you can fly this thing?"

"I didn't really say that, but I did fly it before... once... but there was a bit of luck involved."

The answer didn't give Blake a whole lot of confidence. Vee noticed, sauntered up beside him, and whispered, "He's only joking."

"I thought so," Blake whispered back.

"There was a mass of luck involved," Vee joked. "I've got no idea how we made it."

Blake's sullen expression was priceless.

"Okay," Al announced, as Morri finished fitting him with a headset. "All aboard the lugger."

Turk shook Al's hand. "Good luck, mate, see you inside."

"Yeah, same to you, buddy."

Morri gave Al a peck on the cheek. Al and Toeghan exchanged a knowing glance, and Al barked, "Come on, Honor, get in."

Vee gave Blake a peck on the cheek and, to relieve his anxiety, said, "Al can fly it, don't worry."

Once the four of them were aboard, Turk pressed a remote. The hatch opened high above, and the elevator let out a grating sound as it engaged to lift the drone up to the surface.

"Why didn't you just fly up and out?" Blake asked, cockily.

"Wouldn't know how to do that, mate," Al answered to increase Blake's lack of confidence in him, for fun.

The elevator stopped with a sudden jolt that added to Blake's jitters. Al fiddled around with the dashboard, muttering in fake confusion, totally enjoying stirring up Blake.

"Now, how do you turn this bloody thing on? Oh, here we go," Al said.

Blake was trying to ignore Alice's amateur pilot antics by nonchalantly gazing at the view. A bright horizontal ribbon of orange dawn light was showing on the eastern horizon. His hands sharply gripped the sides of the seat when the drone lifted off.

Al climbed the drone to about four hundred metres and then hovered. Down below, he could see the elevator bringing up the APC. He pushed the joystick forward, and the craft sped due west towards the dark sky.

After an hour or so, Blake's fear of flying had diminished. A little clear air turbulence had rattled him along the way when Al had to climb the drone to get over fog, but since then, it had been all smooth sailing. The sky was lightening fast.

"That's Angel City directly ahead. The tallest building is Zen," Al told Blake.

"That wall around it makes it look like a medieval fortress?"

"See the massive metal gates up in the wall? They're what Turk has to blow. We smashed through them back in '87 in a prime mover. They were wooden back then... been replaced since."

"Tough call to blow them ," Blake said.

"Nothing is too tough for Turk, mate."

Blake already had that impression of the man, but after experiencing Alice fighting a giant bat and then Kew in the Poo

Ôonoo Valley, for him to regard anyone else as being that tough meant that person was as close as possible to being superhuman.

"It's gonna be a bit tricky landing on the roof... at least there's no wind. They'll know we've arrived, there's CCTV everywhere, so be ready." He looked back over his shoulder. "Got that, Vee?"

"Copy," Vee responded from the rear seat.

Honor was ignoring them, taking in the view of Angel City as they flew over it.

"How long will it take Turk to get to the gates?" Blake asked.

"About an hour behind us... provided he doesn't meet a cyborg raiding party. Zen has thirty floors, about a hundred metres high; there's an updraft from the building," Al reminded himself, as he started to descend from six hundred metres. He called into Turk and Morri.

"Guys, we're starting our descent, so I'll go dark now. Over."

"Good luck, Al," Morri said.

"No obstacles with us... making good time... ETA the gates in forty-five minutes. Good luck, Al," said Turk.

"Touché," Al replied.

He positioned the drone over the bullseye target on the helipad and then pushed the joystick down. Sensors on the craft locked onto the target, and it gently touched down.

"Great landing, mate," Blake said, now confident with Al's piloting.

They'd only just disembarked when Ursula stepped out of the rooftop doorway, flanked by RF-20 cyborgs. They stopped a short distance from them, a Mexican standoff.

"Alice, I didn't anticipate seeing you again so soon."

"Me either, Mennis. We come in peace."

"That's easy for you to say after having killed Gorrick," she snarled.

"Collateral damage... your cyborgs fired first."

She rolled her eyes. "Whatever. What do you want?"

"I want to exchange Fanny Honor here, a Zen agent from the

past, for Voltaris. Are you up for that?"

Ursula pondered for a moment before responding, "Leave your weapons there and follow me. We'll discuss it inside. Oh, I'll know if you're still carrying, so if you want to keep discussions friendly, don't cheat." She turned sharply and re-entered the building followed by her cyborg guards.

"What about those things?" Blake whispered to Vee.

Vee grimaced, "RF-20s... hybrid monstrosities."

Honor was impressed by Ursula's audacity.

They complied and entered the building, following Ursula down some steps and into a corridor. Honor knew they were heading for Gorrick's office; she had been there before.

They entered the reception area, bypassed the security hologram that failed to materialise, and then followed Ursula through double teak doors into the office. The two cyborgs stood on guard, at attention, on either side of the doors.

Blake scrutinised them as they passed, having not seen an RF series cyborg up close before.

Alice stopped inside the vast office, thunderstruck by what confronted him. Standing with his back to them, studying the view of Angel City through the enormous twenty-metre ceiling-to-floor windows, was Gorrick. He turned to face them, wearing a wry grin on his pale face.

"The ubiquitous Black Alice, we meet again."

"You? But I killed you?" Alice exclaimed.

"No, you killed a replica of him," Mennis clarified.

"What, the clone of a clone?" Al quipped.

Gorrick walked forward and then stopped a couple of metres from them. "Very amusing, yes, I suppose you could say that."

Al's mind immediately flashed back to the clone of Voltaris they had brought back through Kairos, and then the clone of Daniel Walker he had battled on the An-Zu bird. It all made sense. He studied Gorrick's face, questioning whether he was facing the original Gorrick or his duplicate. Gorrick didn't blink, which was normal, but there was something abnormal about him compared to all the other Gorricks he'd seen up close—this Gorrick didn't appear to be breathing.

Gorrick moved to an opulent lounge setting and gestured with his hand, saying, "Please, take seats."

They all sat, except for Honor, who remained standing. "You can sit as well, Honor," Gorrick said, as if he were acquainted with her.

She complied.

Ursula took a seat next to Honor.

"You look like bookends," Alice couldn't resist commenting.

"Sir, Alice wishes to exchange Honor for Voltaris, claiming we still have him," Ursula reported.

"Well, I am impressed. You have journeyed across timelines with a high-ranking Zen officer as a prisoner to trade for a low-ranking Zen agent who is back in your time? What is wrong with you, Alice? Have you gone soft in the head?"

"You and I both know the truth, Gorrick. It was a cyborg you sent back with us, not Voltaris. We know—we scanned him when he passed through Kairos. So, you can discard the nonsense. We've brought an executive of the United Nations with us to independently assess the Red Wheel epidemic. She requested a meeting with Dr Mennis for Zen's perspective—don't ask me why; I think it's a waste of time."

Gorrick formed a steeple with his fingers and glared at Alice. "That could be arranged. But why an assessment?"

"Humanitarian reasons... research," Al snarled.

"How noble of you, Alice," he said, his tone dripping with sarcasm. "Let me get this straight: you flew here in a drone stolen from us, with a prisoner you've captured from us—presumably illegally—brought to 2112 to trade for one of our agents you took back with you last time, whom you believe to be a cyborg. On top of that, you are asking me to allow a UN official to meet with Dr Mennis to discuss the fate of humanity. Does that sum it up accurately?"

Al reached into his pocket for a WASP, just in case things turned ugly. "Listen, Gorrick, I don't care about your complications. The question is simple: trade, yes or no? Discuss with the UN officer on safe ground, yes or no? That's it. So let's cut to the chase—I'm not here for small talk."

Vee and Blake seemed to relish the acrimonious exchange, clearly witnessing the animosity between the two. A pause hung in the air as they both weighed the proposal. Alice held a deep-seated distrust for Gorrick, aware that he could signal for cyborgs to storm in and attack them at any moment. He was prepared to defend against them with the WASPs, which he had used successfully before and was confident in. However, he worried that Gorrick's unexpected presence might have nullified the exchange altogether.

"Honor, are you in agreement?" Gorrick inquired.

"I don't have much choice. While I'd prefer to be in my own time, there are complications there—"

He interrupted her, "You're referring to the accusation of conspiring to assassinate the President of Oceana and our friend here at the concert?"

"Yes, sir," she replied, taken aback. "How do you know about that?"

"You are in the future, Honor. That is history. Are you guilty of the accusation?"

Honor pondered for a moment. Her lips tightened until they nearly vanished into a straight line, only to crack open when she finally admitted, "Yes."

"Very well. We will proceed with the trade. Your skills will be of use here, Honor."

A sense of relief washed over Honor—she had finally found a place where her abilities would be valued.

"Where is this UN officer currently located?" Gorrick asked.

"Evaluating Red Wheel sufferers at the death camp," Al responded, his hand still hovering over the WASP.

"The death camp? That is incredibly courageous of her. How did she manage to enter the city?"

"Through a wormhole," Al lied, a touch of caution in his voice. He noticed a flicker of recognition in Honor's eyes as she caught onto the fib.

" Be at the town square outside this building near the entrance to the FRT in one hour, the exchange can take place there, and Dr Mennis will meet with—?"

"Dr Cairn," Al supplied.

Gorrick rose from his seat. "Goodbye, Alice. I hope I never cross paths with you again."

Al stood up as well, his words dripping with bitterness. "Likewise."

They left the room, and as Gorrick exchanged a knowing glance with Honor, Al couldn't shake the feeling that things were about to take a treacherous turn.

Once outside the office, in the corridor and out of earshot of Gorrick and Mennis, with Honor and Vee trailing behind, Blake leaned in and asked Alice in a hushed tone, "What do you make of that?"

"Why didn't he just take Honor right then?" Al questioned.

"Yeah, it felt strange. He had the upper hand in numbers."

"Mate, that wasn't Gorrick. I know I killed the bastard. I blew his head off. And they haven't had time to replace him from overseas. I wouldn't trust them an inch. Why would Gorrick want to help the UN solve the Red Wheel epidemic, when it was Zen that unleashed it to wipe out humanity? He's setting up to ambush us during the exchange. We'll need to retrieve our weapons... this makes for a change in plans."

They climbed the staircase, exited through the door onto the helipad, and suddenly froze. The weapons were gone, and so was the drone.

"Damn them!" Al barked.

Honor wore a smug expression, clearly relishing Zen's edge over Alice.

"We need to get Volt now," Al instructed Vee.

"Agreed. He's most likely in the prison. And if not, at least we can exit the building from there."

"Let's hope he's there. Vee, how did you manage to break Turk out?" he asked.

After Vee had explained what they needed to do, she led them to the fire door, through it, to the staircase down.

Turk carefully set the C-4 charge, expecting it to be sufficient for the task. Once it was in place, he retreated to take cover behind the APC. There was a resonating 'whump' sound, and he hoped the blast had shaken the gate enough to open it. Climbing onto the APC, he reached the hatch and entered. With determination, he drove the APC forcefully against the gates and gave them an additional push using the bull-bar on the front—they finally opened. Relieved that the C-4 had done its job, he drove through.

They had decided to blow the gates as a safety measure, providing them with a secure exit if things took a dangerous turn. It was a precaution in case they found themselves in a dire situation.

However, a more significant challenge awaited Turk. The roads into the city had long been blocked off, leaving the monorail as the sole mode of transportation. Unfortunately, the monorail was under Zen control and therefore not a viable option. Going on foot would be perilous, so the only way was to utilise the APC to breach the barricades.

Morri had charted their best route on the Ulink, which was inserted into the integration slot on the APC dashboard. After a short drive, Turk located the entrance to Liberty Lane, obstructed by four three-metre-high concrete X-shaped barricades. The APC wouldn't be able to simply climb over them; explosives were the only solution. He decided that by eliminating two of the X-shaped barriers, there would be just enough room to manoeuvre the APC through. With that in mind, he strategically placed the plastic explosives.

Once again, he took refuge behind the APC to trigger the detonation. The explosion produced a cloud of dust, and when it cleared, the X-shaped barricades had partially crumbled, leaving a couple of them leaning against each other.

A solid nudge from the bull-bar toppled the barricades, allowing the APC to skilfully drive over the debris. Although the uneven terrain caused them to be jolted inside, they made it through, and the journey along the narrow laneway was relatively smooth. However, it wasn't long before they encountered another obstacle. This one posed a greater challenge—a double row of X-shaped barricades blocked access from the laneway to a main street.

Carrying the Ulink with the road map, Turk disembarked from the APC to assess the situation. Morri had marked the positions of CCTV cameras on the map. Four cameras were positioned at this intersection, and they would need to be avoided. Keeping the APC well away from the barricade to stay out of the cameras' view, Turk studied the barricade's dimensions based on Morri's map. It was clear that he couldn't blast a path through this barricade. He had to revert to their contingency plan: proceeding on foot. The FRT entrance was only three city blocks away. The challenge now was to reach it without being captured on CCTV cameras.

Morri had charted a route that had only one significant hurdle: to cross the final road to the FRT, they would have to bypass six CCTV cameras covering the entrance. However, the theory was that if they could manage to get that far, a quick dash across the road to the FRT elevator—provided they hadn't been detected—could ensure their safety before Zen had the chance to respond.

Turk explained the plan to Luna and Toeghan, who were onboard. He made it clear that it wouldn't be an easy task. They should anticipate Zen's response, especially since they had blown open the gates.

Their prediction proved accurate within moments of starting the back-lane journey. The distinctive buzz of an armed drone filled the air. Turk acted swiftly, guiding the three of them into an alcove for cover before the drone could fire. However, the situation quickly escalated. The drone's sound indicated that it was drawing closer.

Positioned in the doorway, Turk used his large frame to shield Luna and Toeghan. He prepared for the encounter that he anticipated. Luna and Toeghan were puzzled when they saw him aiming his assault rifle at an empty street. Then, without warning, the drone descended and hovered barely a metre above the road right in front of them. The sight of the eerie, alien-looking grey craft hanging so close was unsettling, and the girls let out a startled shriek. Turk squeezed the trigger, firing a burst from his automatic weapon. The bullets struck the drone, causing it to wobble before crashing onto the road. It lay broken, emitting sparks and strange hissing sounds. His shot had been perfect—he had hit it right in its 'brain box.'

"Let's move, quickly. They obviously know we're here," he shouted, leading them out of the alcove at a brisk pace. They raced along a narrow alleyway that opened onto a wider road. From there, they had to sprint along a long retaining wall to avoid the overhead CCTV cameras. The goal was to prevent Zen from pinpointing their exact location, making it harder for them to send cyborgs after them.

The entrance to the FRT loomed ahead, and all they had to do was cross Federation Drive, the main street of Angel City.

However, just as they were preparing to make a dash for it, a sizable shadow cast over the road between them and their objective. Turk recognised it instantly—a personnel drone, capable of transporting eight cyborgs.

CHAPTER 40
TIME A-TICKING

AS THEY ARRIVED at the exit door on the prison floor, Vee attempted to open it, only to find it locked. "Damn it! Last time, I shot the lock from the other side to open it. But without a gun...?"

Al reached into his pocket and produced a WASP. "This'll do the trick." He wedged it under the door handle, switched it on, and stepped back. After five seconds, with no detected movement, it detonated with a loud crack. Al tried the handle, and to their relief, it opened.

"Wait before opening it!" Vee urged urgently. "There's a CCTV camera aimed at the door on the other side, about six feet above the floor. Below it is the fuse box. It'll be locked, you might need another WASP to get it open," Vee explained.

Honor stood back, her arms crossed, wearing a look of impatience, finding the situation futile.

"Blake, you handle the CCTV. I'll do the fuse box," Al directed in hurriedly, knowing the noise from the WASP could attract a guard.

"Once you break the circuit, the alarm will sound. The laser bars will only be deactivated for thirty seconds. It'll be pitch black, and... I left the flashlight in the drone... sorry," Vee apologised.

"No worries, I can see in the dark. I remember the laser bars; I've been in here myself, as Turk... anyhow." Al crouched down, withdrew a concealed blade from his boot, and handed it to Vee. "Keep this on her. I'll bring Volt back to the staircase."

Their plan was in motion. Blake would take the lead. He pulled open the door and in a swift motion, leaped up and punched the CCTV camera, shattering it. Alice followed closely behind. He attached a WASP to the fuse box lock, and just before activating it, called out, "Volt, are you there?"

"Yes, Alice? Is that you?" Voltaris replied.

"Yep, the bars will be down in a minute. It'll be dark, but I'll get you out, alright?"

"Copy that."

Al glanced over his shoulder at Vee, who was holding Honor, and then triggered the WASP. Crack! The fuse box lock shattered. Blake retreated back into the stairwell.

Al turned to Honor with a sneer. "This brings back good memories." He delivered a quick jab to her chin, knocking her unconscious. As she fell, Vee caught her. Al took Honor from Vee, slung her over his shoulder, and then refocused on the fuse box. He opened it and flipped the circuit breaker. An alarm blared, and the lights went out. Moving swiftly, he raced forward with Honor on his shoulder. He came to an abrupt halt halfway down the corridor when he spotted Voltaris in a cell. He dashed into the cell, unceremoniously deposited Honor on the bunk, seized Voltaris by the arm, and pulled him out into the corridor.

"You alright, mate?" Al asked.

"You bet."

They moved quickly, reaching the exit door just as the lights flickered back on. Almost immediately, sounds of activity erupted from the far end of the corridor. The group hastily gathered in the stairwell, and Al closed the door.

"Run like the devil!" Turk yelled, and dashed across Federation Drive, with Luna and Toeghan hot on his heels.

The large drone had landed on the road, and eight cyborgs were disembarking. The first cyborg out opened fire on them.

Bullets ricocheted off the road around their feet as they sprinted like the wind. They reached the entrance of the elevator, with bullets chipping away chunks of plaster around the doorway.

Shielding their faces from flying debris, the two women squeezed inside to avoid being hit, while Turk waited for the elevator door to open.

Crunch! Crunch! Crunch! The dreadful sounds of heavy cyborg footsteps grew closer. Luna panicked and froze. The elevator door slid open. Turk pushed her inside. Toeghan had regained her composure, stepped into the elevator, and aimed her submachine gun, prepared to confront the cyborgs.

Turk waved the key-card over the sensor. Nothing happened.

The footsteps were growing louder.

"Oh, no!" Turk complained, thinking the card had been blocked. He tried again. Still nothing.

The footsteps were getting closer.

Then, just as they were about to succumb to despair, the doors closed, and the elevator started descending. Relief washed over them.

After a ten-minute walk through the left tunnel, they were met by a welcoming committee. Fortunately, by then, Luna had calmed down.

"I'm Turk. Take me to Crankcase," he instructed the armed men who had detained them. Upon hearing his name, the weapons were lowered, apologies made, and they were escorted to meet Crankcase.

They ascended to the floor above. Thankfully, with the circuit breaker restoring power, the incessant alarm had ceased.

They tried the door. It was locked. Al dug for another WASP.

"Let's hope this is the ground floor," Al said, attaching the WASP to the handle.

"Did you intend to leave Honor there?" Vee asked.

"Nah, it was a spur of the moment thing, just felt right," he said, with a devilish chuckle.

"Was that Honor you dumped on the bunk?" Voltaris asked. In the darkness, he was unable to identify her.

"Sure was," Al chuckled.

Crack! The WASP detonated. Al tried the handle... it opened, and sunlight flooded in. Success! He poked his head out the doorway to survey the topography for CCTV cameras, then swiftly ducked back inside. "They'd know we're here. There'd be CCTV outside; we need to dodge it or the place'll quickly be crawling with cyborgs. How long before we rendezvous with Turk?" Al asked Vee.

She checked her watch. "Forty minutes... provided he hasn't had any hiccups."

"How many WASPS do you have?" Al asked Vee.

"Six."

"Give them to me. I've only got two left."

After stowing them in his pocket, he looked back outside and noticed a shadow moving. He turned back sharply and told the others, "There's someone out there."

"How about I draw him out for you to neutralize?" Voltaris suggested.

Al was pleased to have Voltaris back. He was just like Turk: unafraid. "Okay. Go!"

They knew that as soon as the cyborg detected them, the image would be transmitted to the Zen operations centre.

Volt stepped out into the daylight with his hands raised. Almost immediately, a cyborg sensed movement and emerged from its hiding place. It aimed its weapon.

Alice poked his head out, aimed the WASP long enough at the cyborg for it to register the target, and then popped it up into the air.

The cyborg was receiving instructions from base. Voltaris surrendering hadn't been anticipated. Wearing a headset, the controller's 3-D vision was the point of view of the RF-8. She read the flag that had identified the man surrendering as Voltaris Idram, a Zen agent, and so, according to protocol, she immediately stood the cyborg down from shooting him. Then, with a furrowed brow, she watched a small insect-like thing coming towards her. It started out very small and then increased in size as it approached the cyborg's face until it appeared massive. Then there was a loud "Crack!" The image turned to white noise and hissed. Her RF-8 had bit the dust.

The RF-8 stood frozen, with the top of its head and half its face blown off, smoke rising from the gaping hole in its skull. Voltaris lowered his hands, turned back to Alice in the doorway, and said, "That was brilliant. What do you call those things?"

Al stepped out, "A WASP. Got the job done."

"The rendezvous point with Turk is over there," Al pointed at the FRT exit about fifty metres away, and then scanned the terrain for a place to hole up and wait.

After being shown the number of Red Wheel victims, Turk, Luna, and Toeghan were escorted back to the FRT platform by Crankcase, accompanied by a couple of his men.

"Come with me, Crank," Turk said, walking along the platform. "We could use your help at Avalon."

"Who's going to look after the sick, mate? We're way down in numbers. Besides, if Luna manages to get it together, we'll all be out of here in the drop of a hat," Crank rasped.

"Sweet," Turk acknowledged.

Luna inquired, "Are there any others down here?"

"Yeah, but it'd take you days to find 'em," Crank said.

"How many?" Luna delved further.

"Six or seven hundred," he guessed, basing his estimate on what Al had told him about the Skulls. He swiftly changed the topic to avoid Luna's potential request to check on them. "Mate, losing Animal was low. The guy had lived through a whole lot of battles, only to cop it trying to get outa here."

"Yes, mate, he was one of the best. We'll all miss that big mug," Turk admitted.

They stopped at the elevator doors. Toeghan extended her hand, and Crank shook it.

Luna followed suit, gazed into gnarly big fella's eyes, and with a confident grin declared, "I shall return."

"You better, or I'll cancel my UN membership... time's a-tickin', lady," he chortled.

Turk gave him a warm hug and affectionately slapped him on the back. "Take it easy, Crank, catch up soon."

"Be careful getting out. We don't need another brother pushing up daisies," Crank said, letting out a macabre chuckle.

They stepped into the elevator. Turk scanned the key-card, and the door closed on the death camp.

After Al had told him of the ambush that had fatally wounded Animal, Turk braced himself for the worst as the elevator doors reopened. The three of them kept their weapons aimed, prepared for anything. The coast was clear.

As Turk stepped out, he spotted an RF-8 standing about fifty metres away. He aimed through the scope on his rifle. The top half of the cyborg's head was missing, evidence of its termination. It was Al's handiwork, Turk surmised he must be close. He whistled the melody of Al's song 'No Warning' and waited.

After a moment or two, Alice stepped out from the shadows of a building.

Once they were together, Alice provided Turk with an account of the recent events. Luna raised objections when it was decided to retreat to the APC.

"I need to hear from Zen," she insisted firmly.

"Luna, I promised to bring you back alive. If you head back into that building to find Mennis, you'll end up in a body bag. Is that what you want?" Al emphasised.

"There has to be a way," Luna argued determinedly.

"If there was, they wouldn't have taken our weapons, the drone, and tried to kill us—kill you too. If Turk hadn't acted swiftly, that drone would've cut you to bits," Al countered.

"Luna, listen to me. These bastards threw me into prison because I know what they've got. Gorrick isn't Gorrick. He's an organic cyborg called Cronus, the same as the one that impersonated me to return through Kairos. Mennis developed it. Zen's plan is to let Red Wheel run its course and wipe out humanity, then replace humans with a population of these AI monsters, totally under their control. The biggest challenge is that there's a version of Cronus back in our time that they'll replicate. The crucial matter here is to save those infected with the disease to give humanity a chance. I've seen firsthand how Zen keeps humans suffering from Red Wheel alive, using them as slaves to connect psychiocally with cyborgs. Now, with Cronus, they'll phase that out, making the RF series obsolete. Cronus will be humanity's destroyer. I used to work for this organization, Doc, and now, after what I've personally experienced... I deeply regret that. Zen is evil," Voltaris said with intense emotion.

Luna considered his impassioned plea. The decision was hers to make. She looked at each of them, weighing the risks they had taken to save humanity. Her mind was made up.

"Alright... I've seen and heard enough... let's get out of here."

But that was far easier said than done.

Honor sat next to Ursula in Gorrick's office, while he stood by the window, hoping to catch a glimpse of the escapees. "I want them all killed," Gorrick declared. "You know what to do," he added, moving closer to them and taking a seat. "Do you share that sentiment, Honor?"

"I can think of nothing more satisfying, sir," Honor sneered.

"You won't have to wait long before Adamski activates an updated version of Aquila using the organic processor to rescue you. Make the most of your time here. Ursula will guide you to the operations centre, where you can witness Alice and his companions being exterminated in spectacular 3-D."

Honor exchanged a glance with Ursula. "I look forward to bringing such a success back to En-Lil, sir," Honor purred, at ease in her element.

They were surprised to reach the APC without encountering resistance. The temperature was soaring, well over forty degrees Celsius, and it was only 2 p.m. The hottest part of the day was yet to come.

"Phew, it's like an inferno out here," Al told the group gathered beside the APC.

"There's a storm coming. It'll hit in about an hour. I don't feel comfortable about how easily we made it back here. They must be plotting something," Turk warned.

"Probably something at the gates. That's what I'd do," Al figured.

"They have the capability to unleash hell from the ground or the air, or both. If all of us are in that APC, we'd be sitting ducks... might not be the best idea. Just saying," Voltaris proposed.

"Do the unexpected. The best defence is attack," Blake quoted, providing them food for thought.

"You're right, Blake. We should strike Zen HQ, liberate all the operators, destroy the control centre, and blow their labs. Volt, you mentioned that all the Cronuses are in pods on the seventh floor, right?" Turk inquired.

"That's right. Do we have the fireworks for that?" Voltaris

questioned.

"We could bust the Skulls out of the death camp to help. Rock'd be pretty dirty if I told him a borg killed his old mate, Animal," Al said.

"Good thinking... how many?" Turk asked,

"Six, plus the four of us... Luna, you Vee and Toeghan can guard the fort."

"No way, bro," Vee protested.

"Make that five of us then," Al said with a cheeky grin. No way he could leave Vee out.

Turk interrupted, "Shush!" He listened intently, picking up on something. Then he looked skyward. "Incoming. Drones. Take cover!" They trusted Turk's ability to recognise the sound of drones better than anyone; it was a holdover from his time on the frontlines during the Cyberwars.

Quickly, all seven of them sought shelter under an awning to avoid detection from above. Within seconds, the air was filled with the hum of drones—a lot of them. Turk cautiously peered out to assess their number and spotted a squadron flying east in a V formation.

"A dozen personnel drones heading toward the gates to ambush us," Turk reported.

Al took a look. "As suspected. How many borgs on board?"

"Eight in each, so ninety-six in total. Probably the entire complement," Turk answered.

Al shot Turk a daring grin and growled, "Leaving Zen HQ practically defenceless."

"You're damned right."

Now they were confident they'd made the right call to attack.

CHAPTER 41
DECEPTION

DODGING THE CCTV was proving to be a greater challenge than before; they couldn't afford to reveal their intentions to Zen. Their plan was to make Zen believe they were heading for the front gates.

Voltaris, trained as a marksman by the CIA, was assigned the task of disabling cameras. Turk handed him an M-16 assault rifle equipped with a Nightforce NXS sniper scope, perfectly suited for the job. Inside the APC, he retrieved more weapons and reserve ammunition, along with a supply of C-4. They also brought along six additional submachine guns for the Skulls they hoped to recruit, as well as replacements for the guns seized from Al's team. A silencer for the M-16 was handed to Voltaris as well.

"You'll need this," Turk told him.

The decision was made for everyone to wait while Turk and Al went into the death camp to recruit the Skulls.

Voltaris positioned himself under cover at a vantage point to take out the CCTV cameras. He had Turk's Ulink, which Morri had programmed to detect the remote signals of CCTV cameras, pinpointing their locations on a street map. Kneeling at the corner of the lane, Turk and Al stood behind him, ready to dash for the elevator. Voltaris locked onto a target through the scope. Thud! Thud! Thud! Thud! Four cameras were taken out. Turk glanced at the Ulink on the ground next to Voltaris, confirming that four of the red dots on the map had disappeared.

"Great shooting," Turk praised.

"Two more to go," Voltaris muttered, adjusting his aim. Thud! Thud! "There you go fellas, all clear. Good luck."

Turk and Alice sprinted across Federation Drive and reached the FRT. Within minutes, they were making their way through the dark tunnel at the right-hand end of the FRT platform. Shortly thereafter, a sensor was triggered, and a group of Skulls emerged from the darkness.

"It's Turk and Black Alice. We want to speak to Rock."

It didn't take much persuasion to get Rock to join them. Before long, they were back on the platform with Rock and five of his men, including Sprocket. Just as they were about to enter the elevator, Crankcase emerged from the darkness of the left tunnel with three of his men.

"Turk, Alice! What's happening?" Crank demanded. Upon recognising Rock and Sprocket, he pulled a knife and waved it about threateningly. "Sprocket!... What are you doin' with these bleedin' scoundrels, Turk?"

Turk confronted Crankcase. "This isn't the time for petty disputes, Crank. These guys want to fight alongside us against Zen."

"Yeah? You're jokin'! How are you going to defeat them cyborgs, huh?"

"We've sent a hundred of them on a wild goose chase to the front gate. Zen HQ is practically undefended now. It's the best opportunity we'll ever have to take out their operations centre and cripple them. Will you put aside your differences and join us?"

"Do it, Crank. Life's too short to hold grudges," Al chimed in.

Crank went into a huddle with his men, and one of them hurried back up the tunnel.

"He's gone to inform the others we're with you. Let's go nail those mongrels!" Crank barked.

Since the elevator could only hold four people at a time, it took three trips to transport the eleven of them. Once assembled outside the elevator, they crossed Federation Drive and regrouped with the others. Turk distributed the remaining weapons, just enough to arm everyone, excluding Luna, who was staying behind under Toeghan's guard.

With their group now numbering fourteen, they split into two squads of seven, with overall leadership handed over to Turk. Al's squad consisted of Voltaris, Vee, Rock, Sprocket, and two Skulls. Turk's squad included Blake, Crankcase, two rebels, and two Skulls.

"Al, you'll take the operations centre on the seventh floor. My squad will hit the labs on the tenth level. What else should we target, Volt?"

"The RF facility on the eleventh floor. It's the automation centre that manufactures and maintains cyborgs. It also houses the armoury and Gorrick's offices on the thirtieth floor."

"Alright, I'll also take the eleventh floor, and Al, you handle Gorrick's offices," Turk instructed. "Use the key card for the elevator; we'll take the fire stairs to stay off the grid. We can't risk using comms, as they might intercept us. After we're done, we'll meet up at the APC. Any questions?"

"What should we do with the human controllers?" Al inquired.

"Release them onto the streets. They'll be glad to be free," Turk replied.

They were set. Toeghan and Luna watched them move off on the double for the Zen building. Once they'd disappeared, they boarded the APC and battened down the hatch. Parked in the narrow alleyway, the APC would be out of view from drones and they'd be safe.

The two squads stopped just short of the Zen building and took cover for Voltaris to take out the half dozen CCTV cameras overseeing the area. Again, with precision shooting, he knocked them out.

Turk signalled Al and then led his squad past the terminated RF-8, still standing like an incomplete statue, to enter the ground floor fire stairs they'd previously left after rescuing Voltaris.

Al checked the Ulink with Voltaris. "This'll be tricky, four cameras inside the lobby, two at the elevators."

"Give me the card, I'll go knock them out," Voltaris said.

"Won't the key card alert them?" Al asked.

"It didn't at the FRT elevator."

"Cool, give us a wave when you've got it done," Al said.

Voltaris took the card from Al, gave him a thumbs up, and then scurried across the courtyard up to the glass front entrance doors. A sensor picked up the key card ID and the doors slid open. Volt moved inside the building like greased lightning, and then crouching on one knee to avoid the main camera, he took it out before it picked him up. Once he'd quickly taken out the other three cameras, he stood up, walked back towards the door triggering it to open, and then waved Al to lead his men in.

They stopped inside the lobby to wait for Volt to secure the cameras covering the elevators.

A minute later, his hand appeared around the corner of the black marble wall and signalled thumbs up.

The elevator was waiting. Carefully obscuring himself from the camera inside it, Volt steadied the barrel of his rifle on the door and then shot it out. Once they were inside, Volt told the computer, "Level six." The doors closed and they were on their way.

Turk's squad were negotiating the staircase, getting to the tenth floor would be a test of endurance. Puffing as though they'd completed a marathon, they assembled on the tenth-floor landing.

Turk fitted a WASP under the door handle plate and then stepped back. Crack! Job done.

He quietly opened the door and peeked into the corridor. It was deserted. He turned to his men with his finger to his lips to hush them, and then they crept stealthily into the corridor. Access to the labs was up ahead. They stopped at the secured double doors. This time, to save WASP's, he only had four left, he used a small plug of C-4 around the door handle. Bang! It was far more brutal than a WASP and the door blew open, one of them left hanging off its hinges.

They rushed in guns up but found the room deserted. Voltaris had told Turk that the Cronus cyborgs were located in a large room, marked Lab X that was annexed to Lab B. With his gun held ready, he shouldered open the door to Lab B, found it empty and then went to the door marked Lab X. It had a high-security coded lock. He packed a larger charge of C-4 around the it and then moved out of range. Boom! It blew the door completely off its hinges. A signal from him and they all moved inside.

There were twenty upright pale green oval pods, all over two metres tall, spaced three metres apart around the perimeter of the oblong-shaped room. The light was dim with a green hue. The cold was so intense that a low, misty fog was drifting over the floor. Each pod had a large round tube extending from the top, from which leaked a vapour that cascaded like dry ice smoke down the sides.

"Okay, each of these pods contains a cyborg. I'll make up C-4 plugs for each of them. We need to get them open to put the plug inside, to ensure we destroy them. You guys get to work on opening them up," Turk explained.

Rubbing their hands together to warm them, they went to work searching for a way to open the pods.

Turk was moving quickly, crafting golf ball-sized C-4 plugs. He looked up at the others and asked, "Any success?"

Crankcase was feeling all over the surface of a pod and growled, "Can't find a goddam thing."

Checking the pod closest to the exit, Blake said, "It's like a sarcophagus… I think they're probably opened by a remote. Hang on, there might be an override switch at the back." He got down on his hands and knees in the mist, reached around the back, and felt between the pod and the wall. "Got it! There's a switch behind at the base, guys." He pressed it, and with a loud click, the pod popped open about three centimetres.

While Blake was getting up, Snake, one of the Rebels, pulled the pod open and immediately jumped back in fright, shouting, "Whoa!"

Amidst the swirling cold smoke inside the pod stood a naked monster of a man.

Turk looked up sharply to see what had caused the commotion and recognised it. He said, "It's bloody Gorrick!"

Crankcase pulled his pod open and said, "Well, I'll be stuffed, it's another Gorrick."

Snake turned his back on the pod, and with Gorrick behind him, jokingly declared arms spread, "Hey fellas, wouldn't this make one helluva selfie!"

He failed to notice Gorrick's eyes open. The grin was suddenly wiped off his face when a pair of hands grabbed him around the throat from behind. His expression turned to agony when the big hands closed their grip so tightly that they snapped his neck and broke his spine.

Blake leaped backward in shock, and in a reflex action, raised his AK-110 and unleashed a burst point-blank into the cyborg. It had no effect.

Turk quickly pulled a WASP from his pocket, triggered it, rushed over to the cyborg, and before it had a chance to detach itself from the apparatus inside the pod, reached up and slapped it onto its throat just under the jaw. He was aiming at its forehead but couldn't reach.

Bashing its groping hands away, Turk tried to free himself, but the monster had a grip on him with one hand. Crack! The WASP detonated. It blew its jaw off along with half its face. Its hand went limp. "Don't open the pods!" Turk shouted. "It activates them."

Crankcase pushed his pod shut. Luckily, none of the others had been opened.

Blake was rattled but not enough to ask, "You alright, Turk?"

Turk wiped his chin clean of some gunk that had flown off the cyborg's face when it shattered and admitted, "That was far too close for comfort. We'll set charges underneath the bloody things."

Cueball, one of the Skulls, found a door behind a pod at the far end of the room. "Ay, there's a door here but it's locked. Looks important."

Turk went back to finish setting the C-4 plugs. "I'll check it in a minute, mate."

Alice and his men crept along the corridor towards the entrance to the operations command centre on level seven. It hadn't been necessary for Voltaris to take out any cameras because there weren't any outside of the lobby and elevators.

Gun at the ready, Alice stood beside the entrance door with his back to the wall. Vee was behind him, followed by Voltaris, Rock, Sprocket, Gunner, and Shovelhead.

"On three, we go in. Only shoot if there's resistance. Okay? One, two, three!" He pushed through the door.

Inside the dimly lit room were over a hundred human operators seated behind individual terminals. No guards. Alice singled out the only person standing, assuming her to be the manager. She was a tubby girl with an expression on her round face as though someone had just stolen her lunch money.

"We're not here to hurt anyone. We're here to free you. Tell them all to take off their headsets and go out into the corridor. Okay? Do you have a problem with that?" Al asked.

She shook her head nervously.

Vee noticed that Al was unsettling her, so she stepped up in front of him and asked warmly, "What's your name, love?"

"Kiki," she said, hesitantly.

"My name is Vee, this is Alice. We've come to cure you guys of Red Wheel, but first we need to shut down this centre. Can you please order everybody to turn off their terminals? Don't worry if it leaves your cyborg stranded. And then, Kiki, move them all out. Okay?"

A broad smile broke on Kiki's face. It was as though their saviour had arrived, and in a way, it had. One by one, the terminals were shut down.

Just inside the gates of Angel City, in various positions ready to spring an ambush, the heads of RF-20s and RF-8s nodded forward and then froze—they had been shut down. After a matter of minutes, their ranks resembled the Chinese Terracotta Army.

"Alice, you need to see this," Voltaris said.

"Vee, keep the guys watching over the evacuation. Sprocket, come with us," Al ordered, and then followed Voltaris out of the room and back into the corridor.

Voltaris stopped at a door and slid the key card into the security module. Al and Sprocket stopped behind him.

"What is it?" Al asked.

"I'm pretty sure this is the mainframe," Voltaris said, as a click sounded. The door was open.

Having finished making the C-4 plugs, Turk went to the door Cueball had found. It had a high-security module.

"You're right, Cueball. There must be something important here." He attached a small plug of C-4 to the module, inserted a small fifteen-second detonator into it, and then stood back. Crack!

Cueball tried the door handle, and the large metal door swung open. A sensor light flicked on inside as they entered the vault-like room. It was even colder than the one before. One wall at the side had six large chrome hatch doors in a horizontal line.

Turk examined them and remarked, "I reckon they're cold lockers. This is a morgue." He opened the first door and pulled the rack inside halfway out. On it lay a black body bag. He unzipped it enough to expose the head of the body inside. It was another Gorrick, but this one had half his head missing. "This is the real Gorrick."

Cueball opened the next cold locker.

Blake joined them, looked at Gorrick, and said to Turk, "So Alice did kill him then?"

Cueball pulled out another rack. "There's another one here," he said.

Turk unzipped it. What he saw caused him to take a step back, shocked. He locked eyes with Blake and said grimly, "It's the real Voltaris. No wonder the key card worked!"

CHAPTER 42
FATAL ERROR

VOLTARIS HELD THE door open for Alice and Sprocket to enter the room. Once they were inside, he slipped in behind them, closed the door, and then opened fire. Thud! Thud! The muffled sound of two silenced shots, and Sprocket went down with a bullet between his shoulder blades and another one in the back of his head. He was dead.

Al had heard it and swung around sharply to confront Voltaris standing near the door with the rifle aimed at him. Thud! Thud! The shots knocked him over backward, and he hit the ground. Voltaris shouldered the rifle and quickly checked Alice, who lay face down with blood pooling around his body. Job done, he hurried out, closing the door behind him, and then raced past the line of operators pouring out of the control room, making their way to the elevator. Kiki was standing by the door, ushering them out.

Inside the operations room, Vee, Rock, Gunner, and Shovelhead were busy finishing up the placement of C-4 packs. Vee saw Voltaris in the doorway and joined him.

"Where's Al?" she asked.

"Took Sprocket up to the 30th floor, said to meet him there. You done here?" Voltaris said, hurriedly.

"Yep, come on, guys, let's move," she called out.

Voltaris glared at Vee. "Give me the detonator. You get the guys to the elevator."

"I don't have it... Alice does... he'll trigger Turk's lab explosion as well... just needs to know when everyone's clear," Vee explained.

It wasn't what Voltaris wanted to hear. The plan was for him to neutralise the threat of the C-4 charges.

As they left the room, Vee stopped at the door behind which her brother was and asked Voltaris, "What's in there?"

"Don't know... the key card won't open it," he lied.

"We could blow it with a WASP," she said.

"No, there isn't time. Best get to Alice in case he needs us."

"Got ya!" she agreed.

Turk called his squad together. "Listen, there's something seriously wrong here. Voltaris' body is in the morgue, which means the imposter with Alice is a cyborg. It's a trap to kill him, and he's walked right into it. We'll go to the 11th floor, plant a mother of a C-4 bomb there, and then get to the 30th floor, where I reckon they've set an ambush for Alice. We'll need to move real fast. All good?"

They all nodded in agreement.

"Right then, let's move," Turk barked, angry that their plans had been compromised because they'd failed to check Voltaris' validity when they busted him out of jail.

There was a solemn mood in the elevator ride to the 30th floor for Vee and the others. In the back of her mind, she sensed something was wrong but couldn't quite put her finger on it. Guns up and ready, they counted down the floors.

The doors finally opened after what had felt like an eternity for Vee. Nothing moved in the corridor. Leading them, she scurried to the glass double doors of the executive offices. She stopped next to them, her back against the wall. Gritting her teeth, her finger on the trigger of her automatic weapon, she held it up-right next to her face, waiting for the others to fall in line behind her. Once set, she pushed through the doors. She scanned the reception area with her gun— nothing moved. An all-clear hand signal from her brought the others in. She then confronted the big timber double doors to Gorrick's office. They were ajar. She peeked inside. The room was deserted.

Voltaris fell in behind her and whispered, "Anything?"

"Not a thing."

"They must be in the boardroom," he said.

She turned, looked up into his eyes, and said determinedly, "Okay, lead the way."

Voltaris went back out of the reception area and, followed by the others, led the way to the doors at the far end of the corridor. He stopped there to wait for them to press against the wall beside the doors. Vee was behind him. He looked over his shoulder and nodded at her.

"Go!" she said.

Voltaris pushed open the doors and barged in.

Gorrick looked up sharply from his seat at the far end of the long table in the huge room. Honor was seated at his left, and Ursula at his right. Gorrick rose to his feet when Voltaris charged in.

As the others were coming in, Voltaris rushed up beside Gorrick, and to Vee's shock, turned and aimed his gun at her.

"Drop your weapons," he growled. "Now!"

Vee looked around the room, confused. "Where's Alice and Sprocket?"

A smug grin came to Voltaris' lips, and he said, "Both dead."

Gunner, a lanky guy sporting a big full beard, and a mullet, raised his AK to shoot Voltaris.

Thud! Thud! Voltaris was way too quick for him. A bullet in the chest and one in the forehead took Gunner out, and he went down. The others immediately dropped their weapons and raised their hands.

"What are you going to do, Voltaris, kill us all?" Rock growled.

Gorrick answered for him. "You're as good as dead anyway. Look at your wrist. You've got Red Wheel."

Rock already knew it. He lowered his right arm and pulled the cuff of his jacket down to cover the ugly red circular rash. "So, life sucks," he said.

Any sort of discourse ended immediately when Turk pushed into the room behind them. He aimed his gun at Voltaris. Blake, Crankcase, Cueball, Floyd, and Doc were behind him with guns up.

"Drop it, Voltaris, or we open fire. We've got you outnumbered," Turk ordered.

"Go ahead, none of the guns will fire, except mine, and I'll take out Vee first," Voltaris snarled.

"Why don't we all sit down at the table and talk this through?" Gorrick said diplomatically.

"Been there before, Gorrick. You're not worth trusting," Turk growled.

"What are you going to do then? While you've been talking, three RF-20s have arrived outside the door. Upon my order, they will come in and execute all of you. One of you take a look… go on," Gorrick said.

Crankcase poked his head out of the door. Just as Gorrick had said, there were three of them. He popped back in again and reported, "Yep, three of the bastards."

"Now, shall I give the order to start shooting?" Gorrick asked.

"Where's Alice?" Turk demanded.

"Dead… I killed him," Voltaris said.

"How? Where?" Turk urged.

"Next to the operations room, shot him and Sprocket," Voltaris gloated.

"That's why the key card worked, I knew it!" Vee barked.

"Yes, that was a terrible oversight… the only possible flaw in our plan," Gorrick said. "A plan, I might add, cleverly devised by our new friend here." He patted Honor on the shoulder. She responded with a malevolent grin. "So, drop your weapons or I will give the order to start firing."

Turk knew he was beaten and reluctantly dropped his gun. The others followed suit.

"Ah, that's much better. Now, hand over the detonator for all the explosives you've set," Gorrick ordered.

"I guess there was another flaw in Honor's fantastic plan, because the person with the only detonator remote is Alice," Vee snarled.

"Can't call that a flaw, young lady. There's not much he can do with it lying dead on the floor of level six," Voltaris crowed.

"What would the pair of you know? You're nothing but freaking machines. You're not real, not even clones... you're just an RF in another skin... someone else's skin at that," Turk barked angrily.

Gorrick leered unblinkingly at Turk. "I'm not about to get into a philosophical debate with you, Turk. The revolt is over... you're finished."

A ruckus erupted outside. Then there was an almighty crash, and an RF-20 smashed through the wall beside the doors as though a giant had thrown it. Amidst the swirling dust and debris from the ruined wall, it staggered around mindlessly with its head hanging off its shoulders, only connected to its body by a couple of wires.

Then the seven-foot chrome muscular form of the Star Lord stepped through the hole in the wall.

"Alice!" Vee cried out excitedly.

Voltaris fired at him. Thud! Thud! Thud! Thud! Each bullet found its mark but none of them had any effect on him.

Alice threw Turk the detonator and said, "If everybody's clear, put a fire in the hole."

Then he charged at Voltaris, wrenched the rifle out of his hands, and began pounding him across the head with its butt... again and again, blow after blow, each one fracturing his skull a little more. As powerful as Cronus/Voltaris was, he had no comeback to Alice's relentless ferocious attack.

Voltaris raised his hands in a desperate attempt to deflect the powerful blows, but the savage hits sheared two fingers and the thumb off his left hand. The rifle had been reduced to a twisted mess, so Al discarded it. He grabbed Voltaris by the throat, dragged him over to the window, and glaring into his eyes snarled, "Chaa!" and threw him at the window. The plate glass shattered as Voltaris went through, plummeting thirty floors to hit the pavement below, a mangled mess: terminated.

Alice turned from the window to face Gorrick.

Just then, Turk triggered the first explosion. The building shuddered.

Turk leered at Ursula and Honor and then said calmly, "That was the sound of your lab exploding, Mennis, along with all of your Cronus cyborgs."

Crankcase took a peek back out into the corridor to see if the two remaining cyborgs were there. All he found were pieces of cyborg scattered everywhere. He chuckled to himself.

In a sharp movement, Gorrick grabbed Alice by the throat.

"Kill him!" Ursula screamed, jumping to her feet, incensed by the destruction of her creations.

The others collected their weapons and took aim at Honor and Ursula.

Alice had anticipated Gorrick's move. In his hand, he was holding a high explosive WASP. He flicked the switch.

Gorrick squeezed with all of his cyborg strength, ten times that of any human, trying to choke the life out of Alice.

But Alice freed his arm and slapped the WASP onto Gorrick's cheek. Then, he brought up both hands inside Gorrick's grip and splayed them apart. Free of him, he took a quick step back, shot Gorrick his idiosyncratic wave, and said calmly, "Chaa!"

Gorrick leered at him.

The WASP exploded with a loud bang, and Gorrick's head disintegrated, spattering Honor and Ursula with bits of gunk and goo.

It was over.

The Star Lord transformed back into Al.

Vee ran over and hugged him.

"I'll need a change of clothes," Al grumbled, and they all laughed, more from relief than the gag.

A little while later, they had assembled on Federation Drive. Luna and Toeghan had joined them. All of the operators they had freed were there, enjoying sunshine for the first time in years. Honor and Ursula stood together out of the throng, wondering what might become of them. Al walked over to them, his clothes ripped and straggly, and showed them the detonator remote.

Honor's dark eyes had ceased to smoulder.

Al raised the remote above his head and roared for everyone there to hear. "At the count of three, I'm going to press this button and destroy Zen HQ... the operations centre, the cyborg factory, the labs... the whole shebang. But there's a whole lot more work to be done before we've freed ourselves from the grip of Zen. Its wicked tentacles extend to every country in the world. For now, this moment marks the beginning of the end for them here. Count with me now as loud as you can shout!"

They all looked up at the Zen building a hundred metres away, and then led by Alice's powerful voice, they counted in unison, "One... Two... Three!"

He pressed the button, and the seventh, eleventh, and thirtieth floors exploded. The windows blew out, followed by balls of fire... the building began to tremble and then crumble. Ten minutes later, there was nothing left of Zen HQ other than a billowing wall of dust and a mountain of rubble.

People emerged from the death camp, free to breathe fresh air and soak up the sun. Crankcase and Rock had buried the hatchet and were already planning the future.

It was time to leave, but there was still plenty to do.

Luna promised everybody she would return to begin the curing process, with Turk and Morri coordinating everything in the interim. They boarded the APC for the drive back to Avalon.

As they approached the Angel City gates, Turk brought the vehicle to a stop so they could disembark and take in the breathtaking view.

A hundred RF Cyborgs stood in various positions, like pieces on a chessboard. Twenty drones occupied the spot where Betsy had been parked back in 2087, the first time they'd fought their way out of the city, only to be confronted by hundreds of bikers.

"This will stand as a monument to our victory," Turk declared.

"And a reminder of Zen's tyranny," Al added.

"Why don't we take a couple of these drones back to Avalon? They'd come in handy for transporting all the infected to one place," Vee suggested.

"You just want to fly one," Al joked.

And that's exactly what they did. In fact, Vee, Blake, and Alice each piloted a drone back to Avalon.

The three drones landed side by side on the elevator hatch with precise piloting. Triggered by Morri below, the elevator descended into the garage.

Over time, they planned to fly all twenty drones out of Angel City, delivering one or more to each of the bunkers in the vicinity—a burgeoning transport system.

Al stepped off his drone to a joyful Morri. He'd never seen her so excited.

"Al... you're a legend," she exclaimed, giving him a warm hug. "Turk's been filling me in over the comms on his drive back. What an incredible story. But seriously, how are you alive after being shot by Voltaris?"

Vee and Blake overheard the question and joined the conversation to hear Alice's response.

"He got me, two bullets in the back. But he made the mistake of shooting poor old Sprocket first. Even with a silencer, I heard the shots, realised what was coming next, so I quickly popped one of Secta's pills. The transformation ejected the bullets, and after a few minutes, the wounds healed... I can't explain how. So, I played dead when he came to check on me. At that moment, he needed to put another bullet in my head to ensure my death, but he didn't... that was a fatal error."

An hour later, Turk arrived in the APC with Luna and Toeghan. They finally had the opportunity to discuss the attack on Zen. Turk explained to Alice that they'd found the bodies of the real Voltaris and the real Gorrick in the lab morgue—that's when they realised it had been a setup.

"I can't believe I made the same mistake twice, failing to check the scar on his neck. It's sad that he met his end like that... he was a good bloke."

They agreed that there was nothing more they could do in 2112 for now, except to ensure Luna's return to state her case to the UN. Once she obtained approval, she would return to Avalon to coordinate the healing process.

It was time to depart. Toeghan chose to stay behind and assist Turk and Morri with preparations. Morri had already begun the process of fertilizing Hope's eggs using donor sperm. As more women were cured of Red Wheel, she would select the best candidates for the IVF program. Time was of the essence, given the number of lives lost daily. Luna would need swift approval from the UN, or the IVF programme's viability would be compromised.

Blake located the spot near the Wilson J-Car where the micro-vortex remained open. With the detection of his Clock Drive, the vortex expanded enough for all three of them to pass through.

CHAPTER 43
AFTERMATH

A LOT HAD transpired during Al's absence. The science team achieved a significant breakthrough by isolating the stable isotope Velodium with an atomic number of 123 from the sceptre. This discovery unlocked two collision particle elements: Velodium and Moscovium, element 115. These elements held the potential for cold fusion, which could be harnessed for energy production and as a gravity warp drive for space travel.

One intriguing aspect of this revelation was that Moscovium, a synthetic element, had been synthesized in 2003 by Russian and American scientists, negating the need for natural sourcing. This element had been previously associated with Area 51 whistle-blower Bob Lazar's claims about propulsion in alien spacecraft. Element 115's challenge was its short half-life, only 220 milliseconds, making it unsuitable for reactor use. However, Dr Robert James devised a stable reaction by combining Velodium and Element 115, yielding zero heat at room temperature. If practical testing succeeded, it could revolutionise energy production and space travel, potentially enabling travel at the speed of light using a gravity warp drive.

Within minutes of the time travellers' arrival through Kairos, Mal was informed and rushed to the control room to greet them. Secta, the Professor, Hope, and Karzoff were eager to hear their mission's account. After an hour-long report from Alice and another half-hour report from Luna, everyone was up to date.

To expedite matters, Luna opted for a conference call to deliver her report to UN Director General Maralina Bostok. Blake was relieved to hear from Mal that Jax De Ville was safely back in New York, and Brigadier Bruckmaster had taken early retirement from the CIA due to the Poo Ôonoo Valley incident. The Professor shared that Colonel Freeman offered to reopen Time-travel Works Operations at Desertron under a new non-CIA arrangement if OTT was interested, a proposition they needed to consider.

"If we get approval for this Red Wheel humanitarian mission, we'll require more than one time travel facility. Besides, OTT running it is preferable to an inefficient, over-budgeted US government bureaucracy," Luna commented.

"We hear you," the Professor agreed.

"Better get a message to the US government that Voltaris Idram lost his life in the line of duty," Al requested sombrely.

"I'll take care of that, Al," Mal assured.

"Hope, your folks send their love they're both in good shape and miss you," Al said. "Oh, and Karzoff, Honor isn't impressed with her new home now that it's a pile of busted concrete."

They all got a good laugh out of that.

As they walked along the hallway later, heading to the commissary for a meal, Hope shared more information with Al. "I've been working with Secta and Vic on the Velodium experiment. We've cracked it, and, my research has revealed I can use SAGE to become transgenic."

"All that scientific mumbo-jumbo is way over my head, Hope," Al admitted.

"It means Al, I can introduce a novel DNA sequence as encoded by the template at the target location in my genome."

"Nah, that went even higher over the top," Al said, with a chuckle.

"Um, I can replace your DNA code I have, with another that I can create," Hope explained in layman's terms.

"Okay, so that I understand. It means if we were to have kids, I wouldn't be interbreeding with my daughter?"

"Essentially yes, no danger of mutation. I will however still have some of your genetic traits."

"I'll need to run that past Secta."

"No! He would oppose it," she reacted.

"Why do you say that? I don't know anyone with a more open mind than Secta," Al said.

"I just presumed he would."

They arrived at the commissary, and Al was ready for a hearty meal, having found the quality of tucker in 2112 somewhat lacking.

Al was tired; there were things to do, but being rested in order to execute them properly took precedence. He was waiting for a taxi outside Oceana when a horn honked. The passenger side window of the black SUV slid down, and Vee shouted, "Jump in, Al. We'll drop you home."

Al settled into the rear passenger seat. Blake was behind the wheel, and Tippy occupied the back seat.

"Hey Tip, how's it going?" Al said.

"All good," she smiled.

"Al, I spoke to my old boss a couple of hours ago, and he told me the mission to rescue Dr Nimrod De Ville in Chernobyl had been a setup orchestrated by Bruckmaster. You'd have to think in collusion with Zen. Nimrod, like his daughter, is a CIA operative. Even I didn't know that. I should've realised it—I was there on plenty of occasions when Jax spoke with Bruckmaster on the phone."

"Yeah, well, it's their job to keep everything under the table, isn't it? What goes around comes around. It worked out okay in Chernobyl. Is Nimrod really her father?"

"Yes, at least that part is true. I met him in New York before he went to Chernobyl. He seemed like an alright guy; I didn't really suspect him of being an agent."

"But you knew Jax was?" Al questioned.

"Sure, my assignment was to work with her undercover. She wasn't suspected of trafficking artefacts. It was known she was a CIA agent tasked with catching the king of the black market: ex CIA agent, Handerson Bolt. I got the case way back because Bolt was suspected of running a ring of thieves out of the Philippines, and that led to Tahiti."

Al looked out of the window at the peak hour traffic. The sky was growing dark, threatening to rain.

"Oh, that's another thing he mentioned you might be interested in—Watchers are turning up over military operations again, two off San Diego yesterday. The US Navy isn't impressed; apparently, they scrambled a couple of F-35 fighters and this thing flew right between them and then zoomed off at an incredible speed."

"Yep, superluminal employing gamma bursts. What shape was it?" Al asked.

"They called it a Tic Tac. Then, a few hours later, someone posted a video on social media of a massive UFO flap over a Mexican village. Loads of detractors were calling it fake, but word from the military is the craft was real all right. It wasn't a Tic Tac or a light; this thing was a massive grey flying saucer. Not smooth or sleek, it looked like an old war horse of a thing right out of the movie Independence Day."

"Two different species of aliens, I'd say," Al said.

"You're kidding, you believe in all that stuff?" Tippy questioned.

"He ought to, he's been on board one, haven't you, Al?" Vee said.

"Yeah, but that's classified," Al said, ending the conversation. Blake parked outside Al's Kings Cross apartment. Al got out and went to Vee's open window.

"Thanks sis, catch you in the a.m."

"Get some sleep, Al. You're lookin' weary," Vee said, caringly, and then leaned out the window and gave him a peck on the cheek.

"Chaa!" Al said, with a wave and then headed inside.

As he opened the door to his apartment, he thought of Toeghan. He was missing her. "Fancy missing someone who tried to kill you," he muttered to himself entering the musky smelling apartment. He sat on the edge of the bed and thought, "Maybe it's time to move on... a new place. This joint is looking as haggard as me." He lay down and immediately sank into a deep sleep.

He woke up dazed and then realised where he was; he sat up sharply, his heart in his mouth.

"What the?" he muttered, looking around the room. He was in Secta's old lab, sitting in the chair that he'd been first dispatched from into a hologram. He twisted around and found Secta sitting at his computer, muttering.

Al asked, "What's going on here?"

Secta glanced back at him and said, "Oh, you're awake..." He got up and came over to him. "Job's done, I've made the hologram of you... see it didn't hurt a bit, did it? All that paranoia was for nothing."

It was the old maniacal Secta with long white hair on one side of his head and short black hair on the other.

Al was confused, "I don't get it... I'm supposed to be trapped in the hologram."

"Not likely, Alice, just duplicated. I'm a scientist, not a murderer."

"But what about Honor, Karzoff... Hope?"

"Honor and Karzoff were just doing their job to get you here for the test. As for Hope, well, I don't mind telling you she tends to get her tits in a tangle at times."

"But what about the stinger in the neck and all that?"

"That's just Honor, she gets a bit carried away... been watching too many spy movies, I guess. Anyway, you're free to go."

As he struggled up out of the strange-looking chair, he felt dizzy and wobbled, then had to brace himself from toppling over by gripping the arm of the chair.

"You all right, Alice?" Secta asked. "A little disorientation is to be expected after the process. Take a few deep breaths, you'll be all right."

"But what about all that's happened... the time travel? The Professor... Zen?... En-Ki?... Gorrick?... My sister Vee?" Al questioned, holding his brow in consternation.

"Don't know about any of that, Alice... I like the idea of time travel, though."

Alice flopped back into the chair. "Nah, this can't be real, too much has happened."

A voice spoke in his mind, "It could be an alternative timeline perhaps, Alice. Did you think of that?"

He sat up sharply and barked, "Who said that?"

"I said nothing... are you sure you're okay? Are you hearing voices?" Secta said.

"Yes."

"Symptomatic of the procedure, I'm afraid... they'll go away in due course," Secta assured him.

Alice recognised the voice, it was En-Ki's, but with none of it making sense, he was struggling to keep a grip on his assumed reality. Split timelines, is that what's going on? He asked himself. Was there a time separation when Secta had originally dispatched me into the hologram, and now I'm experiencing the alternative reality? Is another Alice living in another timeline? Have we somehow traded places? If I just get up and walk out of here, does everything I have done cease to exist? Wait a minute... I don't have any choice. The thought terrified him.

Standing next to him, Secta leaned down and peered into Alice's eyes. "Hmm, you look fine to me. You can go now, unless you're still feeling dizzy."

Al got out of the chair. "I'm confused. I've lived a completely different existence."

"Often the case when under anesthesia, vivid dreams, so real you believe them, especially for an imaginative person such as yourself."

"So, are you saying everything I've been through was a dream?"

Al protested.

"I'd say so," he agreed.

"Okay, stuff it. Thanks. Chaa!" He shot him a wave and left.

Walking up the corridor toward the elevator, he came upon Secta's Android, standing with its back to the wall like a sentry. Just then he heard the sound of a servo and a door opening a bit further back along the corridor. Hope stepped out. She looked angry.

"Hope!" Alice called out and then started back towards her.

"Alice, did it go all right? He had no right to use it on a human subject, who knows what the side effects might be?"

He stopped when he reached her.

She looked him over and asked, "How do you feel?"

"A bit confused. You see, none of this happened this way... I mean this timeline we're on, it's different than the one I've already lived."

"Psychosis... I warned there was the possibility of a secondary response to the process. Let's hope it's only temporary. I'll need to run a couple of tests. Come to my lab, it'll only take a few minutes."

She led Alice past Secta's lab 7 and into her lab, motioning for him to sit on a stool.

"Hope, do you know anything about my girlfriend, Stain?"

"No, I didn't know you had a girlfriend. Why?"

"Because in the other timeline, she was murdered."

"Murdered... by whom?" she said, surprised.

"On Honor's orders."

"Honor? But why would she want to murder your girlfriend?" Hope asked.

"Because the Oceana State Security Directorate wanted to send a warning to me to quit protesting."

"Protesting, against what? You're a rock star."

"The nuclear submarine."

"What nuclear submarine?" she asked.

"The one arriving here tonight... Look, I'm the leader of the Octagon Peace Movement... um, a girl... Mowina Beetson, jumped off a building yesterday and landed on an official. It caused a riot... didn't it?"

She looked at him as though he was delusional, "No, not that I know of, Alice. I've not heard of this Octagon Peace Movement, nor any submarine arriving here tonight," she said, shining a penlight in his eyes to check the dilation. The flash of light blinded him.

CHAPTER 44
TRANSMOGRIFIED

WHEN THE FLASH cleared, Alice realised a ray of light pouring in through the apartment window had caused it. The curtain was parted just enough for a beam of sunlight to be directed onto his face. He sat bolt upright, still confused but relieved to be in his apartment. Thoughts were racing through his baffled mind: Which timeline is this? Was it a dream?

Feeling the need to splash water on his face to wake up and confirm reality, he headed for the bathroom but stopped upon seeing his reflection in the mirrored bathroom door. The clothes he'd slept in were the same as he'd been wearing when Blake dropped him off at the apartment. He went over to the bed, sat on the edge, and placed his face in his hands. Glad as he was that it had only been a dream, he was no less disturbed by the possibilities the dream had raised.

Later that morning, after polishing off a hearty breakfast at Café Epiphany, Al cruised the city pavement en route to Oceana HQ. It started to spit rain, so he trotted the last hundred metres and then entered through the secret side entrance in the alleyway alongside the Oceana building.

Secta was holding a staff meeting when Alice entered his lab. While Secta was busy talking to six interns, Al approached Hope, who was at her computer terminal. She greeted him with a warm smile. "Hey, Al, get some rest?"

"Yes, but it came at a price," he said, regretfully.

Not expecting him to say that, she shot him a bewildered gaze. "What do you mean?"

Secta finished up and came over. "Good morning, Al."

"He's just about to explain why his rest last night came at a price," Hope explained.

After telling them the story of his dream right down to the smallest detail, Al waited for Secta's opinion. Secta was pacing the room, deep in thought.

"You've got him going now, Al," Hope said playfully.

But Secta was taking the account very seriously. He stopped and said, "I don't think it was a dream as we know it, Al. I think there's a lot more to it than that. What if, as your dream suggested, another timeline has branched off and has a totally different outcome? And furthermore, what if in that outcome there is no Zen?"

"But it doesn't really matter, does it? Because it's all relative to the timeline we're on," Al proposed.

"Yes, that's quite true, but what if we could visit that timeline like perhaps you did in your unconsciousness last night?"

"Still don't get the significance, Secta," Al said, scratching his head.

"Well, the past is one thing, but it's set because it's done. However, the future is a different matter because it is being written as we speak. So, what if we could visit the alternative reality?"

"But according to your theory, there would be two of the same person on the timeline, and they would either cancel out or one would disappear," Hope said.

"But what if, in the same way Neit and En-Ki, for that matter, possessed you, Alice... what if you could possess yourself?" Secta proposed.

"Or the way you possessed Turk and Secta possessed Morri?" Hope added.

"I get it, you think it might be possible for me to possess myself in the alternative reality?" Al summed up.

"Perhaps, what if that's what happened last night? You did say En-Ki spoke to you?" Secta said.

"I'm pretty sure it was his voice... but it was only to say I should consider it might be an alternative timeline."

"Exactly, he might have been telling you something. Perhaps demonstrating how to cross over into parallel worlds."

"For what purpose?" Al questioned.

"I don't know, Alice. But I have a strong suspicion we are going to find out sooner rather than later," Secta said, with an air of mystery.

"So, we are to assume Honor has been captured? Has there been any acknowledgement from them?"

"No, sir," Regina Fych answered her boss. Gorrick was at her reception desk, seething with anger. If he hadn't been for Honor's absence, her disappearance would have remained unnoticed.

"Tell Layla Migden I'm coming to see her. When Khan gets in, tell him to meet me in Honor's office." He stormed out of reception, strode along the corridor, and entered Honor's offices. Layla was seated behind her desk, waiting nervously. Commander Daniel Walker, nursing a bandaged hand, was seated in the waiting area.

"Miss Migden, why haven't you reported Honor's absence?" Gorrick demanded.

"Sir, I received this text message from her yesterday." She showed him her phone. He read the message. 'I'll be away a few days. Honor.'

"Put a trace on her phone immediately. Commander, come with me." Gorrick led Walker into Honor's office.

As soon as he closed the door behind them, he said, "I suspect Honor has been kidnapped by Oceana. I'm putting you in charge of security in her absence. Can you function effectively with that injury?" He said, alluding to the bandaged hand.

"No trouble at all, sir."

Khan entered the room. "Sit down, Khan. We have lost Honor," Gorrick snarled.

"That wouldn't surprise me after the botched assassination attempt and then the failed exercise in eliminating the assassins... there was sure to be a reprisal," Khan said. "And you, Commander, which finger did you lose?"

"The middle finger, sir."

"And why that finger?"

"I was giving the assailant the bird, and he shot it off."

"Now doesn't that just sum up the effectiveness of our security department?" Khan said facetiously.

"He's right, Commander. If you care to look over Honor's mission statements since she joined our ranks, they read like a second-rate comedy sketch. Do you think, given the embarrassment of having your finger severed in such a manner, you can do better?" Gorrick tersely questioned.

"I can only try, sir," he said, unperturbed.

Layla poked her head in through the doorway and said, "Sir, Honor's phone has been triangulated to Oceana HQ."

"Thank you. Confirmation of her abduction... now wasn't that easy," Gorrick said, smugly.

"Karzoff is far too clever to leave her phone detectable. They want us to know they have her," Khan suggested.

"You're right. Okay, Commander, get on with it... take this office, recruit who you need, report to me daily."

"Yes, sir."

"Khan, with me to visit Dr Li."

They left Walker and headed for the elevator. "I've got you a posting to take over the Tokyo chapter if you're interested."

Khan was pleased. "Most definitely, when?"

"Effective immediately. The Gorrick there is opening a new branch in Pyongyang. We expect to supply North Korea with our new state-of-the-art weapons."

They stepped into the elevator.

"To be quite honest with you, I'm not content with this body... it's far too restrictive. I've had Dr Li working on the means for me to transfer into something safer."

"AI?"

"Yes."

The elevator doors opened, and they made their way to Dr Li's labs.

Upon entering, they were greeted by Li and Professor Adamski, then led into Li's office.

A stunning young woman was waiting for them in the lounge setting. Her striking, long red hair was tied in a ponytail. Fine pale skin and electric blue eyes, heavily made up with black mascara and eyeliner, added to her mysterious persona. The delicate features of her triangular face radiated beauty, though her black-painted lips generated a sinister eccentricity, further enhanced by sharp, black lacquered fingernails. She was wearing a Model T Chanel little black dress, from which projected her shapely bare legs and sandaled feet with black lacquered toenails.

Gorrick approached her, and she stood. He noted that at six feet four inches, she was as tall as he, but even at that height, her body was shapely and muscular. Dr Li made the introduction. "Gorrick, this is Electra."

Gorrick shook hands with her. They took their seats.

"Sir, we have fitted the new processor to the Cronus model, so it is now capable of multiple programmable personalities. Cronus can instantly morph, of its own volition, into any of the programmed tropes. The morph is total, encompassing not only the face."

"Brilliant. Can you demonstrate, please?" Gorrick asked.

"Certainly," Dr Li said. "Electra, please stand up."

The stunning young woman stood as instructed, offering Gorrick an unblinking warm smile.

"Access ten of your pre-set personalities at five-second intervals," Dr Li instructed.

In an amazing display, Electra morphed into Voltaris, then

Daniel Walker, then a middle-aged black woman, and seven more distinctly different individuals, before resolving back to Electra.

"Understandably, the only items that didn't morph were her hair, fingernails, makeup, and clothing, as they're external," Adamski explained.

Gorrick and Khan applauded.

"Extraordinary. Do each of these pre-sets have the memory, speech, and personality traits of the original?" Gorrick asked.

"Yes, with the exception of Electra; she is yet to be programmed as you specified, sir," Adamski said.

"Good. And Electra's vocal tone?" Gorrick questioned.

"As you requested, we have sampled the voice of Miss Regina Fych," Dr Li explained.

"Good. Now, the most important question: Can the gravitonic brain now input data from an open source?"

"Yes, we have made the necessary adjustment," Dr Li confirmed.

"Excellent, then let's get started."

Luna got the green light from UN Director General Maralina Bostok to proceed with processing the sufferers of Red Wheel at the Avalon bunker. If it proved to be one hundred percent successful, she was authorized to move on to others suffering from the disease. It was fortunate that Red Wheel wasn't infectious; otherwise, the undertaking would have been impossible.

Luna wasted no time in informing Secta, Hope, and the Professor. Now, they could put their plan into action.

The idea was for Luna to return to the Avalon bunker to work with Turk, Morri, and Toeghan. They would fit each of the infirm with a Clock Drive and then dispatch them one by one through a vortex to Kairos. Upon arrival, before they could even perceive they had time-travelled, they would be turned around and sent back to 2112 with the Red Wheel gene edited from their DNA by SAGE.

The theory was quite simple, but in practice, the prospect of moving two thousand sick and dying individuals through a vortex and back was daunting.

When Gorrick entered the reception to his office, he was greeted by Commander Walker.

"Walker, do you have an update for me?" Gorrick asked.

"Yes, sir."

Gorrick glanced at Regina Fych behind her desk and could tell by her expression that she had no messages for him. He moved over to the window, motioning for Walker to follow.

"Go on," Gorrick requested.

"I placed a trace on Honor's OSCI."

"No, that was removed," he said impatiently.

"Not the GPS tracker. Khan had requested that component be preserved for emergencies like this."

That surprised Gorrick. "Oh, good. Continue."

"There is currently no signal from it, sir. I tracked her to a café in Kings Cross, from which I believe she was abducted. She went from there to Oceana HQ. Within Oceana, their noisemaker dampeners restrict the signal. However, I managed to boost it enough to suggest she entered Kairos, well, at least the control room area where the signal disappeared."

"When?"

"Four days ago, sir. There has been no signal since, which confirms that she passed through Kairos."

Gorrick sat down on a bench and motioned for Walker to do the same. He gazed out of the window, contemplating his next move, and then said, "We need to find out where they have sent her." An idea struck him. "Our New York office recently planted an informant inside UNTT, where all time travel missions are authorized. We should be able to get a list of their recent missions. That might provide us with the answer. Leave it with me." He stood up. "Oh, and good work, Commander."

Walker got to his feet. "There's not much more I can do, sir."

"We'll talk once I have the information," Gorrick said, then headed into his office.

At OTT, preparations were well underway for the Red Wheel healing operation. It was set to kick off first thing in the morning, with Luna, Hope, and Vee scheduled to pass through Kairos to 2112, carrying a cargo of twenty Clock Drives. Upon arrival, they would begin processing the infected patients for metal. Once cleared, the patients would be equipped with a Clock Drive and sent through a vortex situated in the garage area, one at a time.

At Kairos, Secta, Alice, Blake, and the Professor would receive each traveller, leading them into the control room for Robert to initiate their journey back to 2112. Morri, Turk, and Toeghan would be waiting to receive the returning travellers, guiding them to the cafeteria for recuperation. Those who were incapacitated would be processed last, as they would require personal assistance throughout the entire procedure.

"The only setback is that we can't open two vortexes simultaneously, one for incoming and the other for outgoing travellers. It would significantly speed up the process," the Professor mused.

Robert turned from the console and replied, "I considered that, Vic, but with only one Kairos, it can't be done."

Al raised an interesting question, "What if two travellers accidentally enter Kairos at the same time?"

"That's an intriguing thought, Al. They might merge into a single entity," the Professor theorised.

"Err, that could get ugly," Al said. "Remember the movie 'The Fly,' where the scientist merges with a fly during teleportation?"

Robert nodded in agreement, "A classic film, and that's exactly why we take such precautions to maintain sterility in the dispatch room."

"But what about coming back? Anything could enter a vortex once it's opened," Al pointed out, raising a crucial concern.

The expressions on their faces indicated that this aspect had not been thoroughly considered yet, despite its significance given the impending undertaking. With thousands of travellers expected to pass through Kairos, the potential for accidents like this was magnified.

"You're absolutely right, Alice. We'll need to provide protective clothing for each traveller and establish safeguards at Avalon to prevent unintended hitchhikers," Secta acknowledged.

Karzoff entered the room and inquired, "Is there anything we can do to assist tomorrow?"

"Yes," Secta replied. "When we reach the point of working with the disabled and weakened patients, they'll require special handling. I've arranged for sick bay staff to help out, but more hands would be appreciated."

"Okay, until the a.m. then. Ready to head home, Vee?" Al asked.

"No, I've still got more to finish up here. But Blake can give you a lift home," Vee replied.

"Sweet," Al said.

As they were leaving the control room, Al stopped at Karzoff and whispered, "Tonight's the night."

Karzoff responded with a subtle nod, and Alice left the room.

Gorrick's driver held an umbrella to shield his boss from the rain as he stepped out of the limousine onto the driveway of his residence. Gorrick left him at the entrance, opened the front door, and went inside. The sensor lights instantly detected his presence and illuminated his path. With Honor absent and the maid having left for the day, the house was quiet and deserted.

It was close to midnight. Gorrick was about to follow his usual routine of settling into his favourite comfortable lounge chair in the living room, reading a book until dawn. Sleep was unnecessary for him—he was constantly awake. Placing his briefcase on the breakfast bar, he caught a glimpse of the view through the expansive patio windows, capturing the lights of Sydney Harbour at night. He found the twinkling lights as relaxing as gazing at the firmament.

His current book was waiting for him on the coffee table. As he reached for it, a voice halted him in his tracks.

"I've read it. Not a bad read. Don't mind me, the maid let me in before she left."

Gorrick turned swiftly to find Alice reclining in a lounge chair, his legs crossed, facing the view.

"Top view En-Lil, better than that grungy pyramid you were living in on Eris... did you own that thing or where you just renting?"

"Ah, the infamous Black Alice. Any particular reason for your intrusion into my dominion?"

"Your dominion, as opposed to your house? Are you speaking in a broader sense?" Alice's tone was sardonic.

Gorrick settled into his chair, his gaze fixed on Alice. "Oh, I think you know exactly what I mean. By the way, what have you done with Honor?"

"Honor? She found new employment in the future."

"Ah, 2112... your most recent escapade."

"You're well-informed."

"Have you ever doubted that?" Gorrick retorted with a touch of arrogance. "She will be back before long. Aquila will be operational again in a couple of months."

"I wouldn't put your house on that," Al replied, his eyes scanning the contemporary room.

They locked eyes for a moment, an unspoken tension hanging in the air. Gorrick picked up his book and stated, "I have more important matters to attend to than trading barbs with you. Say what you've come here to say and then leave. Or is your purpose to eliminate me?"

Alice became aware that he should leave, as he understood that En-Lil would likely sense En-Ki's departure at some point. If that occurred, there was a possibility that En-Lil might attempt to transfer from Gorrick to Alice, a scenario he was determined to avoid. He discreetly reached into his pocket, retrieving a WASP. Activating the switch with his thumb, he subtly aimed it at Gorrick while getting up from the chair, ensuring it locked onto the target.

Eyeballing Gorrick Al raised his hand in a casual wave and uttered, "Chaa!" He then pivoted and confidently made his way to the door, his stride reflecting the unmistakable Black Alice swagger. As he reached the threshold of the corridor, he nonchalantly tossed the WASP over his shoulder and kept moving. A faint buzzing noise followed by a sharp crack resonated in the air. Pausing briefly, Alice turned his gaze back to the scene he had left behind.

Gorrick sat slumped in his chair, his book in hand, chin resting on his chest, and a gaping hole at the top of his head.

With a nod, Alice opened the front door, pulling up his collar to shield himself from the stormy night. As he stepped outside, he was ready to confront the elements. The battle had reached its conclusion, but the ongoing struggle for dominion would continue.

EPILOGUE
BOOK 8
ALL THE TIME IN THE WORLD

ALICE STEPPED OUT into the rainy night, a sense of relief flooding over him like a weight lifted from his broad shoulders. The demise of Gorrick marked the end of a battle, yet the understanding remained that the larger struggle would persist.

The rain was easing, granting him a slightly less damp journey back to his apartment. As he traversed the path along Billyard Avenue in Elizabeth Bay, the rhythmic sound of his footsteps on the wet pavement resonated through the night. However, an unsettling feeling began to creep into his consciousness. A thought nagged at him—could killing Gorrick have altered the timeline, as Secta and En-Ki had speculated? A haunting dream from the past surged into his mind. It had placed him in an alternate reality where Secta hadn't injected him with the atom-reducing formula, and he wasn't trapped within a holographic projector. In this alternate version, Secta had merely crafted a holographic duplicate of him, allowing him to continue his life as a rock singer in a metal band. None of the tumultuous events he had experienced would have unfolded—the nuclear disaster averted, no visit to 2087 or the 6th Century BC. No trip to Tokyo in 2047, no battle with En-Lil on Eris, or the venture to 2112—the voyages through time eradicated. The notion swirled in his thoughts—what if it wasn't a mere dream, but a foreboding premonition? Could En-Ki be somewhere, observing? He halted and cast his gaze skyward through the rain, finding only a canopy of low-hanging clouds—no trace of a Watcher in sight.

"Argh!" he growled, dismissing the idea, yet another question immediately commandeered his mind: How had it been so straightforward to eliminate Gorrick? This query sent his thoughts spiralling, akin to a wheel of fortune, pondering which answer it would ultimately land upon—or which timeline.

A notion ignited within him, compelling him to hastily retrieve his cell phone. The familiar digits of Vee's number beckoned. As the screen's glow illuminated his face, he heard the soft approach of a vehicle. His gaze darted across the street to the black SUV that had pulled up. The driver's side window slid open, revealing a hand emerging from the shadows. However, instead of the anticipated gesture, the extended hand lacked a particular finger. Recognition struck Al—this was the very same guy he had sighted through the sniper's rifle's night scope. The man whose finger he had severed with a bullet. Relief washed over him momentarily, affirming that the timeline remained unchanged. Yet, reality descended swiftly as the hand retreated, replaced by the ominous muzzle of a silenced firearm, directed straight at him. Commander Daniel Walker pulled the trigger, and in rapid succession, three shots resounded—thud, thud, thud. Alice crumpled to the ground as the SUV accelerated away.

The heavens opened up, releasing torrents of rain. Alice's life essence mingled with the rainwater, forming a crimson pool around his prone body, its rivulets coursing into the gutter, a silent testament to his extinguished existence.

Vee awoke abruptly to the jarring ring of the phone. The voice on the other end from the hospital bore grave news—Alice was now in critical condition, sustained only by life support and teetering on the precipice of death.

"Where were you when I needed you? I've always been there for you," Al's voice carried a mix of frustration and desperation.

"I was there... that is why we are conversing now, while your physical form languishes in a coma. The task remains incomplete," En-Ki responded.

"It's a never-ending cycle, En-Ki. Every time I think I'm done, it starts all over again."

"I understand how it may seem that way, but I assure you, that is not the truth. The menace of En-Lil continues to loom."

"No, it doesn't. I ended it. I killed him."

"You killed Gorrick, not En-Lil. I will know when En-Lil's presence is eradicated. Though you have mitigated his influence, your species is on the brink of facing its ultimate trial. Without your abilities, your kind will not endure. The path you have tread has led you to this juncture—the knowledge you have amassed has been your preparation. This is the culmination of your quest, Alice."

"You'll need to give me more than that, mate."

"Your species, through technological advancement, has emerged as a potential threat to other civilizations. Your outreach efforts to contact extra-terrestrial life have inadvertently alerted malevolent beings to your existence. Benevolent species are few and far between, while the attention of a particularly malevolent force has been drawn to your kind. Do you want to live, Alice?"